Good Morning Captain!

A Fictional Biography

DOUG BURGUM

ISBN: 978-1-4834-2730-0 (sc)
ISBN: 978-1-4834-2729-4 (e)

Library of Congress Control Number: 2015904232

Chapter 3 picture courtesy of Paul Beale. Chapter 9 picture courtesy of Karen Davies. All other pictures are those of the author.

Lulu Publishing Services rev. date: 3/27/2015

CONTENTS

DEDICATION

To my Kindred Spirit

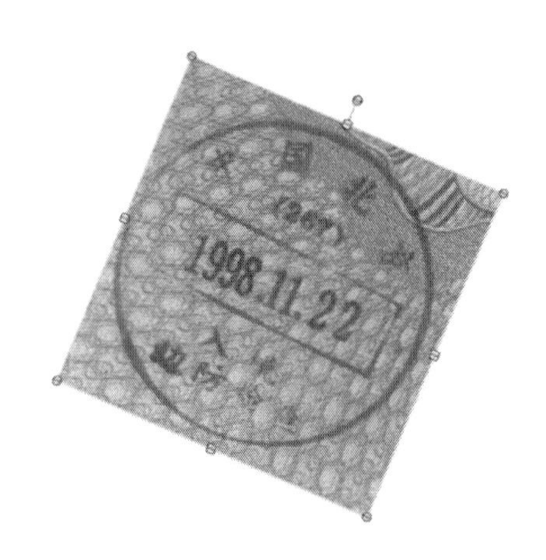

Introduction

Alex Young is a fictitious character born of my imagination. The details relating to family history are entirely true, or as close as I can manage.

Alex is an old man reflecting on his life, while I am a slightly younger man, hopefully with some fuel left in the tank! Whilst it is true that Alex's biography is based largely on my own life, some of this book and his experiences are completely fictional. This is a deliberate ploy on my part to muddy the waters. With the exception of two of my school-teachers who I honour in this book, many of the other characters are fictional, or perhaps composites.

Some who know me, or believe they know me, may think they recognise themselves or others, but I will not enter into a debate about what is true, what really happened and what did not.

I am proud of my life, unashamed and at peace with the world. I am also proud of my family and I have given them as much anonymity as is possible. It could be argued that a book based entirely on my life would be boring and of little interest. However we are the sum of our experiences and I have used these to create a character that I hope is interesting, colourful and a little vulnerable.

I am flawed and I have made mistakes, but I am also one of the luckiest people one might ever meet. This success is not based on anything material, but on my journey through life. My experiences, my family and my friends, past and present; these are the treasures that make me so happy to have trod this earth. I wish I had been worthier, wiser and a better writer, but if you detect any of the compassion and emotion I feel for humankind, and those most close to me, read on...

Doug Burgum

Prologue

"Good Morning Captain!"

Eventually those words became a standing joke between them. From that very first day, Maria had greeted the old man with that very phrase. Now, how long ago that was, he simply could not remember.

The old man raised his head wearily and peered over his spectacles. Standing before him stood a small, young woman with dark skin and jet-black hair. She was plain and slim, but there was warmth in her smile and in her eyes.

"Good morning Captain. My name is Maria. I am here to look after you."

"Where is Isabella? You are not my nurse!" He waved his hands at her dismissively. His words were stern and indignant.

"Isabella is working elsewhere," Maria smiled gently. Her voice was soft, but self-assured. "I will try speaking my very best, Señor. I hope my English will improve as we speak and perhaps we can get to know one another. Would you like some tea?"

"Coffee!" he barked. "I drink coffee in the mornings. Isabella knows I drink coffee in the mornings! She knows how I like it." He banged his hand on the armrest of the old worn armchair in which he sat.

"Isabella is busy Señor. Now, how do you like your coffee?" She presented another, more determined smile.

The old man raised his eyes and stared at the Spanish nurse. It was her eyes that made him pause and consider the woman before him. There was something about those smiling eyes. He saw no anger or irritation in her demeanour; only kindness. She simply stood her ground and waited for him to assess the situation. The silence only lasted a few moments and it was he who conceded, but he would be no pushover!

"Gracias, Maria, coffee would be fine. Not one of those thick, small cups with just one mouthful. No "café solo" for me! A big cup with milk, if you please. Por favor."

Maria gave a small nod of the head and turned on her heels, quickly disappearing from the room. Captain Alex Young (retired) turned towards the window once again. Between occasional naps, the scene beyond the glass was his world. He would look at the parched garden below, stare at the fields beyond and squint at the distant hills. The vines had been green and full with grapes, but now was the harvest. Buckets of grapes, some handpicked, were being tipped into the trailer, now full and almost overflowing.

It was a wonderful sight, but one tinged with regret. The harvest meant that autumn was quietly approaching. There were still warm days, of course, but now the evenings were cooler. Then winter. Winter, once a brief respite from the long hot summer, now felt threatening. It was another season, with the clock speeding away much too fast. There was history, there is now and then; then there will be nothing.

The door reopened and Maria, with a tray in her hands, was a welcome interruption to Alex's bleak thoughts.

"May I join you for coffee?" Maria asked. Alex was pleased to have the company and immediately warmed to the young nurse. He watched her walk across the room. She was pristine in her white-and-blue uniform; comfortable, kind and very slightly assertive. Not too much, mind. However, this woman could hold her ground.

Initially, the two sat by the window in silence, sharing the view. He had watched her carefully as she poured the coffee into the china cups, a dash of milk (*leche*) and two small biscuits placed on a saucer.

"It will be a good wine this year," she said quietly.

Alex sipped at his coffee and nodded. He thought back to last year's harvest. How many harvests had he seen? How many bottles of wine had he opened, savouring the experience - the sound of the cork popping, the rich warm smell and the "legs", the viscous red liquid gripping to the sides of the glass as he held it up towards the light?

Then, of course, there was the taste. French, Australian, South African, Spanish, Argentinean and Chilean. Each country and every wine would have its' own personality and sometimes a surprise or two and, just very occasionally, a disappointment. But that reflected life and red wine had been very much a part of Alex's life.

Torres 'Sangre de Toro' was his favourite Spanish everyday wine, while the wonderful French 'Châteauneuf-du-Pape' he kept for special occasions. These, and so many other red wines, had been his friends during those wonderful times. The dinners, the parties, the quiet romantic reflections and occasionally, seemingly, his only friend when he had drowned his sorrows.

"The summer has been very short," he said. "But very dry. Each day I have watched the hills and there has hardly been a cloud. Sometimes a small fluffy cumulus cloud appears just over the peak, but that soon evaporates away. Very, very dry."

"You must have seen many clouds as an airline captain, no?" Maria asked.

"Oh yes, Maria. I have seen many towering cumulonimbus clouds so large and so high they almost covered an entire country! Flashing and banging away, dropping their rain on the poor people below. We had radar, of course. We would see them as red, yellow, or even purple returns on our radar screen. Sometimes we would route miles off course to avoid them." He smiled as the memories came flooding into his mind.

"Were they dangerous?" Maria asked. "What would happen if you flew through them?"

"Perhaps a degree of danger," Alex conceded, "but mostly a little uncomfortable Maria! Of course, it might be very bumpy and, sometimes, you could be struck by lightning or hit by hailstones. Once when I was descending, with the thrust levers closed, trying to go down, but the cloud had other ideas and pushed us upwards very quickly! It didn't last too long." He chuckled and waved a finger. "That's why you should always keep your seatbelt fastened; just in case you go over a bump in the air!"

"But lightning?" Maria asked. "Can it kill the plane?"

Alex laughed loudly and slapped his hand on his thigh. "Kill the plane? No, no, lightning doesn't hurt the plane! My aircraft were hit several times. Well yes, it might make a loud bang and scare the passengers! Sometimes it can even scare the crew! But no it does not hurt the plane, no. Often it is difficult for the engineers to even find where the lightning has stuck. Still, it was definitely safer to stay away from them altogether. That is why we fly around them; fifty, perhaps a hundred miles or more if necessary!"

"You must have seen so many things, no?" Maria asked.

Alex paused for a moment to look at her. This was not small talk. She appeared genuinely interested in his ramblings! He had no idea why Isabella was no longer looking after him, but this Maria was an interesting young girl. She spoke good English, seemed genuinely pleasant and was always smiling. Not always the mouth and lips, but the eyes. Yes, those interesting Spanish eyes, a deep steel blue; dark, but smiling.

"Yes, Maria, I have seen many, many things. I am a very lucky old man. I have travelled the world. I have seen many incredible places. I have met many wonderful people. I have been very lucky indeed!" Thousands of memories flooded into Alex's mind. Some seemed a little muddled and blurred, while others - others felt as if they were yesterday.

"Will you tell me some of your stories, Captain Young? I would love to hear some of your stories. Please!" Maria was leaning forward encouragingly and those eyes were sparkling and alive.

Alex felt seduced by his young companion. He watched as she stood up and stepped towards the window. For a moment she seemed totally illuminated by the sun as it streamed in through the glass. In resplendent glory he saw her as an angel lit against the sky, bright and white; so bright and white. But even as her black hair shone in the sunlight, the image slowly began to blur. He blinked as misty tears filled his eyes.

Yes, he thought, there were so many stories; what harm could it do? It would pass away the hours. His thoughts raced as glimpses of his life flashed before him as if projected onto a giant cinema screen. So many good times and some bad ones too!

Alex Young liked a good story, but where to begin?

Chapter 1: Mum and Dad

The old Masia had the look of a country mansion, but it was unmistakably Catalan. Unusually its stonewalls rose three floors into the air, its windows decorated with elaborate winding ironwork and huge shutters, supported by rusted hinges that no longer moved at all. The terracotta roof tiles had faded to dull ochre, but still proudly crowned the huge edifice. Tall arches (Catalan 'arcs') stretched down one side of the structure, providing a sheltered walkway into the building.

The long drive leading up to the Residencia Mayores was still flanked by long fields of vines, but the building itself stood proudly, reaching up to the sky. Tall pines provided shade to the baked, dry garden, while silver-leaved olive trees bordered dusty paths that weaved away from the parking area. Just to the north the mountains of Montsant glittered in the morning sunshine. It would be another hot day.

The staff car park was around the back of the building, close to where tired outbuildings crumbled into slow, but inevitable decay. Only one of the sheds here actually had a door and that housed the old ambulance that had once been owned by the Cruz Roja – the Red Cross. It had been occasionally used to ferry patients to the Hospital Sant Joan in Reus but now the doctors came in from Tarragona to check on the patients within the high stonewalls.

Some said it was the civil war that had closed the villa when it was requisitioned by the army, while others claimed family feuds and mismanagement had led to its collapse. Certainly the bank had sold the land to farming neighbours at a bargain price and the house had remained locked up and neglected for years.

The Masia had somehow resisted destruction until a large health care company rescued it in the 1960's. The wine presses had mysteriously disappeared, but the inevitable graffiti (the curse of Spain) was easily removed and the olive groves were rescued from oblivion. There were no longer any chickens in the farmyard, or pigs in the pigsties, although Maria had once seen a stray cat hiding in the shade watching over several tiny kittens. However, there was a strict policy – no animals were permitted in the Residencia Mayores.

Maria keyed in the door code, most out of place in the huge oak door. Its heavy structure seemed more in keeping with a prison, but then…

"So, tell me about your travels. Where did you go?" Maria seemed excited at the prospect of hearing her patient's stories. "Was it exhilarating?" She sat across from him in a wicker chair, her hands folded in her lap. Her bright starched-white uniform contrasted with her dark Spanish skin. Behind her the door to the veranda was open and occasionally a cooling breeze wafted into the room.

Alex smiled. "Life was exciting, Maria. It was a roller-coaster. I just held on and enjoyed the ride! There were ups and downs, of course, but I just held on. It was truly wonderful."

"How did you become a pilot?" Maria asked. "How did you do it? Did you dream of it as a child?"

"Well, it's a long story, a very long story." He smiled; nodding gently, then he closed his eyes and thought back to his childhood. After all, that was where it all began.

Alex was brought up in England during the 1950's and 1960's. The 1950's were a time of innocence when children could go out to play in the local woods for a whole day without fear of harm. Sometimes with friends, sometimes alone, Alex's playground was a huge forest, full of German soldiers, foreign spies, and evil baddies. He was armed, of course; he carried a twisted branch, which fired hundreds of bullets each minute. He and his unit lay in wait, ambushing the invading Nazis.

Then, one crisp Christmas day, all of the boys in the road received plastic machine guns, a generosity much regretted by parents and neighbours alike. The young boys had to add their own sound effects to the guns, but there were many very noisy battles! Elders had witnessed a real world war just a decade and a half before, with no family left untouched. Alex had listened to stories about his parents who had both been evacuated during the war.

Alex smiled. "My father and his brother were evacuated to Cornwall during the war. My grandmother once made a surprise visit to them, travelling down by train from London."

The train had crossed the Tamar Bridge when a German fighter strafed the engine and carriages, although it was uncertain as to whether any of the bullets had found their target. The sound of the shells striking the ground had been terrifying. Eventually the train had carried on to Truro, where Alice Young found people burying a dead sheep that had been killed by a stray bomb.

Finally she arrived at the house, a large terraced building, and opened the wrought-iron gate. The small garden at the front looked well kept, with short cropped grass and several rose trees. *Very nice* she thought. *Very nice indeed*. She gave the door-knocker a hearty bang.

"Hello, Mum, what you doin' here?" A young teenage boy opened the door, almost swinging on the handle. "Freddie, it's Mum!" he shouted up the stairs behind him.

"Well, you goin' to let me in then Billy?" she asked and immediately pushed her way into the hallway. "Where's Mr and Mrs Teague?"

"I dunno," Billy said. He then shouted "Freddie, get down ere now. Quick!"

"Well, blow me!" Freddie came sauntering down the stairs. His long red hair was unwashed and uncombed. "Look what the cat's dragged in!"

"Don't you be so bleedin' cheeky!" Alice raised her hand and slapped the side of his head. "So, how you boys doin' then? Are they looking after you?"

"Yeah, it's all right, in' it Freddie?" Young Billy usually deferred to his older brother.

"Well, it's boring!" Freddie was still rubbing the side of his face.

Alice looked around the hallway. There were three doors off the hall and then the stairs to the bedrooms. "Well, show me around," she demanded.

Freddie went to the first door. "Well this is the best room. We're not allowed in ere." He pushed open the door. Four chairs sat under a wooden polished table. A small tablemat at the centre had an empty vase upon it. Lace curtains hung at the windows facing the street. Black-and white family pictures hung on the walls in elaborate frames.

"Why aren't you allowed in 'ere then?" Alice asked.

"Dunno," grunted Billy, kicking at the carpet. "Cos its posh, prob'ly."

All three of them filed out and into the next room, which had a settee facing the fireplace. A small radio sat proudly on a small table in one corner with a large aerial sticking out of the top. Despite being mid-afternoon and sunny, the room was dark.

At first Alice thought it was the brownish wallpaper with its embossed gold flowers that dulled it, but she then realised a wooden outhouse had been attached to the back window. She peered through the dim glass and saw several wooden boxes sporting garden canes laden with tomatoes. Most of them were still green, but one or two were beginning, just beginning, to ripen.

"Cor lumey, look at them beauties," she said.

"Not allowed in there, niv'er," Billy grumbled.

They stepped back into the hallway and Alice followed her sons into the kitchen. It was surprisingly small, partly because of the old pine table placed against one wall.

"This is where we 'ave tea, Mum" Freddie waved a hand around the room.

"Are you getting plenty to eat? Hope you been sharing some of the stuff in them food parcels what I sent you!" The two boys looked at each other blankly. Freddie looked at the ground and left it to his brother to speak.

"What food parcels?" Billy asked.

"Don't you come it with me boy" Alice snapped at him. "Bleedin' costly to send all that stuff down 'ere every month."

"We ain't 'ad no food parcels Mum, honest, honestly." Billy was looking straight into his mother's eyes.

"Right, show us the rest," Alice took a deep breath and shepherded her boys from the kitchen.

Both boys ran up the stairs two steps at a time then waited on the landing for their mother who was puffing heavily.

"That's the fags," Freddie whispered to Billy, ensuring his mother could not hear. Billy nodded in agreement.

"Toilet." Freddie pointed to a closed door with a small frosted window in the top. Both boys then walked along the landing, passed another two doors, and went to ascend yet more steps.

"Wait a minute, what about these rooms?" Alice asked.

"Not allowed in them, neither," shrugged Billy. "That's the twins' room and that's Mr and Mrs Teagues' bedroom."

"Show me," ordered Alice. The boys looked at each other before Freddie stepped up and opened the first door to the twins' bedroom. Inside, under the rear window, were two neatly made single beds. A huge mahogany wardrobe stood on the opposite wall, with a big silver mirror in its door. The next room was the parents' bedroom, neatly finished with a double bed.

"Never been in ere," Billy muttered.

"Come on, out you go!" Alice ushered the boys out of the bedroom and they both scrambled up the stairs to the next floor. The steps were much steeper and Alice held on tightly as she ascended to the top. The landing was only big enough for one person and the boys had already entered the single doorway. Alice stepped inside and drew a breath.

"What's this?" she asked. She looked around the dark room, dimly lit by a single naked bulb hanging from the ceiling. Two thin mattresses lay on the floor, each with a pile of blankets strewn untidily on top. In the corner on the floor were a pile of clothes, some folded and some screwed up.

"I said, what's this?" Alice asked again firmly.

"Well, it's our bedroom, ain't it," Billy said. He ran over and sat on a large old army box; he then jumped up and opened it. He pointed inside and showed his mother the pile of toys and books that were 'their stuff'.

"How much time do you spend up 'ere?" she asked.

"All the time when we're not at school," Freddie said guiltily. Billy was still fumbling around in the box for his favourite toy.

Alice took a deep breath. The room smelt stale and stuffy; there was no window and the old floor carpet was threadbare. The contrast to the bedrooms downstairs was shocking. It was not what was promised and it was not what was agreed.

"So where is Mrs Teague?" Alice asked again. Both boys just looked at each other and shrugged their shoulders. "I think I fancy a cup o' tea boys. Go downstairs and make us all a drink."

The boys left their mother still standing in the attic room and jumped down the two flights of stairs several steps at a time. By the time she entered the kitchen, Freddie had made three cups of tea. There was a war on and there was no sugar. Alice put the cups on a tray.

"Come on boys, come and open the door for your mother." She stood at the door to the 'best room'.

"Not allowed in there," Billy pointed out.

"Nuffings too good for my boys," Alice said and Freddie stepped forward and opened the door. Alice walked in and placed the tray on the table. "Come 'n sit down boys," she ordered.

The boys each pulled out a chair and sat there in silence. They watched as their mother blew quietly on her teacup before taking a little sip. Both the boys gazed around the room, trying to look at the pictures on the wall, but they knew not to get up from the table. Billy tapped his fingers a few times, but a look from his mother was enough to make him stop.

"Did I tell you about the train journey down? First we had a German aircraft shooting at us, then when I got 'ere, they told me a bomb had dropped on the town and killed a sheep. Killed it dead! I think it's more dangerous down ere than at home, saints preserve us!" Alice crossed herself and the boys looked at each other and raised their eyebrows.

"Was there lots of blood?" Billy asked curiously.

"I didn't see the poor little bugger," Alice replied. "They was buryin' it to stop disease I suppose. But I tell yer, you don't get many sheep being killed in London!"

"Dogs maybe? Or cats?" suggested Billy.

Then the two boys stiffened as they heard the sound of keys turning in the front door. Alice took another sip of tea. Billy now wished he had drunk his; his mouth felt very dry.

"What are you boys doing in here?" bellowed Mrs Teague. She stepped into the room and then stopped in her tracks. "Mrs Young, what an unexpected surprise. You really should have told us you were coming. The boys are not allowed in the 'best room'."

"I told 'em to come in ere. Unexpected surprise is it Mrs Teague? What would you 'ave done then? Moved my boys downstairs into a proper bedroom, would you? Instead of leavin' 'em in that bleedin' pig sty! You should be ashamed of yerself Mrs Teague, I wouldn't keep animals in a space like that!"

"I'll thank you not to speak to me like that!" protested Mrs Teague. "We'll have no profanity in this house, thank you!"

"I'll speak to you 'ow I please," Alice retorted. "And the food parcels, Mrs Teague? I checked with the post office. All were safely delivered. Shared out among the whole family, was they Mrs Teague?"

"Well, it seemed the fairest way," Mrs Teague forced a smile.

"Liar!" It was Freddie who spoke. "We didn't get nuffin', did we Billy?"

"Shut up Freddie!" Alice ordered.

Mrs Teague began to flounder. She had been caught in a lie. "Your boys have been very difficult, Mrs Young, I......" Mrs Teague was cut off in mid-sentence.

"Don't you start lying to me, you bleedin' fat cow! I will be reporting you to the authorities," Alice was now raising her already loud voice several more decibels, but she remained in control. She was gripping the teacup very tightly. "Steal food from the children, keepin' 'em in a tiny attic wiv no windows, sleepin' on the floor. It's like a God damn prison!"

"Mrs Young! I would ask you to..."

"Mrs Teague! If you say one more word to me, I will ram this teacup down your cake 'ole! Now I'm going to start wiv the police. Then I am going to the local authorities. There are laws Mrs Teague. I'm not havin' my boys treated like dossers. It's no safer down ere than back in London. I'm taking my boys back wiv me and if dare you stand in my way, I keep a hair pin ere what can do you a very nasty accident!" Alice was now very angry. Her boys sat, not daring to move, hardly believing their ears. "Boys, I've put most of your clothes in two bags in your room. Go and get them and bring them downstairs."

The boys jumped up and ran past Mrs Teague, who was trembling on the spot. Excuse after excuse came into her head, but each one evaporated before she could even speak. If only her Bertie her husband was here, but he wouldn't be home for several hours yet. She heard the bang, bang, bang as the boys descended the stairs three or four steps at a time. Her instinct was to tell them off, but she could feel her body weakening by the second.

Both boys had removed a couple of jumpers and replaced them with toys from the old army box. They had placed the toys deep into their bags, lest their mother check the contents. They were going home!

"Mum, come on!" Billy called from the front door. He was afraid his mother would change her mind, or that she and Mrs Teague would make their peace.

Alice slowly rose from her chair and walked purposefully towards Mrs Teague. She placed her face about an inch from the woman's face. "You better pray you never see me again, you fat bitch, 'cos if I do, I'll 'ave your guts for garters!"

Mrs Teague jumped when she felt the empty teacup being thrust into her hands. She remained rooted to the spot. She was still shaking as the front door slammed shut. The two boys skipped down the road, swinging their bags with joy.

"Well, your dad will be pleased," she said and allowed herself a brief smile. "…and stop that whistlin'!"

"My God!" exclaimed Maria, leaning forward in her chair. "Was it really safer in London?"

"Probably not!" Alex chuckled.

Somehow the Second World War had held a sort of clarity for Billy. Adolf Hitler and the Germans had invaded a country called Poland. The British Government had got mad and decided to teach Germany a lesson. However, the Germans had lots of men and big tanks and they had chased the poor British back to some place called Dunkirk. Hundreds and hundreds of people sailed across the English Channel to pick up our boys and bring them home. Now Hitler was bombing England to teach them a lesson. This had resulted in rationing, which meant lots of nice things were no longer available. Billy was unsure how Adolf Hitler had captured all their sweets, sugar, milk and eggs, but now most of it had gone. He must be a clever bugger!

"My grandparents owned a pub in East London called the Five Bells and Bladebone." Alex had actually gone back, many years later, to visit the pub in Limehouse, near the London Docks. "When the air-raid sirens went," he continued, "the family would go down to the cellars, which had been reinforced with railway sleepers. They would sleep there among the barrels of beer!"

The boys were delighted to have returned home. The docks and the pub remained a bustling, lively place despite the Blitz. The boys were expected to collect empty glasses and then tasked with washing them, too. Sometimes they ran errands and would linger in the streets to look at piles of rubble where entire houses had once stood. It was an exciting time for young teenage boys.

No one had even considered the irony. The boys had been rescued from Cornwall where they had slept on mattresses on the floor, in a room without windows. Now they slept underground, on mattresses on the floor, in a cellar without windows.

The family would lie there listening to the drone of aircraft engines overhead. They would hold their breath when they heard the loud piecing whistle of a bomb falling thousands of feet through the air towards its target.

"My father," Alex continued, "went back to his room one morning and discovered there was no ceiling to his bedroom! A bomb had fallen in the churchyard opposite, felling a tree. The tree had fallen through the roof of the pub and cut my father's bed in half! And do you know what?" He smiled, watching Maria, and paused for effect. "The bedroom was full of dead birds! They must have been sleeping in the tree when the bomb fell!"

"My grandparents moved to another pub in Canning Town," Alex continued. "By all accounts, my grandmother ran a black market of rationed goods," he chuckled.

"What is a 'black market'?" Maria asked. "Usually for us, this is paying for things in cash to avoid paying tax!"

"Oh it would be cash alright, although Alice was also a money lender. Helping the community out at very high interest rates! No, a 'black market' was where all sorts of goods were rationed and in short supply. My grandparents stored their illicit goods in the garden, in holes covered with corrugated iron. They would buy goods, sometimes smuggled in from the docks by the merchant seamen, and then sell them on to their customers. I think they were probably making a lot of money!" Alex paused and drew his breath. Maria was still leaning forward eagerly absorbing everything he said.

Eventually, after the war, Alex's grandparents moved down to Essex and bought a smallholding, a small farm. They had pigs and chickens and owned acres of ground. With three sons, they had the labour to produce most of their own food, while selling the rest at a tidy profit. When Alex's father, Billy, was in his twenties, he and Freddie would go down to Southend-on-Sea looking for fun."

There was a dance hall in Southend called the Kursaal, which was a favourite with the young teenagers. People would travel all the way down from London for the weekend, just to walk on the beach, eat jellied eels, and dance at the Kursaal. Long queues would form all along the street, men and women keen to dance to the live orchestras and bands. A famous singer called Vera Lynn began her singing career at the Kursaal Ballroom, with the bandleader Howard Baker.

Alex sighed. Maria was too young and, of course, Spanish. How could he expect her to have heard of Vera Lynn? He thought about singing 'White Cliffs of Dover' or 'We'll Meet Again' but then thought better of it.

Billy and Freddie had walked to the Kursaal on one occasion and saw the long queue. Sublimely confident, they began near the front of the line and walked slowing along the straggling queue hoping to see someone they knew. The scene had been described to Alex a hundred times and the image was clear in his mind.

"'ello girls, nice to see yer again." Freddie had a freckled face, ginger hair and a grin that spread right across his face. The girls looked at each other and giggled. Of course, they had never ever seen these boys before. "Cigarette?"

"Don't mind if we do," Betsy replied. She took two cigarettes and passed one to her younger sister Annie. Annie gave her 'a look' as if to protest but took the cigarette anyway. Billy held out a shiny gold lighter and flicked it. He held the flame as both girls drew on their cigarettes. Only then, did the boys light their own fags.

"Bit forward, aren't yer," Betsy flirted. Annie stood silently looking at the two men. She had seen many men like Freddie before, out for more than a laugh and not to be trusted. Billy seemed a little different; quieter and more considered.

"So are you girls meeting anyone? Have you two got a date for tonight?" Freddie grinned cheekily from ear to ear. "P'rhaps you wanna go wiv us?"

"Awl, I dunno, have we got a date for tonight Annie?" Betsy took a long drag on her cigarette, filled her lungs and then exhaled a large cloud of smoke. She'd seen it done like that at the pictures and had been practising.

"Might have a date," Annie said. "Who's asking?" Her heart sank as she realised just how stupid her own words now sounded.

"We're asking, ain't we Freddie," said Billy gently. "So where you girls from?"

As the queue moved slowly forward, the girls used the time to take the measure of these two boys. Well, they were men really, both in their early twenties. Billy had a high forehead and dark black hair, slicked back with Brylcreem. Occasionally the girls would exchange a quick glance at each other when they thought the boys were not looking.

Betsy's glance to Annie meant 'it's just a bit of fun.' Annie's glance meant 'are you sure this is OK?' and 'are you sure *they* are OK?'

Billy was thinking how cute the young one was. Annie had thick blonde hair cascading down to her shoulders, framing a pretty face. The other one, Betsy, was also nice but a bit sure of herself. Freddie, on the other hand, was thinking evil thoughts and had already undressed both girls in his mind. He figured Betsy was spunky and flirty. She might be up for it. The other girl was pretty, but a bit quiet and a perhaps a bit too young.

Alex looked across at Maria. She was totally absorbed in the story.

"Annie was only sixteen," Alex explained. "Before she reached her seventeenth birthday she was pregnant with Billy's child. That was me, soon to be born! My parent's married soon afterwards, much to the disapproval of my grandparents!"

"So young!" Maria exclaimed.

Those first few years were a massive struggle in so many ways. First there was the lack of money, although Annie's parents gave whatever help and support they could. Then there was the problem of Billy's parents who were convinced that Annie had trapped their son into this marriage.

"They even went to the trouble of buying an engagement ring and giving it to an ex-girlfriend of my Dads!" Alex said.

"That's terrible," gasped Maria. "Unforgivable!" she protested.

"Yes, I know," he continued. "They tried to get him married off to this ex-girlfriend instead of my mother but my father, for once, stood firm. It's unbelievable!"

Alice was a matriarch who had controlled Billy's entire life up to this point. Until the day she died, she continued to interfere. When she clicked her fingers, Billy would always come running. Both she and her husband made Annie's life hell and they made it very clear they disapproved of her. Somehow Annie had stood up for herself, fought her corner, and gradually grew stronger and harder.

"We were a poor family and, mostly, I just remember my parents working so very hard. My father worked very long hours and would come home exhausted and tired." Alex wondered how it must have felt for his parents, a new baby and hardly any money at all. Two years after they married, his sister was born.

"Growing up, I can't actually remember my father ever playing with us or giving us any affection," There was a sadness in Alex's voice. "He was a very strict disciplinarian and we knew when to keep out of his way!"

Alex looked across at Maria. She seemed very distant and was now staring out of the window at the vineyards. Perhaps she is tired, he thought. He closed his eyes and thought about those early years but, before the memories came to him, he was asleep.

CHAPTER 2: THE EARLY YEARS

Alex was staring into the air. His thoughts were filled with vague reminiscences from his distant past, but they would fade away just as quickly as they came, only to be replaced by another previously lost memory. He drifted, confused, remembering and then forgetting.

Somewhere a door closed. The sound was not loud, but it startled the old man and he turned his head towards the window. He recognised the curtains, half closed against the burning sun, the small table beside him and the bed across the room. He turned his head the other way and was shocked to find he was not alone.

Seated quietly across from him was a young woman. She was dressed in a white and blue uniform, a silver watch hanging from behind the lapel.

"Would you like a rest Captain? I think perhaps you were perhaps drifting off." The nurse smiled kindly. "You were telling me about your parents Annie and Billy."

"Ah yes," Alex nodded. His thoughts settled and he smiled back at the nurse. 'Maria,' he told himself. 'You are Maria, the new nurse.'

"Would you like to know about my school years?" he asked. Maria smiled agreeably and he continued.

Going to school seemed such a good idea when you are five. It meant that you were grown up and everything would be fine after that first bout of nerves. It was an opportunity to make friends and play. You were taught lots of useful things such as how to colour and paint; teachers even read you stories. Those early years were a bit of blur, but an incident happened that was to affect Alex for the rest of his life.

"My mother had a cleaning job," Alex explained. "An aunt (not a real aunt, just a friend) had picked me up from school and was taking me back to her home, just a few houses down the road from where we lived. We had stopped at the shop in the village and she had bought me an ice-lolly. I was just five years old and was wandering along behind her, licking away at my lollypop. Well, I failed to see a wasp that had landed on it and, on my next lick, the wasp stuck its sting deep into my tongue!"

"Ouch!" Maria grimaced.

"Yes, ouch! The pain was terrible" Alex continued. "I screamed loudly, but then I began convulsing. My tongue was swelling up fast and soon began blocking my airway. I started choking and gasping for air. Auntie Winnie saved my life that day. She ran to the house of a local midwife who lived very close by. The woman had tea and cakes laid out on the table and, to my astonishment, it was all swept onto the floor to make room for me. I can remember the cups smashing as they hit the floor and the noise added to the drama and my fear!

I was lifted onto the table, placed on my back, with my neck and head hanging over the table. I continued to gasp for breath. Suddenly I found a bottle of liquid being poured down my throat. It was whisky, I think. I choked and probably coughed much of it back out, but I certainly swallowed some. It was ghastly!"

"But it neutralised the sting," Maria said.

"It *should* neutralise the sting was exactly what the midwife had said to Winnie!" Alex nodded. "Otherwise I might swallow my tongue and die! I'm not even sure it's possible to swallow your tongue but, anyway,

I lay there thinking I would die, still fighting for air. I was also worried about the broken crockery and wondered just how much trouble I might be in! My throat continued to burn, as did my lungs, but gradually my thrashing and screaming turned to sobbing."

"Ever since then I have had an extreme fear of choking or being sick! Even now, if I were to vomit, I would shake with fear and probably cry. Yes, even now!" Alex laughed.

"I'm not sure we have that on your medical notes," Maria joked.

They both chuckled at the thought and for a moment their eyes met. Then there was that look. What was that, Alex wondered? Was it compassion? Or pity? It had only lasted a second, but Maria had been caught out and she glanced away.

"Gosh, I've just remembered something else that happened that year Maria! It just came into my mind. I think that was the year we had our very first holiday! My parents took my sister and me to Butlins at Bognor Regis! It was a holiday camp where families went and stayed in chalets. It was completely self-contained - there was entertainment, a swimming pool, childrens' activities and Red Coats!"

"What is Red Coats?" Maria asked.

"They were the helpers," Alex explained. "They would always be around assisting people and at night they provided much of the entertainment, singing and dancing. Radios would announce when breakfast, lunch and dinner were being served! 'Hello Campers!' they used to say."

Alex had never ever been to a restaurant before and they all sat in a huge hall, full of rows of tables. There were eight people to each table and waiters rushed up and down the aisles handing out the plates of food and collecting them in afterwards. Hundreds of excited holidaymakers chatted about their day and the noise was deafening. He had never experienced anything like it in his life!

He was about a third of the way through his meal and had paused to talk. Trying to be polite (he must have seen it somewhere) he placed his knife and fork together. He did not know that this was a sign to indicate that one had finished and the waiter removed his plate, despite it still having lots of food on it! He nearly cried and spent the rest of the day hungry!

"Oh, you poor boy!" Maria exclaimed. "But what did your parents say?"

"I don't think they knew much more than me. Anyway, my meal was gone, and that was that." Alex paused a moment. "I don't even know why that came into my head."

Maria just gave an encouraging smile and Alex continued with his story. The family moved to another nearby village and Alex attended a new primary school. This school had a large playing field backing onto the woods and, at one end, was a children's playground with swings, a slide and a roundabout. Alex easily made new friends.

At age nine he met a girl whose name was Janet. Janet's brother was in his class at school and he had visited their house several times before. Janet was tall with a beautiful face and long flowing blonde hair. The hair fascinated him, reaching down her back to her waist. Almost every time he saw her, the hair was different - bunches, a single ponytail, tied up, or perhaps draped over one shoulder. She was two years older than her brother, and consequently two years older than Alex. Totally out of reach. Actually the reason was she was out of reach was because she was a girl!

Alex, trying to find his way in the world, eventually got a surge of courage (or madness) and bought Janet a ring that at cost him sixpence in the local village. He earned a small amount of money, first by doing odd jobs, then later by getting up very early every morning and doing a paper round. He would race around on his bicycle before breakfast delivering newspapers, combating the cold, angry dogs and tiredness. Having money of your own was liberating and he did not want to rely on handouts from his parents, who could ill-afford pocket money.

Sixpence was a lot of money to him but, as soon as he saw the ring, Alex knew what he must do. Several times he found himself in the 'cheap' little shop with his sister or perhaps a friend. They would browse the confectionery counter and sometimes buy a penny worth of sweets from the line of tall jars. A Mars Bar also cost sixpence, but it would be several years more before he could allow himself such an extravagance. Little plastic toys were also too expensive.

Finally he plucked up the courage and found an opportunity to buy the ring. Alex told himself reassuringly that she was worth it. He presented it to her one day while on the playing field at school and her smile was a joy to behold. Her eyes shone and she seemed so happy and kissed him on the cheek.

However Janet's instinct was to run off and show all her friends. Within seconds her happiness turned to discomfort. Suddenly there was laughing verging on ridicule as the group of girls pointed towards Alex and danced around Janet. She had shot an apologetic smile towards Alex, but the sincerity and happiness was now fading rapidly. Slowly she was being drawn into the derision and cruelty that Alex was now to face. He wanted to run away and hide, but this was school and there was nowhere to go. He ran off to a group of boys playing football on the field.

Alex stood and watched and was soon invited to play, provided he was the goalie. He looked over at the huddle of girls with Janet at their centre. He wanted to die and wished the world would swallow him up. His anguish was interrupted as the boys began shouting at him. He turned back, just in time to see the football trickling slowly past his feet and into the net.

As the years ticked by, the lessons gradually became more and more serious. There was talk of the 'Eleven Plus', an exam that decided whether you would go to the local comprehensive school or to one of the grammar schools situated in a neighbouring town.

"I can't remember whether something was *actually* said," Alex explained, "but it was clear to me that the grammar school option would incur significant costs and my parents were very poor. I would have had to travel to school by train, so there would been a significant cost with the tickets. The grammar schools had 'real' school uniforms, rather than the less expensive grey trousers and white shirt option. Certainly, it would have been more expense.

Added to that was my own lack of motivation. Why would I want to travel further to another school? If they had high standards as they claimed, I would have to work even harder and what was the point of that. No, my parents' poverty was a good excuse for me not to work hard at all." Alex did not pass his 'Eleven Plus' and attended the comprehensive school in 1964. Nobody expected anything else.

The 1960's were a time of cultural and sexual revolution, but this all passed him by. His life consisted of the torture and tedium of school, interspersed with playtime on summer evenings and the weekends. Despite having sisters and mostly female cousins, he was very shy and uncomfortable around girls. He lacked confidence and the tall, lanky boy he saw in the mirror simply did not fill him with confidence.

Two years had passed since his public humiliation, but Alex remained convinced that girls were a significant problem and best avoided. So, at age eleven he had graduated to the 'big' school, the large modern comprehensive school down beyond the railway station. It was huge and, initially, quite scary but Alex soon learned that it was easy to hide in this jungle of people. His school chums were OK, nothing special, but they did at least share his hatred of school and teachers.

For a few weeks he became close with Steven and, after school, they would wander across the brickfields looking for newts. Then he and Steven drifted apart, and he became close friends with Toby. They would also play together after school, until Toby decided that Paul was much more interesting than Alex. Eventually he drifted back to the schoolboy pack once again, where his earlier absence went completely unnoticed.

Seb and Gary eventually concluded that they wanted Alex to be their mate and this was a real honour. However they explained that he must prove himself worthy of their friendship and they took him right across the brickfields site to the railway line. The area was well known to Alex, but the acres of rubble, ponds and scrap metal suddenly felt very threatening and hostile. The boys explained that to be truly in their gang, he would have to complete a task.

The mission, the two boys explained, was to cross the railway line. This involved climbing over a high fence, then sliding down the steep embankment through the stinging nettles to the railway line itself. There, he would have to wait until the train came around the corner. Then, and only then, he would have to run across the two sets of rails, leaping the live rail, and climb up the other bank. Over the next fence was a footpath, leading back through the woods, eventually leading to the small village railway station. Seb and Gary would meet him there.

Alex knew the railway was strictly off limits. If he were discovered, the consequences would be awful. Perhaps the police would be involved; his father would certainly kill him. Alex liked Seb and Gary, but not that much. He invited one of them to show him how it was done. Seb and Gary looked at each other in silence for a few seconds and then realised they were late for tea. They left Alex standing there and wandered off, kicking broken bits of bright red brick that seemed to litter the dusty ground all over this area. Alex held back and then chose a different way home.

Three months later another boy, named Mark, was killed running the gauntlet of death. The train took half a mile to stop. Alex wondered whether Mark had been alone that day. More likely Seb and Gary had been crouching in the bushes at the top of the embankment, but he could never bring himself to confront them. Every parent in the village summoned their children and lectured them on the dangers of the railway, but the incident soon faded into history.

Other friends came and went, but life seemed dull and boring. Homework was a punishment, school was dreary, and the future seemed bleak. Alex had noticed that people who had money already had money, while poor people such as his parents worked all hours just to survive. People commuted on the same bus or train every day, working in the same factory week after week, just to get a pay packet that would just about do if you were lucky. He knew that a few people in his road had cars, but those were apparently owned by the bank. Mr Mathews across the road sold vacuum cleaners but, for some reason, the bank had given him a car. Alex just couldn't understand it.

One day Alex was standing in the corridor looking for a boy he knew. They had been told off during chemistry and now they both had an appointment with the headmaster. However, Geoffrey had vanished and Alex was reluctant to face the music alone. It was then that 'she' walked by.

Alex had observed that all people bob up and down as they walked. Just watch their heads, up and down, up and down. However this girl appeared to glide, her head remaining on one level, her entire body simply floating across the floor. Alex stood and stared. He watched as this apparition, moved in slow motion, from right to left just before his eyes. His heart raced as he studied her. She had short jet-black hair, a tanned complexion, stunning eyes (he was uncertain of their colour) and her clothes looked smart, trendy and new. She was the most beautiful thing he had ever seen. He was too absorbed to realise just how hard his heart was now pounding.

Outside the headmaster's office Alex dreamed about the girl he had just seen. Who was she? How could he find out more? Of course, he was much more experienced now and he knew not to get involved. No rings, no slick chat-up lines, no confiding in fellow pupils. He would try and find out her name and would then attempt to find out something about *her*, but he knew that his mission would be to simply love her from afar and then suffer his long and lingering pain in silence.

First there was the matter of the dreaded headmaster. Various pupils walked past the office and looked sympathetically at the boy leaning forward on the middle chair, staring down at his shoes. One or two teachers also wandered past and Alex imagined their immediate condemnation. Guilty as charged; no surprise seeing *that* boy outside the office! Finally a voice bellowed his name from beyond the door and he stood up and straightened his clothes. He looked again at his shoes and gave them a final polish against the back of his legs. He then entered the room.

A large red face stared at him from behind the huge desk that was covered in papers and exercise books. Mr Robert had a bald head with a long strand of grey hair growing on one side. This lay across the scalp as if to disguise the baldness, but the long tufts had other ideas and frequently fell forward. If a boy placed his hand on one side of his head and ran his fingers over the top of it, everyone would know at once he was mimicking Mr Roberts' comb-over.

Alex stared straight ahead, trying not to look at the hair. Instead he looked beyond and through the window. He just saw the roof of a blue and white double-decker bus race by towards the railway station and wished he was on it. That would be a number seven going to Ashingdon, Rochford, Prittlewell and finally Southend. Southend – beaches, a pier, and slot machines!

"And where, pray, is your accomplice? Where is Meadows?"

Alex tried so very hard not to look to his right, where Mr Roberts kept his collection of canes. Alex explained that he had no idea where Geoffrey was. He also considered that Geoffrey's absence was hardly his fault but, of course, he could not say so.

"Are you talking back at me, boy?" Mr Roberts had screamed at him.

In his mind Alex placed himself in the secretary's office, along in the corridor, and then perhaps down the far hall near the toilets. He was sure in each of these places Mr Roberts' voice was causing doors, windows, pupils and possibly other teachers to shake. There was genuine rage in Mr Roberts' face, but really Alex didn't feel he had done anything particularly bad. He was cross that Geoffrey had dropped him in it, but he knew that to say nothing and stand up straight was by far the best strategy. He had even thought to polish his dirty shoes because he knew that Mr Roberts was obsessed with such things, and was frequently known to double the punishment for such an offence. This proved to be the ultimate irony. A year later, following ill-health, Mr Roberts took a year off. His deputy, Miss Holbert, promptly banned boys from having shiny shoes, claiming they were using the reflection to stare up girls' skirts to see their knickers!

In the event Alex got away with a warning, while Geoffrey got the cane a few days later. Alex was learning more about life and survival, but perhaps far less about chemistry and other such subjects, which were obviously a complete waste of time. Let's say one child in a hundred actually became a chemist. That would mean ninety-nine children had wasted years of their lives learning rubbish. It seemed so obvious, but why couldn't adults understand that?

Anyway, now there was a much more important job to hand. The love of his life was called Penny Chapman and she lived up the hill towards Rayleigh, in one of those big houses. She was in the year above him at school in Mr Baker's class. She had a younger sister and their Dad had a very large blue car. Occasionally the Dad picked Penny up from school, but mostly she took the school bus. He also noted that she was very friendly with Suzy, who was in his class. He had considered the strategy of becoming friendly with Suzy, but she was a girl and that presented all sorts of problems. It was complicated.

So Penny was beautiful, she glided like an angel, she was rich and she was older than him. Perfect! He concluded that none of these were a problem because he was going to love her in secret. That summer Alex began taking his bike up the Rayleigh Road, slowly cycling past the house. One day he saw Penny's mother walk out and climb into that very large blue car. She was incredibly beautiful, immediately explaining why his love was so attractive.

On another occasion, Penny's father was standing over that same blue car washing off soapy water with a hosepipe. He even looked rich in his old clothes. Alex sat listening to soft ballads and immediately empathised with the broken-hearted vocalists. He shared in their sad despair and the terrible world that had dealt this cruel hand. Sometimes he even imagined sex with her, gentle, sensual love-making, but they were better than that. Why devalue such a perfect relationship? So perfect they never, ever argued. Well, actually, they never spoke at all. Once, he even considered the possibility that she might eventually get a boyfriend and have sex with him, but that was so awful, so he decided not to think about sex at all.

That summer was terribly and painfully tormenting. Alex found out sometime later that Penny was only, in fact, nine days older than him. However, the academic year had cruelly chosen to fall between them, creating a barrier too high for Alex to even consider risking painful humiliation again.

Several visits to the house confirmed that the Chapman family had probably gone away on holiday. The curtains remained closed all day and the car was never in the driveway. Alex cried himself to sleep a couple of times and realised that from birth until death people worked and slaved, with broken hearts, until nature was kind enough to put them out of their misery.

Alex's grandparents owned a small farm with pigs and an orchard that grew apples, pears, Victoria plums and damsons. Thirteen acres with near perfect lines of fruit trees, separated just far enough apart for a tractor to cut the grass in between. Often at the weekends his family would visit the farm and Alex would disappear into this vast playground of adventure.

This was his retreat from school, the village, his broken heart and all things terrible. Alex loved the pigs and the chickens, but the old dog Paddy was simply too old for anything other than sleeping. Beyond the rows and rows of apple trees, pears, damsons, and Victoria plums the farm had a huge field, right at the bottom, where they grew wheat and barley. After the harvest, the straw was collected and piled into haystacks.

"I would hide," he explained to Maria. "I would climb to the top of the haystack and lay on my back, unseen from the ground. Watching the sky and the clouds, I would sometimes see the condensation trails of the airplanes cutting across the sky. I would wonder where they were going and dream about the crew, their magical and glamorous lifestyles, travelling to far off destinations." He closed his eyes and imagined the "con trails" etching across the sky.

"So, then you decided to be a pilot, no?" Maria asked.

"Oh, I dreamed of it," he continued, "but I never really believed it. My family was quite poor and I was not especially bright at school. When I talked about becoming a pilot my parents, and others, would smile, pat me on the head and say 'of course, you do.' No one ever believed it, least of all me."

"So what happened?" Maria asked. "What made the difference?"

"Well, I drifted at school. I had no real goals; no real expectations. Then one day my parents went to a school meeting, where they were told

I would be a failure. I was in with the wrong crowd. I had no interest in learning, I wanted nothing and, therefore, I would end up with nothing."

Maria nodded, but said nothing. She looked at the ground.

"I saw the disappointment in my parent's eyes as they told me what the teachers had said. And, for me, it was totally unexpected. I really had no idea who the person was they were describing. I felt so ashamed, but I guess I must have realised there was some truth to what was being said. I was predicted to fail."

"You had no idea?" Maria asked.

"None," he said. "I thought school was a punishment because we were children. No one ever said to me 'best marks equals best job' and 'best job equals best money'. That day I realised I had to change, if I was going to get anywhere, so change I did. I guess I had an epiphany."

"Pardon, Captain Young. My English is not so good." Maria shrugged her shoulders. What is it you had?"

"An epiphany - a revelation. Suddenly I woke up to what I must do. It was as if someone had switched a light on in my head!"

Maria nodded thoughtfully.

Alex explained how he had planned to change his life. He began studying harder, of course. Then he took the decision to change his friends. In an extraordinary act, he turned his back on 'the crowd' and looked around for new friends. He found one very serious young man who was a loner. A studious fellow, level headed and probably a little boring! Having befriended him, he discovered that he was far from boring. They spent their time debating all sorts of things and discussing subjects he didn't even know he had an opinion about.

Over time he began dropping the slang that had been a part of his culture and began listening to the radio. He soon concluded that you had to 'speak posh' to be a pilot. So began a journey through the education and maturity that was to lead him down the path to his career. His slow metamorphosis did not go unnoticed. Two teachers in particular changed his life.

Teachers began to give him more attention and his English teacher, Mr Duncan, rewarded him by giving him a job as a librarian. This was a bold move, but Alex embraced the responsibility and worked even harder, both in the library and during lessons. There were no prefects at this school and the job of librarian was considered to be an important appointment. He found himself driven, seeking knowledge for knowledge sake. He was probably not as bright as the others, but he was determined to make up for it by working harder. Only later did he realise how much he owed Mr Duncan.

A second teacher also took a keen interest in him. Mr Taylor taught metal work, but his hobby was designing and building aeroplanes. He had already designed and built one aircraft, the Taylor Monoplane, and was now working on an even more powerful, aerobatic aircraft called the Taylor Titch.

Much of the construction was wood, but some parts were metal and Alex sometimes helped as John Taylor worked spare parts on the school lathe. The talk was of aircraft, of wing sections and of landing gear. Mr Taylor encouraged Alex to join the local Air Training Corps, which was based at the very same local airport from where Mr Taylor did his flight-testing.

It was eight miles from the family home to Southend Airport and Alex would cycle there and back three times a week to attend the Air Training Corps. Sometimes on a Sunday, or perhaps on a long summer's evening, he would see John Taylor flying the Taylor Titch, which looked like a small Spitfire, high above the fields near Rochford. On one such test flight, the Taylor Titch went into a tight spin and failed to recover. Mr Taylor, his Mr Taylor, was dead.

"Oh, my God!" Maria looked across at Alex who had stooped in his chair. The old man then raised his head, blinking away the tears.

"Those two men, Maria. These two teachers, they..." Alex sucked in more air, but was unable to speak.

"You must rest, Señor." Maria began to push herself up from her seat.

"No, no, I'm fine," the old man forcing a smile. "I've nearly finished; while it is fresh in my mind." Maria sunk back into her seat and waited. She did not want to see her patient distressed, but he was calmer now and appeared keen to go on.

"Ah yes, the Air Training Corps," Alex finally continued. "I guess it was also a school of sorts but we, the students, were all enthusiastic volunteers. The opportunities were just fantastic! In fact, later on in life when I lived in Gloucestershire, I returned to the Air Training Corps and volunteered as a civilian trainer. I was able to teach a new generation of young men and women, giving something back for my own good fortune, you know. Some joined the Royal Air Force, at least one became a pilot and another an air traffic controller, but whatever they did, most of them enjoyed the experience!"

At Southend Airport, the ATC instructed Alex in the theory of flight, engines, airframes, instruments and meteorology. Discipline was taught with square-bashing (actually marching), rifle-drill and military exercises. Alex saw things he had never seen before. The Squadron owned a real Rolls Royce Merlin engine, originally from a World War Two Spitfire, and they were sectioning it. This meant cutting holes in it to expose parts of the cylinders and the ignition system. Every time Alex saw it, he thought of John Taylor.

Eventually a reconditioned electric motor would turn that old Merlin engine and revealed how the pistons drew in air and fuel, commencing the four-stroke cycle.

SUCK – the piston pulls downward, drawing air and petrol fumes into the cylinder.

SQUEEZE - the piston goes up again, compressing the fuel/air mixture and also raising its temperature.

BANG – the mixture is ignited causing it to expand rapidly, pushing the piston down again.

BLOW – the piston would rises again, expelling the gases, just before the next air/fuel mixture is sucked and compressed again.

Alex had no idea how a car or aircraft engine worked, but here it was being explained to him in simple terms. Easy! The Squadron had a marching band with drums and trumpets, so marching and drilling with rifles became a regular event. There were even inter-squadron competitions. These extended to sports days, so soccer practice, cross-country running, assault-courses and night exercises all became regular events. Alex hated sport at school, but suddenly he discovered he could run fast, shoot a football or save a goal. They even had him doing the long jump!

He found himself travelling all over the UK and attending athletics meetings in Wales, flying in Suffolk and gliding in Essex. His confidence began increasing, albeit slowly and it was soon recognised that he had leadership qualities. Being tall helped, too! Soon after, he was promoted to corporal, sergeant, flight sergeant and finally cadet warrant officer. He learned how to shoot rifles, how to dismantle and assemble a Bren Gun (a type of machine gun) in the dark (that was always useful in Southend!). He now found himself in charge of other cadets, shouting orders to them across the parade ground.

Then there were the ATC camps. He went to RAF Binbrook, from where English Electric Lightning aircraft defended the skies above the UK. Another year he went to RAF Coningsby, in Lincolnshire, where pilots flying RAF Phantoms trained for a ground attack role. They met with RAF personnel, including the pilots and engineers. They went shooting and flying, and got taken up in small Chipmunk aircraft to do aerobatics.

Many instructors were happy when Alex asked to fly the plane himself. Perhaps the biggest adventure was at RAF St Mawgan, near Newquay, in Cornwall. Avro Shackleton aircraft were operating there in a maritime reconnaissance role, but the runway was already being lengthened for the brand new RAF Nimrod.

One evening the older cadets were released from camp and decided to walk into the nearby village. In those days Alex and his fellow cadets were very fit and athletic, often drinking pints of milk for health, energy, bodybuilding and strength. They had never heard of cholesterol and their food and milk intake was considered healthy at the time. A few beers were permitted from time to time, but only in moderation. The squadron and the competitions came first.

Many of the old huts where they were billeted had triangular steel girders supporting vaulted roofs. The horizontal metal struts were frequently used for pull-ups hanging by your arms; sometimes pulling and lifting your body up with both arms and, occasionally, with just one arm!

Alex and his friends found their way to a local pub, generally avoided by the officers because of its close proximity to the RAF Station. It was a quiet, sleepy establishment that had probably not changed very much since the war. As the group of six young men sipped slowly on their beers, they reflected on that.

One of their number pointed towards the half glass-frosted entrance door, dimmed with age and dust. Each took a turn to speak.

"Man walks in – 'Hello everyone I've some bad news,' he says. 'I'm afraid Ginger didn't make it.'"

"What, you mean Ginger's bought it?" another exclaimed.

"You mean he's gone shopping?"

"No you fool, Jerry got him!"

"For how much?" The laugher was raucous and loud, with some bent double.

"No, no, Ginger's bought it, not Jerry!" another insisted.

"So Jerry paid?" Puzzled.

"No, Ginger's paid! With his life!" Loud and indignant.

The few locals shot disapproving glances at the six lads so they reduced their boisterous laughter to a gentle snigger. Someone suggested they change the subject. They began talking about their day and the program for tomorrow. They were going to climb around in a real Shackleton aircraft and there was even talk of a possible flight.

"You the Southend mob?" Two young men, were standing at their table, having been hidden in a booth towards the back of the pub.

"Yes, actually, we are." It was the sergeant who replied.

"Please to meet you," one said, offering his hand. "We're with the Billericay 2393 Squadron."

It was obvious from their demeanour and short hair cuts that they were also at the camp.

"Didn't realise there were other squadrons here," someone stated.

"Maybe you chaps fancy a kick about after Mess tomorrow."

"That would be great, see you tomorrow then." The two chaps from Billericay turned and sauntered out into the night.

No one had recognised them, even though the two Squadrons were near neighbours back home in Essex. Around the table the six boys discussed just how many they could round up for a football match tomorrow afternoon and concluded that only a full team would do.

The pub door opened and an old man staggered to the bar.

"Hello Jim," he growled. "The usual please." The old man looked around the room. Then to no one in particular he said – "There be two young fellers out there, bein' done over. Someone stealin' their car, I reckon."

Alex and the others looked at each other. Each picked up what was left of their pints of beers and swallowed them straight down. They looked at each other, and then rose as one.

"Thank you and good night," one said, waving and smiling at the barman. Their walk was slow and purposeful. No running; no rushing.

Outside the dimly lit car park was a sight to behold. Off to the left was a Mini, apparently owned by the two young men from Billericay. They were both lying on the ground trying to defend their heads, while a crowd of young men in leather jackets shouted and jeered, encouraging others who stood over them. There was a sickening thud as another kick landed into the body of one. Alex began running, knowing his friends would be right beside him; there was no need to look. As they grew closer, he could see that some of the 'louts' were carrying weapons. One had some sort of chain hanging from a gloved hand. Another had a baseball bat, or was it a cricket bat?

"Hey!" one of Alex's colleagues called out. Alex winced, feeling it was unnecessary to call out anything until they had at least made it across the expanse of darkened car park. He estimated there might be about 16 of them, although he really hadn't had time to count. Anyway, this was not the time for arithmetic. Long hair and beards, they were known as 'greasers' and he had just noticed their motorbikes off to the left. Alex was now jogging gently, clenching his hands and he could now hear the steps of others running with him.

The thugs turned their attention from the two lads on the ground and moved to confront the new intruders. They remained in a group, some glancing at one another and, for a moment, Alex hoped they would turn and run. But they didn't.

First the guy with a chain thrust it towards Alex like a whip, but it was short of its mark by a good foot. By the time it was raised again Alex had grabbed it, twisted it and pulled the slob towards him. He spun the chain around the man's arm and then jumped sideways. He pulled hard as the man's arm was pulled backwards and up. There was a blood-curdling scream and the man went down holding his damaged arm. Another man now stood right in front of him, but was uncertain of what to do. He had his fists raised, but had poor posture. Alex raised his foot and stabbed it at the man's knee. The man buckled, falling onto the crippled patella, rolling over in abject agony.

Alex had time to look up and survey the scene. Several men had run away towards the motorcycles. Several others were standing, watching the carnage. He knew it was an unfair fight. His group, although outnumbered, were very fit and very strong and were trained in self-defence both physically and mentally. The opponents were not men or individuals. They were the enemy and it was crucial to take them out cleanly and efficiently. All his boys were still standing.

He hesitated for a moment as he saw the police car enter the car park. It stopped almost immediately but, to his astonishment, the two officers inside did not get out. He then noticed someone, one of his friends, stagger and fall over. A huge, hairy, leather-jacketed guy fell on top of him.

Alex ran over and initially grabbed the hair. It was greasy and horrible, slipping through his fingers. Then he noticed the silver chunky chain around the man's neck. He had enough time to check behind him; no one was near enough to do damage. He grabbed at the chain and twisted it around the man's neck. He then used his body weight, leaning backwards, to pull the man away. It was Graham on the ground who then raised a knee quickly into the man's groin.

It happened so quickly that Alex failed to notice the second police car, or rather a van, the 'paddy wagon'. A loud whistle blew. It was just as if the referee had blown for full time. Everyone stopped immediately, although several people were still rolling around on the ground, groaning in agony.

"Weren't you frightened?" Maria asked. "That is horrible! Why didn't the police stop it as soon as they arrived?"

"The police were waiting for their colleagues to arrive. I guess they thought they might have been set upon themselves! We had seen these guys kicking two men on the ground! They might have killed them!" Alex smiled. "We thought we were heroes!"

"Sadly," Alex continued, "the police didn't quite agree. They arrested most of the guys in leather jackets. Nearly all the motorbikes were still there the next morning apparently. The publican told his story and was very sympathetic and supportive towards us. The Billericay guys explained how they had found these bastards stealing the battery from their Mini and they had been set upon. In the end, we were sent back to our barracks with just a few cuts and bruises." Alex grinned. "We got another roasting from our own officers and then again from the Station Commandant. Oh, and we won the football against Billericay the next day!"

"Captain, I want to hear about your life," Maria said gently, "but please, not about primitive fighting. It's horrible!"

Alex smiled and thought about the moment once again. Yes it was horrible, but that is how it had happened. He had felt fear, but only after it was over. He was most concerned, and then finally indignant, that the authorities were less than understanding about what they had done! Still, he had learned that he could protect himself, and others, but it had been a risky business. His advice after that was - if you can walk away, do so. However, he was quite certain it would have been impossible have ignored the brutality they had witnessed that night; there had been no alternative but to intervene. It was a good lesson to learn.

At school Alex continued to learn by reading books, of course, but suddenly a new world opened up to him. He read about countries and people, and then would search the pages of an atlas to learn more about South Africa, Australia, the Soviet Union and United States, the places where these stories unfolded. It is hard to say how long it took for him to realise that school and knowledge were common bedfellows. There was no sudden gift of intelligence, just a hunger and a drive that led to hard work; lots of hard work. He did not suddenly become a star, nor did he suddenly soar to the top of his class. Instead, he slowing climbed from near the bottom, to somewhere near the top of his class subjects.

"When I went for my interviews, I soon realised there were thousands of gifted young men keen to be pilots. Many were brighter, some even having private pilot's licences. I felt totally out of my depth. However, I passed each set of interviews and then went on to the next set of interviews a few months later. After getting through those, I had to wait another three months for the next round.

There were tests of all kinds, aptitude, science, common sense – somehow I finally got to the Pilot Flying College." Alex paused and thought. "I spent two years studying really hard," he explained. "I guess I was probably struggling compared to most of the other guys and I just waited for a tap on the shoulder to tell me quite simply I was not good enough. Others did fall by the wayside, but somehow I managed to do enough. I made it!"

"It must have been horrible!" Maria exclaimed.

Alex smiled. "It was hard. It was frightening, but please remember I had been frightened before! But, Maria, it was wonderful, too! This door had been opened for me and left ajar. Eventually I was able to push it wide open. Somehow, inexplicably, the tap on the shoulder never ever came and

I became an airline pilot. Over time I became a good one too, but there was just one more problem!"

"¡Oh dios mio! ¿Cuál era él problema?" asked Maria.

"I thought you were practising your English, Maria?" Alex chuckled. She pulled a face and tilted her head comically.

"The problem was, Maria, I had graduated as an airline pilot, but there were no jobs! We were told by the airline that we would be laid off for three years without pay!" Alex could see Maria looking at her watch.

"I am so sorry Captain, this is very interesting, but I have to go! Where does it go, the time? Tomorrow you will tell me more. I want you to tell me everything! Tomorrow then! Ah, I am so late! Thank you, thank you, it was most interesting!" She picked up her papers and hurriedly tidied the coffee cups, picking up the tray.

The tired old man watched her walk the few steps across the room to the door. She paused and looked back at him, smiling gently. He smiled back but, in an instant, the door was open and closed, and she was gone.

It was like a light going out or the sun suddenly setting behind the hills. He twisted his body and turned his head towards the window and the veranda doors and felt confused. Had those doors not been open? Had he not felt the cool breeze against his face? Certainly they seemed firmly shut. Perhaps Maria had closed them and he had not noticed. He screwed up his eyes and looked through the glass. He could see the sun disappearing ever so slowly behind the distant peaks, a few wisps of cloud glowing red in the sky.

"Red sky at night, Captain's delight!" he chuckled to himself and his eyelids slowly set like the sun.

CHAPTER 3: TAKING TO THE AIR

"Good Morning Captain, did you sleep well?" Maria breezed into the room like a breath of fresh air. In her hands was the tray, as usual, set with coffee, coffee cups, milk and biscuits all perfectly placed.

"Si! Muy bien, gracias Maria." Alex had already warmed to his new nurse and gave her a broad smile.

"I was telling my friends about your story yesterday," she said full of excitement. "I can not wait to hear more. So extraordinary! You went to all that trouble and did all that hard work to train as a pilot and the company did not give you a job!"

Alex smiled again and watched intently as Maria rearranged the items around the tray as if she were playing chess. 'Checkmate in two moves,' he thought.

"Is there a problem? You want coffee, no?" she questioned.

"I want coffee, *yes* Maria!" Alex beamed. "I was just watching you make the coffee. Everything is perfect. Perfecto!"

The coffee was poured carefully and then the milk was added. 'Café con leche' in a sensible size cup! Maria had a 'café solo' a small, but very strong black coffee. That smaller cup (just a couple of mouthfuls) was a Spanish tradition, but just not to Alex's taste at all. Maria prompted him again, recalling the last part of his story, and asked him to continue.

Alex had graduated as an airline pilot, but all was not well with the world. In 1973 the Yom Kippur War in the Middle East caused massive uncertainty and the price of oil rose sharply. 1974 was the year of the three-day week in the United Kingdom, introduced by British Prime Minister Edward Heath, following the Miners' strike. He then called a General Election and promptly lost. Harold Wilson was left to form a minority Labour Government instead. Meanwhile the IRA were wreaking havoc, bombing the cities of mainland Britain. Then, in 1975, Margaret Thatcher replaced Mr Heath as leader of the Conservative Party. Recession loomed and the future looked very bleak with inflation exceeding 24%.

Alex was twenty-one years old. With the prospect of being out of work for the next three years, Alex set about writing to every airline and air taxi company in the UK and several abroad, but there were no flying jobs or at least very few. He literally wrote hundreds of letters to companies who owned aircraft; airlines, air taxi companies, anyone. He was trained, but crucially lacked actual airline experience. Some hard decisions would need to be made. The first was that he and Carol would get married.

Living together would, they hoped, reduced costs and make things easier and cheaper. The second decision they made was to spend their entire savings on an Assistant Flying Instructors' Rating for Alex in the hope that a flying job might still be possible.

The money was spent, instructor training complete, and he sat down again and began writing still more letters. This time he wrote to dozens of flying schools scattered around the country. Then one day, out of the blue, the telephone rang. Was he still looking for an instructors' job? When could he start? Could he start tomorrow?

The next morning, bright and early, Alex made the two-hour drive across London to his new job. The airfield lay in the country and was surrounded by trees and a golf course. The owner had no interest in his licence and aircraft logbook and immediately ushered him outside to meet his first student. By nine o'clock he was walking around a Cessna Aerobat, inspecting the aircraft before his first flying lesson at this new flying school. The student, a small little man in his forties, hung on his every word.

"I was actually being paid to be a pilot!" Alex smiled proudly. "The pay was very poor, barely paying my petrol money, but I was flying and accumulating those important flying hours and getting some real experience."

Over the next few years Alex took students up and taught them how to take-off, fly a circuit and land. He taught them how to turn - thirty degree turns and steep turns (without losing height), each was equally important. He taught his students how to stall and spin and more importantly how to recover the aircraft afterwards. He showed them how to turn the aircraft accurately using just the flight instruments, in case they should accidentally fly into cloud. He would take them on cross-countries, flying from A to B and next to C and then, hopefully, back to A again. This involved map-reading, looking for railway lines, motorways, towns and cities, lakes and coastlines, navigating by the magnetic and gyro-compass with consideration for the forecast wind. Smoke from a field or a factory might sometimes give a clue as to the real direction of surface wind.

Arithmetic, airspeed plus or minus the wind speed gave a ground speed and from that an 'Estimated Time of Arrival' or ETA could be calculated. What if there was an engine failure?

Periodically he would simply close the throttle and then make a radio call – "Practice Pan, Practice Pan, Golf Charlie practice engine failure, now passing three thousand, descending one thousand…." Which field would they land in? What is the current wind direction? How do we plan a circuit and maximise our height as we glide earthwards? Remember to watch out for power lines, trees and other obstacles!

It was a living. Enjoyable (sometimes), demanding (all of the time) and quite tiring (seven days a week). Release came at the end of the day when the sun began setting, or the weather closed in, or after the last student went home. Across the road from the flying school was an old country house, several hundred years old, whose original estate probably included the airfield. Farmland had been converted to a grass strip during the Second World War and had never returned to grazing sheep or cattle ever again. The country house now sported a bar and an outdoor swimming pool, doing good business with the 'nouveau riche' who parked their Mercedes, Aston Martins and Porches outside the flying school. After their flying lessons they would cross to the "club' for a drink before going home.

These same students and private pilots were keen to buy their flying instructor a drink and talk about their day, their flying lessons and their progress. The instructors, in turn, would smile and complement their students, offering further advice, while telling their own tales of daring deeds in exchange for another pint of Tetleys Ale. Gradually the customers melted away back to their businesses and loved ones and the instructors would group together to exchange the real horror stories! 'Flies like a ploughman!" "Doesn't know which way is up!" "Well, he's wasting his money!" These were all expressions that Alex heard time and time again.

The temptation of a drink or two proved too much and those instructors with wives or girlfriends frequently fell foul of their loved ones, getting home late, often with 'one' quick beer on their breath. The answer, of course, was to invite the loved ones to the club for a drink or two themselves and these 'orphans' became frequent visitors, waiting for their instructor partners to finish work. They also became 'nominated drivers' as the guys unwound after their stressful day.

Carol became such a person. When possible, she would arrive at the airfield sometimes to find Alex had just taken off on his last evening sortie. However, there was never a shortage of people in the bar, including several of the other young instructors. They were more than happy to entertain her while she waited for her hard-working husband to return to *'terra firma'*. She was young and keen to have fun and there was something romantic about aircraft, steely-eyed pilots and posh expensive cars.

The instructors would have to compete with rich company directors, businessmen and entrepreneurs whose chariots graced the car park. However the instructors were young, adventurous daredevils who spoke a language normally heard in the movies. They would tell of daring exploits, hazardous mishaps and near misses that would captivate most audiences with a love of flying. With the inclusion of alcohol, table tennis and snooker, it was inevitable that Carol would not mind in the very least if the lesson overran.

Alex finally strolled in with his student, who was keen to thank him (and everybody else!) for the 'rush' he had experienced during today's lesson. Alex had rolled him, the student explained proudly. He had experienced amazing barrel rolls and aileron turns, watching the entire world turn upside down before his very eyes. This, he explained, would give him the confidence necessary should the aircraft not be completely upright. He admitted to losing his stomach (very slightly), but he had overcome his nerves bravely. After that, stalling and spinning was easy, he boasted; the lesson had gone very well indeed. Drinks all round and the audience was enthusiastic and thirsty, happy to drink and listen to this man's success.

Alex, naturally, had been apologetic to Carol – "Sorry I'm late" - checked she was OK and then began sinking pints of beer. He was mentally and physically exhausted. Now here they all were – the instructors, girlfriends, students and others; yes, it was almost like family.

Perhaps it was there that the ground rules between he and Carol had begun to change rather subtly. Perhaps it was there that the concept of going to a party and parting at the door was first considered acceptable.

They would find themselves separated, speaking to different people, in the scrum of the busy drinking house. Carol would dance and flirt while Alex drank and talked of aircraft and flying, but always they would leave together and it seemed so, so natural.

Was that the first death knell? Later in life, those separations spread into the rest of their lives, slowly like a cancer growing beneath the surface. But it happened so imperceptibly, so subtly, that neither of them really noticed. Separate careers; separate lives. Was that where they were eventually to go wrong?

There were significant contrasts to the job. Flying around the circuit, watching some accountant thump the aircraft into the ground on touchdown, time after time - despite all the advice and guidance. It was soul-destroying. Then there was the guilty doubt of taking off in poor visibility, under pressure from the boss to make money, knowing that the student was probably not really learning anything in the grey murk. That was disturbing. Occasionally, however, something would happen to brighten the day.

Once, a famous England cricketer batsman walked into the flying club and asked if we could get him to Fontwell Park by two o'clock! Alex had no idea where Fontwell Park was!

"It's near Goodwood Airfield," Ted had explained, eager to be on his way.

After a little form-filling Alex and Ted were in an aircraft climbing away from the trees and fields beneath them and turning south towards Goodwood, near Chichester. They passed over busy roads and traffic jams, over road works and traffic lights, free from the restrictions imposed on the ground. It transpired that Ted had previous flying experience and Alex was very happy to hand over the controls to his guest. The sportsman proved to be a very good pilot. Fontwell Park was a horseracing course and several other sporting celebrities were there for the race meeting.

"After landing, he asked me what I would do next," Alex grinned at Maria. "I told him I'd probably read the newspaper and just wait for him. Ted suggested I should accompany him, provided I didn't mind being introduced as Ted's private pilot!" There was an element of pride in Alex's voice, which made Maria gently smile.

Alex witnessed all the joys and pleasures of sporting success walking around the Members' Enclosure. He was introduced to a well-known golfer, a famous footballer, several cricketers and the Formula One racing car driver James Hunt They were all indulging in the sport of Kings.

Champagne and betting at Fontwell Park; how the other half lived! Alex, of course, drank water!

Alex flew Ted back to the airfield after the race meeting and the talk was of geldings, fillies, jockeys, owners and trainers (horse trainers, of course). Alex explained how his career was temporary, waiting for the move to the big airlines. The sportsman listened and smiled politely, occasionally glancing at his watch. He had a dinner to get to. After landing, a shake of the hand, and the cricketing legend had gone, but Alex had something special to talk about in the bar that evening.

On another occasion, a beautiful young woman walked into the flying school, asking about flying lessons. She was tall and slim, with longflowing hair. The instructors fell over themselves, almost fighting to attend to this young woman before Alex finally stepped in.

She was a fashion journalist and she had been encouraged to spend her success learning to fly. For a period of about four or five months he took her flying and watched her progress. She proved to be an intelligent, attentive student and Alex really enjoyed her company. However, when one flying instructor, and then another, begged and begged him to be allowed to teach her, he finally relented.

"One of the instructors left his wife for that beautiful girl," Alex explained to Maria. "Then another instructor ran off with her and they were never seen again! Can you believe it? The 'soap opera' was complete!"

Maria smiled encouragingly, her eyes wide and attentive, so Alex continued to tell his story.

The two-hour drive across London and, worse, the two-hour drive back, eventually began to take its toll. It was too tempting to go to the bar and far too alluring to have just one more drink amongst people he knew. One night Alex closed his ears with his fingers and watched the animated conversations. In the silence he looked at the hands in the crowd held skywards, becoming airplanes flying through the air. Above their heads, palms down, the fingers would achieve a steep-turns or a stall or perhaps a perfect landing.

You didn't need to hear the conversations to understand the stories being told. Flying was in the blood, thrilling and exciting, and everyone here had the disease. It was also cathartic after the long arduous day! Alex returned home to find Carol already in bed, asleep. Tomorrow morning he would have to wake early, about 6.30am, in order to get to his first flying lesson of the day. Carol was still asleep when he quietly pulled the front door closed.

Henry was a successful architect who had taken up flying some time ago. He had a large expensive house, an expensive car and expensive tastes, but his business funded it all comfortably. He was lucky. He had suggested that his flying instructor was also very lucky, but Alex didn't feel very lucky and said so. The long commute, getting up early and getting home late, a strain on the marriage and the poor wages; no, not so lucky, he said. But Henry was a practical man.

"Well, do something about it, Man!" he suggested. "Move nearer the airfield."

"I work seven days a week!" Alex complained. "I don't have time to look at properties and I probably couldn't afford to live near here anyway!"

The checks were complete and they were now ready for take-off. Alex put his problems to one side and concentrated on the lesson. First he cautioned Henry to check more thoroughly before lining up on the runway; there had been no other traffic on the radio, but you wouldn't pull out of a side road without checking first, would you? Henry did his final checks and opened up the throttle. The propeller roared as the aircraft accelerated and began bumping down the grass strip. At seventy knots he rotated, pulling back gently on the control column, and they were airborne. Alex was looking out of the window, checking for other traffic that might be joining the circuit. Speed was good. At three hundred feet he reached across and closed the throttle.

"Oh Henry, you've had an engine failure on take-off!"

Henry pushed the nose forward, regaining the speed that had begun to decay. With the nose lowered, the view at the front of the aircraft became much clearer. They were now gliding towards the ground, the engine coughing and spluttering at idle.

"So where are we going to go?" Alex asked. Ahead lay trees separating the perimeter track from the flooded gravel pits beyond. "Shall we turn back?" he asked. Henry shook his head and pointed to his right. He headed for a narrow strip of grass opening up into a field. He placed his hand on the flap lever, but knew not to pull any more flaps.

"Good, Henry, good!" Alex reached across and pushed the throttle back up to maximum. The speed began to increase and they were climbing again. "I have control Henry."

"You have control," Henry repeated, removing his hands and feet from the flight controls. His shoulders visibly relaxed as he watched Alex turn the aircraft gently towards the north, raising the flap as they accelerated.

"India Papa changing to Radar - one two six decimal one," Alex said into the radio and then changed channels. "OK Henry, very good. Nice piece of ground to land on. What are we looking for?"

"Trees, power lines, obstructions," Henry answered. "But I forgot the carburettor heat again, didn't I?"

"You did, Henry, you did. But the flying was excellent. Don't be afraid to get that nose down firmly. We don't want to stall. And here's the Government Health Warning – you must never practice engine failures on take-off on your own; only with an instructor! OK?" Alex paused to look at Henry and get a firm nod.

"And remember to check that carburettor heat! It might be miss-set, it could be ice and it might just get that engine going again, OK?" Another firm nod. "OK Henry, you have control. Level off at two thousand five hundred feet, heading 330."

A week later Henry was back for his next lesson but, before they started, he had a proposition to put to his instructor. He owned a street in Harrow. (A whole street?) There were rows of semi-detached Victorian houses, converted to flats, mostly empty. Henry was waiting for the last few residents to sell up, or die, so that he could demolish the entire street and redevelop the site. It might take several years but, meanwhile, this flat was empty. It wasn't much, but he could let Alex have it for a token rent. He should go and see it as soon as possible. There was one problem (there usually is!), but it was solvable. His lawyers would not allow him to rent to an individual. Squatting rights! But, if it was rented to the flying school…

Two weeks later, Alex and Carol moved in to their new home in South Harrow. It really wasn't much, but nor was their first flat in Tooting Bec! The kitchen was very basic. Four planks of wood placed across the bath made their kitchen table. A tablecloth failed to hide its true identity! However, remove the planks, boil numerous kettles and saucepans on the stove and, hey presto, you could have a bath! Still, what could be worse than having no running hot water? Well, there wasn't a toilet either, at least not in the house!

Carol had never seen an outside toilet before and the prospect of rushing out to this little brick cabin with an ill-fitting wooden door in the middle of the night appalled her. It was a dry late summer's day, but Alex resisted the temptation to mention the possibility of rain, wind, or even snow in the months ahead. She would experience all three soon enough! Still, it was home, it was cheap and it was much nearer work. Well, for Alex at least.

The Harrow flat improved the situation immensely and, while Carol taught school, Alex taught people to fly. It freed up much more time and they explored the local area, mainly parks and shopping centres, both zero cost items provided you didn't actually buy anything. However, as winter grew ever nearer, the Harrow flat revealed its true character. It was possessed! Not by ghosts or ghouls, but by nature itself. Every morning the walls were covered with visible moisture. You could scoop enough with your hand to fill a pint mug. The fireplace was unusable and the electric heaters hungrily consumed energy and money, but still the flat did not warm up.

One wintery Saturday afternoon Carol and Alex decided to go to the pictures; the cinema. They didn't care what movie was being shown, they just wanted to get warm! Dressed in double layers of clothes, jumpers and thick coats they paid for their tickets and waited for the film to begin.

In the half-light of the cinema a small round man waddled down to the front of the movie theatre and onto the stage. He walked like a cartoon penguin and looked tiny in front of the towering deep red velvet curtains. He peered out into the half-lit darkness, unable to see his customers, and looked down to the microphone that had appeared in front of him. He tapped it twice. Two loud bangs echoed around the almost empty theatre.

"Hello ladies and gentlemen, welcome to the Harrow Cinema. I am the assistant manager and we would like to apologise to you all as the heating has broken down and it is a little chilly in here." He paused and then added, as an afterthought, "We hope this does not spoil your viewing of today's presentation."

The frozen couple could not believe their ears, indeed, they could not even feel them! It was freezing and gradually the cinema got colder and colder. The movie was terrible and Alex and Carol went home in silence. They sat on the draughty double-decker bus as it bumped its way back to South Harrow. The driver appeared to be in a big hurry to get home, but the couple barely noticed. They huddled together tightly as they walked up the dark street to the house.

It was colder inside the building than outside, but it was also felt damp and musty. Alex was convinced the water on the walls had probably frozen. The unhappy couple went to bed at six o'clock in the evening, not for sex or romance, but simply to try and get warm. They cried each other to sleep. Things could not get any worse, but they were about to.

"Surely not!" Maria protested. "Is this true?"

"Of course!" The old man lifted his head and forced a wry smile. "It's OK to be poor, but when you are cold, damp and hungry, things seem much, much worse. The outside toilet, no running hot water, freezing cold rooms, it was pretty bad!"

"But you said it got worse!" Maria protested. "How could this be?"

Alex smiled and continued with his story. At work, his boss had become more and more difficult. Maybe the boss had his own problems, but he certainly made life more difficult for the instructors and the students. A flying lesson was usually prefaced with a lecture at the blackboard, explaining the theory of the lesson and the practical behind the day's tuition. Now the instructors were being told to 'just get them in the air'.

'Talk to them in the aircraft,' they were told; it will cost them more, increasing his much needed profits. 'Screw the customers. Screw you!'

The wages were poor, resources were low, and Alex and Carol could not continue as they were. His work had become untenable and they considered their options. It was clear he would have to get a real job, one that paid real money. He was sure he could probably get a flying instructor's job somewhere else at the weekends, when most students wanted to have their lessons. Together they gradually hatched their plan.

At the flying club things had become impossible. There were several incidents, some of which could have easily become accidents. Alex had a genuine engine failure on take-off, a huge bang with no resemblance to the practice failures he had taught his students so many times before. The spinning propeller had acted as an airbrake, slowing the plane and making the problem much worse. As the speed rapidly decayed, he immediately took over from the student who had been flying the aircraft. He glided it earthwards, aware that his options were diminishing by the second and the trees were going to be very difficult to avoid. It was very dangerous.

Another of his students was compelled to do a forced landing while on a solo practice cross-country flight, after the cockpit filled with smoke. It was a perfect emergency landing, save for the atomic power station adjacent to the field. The authorities were not pleased! Alex was convinced the aircraft were not being properly serviced. Corners were being cut both in engineering and in the air.

Alex finally resigned. Enough was enough; he could take no more. He began looking for a real job; one that actually paid money! He went to the employment exchange, but sadly they seemed more interested in giving him money, rather than finding him a job. They told him if a pilot's job came up, he would be contacted! He insisted he would be happy to do almost anything, but they simply smiled at him and sent him on his way.

It proved extremely difficult to find work. He was too well qualified for most jobs; too many 'O' levels and 'A' levels! He had very little practical experience (except in flying). Fords refused him a job on the assembly line lest he become an agitator. Others claimed he would not last five minutes They reasoned he would readily leap at the first airline company to click their fingers and offer him his dream job. He tried patiently to explain that that was not going to happen in the current economic climate, but they just smiled knowingly. He would say that, wouldn't he?

Then the bombshell arrived. Alex received a letter from Henry. Their flat had been let in the name of the flying school and his ex-flying boss was now insisting to Henry that Alex be removed from the premises. Henry had tried to reason with flying school owner, but vengeance was sweet and too good a motive to resist. There had been an insistence that the ex-employee be removed by Christmas. Henry apologised profusely, but there was pressure from the flying school and the lawyers. There was nothing else he could do.

Alex and Carol were evicted from their Harrow flat on Christmas Eve! They had resisted for as long as they possibly could, hopeful that something would come up, but now they had nowhere to live. Their worldly possessions were packed into a small van and driven down to Carol's grandparents in Wiltshire, where the contents were unloaded into the unused garage. It didn't take long.

"This is not possible!" Maria banged the table incredulously. "This could not happen!"

"Ah, but it did happen, Maria." The old man was no longer smiling. The memory was still painful five decades after the event. "It was so shocking; we really couldn't believe it ourselves."

Christmas that year had seemed rather unreal and they spent it with Alex's parents in Devon. A Christmas tree, the carol singers, the Christmas dinner and the Queen's Speech, all masked the reality of what was going to happen next. A fellow teacher of Carol's offered her a small room in her flat in London, close to the school, at a very reasonable rate; but there was a catch. The young female schoolteacher had a young daughter and would not allow men into the flat! Any men!

Alex would not be able to stay there or even come to visit! But to refuse the accommodation would have put Carol's job at risk and they could not even contemplate the possibility of both being out of work. Between the opening of presents on Christmas morning and the Boxing Day leftovers, the married couple discussed their enforced separation.

Carol would accept the offer of a room and keep her job in London. Alex would live with Carol's grandparents in Salisbury, one hundred miles away, and search for meaningful work. It would only be for a very short time, wouldn't it? The price of becoming an airline pilot was becoming extremely high indeed.

"I had learned a lot about flying airplanes," he continued. "But the life of a jet-setting pilot, staying in lovely hotels around the world, pretty stewardesses, with lots of money and fast cars; all that seemed a million miles way. Of course the job was not really like that anyway, but I was yet to discover that for myself."

"Carol and I were separated for about five months. We could only afford to see each other about once a month, sometimes less, because of the cost of the petrol. Again the Employment Office gave me a small amount of money, but I wanted and needed a job!"

Carol spent her weekends in London searching for a cheap apartment and eventually found one in Forest gate, in East London. There had been a misprint in the newspaper advertisement and no one else had even bothered to view the property. Was this the stroke of luck they had been waiting for? The flat was close to her school, clean and tidy, and it meant Alex could move up to London and join her.

Once established in East London, he recommenced his search for work and one day entered a private Employment Agency in the High Street of a town just a few miles away. A delightful young lady charmed him into giving his details, reassuring him that placing such a 'high flyer' would not be a problem. She had not intended the pun, but Alex knew that his work history would be a significant barrier. The alternative was to not mention the flying at all but, with such a big hole in his past, people would assume he had been in prison!

The young lady had wonderful customer service skills and had almost convinced Alex that he was the catch of the century. She smiled as she began ringing all her local contacts, enthusing about her latest find. He watched her with interest. She was charming and she had persistence, a deep belief in herself and an even deeper belief in him. He sat there patiently wondering how long it would be before she recognised and understood the problem. Over an hour and countless calls later, he could not help but admire her tenacity.

"Mr Hevers," she spoke in a slightly different tone to this one. "Mr Hevers, I have a problem." Well, this was a completely different approach, almost an admission of failure, and Alex wondered what sort of job this might be. "I've got this guy, twenties, three 'A' levels, about sixteen 'O' levels, no, really! Yeah, well I've been working him for over an hour now and got nowhere. Yeah, really nice. Yeah, that too." She glanced up and Alex wondered what had just been said. She placed her hand over the telephone, but did not cover the mouthpiece.

"Mr Hevers wants to know, would you be interested in this job?" the girl pointed to herself. "Recruitment?"

"Yes, I'll do anything," Alex insisted. "What does it entail?"

"Keep 'im there," came a voice from the telephone. "I'll be around in five minutes."

Fifteen minutes later, a rather large Mr Hevers walked into the office clutching an open box of doughnuts. He was wearing a grey linen suit, whose seams were straining in every direction. He dragged huge brown Hush Puppy shoes across the room, his feet scraping along the floor.

"Make us a coffee, darlin'. Doughnut?" he offered Alex the box, but appeared rather pleased when Alex said no. Mr Hevers picked up the CV and began to read. It was merely a glance at every line, but he had seen enough.

"So tell me something about yourself."

While Alex gave a brief history of his short career, Mr Hevers took to demolishing the rest of the doughnuts and, by the time the coffee arrived, the box was empty. Alex continued talking while Mr Hevers swilled the coffee around his mouth and sucked sticky sugar from his teeth. Alex had not yet finished describing his short career history, but he was interrupted anyway.

"OK, that'll do, Boycie. I've heard enough. So, do you think you could do 'er job? Piece a piss really. Interviewing, bit of telephone work, cold calling and creating contacts. You speak posh anyway. It's easy, isn' it love?" Mr Hevers had drunk his coffee in about three gulps and Alex thought the huge balloon in front of him was about to belch.

"Well, if you think I could do it…" Alex began.

"Whooo, stop there!" Mr Hevers now raised a huge sticky hand to Alex's face. "It's all about confidence, sonny. Uv'ers fink – WE DO! No 'perhaps', no 'mights', and no 'maybes'. Of course you can do it. You know you can, don't you!"

"Yes," Alex asserted. He felt he was being coached for an acting role. "I can do it and I'd be good at it. I'm very good with people…"

"OK, OK, that'll do, don't go overboard..." Mr Hevers paused to suck his fingers one last time and then wiped them on an off-white handkerchief he had pulled from his pocket. All this time Julie has sat there listening, learning from the master. "Ok, now there's good news and there's bad news. The next course is in two weeks' time. It lasts one week, nine to five, in the City and you don't get paid. Not a penny, not even expenses. Savvy? Graduate from that course and you've got a job with us. What'ya think?"

"Excellent. What do I have to do now?" Alex reached over to shake Mr Hever's huge hand, which was inevitably hot and sticky. It was a very firm handshake.

"Julie will take more details and set it all up. No screwing around now! If you decide not to go on the course, you get another job or somethin', you'd better bloody ring us Boycie, and I don't mean the day before!" Mr Hevers stood up and looked at his watch. Alex was to learn later that Tony Hevers had been checking that he still had time to get to the betting shop for the three o'clock race at Doncaster.

The training course was held in Holborn, in central London and Alex had taken an early train in from Forest Gate. He did not want to be late on his first day. There were about twenty new recruits, all very different, but all keen to do well. He was unsure whether they were actually meant to be competing against each other, but some of the personalities were surprisingly ruthless. The presenters were somewhat evangelical in their approach. They began by talking about the humble origins of the owner, who had begun with just one small office and developed the company into a High Street brand.

Lectures and presentations were followed by workshops. Tasks were assigned, goals identified and much was made of the role-play. Some were given cards that describing their role as job seekers. Others played the managers of a particular company, brusque, busy and impatient. This manager needed recruits with particular skills, but did not want to have to spend time or energy on the process.

How, exactly, are you going to 'sell' your applicant? Open questions, closed questions, cold calling, building trust; these were processes that could not be left the chance. Each and every workshop was analysed. Who said what? There was a balance between charm and assertiveness when dealing with the bosses and the managers. There was the building up of the applicants' confidence and teaching them how to do well at interview. It was all very intense, taken very seriously and strangely enjoyable.

Two weeks later Alex found himself working alongside Julie in the very office that had recruited him. They were now a team of four and very soon it became the most successful company branch in the whole of the UK. They really were a terrific team with high moral and confidence and this fed through to the applicants and clients they dealt with daily. However, senior management eventually got greedy and, after six months, decided that if they split up the team, they might quadruple the success. Alex was promoted to branch manager, received a very welcome pay rise and he was given his own office nearby with his own staff. However, none of the offices were ever able to replicate the success they had enjoyed as a team together. The Dream Team.

"Why was the team so successful?" Maria asked.

The old man sat, closed his eyes and considered this for a moment. Finally a smile came to his face, although he paused for a moment to reflect upon the story he was about to tell. He would give the example of Tina Collins.

Alex had just got off the telephone to a client who made foam packaging for electrical goods. Julie had been interviewing a young girl across the office. Hundreds of girls like Tina came through the office every week. Julie had just arranged for this girl to go for an interview at another local company, but the girl had very little spark and even less enthusiasm. Alex had been called over from his desk and he was shown the job specification. He knew the job, of course, but stood at the desk pretending to read it again. Every now and again he would look up and smile a bit but, in fact, he was reading the girl's résumé upside down.

"Wow, what a great job!" he declared enthusiastically. "Only..."

"Only what, Mr Young?" Julie asked so innocently.

"Well for a job like this," he continued, "a successful applicant would probably have to have maths and typing!"

"Well, that's great, Mr Young! Tina actually has maths and typing!" Julie smiled back at him knowingly. Such amateur dramatics had proved to be very effective and were well practiced. Alex turned to the young innocent and looked her straight in the eye.

"Tina..." He paused for best effect, taking a deep breath. "Tina. Now, many other people will be interviewed for this job. At the end of the interview, you will be asked if you have any questions. You will need to say - 'I would just like to say that if you offer me this job, I would accept it immediately!' Now we will be ringing Mr Pettit afterwards and we will ask him if you said it, so don't you dare come back here without saying it! OK?"

Alex wagged his finger at the poor girl, who nodded rather shyly. She took her appointment card and left rather hurriedly. Later, towards mid-afternoon, Julie had rung Mr Pettit and asked how the interview had gone.

"I'll be brutally honest Julie," he had said. "I've seen about six girls, all with typing and CSE maths; not a matchstick between them. I'll let you know."

Young Tina did not return to the office after the interview as she had been instructed to do. This often happened - sometimes you win some, sometimes you don't. However, at a quarter to five that evening, the telephone had rung and Alex had answered it.

"Mr Young, hi, I thought you might like to know that we are taking on your girl. Err, Tina Collins." There was a pause and Alex sensed that Mr Pettit had more to say.

"Can I ask why you chose our girl Mt Pettit?" Alex asked. "I understand they were a much of a muchness."

"Well," Mr Pettit explained. "She returned to my office about ninety minutes after her interview - after Julie had rung me. She was sobbing and her mascara had run all down her face. She stuck her head around the door and sobbed 'I would just like to say if you offer me this job, I would accept it immediately'! That takes character, Mr Young. I don't know what you did to her, but it bloody well worked!"

Alex put down the telephone with a smile all across his face. It was against the rules, but the team had kept a couple of bottles of sparkling wine in the fridge, wrapped up in paper. Tonight after work they would all celebrate with a paper cup and toast their success.

"To the Team!" Julie, he knew, would take a sip and then spill the rest down the sink when she thought no one was looking. She didn't drink and wanted to keep it a secret. Sometimes Marion, branch manager at that time, would take Alex around the corner for a quick pint.

"Silly bitch!" Marion complained while holding a pint of lager in her hand. "I don't mind her not drinking, but it's a bloody waste of Champagne!"

About nine months later Alex had rung up the same Mr Pettit over another matter, relating to a bookkeeper's job.

"I'm sorry, Mr Pettit is engaged at the moment. Who shall I say is calling?"

"Could you tell him it is Alex Young." Alex noticed a slight hesitation.

"Mr Young?" There was hesitation in the female voice.

"Yes?"

"Mr Young, it's Tina here; Tina Collins."

"Hello Tina, how are you?" Hundreds of bodies had passed through his office and Alex was trying to remember who Tina Collins was.

"Tina Collins, Mr Young. You made me go back and say I really wanted the job. I'm Mr Pettit's personal assistant now. I just wanted to say thank you so much." The voice was so assertive and confident. Could this be the little shy girl who had been in his office all those months ago? He knew that those small details made all the difference, but here it had actually changed someone's life.

"I am putting you through now, Mr Young. Thank you again."

Alex wondered if he had changed anyone else's life.

At the weekends Alex and Carol would drive down to Southend on Sea, in Essex. Alex had walked into one of the flying clubs at Southend Airport and spoken to the Chief Flying Instructor. Ted had almost bitten his hand off and asked him if he could start the very next weekend; Saturdays and Sundays. It would now mean, Ted had explained to him, that he would be able to have regular weekends off for the first time in a very, very long time!

While Alex flew a full Saturday and Sunday program, often running the flying school, Carol would go shopping or visit old friends and relatives. She would then turn up at the flying school and just sit in the corner, sometimes simply reading her book, waiting for her husband to finish work. These were happier times, more stable and more financially secure. Both of them had real jobs now and the flying, well the flying was the means to an end. Keeping in practice and accumulating flying hours, that was the key. Experience is also a learning curve and Alex was learning a lot. He was no longer the raw graduate who had left the flying college several years ago.

Ever so slowly the weeks and months ticked passed. During the entire layoff, the airline had never contacted him once, but finally the letter arrived. Quite formally it stated that he was to be offered the job of an airline pilot, beginning as a Second Officer. He was being given three months' notice of his start date, 1st March 1978, exactly three years after his graduation from the Airline Training College.

Alex was asked to report to Heathrow Airport, but for some technical reason they were unable to receive him until 2nd March. They regretted that no flying course was currently forthcoming, but alternative employment would be found until such time as a course became available. However from the 1st March he would be given a Second Officers' contract and a Second Officers' salary. He would not be flying aircraft, but it was a start.

Chapter 4: Carol and Lake Page

Coffee time was usually filled with general chit-chat and Alex began to relax. He had felt a little drained, a little tired, but he did enjoy their talks.

Maria sensed his weariness immediately and she changed the subject, telling Alex about her little Mini. It was old and sometimes she would have difficulty starting it. There were also several rattles beneath the car, which she successfully fixed by simply turning the radio up louder. She listened to the local modern pop channel called Radio Flashback, playing old songs from the past. To Maria any song much over a year old was an old song. Alex thought for a moment and considered the irony of a "modern" pop station playing all the old hits. Nostalgia was not what it used to be!

"There, we are settled," Maria said, taking a deep breath and placing the coffee and the two biscuits in front of Alex. "So tell me Captain, how did you meet your wife?"

"Ah, but which wife?" Alex retorted. "I had two, you know!"

"Well, not at the same time I hope!" Maria giggled; the thought was amusing. "Well, let us start with your first wife. How did you meet her?"

"At school," he chuckled. He was still thinking about having two wives at the same time and it tickled him t for a moment; perhaps not though - too much like hard work! Maria sat patiently, waiting for him to focus back onto the story.

"Yes, it was at school," he said. "I was sitting on a coach with a friend. We were going on a geography school field trip to South Devon, in England. It was to a place called Torcross, near Slapton, on the south Devon coast. My friend asked me if there was anyone I fancied on the coach. I pointed out the two girls in the front row on the right, sitting just behind the driver. One had short dark hair, while the other had long blonde hair. The dark-haired one actually married the teacher taking the field trip! I married the blonde!"

"The pupil married the teacher!" Maria exclaimed. "In Spain this would not be allowed!"

"In England, also, it would not be allowed," Alex said. "They didn't go out until after she had left the school. It was very proper, I think. Anyway they had several children and their marriage lasted much longer than mine!"

Alex had not considered this point before and paused for a moment to absorb it. He munched quietly on a biscuit. Suddenly he realised his mouth was dry and he reached for his cup of coffee. His hand shook a little, so he used two hands to steady it and bring the drink to his lips. The coffee was warm and comforting.

"Anyway," he went on, "one evening on that trip a group of us were talking in the pub. I think it was called 'The Anchor'. There were no teachers present that night, just us teenagers and there was a sense of bravado. I suppose we were all trying to impress the opposite sex. Anyway, some fool came up with the crazy idea of swimming in the sea the next morning. Several of us felt this was a very silly idea indeed, while others agreed to the challenge and we finally made the arrangement to meet up at seven o'clock the next morning."

"In the event, only two people turned up that morning - Carol and myself. Clearly I was trying to impress her but, she too, was out to impress and so there we were. The problem was it was a very cold mid-October and the English Channel was absolutely bloody freezing! The air temperature on the steep shingle beach was not much warmer, but neither of us felt we could back down. We both stripped off to our meager swimming costumes and charged down into the waves. It was a crazy idea, but there began a relationship, which lasted well over thirty years."

Alex reached down and placed his coffee cup back onto the table. He stared into it for several minutes looking at the thick brown stain that was left at the bottom. Maria just sat there, patiently waiting for him to continue with his story. Silence, she had found, helped him hold his concentration and that was the best form of encouragement.

"You may recall I was appointed a librarian at my first school," Alex watched as Maria nodded having just taken a sip of her own coffee. "Well, I had done sufficiently well to go on to the Sixth Form College, which was attached to the Grammar School."

"So you made the Grammar School after all," Maria said.

"I guess I did," he smiled broadly. "Maybe because I had been a librarian and, having been good with responsibility, I was made one of the head prefects. I remember I had been on duty in the school corridor, checking up on my team of prefects, when someone had asked me what I intended to do with my life. I told them, of course, that I wanted to be a pilot and apparently Carol had been one of that small group. Apparently I had impressed her, so I guess I was pushing at an open door."

"You were pushing at her door?" Maria asked.

"No, Maria, it is an English expression. I was chasing this girl, but all of the time she wanted to be caught. I just didn't know it! Women are very confusing to me, Maria. They say one thing, but mean another. Sometimes they say nothing and that means something too." Alex chuckled. "A whole lifetime and I was never able to fully work it out!"

"It was a wonderful life," he continued, nodding his head with some sort of approval. He paused for a few moments, trying to gather his thoughts. Maria watched as Alex struggled tried to make sense of the memory fragments in his mind. Her eyes remained fixed on his old wrinkled face, willing him to speak.

"There was a movie. Did you ever see that movie, Maria?" He asked. "It was called 'It's a Wonderful Life'?" She shook her head.

"It's a Wonderful Life was about a man named George Bailey who lives in a small town somewhere in the USA. He runs a savings and loan company, but things go terribly wrong and he decides to end his life. But, before he can, an angel intervenes and shows him what life would have been like had he never lived at all. Only then does he realise the impact he has made on his community and his family and friends and, of course, everyone lives happily ever after."

"I think I know this movie!" Maria exclaimed. "It is American, but the words are dubbed into Spanish. I think it is a Christmas movie. Is this your favourite movie Captain?"

"I guess it's one of them, but no, Maria, it is not my favourite movie." Alex smiled and stared at the ceiling. "I don't even have to think about that one, although it has the same actor in it - James Stewart. My favourite movie was called 'Harvey', about a six foot white rabbit!"

"Your favourite movie was a cartoon?" she asked.

"No, no, it is a comedy with real actors! Harvey was about an eccentric old man, who liked a drink or two."

"Ah, now I know why you like this movie. It is about you, no!" Maria laughed at her own joke.

"I don't know what you mean!" he beamed. His mouth was still very dry today and he reached down to pick up his coffee cup. It was empty. Maria poured him another, with milk, not too full. He took it gratefully.

"This man tells everybody he can see this large white rabbit, which no one else can see of course, so his family decide to put him in a mental institution; a hospital. While he is there, a mistake is made and he walks back into town on his own. Everybody searches for him, thinking he might be dangerous but, in fact, he is very gentle."

"Eventually the assistant doctor finds him and asks about the white rabbit. He is asked how he met the rabbit and he explains that Harvey had been standing on a street corner and had said 'Hello Mr Dowd'. The doctor asks if this is not just a little strange and Elwood P. Dowd replies that he was not at all surprised because lots of strangers knew his name!"

Maria smiled gently and nodded for him to go on. Alex was in his element!

"Well, Maria, the doctor then asks him how come the rabbit's name was Harvey. 'Now that's the strange part,' Mr Dowd says. 'He asked me what name I liked and with no hesitation I said Harvey.' 'That's a coincidence' the rabbit had said, 'that's my name too!' The doctor then suggests that maybe Harvey was his father's name or his best friend's name." Alex loved doing the voices; he so enjoyed his role as a storyteller.

"Elwood, played beautifully by James Stewart, then went on to say that he didn't know anyone with that name, which was why he had such hope for it!" A tear appeared in Alex's eye and he drew a deep breath.

"Years later Maria, I saw James Stewart, the very same famous actor playing 'Harvey' on the London stage!"

"That must have been wonderful," she said glowingly.

"It was," he replied. "Carol and I actually went to the stage door afterwards and met him. I actually got to speak with him! Did you know that James Stewart had been a pilot in the United States Air Force! He went on to get a commercial pilot's licence."

"He is your hero, no?" Maria asked.

"Yes Maria," Alex affirmed. "Why was I talking about him? Ah yes, I was talking about my wonderful life. I've had a great life Maria. I had two lovely children, a series of nice houses and a very pleasant circle of friends. A fine life indeed, but I was travelling all the time. I was flying around the world and staying in some lovely hotels, but it was also tiring too. Carol was at home, bringing up the boys, and I would arrive home, jet-lagged and exhausted, with a suitcase full of dirty washing." Alex sipped again on his coffee. "We had two very different lives. I would have my list of chores, building things, fixing things, so much so I looked forward to returning to work for a rest! Carol would talk about things that were less interesting to me, such as what little Johnny had done at school today."

"Who is little Johnny?" Maria asked, confused.

Alex laughed. "It's another English saying! The name is made up. Carol would tell me about her pupils at school. It was important to her; it was her life and her job. It just was not so interesting to me! Occasionally she would come on a trip with me. As a schoolteacher, she got really good holidays. She had long holidays. She would see the glamour; have a nice seat on the aeroplane and a first class hotel at the other end. We might go drinking and dancing with the crew, or visit some tourist attraction, but it all seemed so far removed from her domestic life of children, cooking and cleaning."

"Did she resent that?" Maria asked.

"Well, the first problem was that Carol thought that all my trips were like that! When I came home tired, she was convinced it was because of late-night parties. If she came on a trip she would sit in her comfortable seat on the aircraft, have a glass of champagne and watch a movie, while I was working and flying the plane. She would have a sleep and still be exhausted when she got back. It would take her a week to recover from the jet lag! I would sometimes only have one or two days at home before going back to work again. I would go to work, still with the jet lag from the last trip. But she would forget that!"

"Then, there was a second problem," Alex sighed sadly. "Carol began creating her own life. She would find time to meet up with friends. She would have her own routines, before settling down to a good book or an evening of television. I think Carol enjoyed the life she had created for herself, but eventually she began to dislike, perhaps resent the disruption I might cause by coming home. Over the years 'her' world became more attractive than 'our' world. Cracks began to appear. Little arguments became big arguments. We began to disagree on so many things. How dare I come home and suggest how we bring up the children! How dare I come home on the night when her best TV program is on! How dare I come home at all?"

Alex finished the last of his coffee. It was cold, but he did not really notice. He understood there were two sides to every argument. He knew the blame, if there was any blame at all, lay on both sides. He looked at Maria as she waited patiently for him to continue his story. She just sat there, as always, still and motionless. Only those eyes, those bright and smiling eyes.

"Don't get me wrong Maria," he continued. "We had been married for over thirty years, which I think is rather a good innings. We grew together, we went through some pretty rough times together and we had our children together. We had many happy times and I wouldn't have changed any of it!"

Alex paused for a moment to place his empty cup on the table beside him. He did not notice Maria leaning forward, pulling the cup away from the perilous table edge.

"I think life is like a pathway," he mused. "If you come to a fork in the road, do you go to the left or the right? But are the paths so very different? When they twist and turn, do they take you off in different directions and go somewhere else, or do they eventually lead back to the same place? Perhaps uphill, sometimes down. I have had such an incredible time and, had I taken a different path, who knows where I would have ended up."

"With another nurse, perhaps," Maria joked.

Alex chuckled. "Would another nurse make another coffee?"

"Captain, you are impossible!" Maria tried to scowl, but her eyes gave her away. She stood up and placed the cups back onto the tray. "I will be a few minutes. Then you must tell me more about this story. Do we have a deal?" Maria raised the tray and paused. Alex nodded and suddenly she was gone.

Alex looked around his room as he did every day. The bed was always perfectly made, with brilliant white starched sheets. A number of things lay on the side table, but he could not remember or make out what they were. His watch, perhaps, but he had little use for the time. There was a fireplace with logs, although Alex had never seen it alight. The walls were bright white, while the floor tiles were more of a cream colour. Curtains hung on one wall, where glass doors were his window to the outside world. He thought he remembered the doors opening onto a small balcony, but he could not be sure. He thought again about this question, but still he could not remember if the doors opened, or not. Perhaps he would ask Maria.

Alex examined the chair he was sitting in and rubbed his hands across the soft green cushion beneath him. Laura would call it lime green. His elbows were perched on armrests making this the most comfortable of positions. Yes, he felt very much at home in this chair. The table looked very old, but was highly polished. He turned and looked over his shoulder. Yes there, there is the bathroom, just where he thought it was. A shower, a toilet and thick white towels, he could remember thick white towels.

How long had he been here? Why was he here at all? That was something else to ask Maria. However, when she eventually walked back into the room, the questions were already forgotten. Now there was more coffee.

"Where did you take your wife? You must have had some wonderful holidays, no?" Maria appeared to be searching for a new direction to this story.

"Oh, so many places, Maria. Once we flew to Denver, in Colorado, and drove across half the United States of America to the Pacific Ocean. We hired a car and just pointed it in the right direction. We had three weeks to get to San Francisco, but only a rough idea of our route. If we saw something interesting we would stop. Perhaps, if there was lots of desert, we would just drive and drive, putting the miles behind us. Often we would get up and drive for a couple of hours before breakfast. Then we would stop and have pancakes, egg and bacon, and lots of coffee; we rarely needed lunch!" Alex stopped and sipped his coffee while it was still hot. He was very thirsty today!

"We drove through the Rocky Mountains, laden with snow. Some of the mountain passes we drove over were eleven thousand feet high and still the peaks towered above us! One evening we went to a hot natural springs. The area was buried in eight feet of snow, although the pathway to the springs had been dug out. We sat in the mineral salted water, surrounded by snow, enclosed by the mountains, looking up at one of the clearest skies I've ever seen. Millions of stars! It was just stunning!"

"After that," Alex said, "by each afternoon when we began looking for a motel for the night, we would try and find one with an outdoor spa pool. We also hoped there would be a bar nearby, of course!"

"Of course," Maria chuckled.

"We went to a remarkable place called the Black Canyon of the Gunnison, which we thought was every bit as good as the Grand Canyon. It was much narrower than the Grand Canyon, making it look deeper and more dramatic. The most amazing thing," Alex said, waving his wrinkled hands around him to emphasise his point, "was that there was no one else there. Not a single soul! It was incredible! We stood at the top of this massive canyon – such beautiful colours - peering down on a huge river, which actually looked tiny because it was so deep, down on the valley floor. Then small little chipmunks came right up to us and ate nuts out of our hand!"

"Were you allowed to feed them?" Maria asked.

"Probably not, but there was nobody else there; not one single soul. The chipmunks were actually smaller than my hand." Alex spread his fingers, illustrating the size of his hand. "We also found an old mining town called Silverton, which looked like something from the Wild West. There were even poles in front of the buildings for tethering your horse! Thousands and thousands of people once lived there, looking for gold and silver. Now, there was a population of just a few hundred. Nearby we found a ghost town – I think it was called Eureka – and certainly no one lived there now! The ruins of old wooden cabins, mines dug in the side of the mountain, a fence here and there; it was just incredible!"

Alex stopped and looked at Maria. "Is this boring you?"

"No, no!" Maria protested. "It's very interesting! It is good that you remember all the details; it is good for your mind to think back on all these things. Please, go on."

"Well, here is a good example of how we did things," Alex explained. "We came to a town called Durango, full of character. We drove out to the edge of town, but finally decided we would stay right in the town centre. We found a nice hotel on the corner of the street and I remember the entrance to the bar had swinging half doors just as they had in the old western films! We had walked along Main Street, imagining how it might have looked a hundred years before. We found a nice little place to eat and I had a juicy buffalo steak. It was fantastic! Then we walked back to the hotel and through the swing doors into the bar."

The bar was highly polished, fronted with stools and a brass footrest all along its length. Behind it was a vast mirror, and rows and rows of bottles of liquor. Carol and Alex decided to sit at the bar and climbed onto two of the stools. The walls were covered in old sepia photographs of famous cowboys, outlaws, and lawmen, some of whom (it was claimed) had visited this very bar!

A man sat in one corner at an upright piano, playing tunes Alex had only ever heard in the movies. The man was wearing a grey-white shirt with garters around the arms. Alex nudged Carol and pointed to the ceiling. Wagon wheels hung down flat on long, rusty chains, supporting candle-shaped electric lights to illuminate the room. 'It looks like a stage set' Alex had whispered to Carol.

"What'll yer have?" The barman was acting in character too, wearing a white apron tied at the waist, protecting grey and white striped trousers and a white open-neck shirt. He also hosted a thick handlebar moustache perfect for the part.

"Do you have a drinks menu?" Carol had asked.

"We're a bar, we got everything," the barman drooled. "What'll yer have?"

Alex thought the barman was going to spit tobacco. Carol, by now, was completely flustered.

"I'll have a Coors," Alex requested. He turned to Carol, who just managed to mumble a request for a Margarita.

The barman sniffed and turned away. Alex wondered whether he was genuinely rude, or just playing a character. He watched the barman make the Margarita. He inverted the glass, dampened with lemon juice and dipped it in a bowl of salt. Carol was also watching and had already begun searching for a tissue in her handbag in order to wipe it from the rim. The Margarita was placed on the bar, in front of Carol, with a sharp thud; enough to make her jump! Alex chuckled. The barman then poured the beer and called something that Alex didn't understand. Five people sitting along the bar to his right all lifted their drinks. Alex's beer came sliding along the bar, stopping just short of the glass of Margarita, stopping inch perfect in front of him. The other customers sitting there replaced their drinks on the bar as if nothing had happened.

"Wow, did you see that?" Alex exclaimed. "Isn't this place great!"

Carol was a great sport, but she was still uncertain about the gruff barman. She nervously began wiping the salt from the rim. Within seconds the barman walked down towards them. In his hand was another Margarita, this time without salt.

"You only have to ask honey," he said, removing the salted Margarita. He grinned. "You folks ain't from around these parts?"

"Thank you," Carol said, visibly relaxing. "No, we're from England."

"Enjoy your stay," The barman smiled, placed the bill in a glass at the back edge of the bar.

"Where you goin'?" The question came from a middle-aged man sitting the other side of Carol. He had a cigarette in his hand, a small beer and a shot glass full of some yellowish liquid. Every now and again he would tap the bar with one finger as if he were sitting at a Blackjack table and asking for another card. The barman would then step up and refill the shot glass.

"San Francisco," Alex answered.

"You lost?" came the reply.

"No! We're driving from Denver to San Francisco. It's about three thousand miles." Alex picked up his beer, ice forming on the outside of the glass. It was very refreshing.

"Jake Baxter," Mr Baxter placed his cigarette in an ashtray and offered his hand. Carol shook the hand and then Alex reached over and shook it too. Mr Baxter had a very firm grip. "I'm from Wichita."

"Do you working locally?" Alex asked. Carol was happier just listening, unless she was directly asked a question.

"I work all over," Mr Baxter said. "I sell pharmaceuticals. I go and tell the doctors that our products make people better, quicker and the doctors richer, quicker!" He smiled broadly and Alex figured this guy could probably sell anything to anyone.

"Which way you headed?" Mr Baxter continued.

"Arizona, Grand Canyon, Death Valley," Alex explained. He took another swig of beer.

"You goin' to Mesa Verde?" Mr Baxter asked. "It's just a ways west of here."

Alex and Carol looked at each other blankly. They normally planned their next day's activities before going to bed, or at breakfast, but always remaining flexible. Neither of them had ever heard of Mesa Verde.

"They're really worth the trip. They're Indian cave dwellings. Houses built on the cliff walls, real high up. Just haul up them ladders and the enemy can't getch yer! It's a National Park. Go west along the 160 towards Cortez and its sign-posted. The Injuns got chased off, I guess, but the dwellings are really something!" Jake Baxter downed another shot in one and then took a mouthful of beer. He tapped the bar top lightly and the barman refilled his shot glass. "And another round for our visitors please Tommy."

Alex and Carol protested, but neither Jake nor Tommy were in the mood for an argument. A fresh iced beer and a Margarita were soon presented with Tommy making a point of placing the chit in Jake's bill glass. Alex noticed there looked to be rather a lot of chits in there already!

The talk moved to the economy and how lucky we Brits were to have Margaret Thatcher. President Regan liked her and that was good enough for Jake. Alex knew that Carol would be bored, with little knowledge or interest in politics. He asked for his bill, arranging to buy Jake another beer at the same time. Another firm handshake, a dollar and some coins on the bar for the barman, and Carol and Alex shuffled upstairs to their bed.

"Were you really bored?" Alex asked.

"No, I thought he was really interesting!" Carol replied. "I think we should sit at the bar more often. You never know who you might meet!"

Alex could not believe it. He could have had another beer! He had rescued Carol, when no rescue was necessary!

"Mesa Verde was astonishing," Alex said to Maria. "The dwellings were carved out and built on the cliff face, creating an entire village. Ropes and ladders still hung from the cliff tops above. It was much larger than we had imagined! Just beautiful!"

The Pueblo and Hopi Indian tribes had been farmers, growing crops and collecting berries. Occasionally they would also hunt for meat. The inaccessible location of their dwellings, built with defensive walls, protected the tribe to some degree. Eventually more aggressive Indian tribes moved into the area. These new tribes had begun by trading with the peaceful Pueblos, but the new tribes began stealing from them, sometimes raiding them. The defences worked reasonably well, but the women would have to climb the steep cliffs every day to get water. They would also have to haul food up the cliffs, or lower it down in baskets from above, in order to keep a full stock of supplies. In times of danger they completely isolated themselves by removing all the ropes and ladders.

"Several incredible things happened to us on that journey," Alex beamed. "We were driving down through Monument Valley, from Utah and into Arizona, where John Ford filmed all those John Wayne westerns. It's where those big rocks, buttes and mesas, just rise out of the desert looking completely amazing! Anyway, we had stopped at a roadside café to have a snack of coffee and blueberry pie. I remember there were two Highway Patrolmen, sitting in the corner. They were having lunch, sitting in their police uniforms with big guns hanging from their belts. After a while they got up to leave and, to our amazement, one came over to talk to us!"

"Hi there, where you folks from? Are you travelling north or south today?" the policeman had asked.

"Er, we're British. We're going south to start with, down through Monument Valley, and then probably going over to Zion and Bryce National Park. Something like that." Alex was still looking at the huge holstered gun the officer was resting his right hand on. In his other hand he played with his super cool police-issue sunglasses.

"Well, don't you folks go pickin' up any hitchhikers on these roads today. Especially Injuns! There's a tribe on the warpath today!" Alex and Carol both looked at each other and burst out laughing.

"Hank, you got a moment?" he called to his colleague. Hank was pushing his change into his tight trouser pocket and strolled over. His arms were so huge, it looked as if his grey shirt would simply burst at the seams. "Would you tell these British folks about those Injuns."

"Sure. Hi folks. There was a court case in the Supreme Court, in Washington DC yesterday. It involved two Indian tribes fighting over a disputed bit of land. Been disputed for nigh on one hundred years. Anyways, one Native American tribe won and one Native American tribe lost and that one ain't happy. They've gone on the warpath and that's the truth. Might be nothin' but they've been threatin' all sorts of trouble. We have extra police patrols out, but it would be very unwise to pick up any Indian folk." The first officer placed his hand on Hank's shoulder.

"Couldn't put it better myself, buddy. You folks be careful and have a nice day. Come on Hank, let's rock'n'roll."

"Oh, are you making this up?" Maria protested. "Really? Wild Indians on the warpath! You maybe think I am stupid, no?"

"No Maria, God's truth!" Alex said.

"You must not take God's name in vain Captain Young!" Maria crossed herself. "Please, please go on with your story!" She waved her hands at him, as if dismissing or admonishing him.

"Well, Monument Valley was beautiful and we didn't see any hostile Indians. We did switch the radio on and it was actually giving out warnings, with news about the Indians and the court case. It was very exciting though! We were driving down to Zion National Park and Bryce

Canyon National Park. They were meant to be spectacular with natural rock formations and, indeed, they were.

On the way we were going to pass a town called Page, close the site of the Glen Canyon Dam, and thought we might stop off for a look. The dam is across the Colorado River and it has created an amazing lake, Lake Powell, a hundred and eighty six miles long, right in the middle of the desert." Alex was beginning to feel thirsty again, but he wanted to finish his story before he forgot it.

Alex and Carol arrived in Page and discovered it was possible to hire a boat and it wasn't too expensive. It was a beautiful day, and they had been seeing an awful lot of desert and so decided to have a break. They bought some bottles of water, got issued with life jackets and had a two-minute lesson on how to drive a boat. The couple headed northeast up Lake Powell and soon found themselves out of sight of the boat quay.

Alex stuck reasonably close to the shore because the rock formations were so pretty. He found a little bay and threw a little drag anchor into the water, switching off the engine. They had not seen another boat or another living soul.

"Swim?" Alex asked. Carol smiled and began undressing.

The couple had no swimming costumes, so stripped off naked and dropped into the water. It was cooling, without being cold and they swam and floated, kissed and cuddled and concluded that this was truly Paradise. Finally they climbed back into the boat and lay there naked on the bench seats, allowing the sun to dry them. Alex closed his eyes and his mind drifted, with not a worry in the world."

It was Carol who had brought them back to earth. "We ought to get going," she suggested. "By the time we get back to the quay, it's probably a couple of hours drive up to the park. We're going to want to find somewhere close so we can get a full day tomorrow."

She was right of course. Carol could be irritatingly right sometimes, but it kept Alex on track. They had experience of driving around looking for motels after dark and it was sometimes difficult. There weren't many towns after Page, so finding a motel, any motel, might just be very challenging.

Such challenges often led to short tempers and recriminations. Yes, it would be a shame to spoil such a wonderful day.

They both got dressed and had a final drink of water. Carol was putting her life jacket back on, while Alex checked the ignition. The light came on, but the key did not turn any further. Only then did he realise it was not electronic ignition. He moved towards the back of the boat.

Sure enough there was a rubber pull handle connected to a rope. Pull the rope, spin the engine and 'hey presto!' Alex pulled at the rope. The engine rotated sluggishly, coughing a little, just to tease him. The rope rewound itself onto a spring and Alex yanked at it much harder. Suddenly he was flying through the air; the back of his legs catching on the seat. He was lying on his back staring straight upwards at the sun canopy. Carol had checked he was OK before laughing at him.

"Whoops," he said as he raised his right hand, showing the rubber handle and the rope in his hand. "It came off in me hand, Governor!"

"Better put it back then," laughed Carol.

Alex climbed back to the rear of the boat looking for the place to put the rope. He examined the mechanism.

"Oh Shit," he gasped.

"Problem?" she asked.

"The fly wheel, the thing the rope winds around, it's a sealed unit!" Alex looked at Carol. "Can you see if you can find a tool kit?"

They both searched and searched. They opened every panel, lifted every seat, but they could find nothing at all to help. They were on a lake, in the middle of a desert, a long way from the boat yard. Already he was feeling the slightly cooler air. At night, he guessed the temperature out here would drop considerably. How cold would it get? He had no idea.

They had no extra clothes, no towels, no radio, nothing! He looked at the shore and wondered if they could swim ashore, but what then? Walk through the desert at night? Fall into a ravine? They might find themselves still walking tomorrow in the desert sun. No, that would be crazy. Stick with the boat. Would they send out a search party? The lake was enormous, although Alex had no idea how big. Later he looked it up on a computer. They were lost on a lake of over two hundred and fifty square miles.

Carol just sat and watched Alex. She knew he would consider all the options and if she made a stupid suggestion, he would probably shout at her. Anyway, she didn't have any ideas; none at all. She had seen the rope detach from the engine and understood fully that the boat was broken. She stared out across the huge lake, where the fading blue sky met the lake on the horizon. Then to her right she saw movement. She stared at it for a few moments just to be sure.

"Alex!" she said, standing up and pointing. "What's that?"

Alex turned and strained his eyes. Getting nearer and larger was a boat. Was it coming directly at them? Had it come to rescue them? Alex pulled off his T-shirt and began waving it above his head. He began calling, although he imagined the other boat's engine would drown out his shouts of help.

"You should take your teeshirt off," he called to Carol. "He's more likely to stop for them." He pointed to her breasts and grinned. He continued to wave, with the occasional call for help. If anything, the other boat was slowly moving from right to left, but it was getting larger all the time. Their boat rocked from side to side as he spun his shirt above his head. Also down by his side, he noticed his life jacket, which he had not put back on.

"Carol, wave the life jacket. Maybe the colour will be easier to see."

Carol began waving the life jacket around her head, but their activities were out of sequence, destabilising the boat. Both of them paused to grab hold of the sun canopy support. Again they began to wave and scream for help.

"Yes, they've seen us!" Carol shouted, leaping up and down with one hand still holding on to the rocking boat.

Alex thought he could see at least one person waving at them, but he remained concerned. The other vessel had not changed course and had not slowed.

"Keep waving," he insisted. "Those idiots think we are just saying hello!"

It seemed like forever, as they shouted and screamed, waving the items above their heads. Alex was gently cursing at the idiots who were laughing and smiling back at them in the distance. Perhaps someone at the boat yard might approach them and ask, by chance, had they seen a young couple on the lake? 'Yep, they were fine!' these idiots would say.

Alex's arms were getting tired and Carol had given up waving, simply holding the jacket steady above her head. Perhaps it was that, Alex later thought, because soon after the boat began a slow gradual turn towards them. It veered off slightly to the left so that it could pass close to them side on.

"Howdy" a man waved from the deck. "You folks OK?"

"No, we've broken down! Can you help us?" Alex shouted.

A woman joined the man on deck and stared down at the shipwrecked couple.

"How you all doin'?" she asked.

"Not great," Alex repeated. "We've broken down."

The people on the boat were talking to each other, but Alex could not hear a thing due to the two large engines spluttering at idle at the back. Suddenly one engine increased in revs and the boat began turning away from them. Then neutral, then a little chug chug as the boat began backing up towards them. The woman had taken the helm and the man appeared at the stern. Slowly the boat reversed towards them. The man disappeared for a second, then reappeared carrying a rope.

"Grab the halyard," the man called.

Alex had no idea what a halyard was, but as the man was holding a rope, he guessed that was what he should grab. Yards of rope hit the boat and bounced into the water beside them. Alex grabbed at it and hauled a dripping, wet rope out of the water. He turned to Carol and passed her the rope.

"Whatever you do, don't drop the rope!" Alex ordered.

Carol reluctantly took hold of the dripping rope, wondering what she would do if the other boat began moving away. If she didn't let go, she would be pulled through the water like a water skier but without skis. Alex moved forward to the front of the boat. There were a number of grab-rails near the front, either side of the bow, and Alex took the 'halyard'. He threaded it under the grab-rail and tied a knot, a sort of slipknot he had been taught, and yanked at it. It seemed sturdy enough. He then remembered the anchor and quickly pulled it up before Mr Birdseye tore their boat in two!

The woman opened up the engine very slowly until the line went taut. Suddenly another head appeared from the roof or top deck of the rescue boat; a second woman. She appeared to be completely naked and, after a minute spent staring down at them, resumed her sunbathing. Alex, distracted for the full sixty seconds, decided he should perhaps be at the steering wheel. He suggested that Carol sit down. He took another moment to put on his life jacket. He pulled it tight. He had a bad feeling about this. Finally the man went to the helm and took control from the first woman. He looked back and nodded. Alex nodded back.

In the next few seconds Alex and Carol both saw their past lives flash before their eyes. The two very large outboard motors roared loudly. Neither boat appeared to move, but the larger boat's propellers gouged a large hole out of the water in front of them. The hole grew threateningly bigger and deeper and their small boat began moving towards and into it. The damn Americans were going to sink them.

"Hold on!" Alex shouted anxiously to Carol. "If we do end up in the water, keep away from the bloody propellers!"

Carol looked across and Alex saw real fear in her face. He tried to smile, but it most probably resembled a grimace. Up on the other boat, the woman was shouting and pointing behind her. The outboard motors stopped their roaring and began chugging gently again. The hole of water disappeared within seconds and, this time, the engines opened up to just half throttle. Both boats slowly moved forward. Alex looked down at his hands. They had both turned white where he had been gripping the steering wheel so tightly. Slowly the colour began returning and he relaxed. He turned to smile at Carol, but her eyes were locked on the boat in front. There was nothing funny about this!

Alex was surprised quite how far out they had been from the boatyard. Eventually it came into view and two men wandered out and tied up the two vessels. Carol was already in the office demanding the bill be cut for the two hours we had been stranded. Finally they were all ashore and Carol was marching back to the dock. She had negotiated a huge discount to the bill and had obtained an apology, although her face still reflected the anger she felt.

As she approached, our American rescuer introduced himself.

"Hi, I'm Randy" he declared.

"I'm not surprised!" Alex retorted. "With two lovely ladies on board!" Carol was now standing beside him and she rolled her eyes. Randy, however, loved the joke and almost burst at the seams.

"No, no!" Randy protested with a grin. "This is Millie, ma wife, and this is Sandie, ma sister." A complex web of arms formed as everyone tried shaking everyone else's hand.

"Thank you for rescuing us!" Alex said. "Is there somewhere around here where I can buy you guys a drink?"

Carol looked at her watch. It was now certain that they would not make Zion or Bryce Canyon tonight. Having a beer or two would probably mean they wouldn't even get out of Page. He heart sank.

"There's a bar just up the road," Randy pointed towards the exit. Just up the road proved to be about fifteen miles west but, as Alex pursued the large green Dodge Pickup at high speed, he tried to justify himself. "I just want to thank them," he explained. "And I could sure use a drink. That was very stressful!"

Carol stared out of the window knowing the argument was lost and, probably, the rest of the day. Suddenly the green Dodge braked heavily and signalled right. The two cars pulled into the 'Big Water' Saloon, a large wooden building in the middle of nowhere.

"I wonder if it gets many customers," Carol muttered as she struggled to unbuckle her seatbelt.

In the failing light, several neon signs were glowing on the walls of the long narrow cabin. They advertised Bud Light, Coors and Michelob. Steps led to the veranda and an old wooden door with 'OPEN' on it. The inside looked more like someone's living room, with settees and small tables. There was a bar to the left sporting rows of bottles while, in the middle of the room, stood a huge fireplace. In one corner, a multi-coloured Wurlitzer Jukebox was playing country and western music.

"What will you have?" the barman asked. Alex rubbed his hands together, just for something to do.

"Two draught Coors, er, a gin and tonic, a Jack Daniels on the rocks, and a vodka club soda; I think that's it." Alex paid for the drinks and the barman helped him carry them to the table.

"Well, cheers and thank you again for saving us," Alex raised his glass. Everyone held their drinks up in front of them, muttered a toast and took a sip, except for Sandie who downed her beer in one. She was already waving to the barman for another. As they were the only customers, it wasn't difficult to catch his eye.

"So what you folks up to?" Randy asked.

"We're driving from Denver all the way to San Francisco," Carol explained, still wincing from her fifty-fifty gin and tonic.

"You guys frightened of airplanes?" Randy asked. "Its cheaper and sure a whole lot quicker!"

"No! Actually I'm a pilot." Alex glanced at Carol, who smiled with more than mild satisfaction. She drew a number one in the air with her finger. He knew exactly what she was thinking. 'How do you know when a pilot is in the room? – He tells you!'

"Ah hell, so you guys are on vacation." Randy slapped his leg as if he had just discovered gravity. The barman arrived, not with one beer, but an entire round of drinks. Everyone seemed happy except for Carol, who made a point of looking at her watch for the third time since they had been there.

"You ain't goin' nowhere honey." That was Millie speaking and Carol went red, flushed with colour.

"Ma wife has spoken!" Randy declared and took another sip of his Jack on the Rocks. "So what do you do young Missy?" Carol was uncertain whether she was happy with the term 'Missy'.

"I'm a school teacher," Carol explained. "I teach seven to eleven year olds."

"A noble profession!" Randy declared.

"So what do you do?" Carol retorted. She was very close to being rude and Alex glanced at her nervously.

"Well, I fix cars; and sometimes tractors; and sometimes trail bikes." Randy replied.

"And sometimes nothin'!" Sandie added dryly. She pulled a cigarette from her purse and lit it. He watched to smoke blown through her lips. Alex looked at her with some interest. She had been sunbathing naked on the roof of the boat and had a terrific body. Perhaps she wasn't beautiful in the traditional sense, but there was definitely something extremely sexy about her. He reckoned she was probably quite dirty!

"I was in Vietnam," Randy continued. "I had a normal regular job before I left home but, when I came back, all them regular jobs had disappeared. It was like I was a leper! People will still pay when something's broke, so that's how I make ma living."

Millie scoffed and drew hard on her cigarette. Everyone stopped for a few seconds and watched the smoke rise in swirls.

"What was Vietnam really like?" Alex asked. He was genuinely fascinated.

"Well, it was not a nice place to be." Randy said quietly. "I saw my buddies shot to hell, their flesh and blood splattered all over me. Couple of guys died in my arms!"

"That's 'cos you cooked chow for them!" Millie intervened. Randy ignored her.

"It was crazy," he continued. "We did our job and loved our country. But it all seemed so insane. Half the guys were high, 'cos there was nowhere else to be."

Alex wanted more, but Carol was looking tired and pissed off. He then remembered Durango and figured she would just have to look after herself. Randy seemed to sense it too and spoke to Carol directly.

"Honey, I'll give you one hundred dollars if you can tell me what my sister here does for a living." He grinned, looked at his sister, then back at Carol.

Carol looked curiously at the sister. Sandie raised her eyes from her beer and stared directly back at Carol and smiled. She took another large mouthful of beer, her eyes now fixed on Carol. Alex was intrigued too, but this was Carol's game.

"Are you a teacher, too?" Carol asked. There was a shake of the head.

"Do you work in a shop?" she tried. Another shake of the head; Johnny Cash was the only person making a noise in the room.

"Do you fix up cars, like your brother?"

"Nope." Sandie smiled, her eyes still fixed on Carol.

"Do you work in an office of some sort?" Carol asked.

"Nope."

"Are you a cook?" Carol was intrigued, but was already short of ideas. She knew she couldn't win otherwise she would not have been challenged in the first place. Still, what could it be?

"Are you in the Military?" she asked.

"Hey, that's a good one!" Randy said. "Do you fancy wearing a uniform?" Sandie smiled and slowly shook her head.

"No uniforms." Sandie continued her enigmatic smile.

Alex stared down at his beer and wondered whether it was drugged. He had begun to fancy Millie and now he had begun to see Sandie in a new light. This was a very strange family indeed, but he was definitely drawn to them. Perhaps he had had too much sun. Drugged, or not, he took a large mouthful of beer and hoped it was.

"Is it manual work?" Carol asked.

"Good question!" Sandie chuckled and lay back in her seat. "There's a bit of screwing involved."

Alex almost choked on his beer and this time Carol's face had really turned scarlet. The Americans seemed to relish the discomfort and chuckled knowingly to one another.

"She ain't no hooker!" Millie smiled. Alex was mesmerised and tried to understand the chemistry of this situation. They seemed to be deliberately embarrassing Carol and he wasn't sure whether to rescue her and spoil the joke.

Carol, however, seemed to have been really caught up in the mystery and, save for the red face, her inhibitions seemed to have gone.

"You'll have to give me a clue. A little clue." Carol was staring back at Sandie and the smile had returned to her face. "OK, are you a carpenter?"

"Screw! Carpenter!" Randy was enjoying this enormously. "I'll give you a clue. I ain't ever met another one! Never likely to, neither."

Carol was totally absorbed and didn't even notice the third round of drinks being placed on the table. Absent-mindedly she picked up her third gin and tonic and began drinking it.

"Probably manual work. A bit of screwing involved – it's an unusual job. Is that all correct?" Carol watched as Sandie smiled and nodded at her. "Ah, do you breed cattle!"

"Whah, hah! Damn it girl, you are really good at this!" Randy was very animated. "No!"

Carol sighed. She was enjoying the game and, she too, was feeling a strange chemistry, there seemed a strange interaction that she didn't understand, but rather enjoyed. Also she was at the centre of the game for once, instead of being at the periphery.

"Is it anything to do with animals or plants?" Carol watched intently as Sandie slowly shook her head. What was manual work? What wasn't manual work? No uniform, not in an office, possibly manual work, but not cars, not a cook.

"Do you work in a bar?" Carol felt triumphant. "Do you work in this bar?"

"Sorry, honey," Sandie smiled. Randy slapped his thigh again and said 'damn' while now it was Millie lost on a cigarette. Alex didn't intervene, indeed he couldn't intervene. He had considered several possibilities, but each had been dismissed.

"I think I am going to have to give up," Carol sighed. "You'll have to keep your hundred dollars Randy."

Randy whooped with joy as if he had won a lottery. The three Americans looked at each other and smiled. They had had their fun and now it was time to divulge the truth. It was left to Randy, who after all had begun the game, to reveal the answer.

"My sister," he announced proudly, "is a plumbing nun!"

Alex and Carol looked at each other, attempting to digest this piece of news, while the Americans chuckled to themselves.

"I joined a Convent when I was in my late teens - The Holy Sisters of Mercy." Sandie addressed Carol directly. "I spent years there, preparing myself for a lifetime's service to God. Then, one night, God came to me in a dream and said 'Go forth and plumb!' I told the Reverend Mother about my dream and she told me I should follow my heart. The Sisters arranged for me to do a plumbing course and, upon graduation, I left the Convent. Now I install and repair bathrooms while passing on the Word of God."

"Well, we would never have guessed that, would we Alex?"

Alex listened to the raucous laughter, while Glen Campbell was singing about Phoenix. He tried to focus his eyes, but his head was beginning to spin - alcohol, dehydration, too much sun, jet lag, or drugs. He tried to go through the list a second time, but found he couldn't remember a single item from the list. Glenn Campbell had reached somewhere else now, but as the song faded, so did Alex.

Alex was awakened by the conversation next to him. He opened his eyes, but bright sunlight was blasting through the blinds. His head was sore and he closed his eyes again to relieve the pain. He lay there for a few moments and then forced himself to open his eyes once again. Carol was sitting up in bed beside him drinking coffee.

"Breakfast is ready, Honey, just when you want it." A naked woman walked from the room.

"Who was that? Was she naked?" Alex asked. He commanded his limbs to move, but they were not very responsive.

"That was Sandie," Carol said. "She says they'll do us a nice breakfast. There's a coffee here for you."

Alex pushed himself up. He was lying on the top of the sheets, also naked. The room was hot and stuffy.

"Where are we?" he asked, cradling the coffee mug with both hands.

"We went back with the Americans. You were keen to come back for the party! You weren't in a fit state to drive anyway!" There was chastisement in her voice.

"Party? Really, what party? I can't remember anything," he muttered.

"Yep, we had a party. You kept telling them you were up for anything!"

"All I can remember is something about a plumbing nun!" he mumbled.

"It was a very strange day Maria. What with plumbing nuns and goodness knows what!" Alex peered across the room at the empty chair. Maria was gone.

Confused, Alex looked across to the window. The sun was well below the mountain and the landscape was gradually fading into full darkness. A single slither of cloud shone bright red in the fading sky. He slowly moved his head back to view the rest of the room; his room. Long shadows had begun to form in the corners and the high ceiling now seemed very dark and oppressive. He was alone.

Quite alone.

Chapter 5: Joining the Airline

"Good Morning Captain!" Maria came bounding into the room. "I am a little late this morning! The weather! Such rain! Have you looked out of the window today?" Maria walked to the window and pulled back the curtains. The sky was grey and rain poured from the sky.

"It looks like England" Alex grumbled.

"Ah, but we need the rain. It has been very dry this summer. It has been raining all night and perhaps all day today. It will also be cool."

The Spanish enjoyed the cooler weather and rain was always something to celebrate. Even the thunder and lightning was welcome, although it was common to lose the electricity or the telephone line during the storms. Flash floods could also wash gravel and rocks down the hillsides and onto the road, but it was still rain!

Alex liked to see the hills and the vineyards. He loved wine. He loved the smell, the taste, the effect and even the look of the vine. It was an art, a science and a romance all at the same time. He had often walked over the Garraf, and elsewhere, turning a corner to find half a dozen rows of vines bathing in the sunshine. Taking sunshine from the sky each season, goodness from the earth and occasionally water from the ground, it would finally give it all back as Rioja or some other magical wine.

"So you joined the airline, finally!" Maria said. "Finally you achieved your dream, no?"

"Well, not quite Maria." Alex sat back in his chair refreshed and relaxed. A male nurse had helped him shower and wash his hair and he was feeling terrific. He had eaten a full bowl of cereal with nuts in it together with some sort of fruit juice. He had taken his pills (he was a model patient) and was now ready for the day. Of course, his day never really started until Maria had arrived. He thought back to those halcyon days; well nearly.

"The airline had promised that we would be pilots and we were! We were qualified, given pilot contracts and pilots' pay, issued identity cards and uniforms; only one thing was missing. Can you guess?" Alex asked the question and waited for Maria to reply. She shrugged her shoulders.

"No, I don't know," she said.

"Aeroplanes, Maria. Aeroplanes!" Alex slapped his hand on the table in front of him. "They promised we would be pilots. We had a contract to say we were pilots! We even had uniforms with just one stripe on the sleeve! But they didn't promise us an aircraft. So they put us in an office! Sure, we would be given a course just as soon as one became available but, in the meantime, we would have to earn our pay doing something else within the airline."

"So what did you do?" Maria asked.

"Well many of the pilots were angry. Some of them had been flying for other airlines in the UK and overseas. They had left their jobs and reported to Heathrow to fly aeroplanes and they were not about to work in an office! Many of them resigned and found flying jobs elsewhere.

I hadn't been so lucky and I decided to bide my time. Several of us were placed in an office doing basic clerical work. Still, our boss had explained that he understood our position. He suggested we were probably a little brighter than the average clerk and would probably find the work easy. He told us that he would give us a weeks' work each Monday. If we finished it early, we would probably be able to go home early on the Friday."

"That seems very reasonable," Maria suggested.

"It does seem very reasonable. Except we finished our weeks' work on Tuesday afternoon! Our boss carefully checked the work and it was complete. But, he explained, he could not give us the rest of the week off, it would upset the other staff. Besides, he continued, we were getting loads more pay than the rest of the office staff!" Alex paused for a breath. "Of course we are, we said to him - we are not clerks, we are bloody pilots!"

Alex was now becoming very animated and Maria was loving it. She was grinning!

"Anyway he gave us more and more work, but still we could not go home. We decided instead that we would go on a 'go slow' but that didn't work either."

"How is a go slow?" Maria asked.

"A 'go slow' was where we worked as slowly as possible, but even when we were working slowly, we were still doing more work than the normal staff, it was crazy! In the end we took a chess set into the office. We would complete our work and then play chess. At first we hid the chessboard and played in a desk drawer, but soon we just played chess on top of the desk. Our boss would complain and we would explain that we had completed all our work. He would just give us more. Once he gave us hundreds of sheets of computer paper and asked us to add up all the numbers in the columns. After several days we asked him why the computer did not add up all the numbers. Do you know what he said?" Alex watched as Maria shook her head and shrugged her shoulders.

"He said, if the computer added up all the numbers, we wouldn't have anything to do!"

Maria laughed. It was a bad thing, of course, but Alex told the story in such a way, she could not help but laugh. He continued by saying that the rest of the staff were lovely. They understood these pilots didn't really want to be there. They did not mind the antics. For the boss, however, it was very difficult.

Eventually the boss complained to the pilot managers, but they were sympathetic to the pilots and told the manager to be a little more understanding. This gave the grounded pilots even more of an opportunity for humorous disruption. If they were going to waste their time in this office, they were going to have fun wasting it!

"I met some wonderful people while I was there," Alex told her, slowly nodding his head. "Some of them I will never forget."

Finally the flying courses came.

Some of the pilots were given jet courses but Alex, as one of the younger men, was given the Vickers Viscount. The Viscount was a four-engined propeller aircraft from another older era and Alex was very disappointed. However, that disappointment did not last long. The aircraft was based at Heathrow Airport, but did five-day tours around the UK. They would begin in London but fly to the Channels Islands, Bristol and Cardiff, Dublin and Belfast, the Isle of Man, Manchester, Leeds, Newcastle and Scotland. That included the Highlands and Islands of Scotland – Stornaway, Benbecula, Inverness and Aberdeen, Wick, Orkney and Shetland. They would fly several sectors each day but night-stop in nice hotels each evening. The bars and pubs served British beer and the food was traditional fare. What more could a man want? It was hard work, but the five days passed quickly and they would only ever return to London on the fifth and last day.

It was real flying too! The weather was changeable to say the least. You could experience low cloud, fog, and gale-force winds all on the same day. Alex was learning more and more from the Captains he was flying with every day. So many great experiences! He had flown into Stornaway, on the Isle of Lewis, where the airport was close to the beach. They would shut down the aircraft engines and the passengers would disembark for their hotels and cottages. The airport would return to almost complete silence, save for the gulls squawking overhead. It was several hours before the return flight to Glasgow. Sometimes the crew would be given a taxi to a local country hotel where they would take afternoon tea. Sometimes Alex would just walk across the tarmac to the beach and watch as seals sunbathed on the shore.

For five days, two cabin crew and your Captain would be your best friends. You might have a meal together and a couple of beers. (That was all that was permitted). Most people went out, so it was a sociable time. Alex just loved it! Some cabin crew were actually based in the city where the pilots were night-stopping and went to their homes. However, in these larger cities, there might be more than one flight crew staying there; a chance to meet friends and colleagues. The lifestyle was simple and the flying often challenging because of the weather, but Alex was now a real airline pilot!

Alex flew Viscounts for about two years but, for that entire period, the rumours were that the Viscount aircraft were going to be sold. Bases, such as Jersey and Newcastle were sold, routes were given away to other companies and the aircraft were indeed sold. It was a cliché but it was, literally, 'the end of an era'.

Following a period of uncertainty Alex was informed he was to be transferred onto the BAC 1-11 (One-Eleven). He thought there must be some mistake. This was considered a senior fleet with many of the routes operated out of the walled city of Berlin, still isolated like a small island in communist East Germany. But it was no mistake.

It was sad to see the Viscounts go, but this was very easily compensated by the prospect of flying the One-Eleven aircraft. It was a hundred-seater tube, with two jet engines at the back. First there was the ground school, where they had to learn everything about the aircraft. They were taught the location and function of every switch. The hydraulics and pneumatics were explained to them, and then there was the safety and equipment training. Exams followed before the simulator training could take place. The simulator was exactly that, a fully functioning cockpit with the same switches and flying controls. It could be changed from night to day, from sunny to foggy, at the flick of a switch. In 'the box' (as the simulator was called) it was safe to practice engine failures, engine fires, emergency decompression and control difficulties.

This was to become part of Alex's life. Every six months he, and every other pilot, would face two days of gruelling procedures in the simulator, flying different types of approaches in varying weather conditions and wind strengths. It was a significant test of memory and recall skills, their flying ability and their temperament under pressure. He and another pilot would deal with emergency after emergency, while still keeping the aircraft safe and in the air, using so much brain power and concentration that it was easy to forget you were not in a real aircraft. The trainer sitting just behind you was teacher, examiner, air traffic control and chief cabin crew all at the same time. It was hot, sweaty and intense, but sometimes actually fun! However there was always relief when the final debrief was complete with the knowledge that you wouldn't have do it again for another six months.

Having completed the ground school and after several weeks in the simulator, it was time to go for base training. Before you would be permitted to fly a real One-Eleven aircraft, as part of a crew carrying passengers, you would have to do base training. Alex was informed he would be one of six pilots flying out as a passenger to Berlin, in order to complete base-training at Berlin's Tegal Airport. The six pilots were led to an office and briefed about their task. Each of them would do a series of take-offs and landings, initially on two engines, but they would also be practising simulated engine failures on take-off, a one-engined circuit and a single-engined overshoot (a go-around) finally followed by another landing. Simulators in those days were not as sophisticated as they are today and landings had to be practised on the actual aircraft. The other new pilots would sit in the passenger cabin, waiting to be summoned for their turn. Everyone prayed for good landings knowing a jury of your peers was assessing every touchdown.

Finally it was over. Everyone had passed and they were all to be taken into the city to stay overnight at the crew hotel. It was all new and exciting and, after the tension and nerves of the last few hours it was time to let off steam. Enclosed within a high wall, and surrounded by armed East German guards, Berlin was one of the most exciting cities in the world. It had a unique atmosphere and Alex loved it from Day One.

The BAC 1-11 operated out of Manchester, Birmingham and London flying to various airports all over Europe. But, for one week every month, Alex would fly to Berlin and spend five days flying down the Berlin Corridors.

Alex was fascinated by the history. Following the Second World War Germany was divided up into zones. The British, French and Americans took responsibility for the western zones, while the Russians took over the running of the zone in the East. The capital city, Berlin, was deep in the Russian zone. Berlin was likewise divided up into zones. At first the Allies had free access between the various zones by road, railway and air, but in 1948 the Russians decided to close the roads and railways, effectively cutting Berlin off from the West.

In the Eastern Zone the Russians had enforced a communist doctrine. By cutting Berlin off from the West, they would be able to have political and practical control of the city. However, the Western Allies decided this was unacceptable and organized the Berlin Airlift. For nearly a year pilots flew, on average, six hundred flights per day delivering food, supplies and fuel to a city under siege.

During the airlift over a hundred pilots died, mostly from crashes. It was one of the first major conflicts of the Cold War and it had resulted in the formation of two separate and divided countries - West Germany and East Germany. Restrictions on travel gradually increased between West Berlin and East Berlin culminating in the construction of the Berlin Wall in 1961.

This made the city of Berlin a fascinating place. Three narrow air corridors were created, with a height limit of just ten thousand feet. Alex and his colleagues would fly the Northern Air Corridor to Hamburg and Breman, then the Central Air Corridor to Hannover, Dusseldorf, Cologne and London, and the Southern Corridor to Frankfurt, Stuttgart, Munich and Nuremberg. Sometimes a large thundercloud would sit directly over the airway and some delicate negotiations would have to take place with the Soviet and East German authorities! It was all taken very seriously but Berlin, the city, had a magic all of its own.

Alex loved walking around the Tiergarten, the huge park with its zoo in one corner. Near here was the old Embassy sector, with houses still in ruins since the Second World War. The era of the Cold War, Check-Point Charlie and Russian spies fascinated Alex. But there was so much more. The Kurfurstendamm was a huge street stretching for miles containing showcase shops, in contrast to the empty shops of East Berlin. The KaDeWe was perhaps the most amazing.

"I think the food hall was on the sixth floor," he said to Maria, trying to remember. "We used to say it made Fortnum and Masons look like the local VG store!"

"Captain, I have no idea what you are saying! Fort what? VG? What is this? Please speak in English!" She chuckled and raised her arms questioningly. He studied the broad grin on her face and felt the warmth that was becoming familiar to him. For a moment he thought about his last nurse, but then realised he could not even remember her name!

"It was thc most amazing food hall I have ever, ever seen!" he exclaimed. "In fact, I took an East German girl there once. She had been given special permission to visit West Berlin for her sister's wedding. It was sad, a family divided by the Wall. Incredibly the East Germans had placed plain-clothes policemen outside her house in East Germany to guard her children and make sure she returned home again after the wedding! I took her to the KaDeWe thinking it would impress her, but instead she simply cried and cried. Such splendour was too much after the bare shelves of her home town."

"So sad," Maria agreed.

Over time, Alex ventured further afield. He visited Spandau in search of the famous prison. He went windsurfing on the Wannsee, a large river and lake that serviced West Berlin down towards Potsdam (outside the Wall) and the Grunevald Forest (inside the wall). On a number of occasions he visited East Berlin, passing through Check-Point Charlie, then wandering the streets in search of East Berlin's famous museums. The shops were generally bare (and closed) and the few restaurants were poor. One day with a friend he surveyed the menu at one typical restaurant, listing steak, fish, pigs' knuckle and chicken. The waiter patiently waited until we had made our choices, then informed us they only had chicken! They always only had chicken!

The nightlife in West Berlin was famous for its decadence and its diversity, creating an atmosphere that anything goes. Alex found this reputation had continued inside the walled city where parties and pleasure allowed the people to demonstrate that they were not the prisoners. The Berlin Wall was built to prevent East Germans from escaping into it; it was they who were imprisoned by communist dogma. Jazz clubs, nightclubs, bars and beer gardens, Irish bars, punk and rock, it was all there. Berliners knew how to enjoy themselves!

"It was an amazing place, Maria" Alex continued. "We spent so much time there, working and enjoying ourselves, that it seemed like a second home. You could walk into certain bars in Berlin and you would be greeted by your name like a long-lost friend. It was said some pilots even had part-time girlfriends in Berlin!"

"Disgraceful!" Maria admonished. "I hope you were not among them!" Alex chuckled.

"One Christmas, many years ago, we were staying in a hotel in Berlin. We had completed our flying for the day and we were having dinner in the restaurant. I was a young First Officer, somewhat quiet and a little shy. My Captain was very amusing, the life and soul of the party, and we all listened as he told his amusing stories. The men all respected him and the girls loved him and I remember thinking that perhaps, one day, I might be a fine Captain like him."

"I'm sure you were a fine Captain!" Maria assured him. "So what happened in Berlin?"

"Well we laughed and laughed at the Captain's stories and jokes when suddenly he declared it was time for him to go to bed. Everybody around the table sighed and said their goodbyes and their good nights.

The Captain stood up and walked around the table. He shook everyones' hand and kissed every girl, either on the cheek or the hand. When he left the room it was as if he had taken a bright light with him. The room seemed a little darker, certainly quieter, and the atmosphere more subdued than before. People continued to chat, to laugh and joke, but it was not the same." Alex paused and took a mouthful of his coffee. It was cold and slightly bitter, but it quenched the dryness in his throat.

"About twenty minutes had passed before I heard the gasps from around the table. I turned to see the Captain at the door, his arms full of flowers. Our bright light had re-entered the room. He announced he had found the flowers and thought the girls should have them. There were cheers and clapping as he staggered around the room handing out individual flowers to each of the ladies. His little pantomime last only a few minutes, but it was both funny and really quite moving.

With the flowers handed out, he rubbed his hands together and again said good night. He waved goodbye as he walked slowly and carefully towards the door. Someone thanked him for the flowers and then asked him where he had found them so late at night. With a wry smile he turned and grinned. With perfect timing he told us he had picked them from the hotel's own garden. There was a roar of laughter as he left the room!"

"Ten minutes later he returned. This time he had two huge pot plants and everyone creased up laughing as he struggled to drag them to the table. Each contained a palm tree about two metres high; they were huge! Finally the Captain retired to his room. It had been an amazing evening. Strangely enough those palms trees were found in his hotel room the next day!" Alex chuckled at the memory.

"How did they get there?" Maria asked.

"I really can't imagine, Maria. I can't imagine!"

Chapter 6: The Snow Storm

"How are you today?" Maria had poured the coffee in silence, but finally asked the question. There was a routine, it was good to have a routine, but the old man seemed different. He had sat and watched her without saying a word, hardly moving. Usually there was banter, some sort of small talk, but not today. "How do you feel?" she asked gently.

"I feel tired. Very tired." That was all he said.

Maria added a small amount of milk to his coffee and pushed the cup towards him. She took hers black. She sat quietly, blowing gently on her coffee. Yesterday, during her last visit, he had simply sat there, daydreaming at first, but then falling into a deep sleep. She had made a note of it for the night nurses to monitor his sleep patterns during the long quiet nights. Actually there was complete silence now. The building was very old, with thick stonewalls, but it sounded as if everyone else had left the building. Could all the staff and patients just vanish?

Alex sat there breathing heavily. He tried to think, but it was hard. The air was heavy today pushing down upon every part of his body. He told his hand to reach forward, but the effort was too great and he remained still. His mind was full of thoughts, but it was like peering through frosted glass. He thought he could see things beyond the glass, movement perhaps, but everything was blurred. The harder he tried to read his own mind, the harder it was to see or think of anything. Just fatigue. His eyelids began to feel heavy and he strained to keep them open; these were his window on the world and he did not want to shut out the light; not yet. But fall they did…

"Qué hora es?"

Maria was sitting by the window writing notes in a large black file. She closed the file, clicked the pen and put it in her pocket. Only then did she turn her head and look at the old man.

"Son las tres," she said. "It is three o'clock. You have been asleep a long time. Would you like some coffee now? Something to eat?" She stood up and, with the bright sun behind her looked like an angel. He had thought that some time before, had he not? He just could not remember.

Alex nodded at the offer of food and coffee, but something was wrong. Maria picked up her file and left the room, but Alex had noticed there had been no smile! That was it. Maria always smiled, her mouth, her eyes, always a smile. Had he done something wrong? Was she upset with him? He moved uncomfortably in the chair and pulled himself up onto his feet. At first he was unsteady, his legs a little wobbly, and so he waited a moment or so to catch his breath before shuffling to the bathroom. He urinated in the toilet and then washed his hands. He splashed cold water over his face and stared into the mirror. He was shocked to see a stranger staring back at him.

Who was that old man? He studied the grey thinning hair and the stubble on his face. His once tanned skin was now pale, with blotches of freckles and moles. His eyes were dark and sunken. He had seen this face before, of course, but it was always a surprise and a shock to him. It was no one he recognised. He lifted himself onto his toes and tightened his leg muscles. He had once been an athlete with young, firm tight limbs, but now he was weak and sometimes his legs trembled. He should tell the nurse that he needed to go for more walks. Perhaps they should go to the mountains and walk to the top. That would be good exercise. Perhaps Maria would find the going hard; maybe he should suggest a gentle hill to begin with.

Alex shuffled back into the room and went to the window. He tried the glass doors to the balcony, but they were still jammed shut. He needed to get those fixed. He would tell the nurse when he asked her about the other thing. The other thing, what was the other thing? He stared across the valley at the vineyards bathed in sunshine and tried to clear his mind. What did he have to ask? He would ask Maria, she would know.

The door opened and a different Maria entered the room holding the tray. She cleverly closed the door with her bottom so that it clicked gently shut and then she went to the table.

"So Captain, did you enjoy your little nap?" Maria's eyes were sparkling again and, dressed in her perfect white uniform with a touch of blue, she smiled at him warmly. She had rid herself of her concerns and become her professional, cheerful self once again. It normally came naturally to her, but the old man had been so tired for several days now and she feared for her patient.

"I slept very well Maria, thank you." He stretched his arms and legs before shuffling back and slumping into his chair. Maria was pouring the coffee. Also on the tray was a selection of cheeses and meats. Excellent, he was feeling rather hungry now and he rubbed his hands together as if washing them again, before tucking into his feast. He spoke a little about the weather and the impending wine harvest, an obsession with him, but she skilfully steered him back to his memories. He had mentioned an incident in the snow?

Alex peered through the windscreen at the blinding snow. The traffic ahead was stationary, defused brake lights ahead flashing on and off occasionally as someone moved forward another inch or two, before stopping again. Eventually he made out another pulsating light, dim and distant. It was moving very slowly, almost indiscernible in the blizzard.

At first it appeared white, but as it got closer he made out the blue light of a police car. It appeared to be pausing at each car and finally it moved alongside his car. Alex unwound his window and a spray of icy snow blasted the skin on his face, stinging him.

"The road ahead is closed," the policeman shouted as more icy snow blew into the car. "The road behind is completely closed. Drive carefully down the hill and pull onto the garage forecourt." Some of the policeman's words were lost on the icy wind, but Alex understood what was being said. Before Alex could say anything, the policeman had moved on to the next car behind them.

Alex looked at Carol, but said nothing. She didn't have to say anything; it was written in her face. Alex left a good distance between himself and the car ahead, but still the car slid sideways several times as they descended the hill. He wished the bloody driver behind would be equally cautious, but he found himself transfixed to the rear view mirror as the idiot at their rear got dangerously close. It was with relief that he finally pulled onto the garage station forecourt. Several more cars tiptoed down the hill and pulled in alongside them.

Thc garagc pctrol station was closed and only a small dim light illuminated the tiny office, presumably for security. Even though a large canopy covered the petrol pumps, snow had drifted across the forecourt, making it very difficult to see outside. Most cars had left their lights on, but Alex wondered whether they had switched off their engines or left them on for warmth. Finally he switched off the ignition. There was no sound, save the howling wind, but within a few minutes the temperature inside the car had began to fall.

"Can't we just keep the engine running," Carol asked. She emphasized the point by pulling her coat more tightly across her body.

"We can't keep the engine running all night," Alex protested. "And besides, if snow starts accumulating near or around the exhaust, the carbon monoxide fumes from the engine will poison us. Listen, I'll be back in a minute."

Alex grabbed his coat and got out of the car. He struggled to get his coat on as the wind tried to rip it away. The snowflakes hitting his face felt like grit, stinging at his skin. It was really quite painful. He peered around and finally saw a policeman. He imagined it was a policeman, urging another couple to remain in their car, but it was difficult to be sure in the blizzard. He strode towards the officer, but found the snow was already deep enough to make walking difficult. His shoes crunched loudly; the only thing he could hear above the howling gale. As he approached, he called to the man, but his first words were stolen by the wind. He stepped closer.

"Officer, hi, how long are we going to be here?" Alex was startled to discover there were, in fact, two police officers standing there. The darkness, the blinding snow, and the bulk of the first man had hidden the second person.

"You need to stay in your car sir," a voice shouted. It was a woman's voice.

"How long do you think? How long before the road is cleared?" Alex persisted. He was shouting.

"The snowploughs and gritters are out now, but apparently they are being impeded by abandoned vehicles. It could be some time." This time it was the policeman that spoke.

"You need to open up the restaurant," Alex shouted back. "You can't leave these people in their cars. Where does the owner live?" He pointed to the Little Chef Restaurant just up the slope, next door to the garage. Shrouded in darkness, he had not seen it at first.

"We are trying to contact the key holder. The roads are blocked, of course, but we might get him in by helicopter."

Alex was unsure whether the officer was smiling or grimacing, but he realised that he was actually serious. Alex shot his eyes upward, but the snow again stung his eyes. He knew that the thick, dark snow clouds were not very far above his head.

"Look, I am an airline pilot. The cloud is far too low for a helicopter, and if the roads are impassable..." Alex paused just for a second and then began striding towards the Little Chef. "Hey, come with me."

If there were protests, he did not hear them in the wind. He pulled his coat still tighter, the wind taking his breath away. His shoes slipped slightly as he strode up the slope and he corrected himself by taking smaller steps. Before him stood the entrance door, a sort of porch that then led into the main dining area of the Little Chef. The inside was pitch black. To his right, he could make out a window, with a smaller opening window above it. He had not heard them, but now the two officers were standing right behind him, just as he had requested.

"We should break in there," he yelled. "If we break that small window up there, I reckon you are small enough to climb through." He pointed to the female officer, who glanced up at the window. She then turned and looked at her colleague for some support, but he said nothing, staring at the window. Eventually she pushed at his arm and he looked down at her and shrugged.

"People could die out here," Alex insisted with his raised voice. "If the cold doesn't get them, the fumes from their cars might. Either way, it's dangerous." Without waiting, Alex looked around on the ground and immediately saw a brick edging a flowerbed under the window. He bent down, pulled the brick clear and raised it. He did not look back at the police officers, fearing they might yet intervene. Unhesitatingly, he struck the window hard, but the brick just bounced off in his hand. A second blow had similar results. A third harder blow resulted in the glass giving way, with shards threatening close to his hand. He tapped at those and they fell silently into the dark room inside. Finally he turned and faced the policewoman.

"Try climbing through there," Alex pointed to the broken window he had just created. "But be careful of the glass!"

"Do you do this for a living? Breaking and entering?" she asked. She looked again for support from her colleague, but found none. "Oh, well," she said and pulled herself up onto the window ledge. She checked for broken glass around the rim with her gloved hand before pulling herself up still further. She was unlikely to injure herself, but she could end up tearing the uniform she had just had cleaned! However, when she pulled herself up and then forward, nothing happened. Although fairly small, her frame was encumbered by the huge thick coat that was wrapped all around her. The other officer attempted to push her upwards and inwards, finally pushing at her buttocks.

"Enough already!" she shouted down angrily. The policeman backed off immediately. "Enough!" she repeated and jumped down. She gave Alex a sharp, stern look. She looked very cross!

"Bugger this," she said and began undoing her coat. Within seconds the coat was loose in her hands and she threw it aggressively to her colleague. She then leapt back onto the window ledge and pulled herself up with the agility of a cat. Within in a few seconds she her head and shoulders had disappeared through the window but now she had reached her hips. There appeared to be a flaw to this plan.

Alex looked at the policeman, but neither felt brave enough to assist further. It was tempting, but quite simply not worth the risk. After a pause, the struggling began again and suddenly she was in, head and hands first. Alex could hear her swearing angrily, but could not make out the words above the wind. A full minute passed until a torchlight darted about the room. In another minute she was at the door. It opened and Alex drew a breath.

"Coat!" the officer held out her hand and snatched the coat, before a little smile broke across her face. She was clearly pleased with her achievement. "Didn't think I could do it, did you?" she challenged her colleague. He knew this was no time for an argument!

"Right," Alex said. "Can you get everyone up here? They need to bring everything with them. Coats, books, bags, anything they might need. Tell them they will not be allowed back to their cars. We can't have people wandering around outside. Oh, and can I borrow your torch?"

The officers looked at each other, but said nothing. The torch was thrust into Alex's hand and he stood and watched as the two dark figures quickly disappeared into the blizzard. Alex turned and entered the restaurant. On his right was a counter with a cash register. Two open boxes displayed Kit Kats and Mars Bars. To his left was another door, with glass in the upper half. Beyond the door was a payphone. He tried the door but it was locked. To the right of the door was a single light switch. It illuminated the immediate entrance hall, but the rest of the restaurant remained in darkness. Stepping behind the counter, he found another bank of switches. He flicked the first switch and the rest of the lights came on; all of them. The restaurant was large with booths and tables. At that moment the first "guests" began to arrive.

"Wow, that was quick. Please find a seat and make yourselves comfortable," he suggested. The people filing through the door were carrying bags, coats and blankets; they looked like refugees. All were covered with a sprinkling of snow. Carol was with the first group.

"Hi," she said wearily. "Is this your doing?" Alex grinned and nodded.

"Need some help?" she asked. He nodded again, the smile still full on his face. He was in his element!

"Can you get round here and hide the chocolate?" Alex pointed to the counter. He pressed a couple of buttons and opened the cash register. It was empty. He then turned his attention to the rest of the switches. He began flicking everything on.

"What are you doing now?" Alex turned to see that the female police officer standing at the door holding a folded pushchair. Her face was puffy and red from the cold. Please, no more breaking in!"

Alex smiled. "I'm switching on the power. Heating, lighting and, I'm guessing, power to the boilers. These people are going to need hot drinks inside them." He continued along the line of electrical switches.

"Carol, do you know how these boilers work? We could do with making some tea and coffee." Alex began opening cupboards, finding cups, saucers and plates of various sizes. Behind the counter was another door and Alex tried it. It was locked. He looked behind him. The two officers were crouching over a young couple with a baby, over in the far corner of the room. Alex tried forcing the door with his shoulder, but it was shut fast.

"I can help you with that." Alex turned to see a well-built man in his thirties standing at the counter. He had hundreds of freckles and bright red hair, shaved very short. "I'm a fireman. I can open that door for you." He moved towards the door, pushing it near the top and bottom, looking for other locks or catches.

"Just a straight mortise lock," he said. He stood facing the door, drew a breath and then kicked at the door. He wore heavy-duty boots and, with that single kick, the door crashed open. Alex glanced across at the crouching police officers, but there was simply too much commotion, chatting and movement in the room. They did not even look up. The fireman stood aside to allow Alex to enter.

"I'm Paul," the fireman said, offering his hand. Alex shook the outstretched hand and introduced himself. He then pointed to his wife. "This is Carol." Switching on yet another light, Alex found himself in a large walk-in cupboard. On the open wooden shelves were loaves of bread, loads of pots of jam, tins of ham and some cheese. There appeared to be a bank of freezers or fridges, but each had a bar across its' door, which was padlocked.

"Why would you padlock refrigerators?" Alex asked. The fireman shrugged his shoulders. On another shelf was a brown plastic tray with a lid on it. Alex lifted the lid and found it to be the drawer to the cash register. Inside looked to be the day's takings. He turned to Carol, who was standing at the doorway.

"Could you ask one of the police officers to come in and see me?" he asked. He turned to Paul, the fireman. "Will you help me take all this stuff out to the counter?" Alex asked. "We can some helpers to make up some sandwiches."

"You wanted to see me Governor?" It was the policewoman.

Alex looked up with some surprise. Maybe he had misheard. "There's a till drawer here with some money in it. Would you mind counting it and bagging it? Perhaps you could look after it for us?"

"There's money in the till?" She looked surprised. "That's a bit casual isn't it? OK, we'll do that for you, won't we Gary." The male officer was now standing beside her. He nodded and smiled.

"What did you call me?" Alex whispered as they were about to leave. The policewoman glanced backwards and saw that the fireman off-loading an armful of loaves of bread along the counter. She turned back to Alex.

"Look," she began. "Gary and I figure we will need to go out and search for more people. We're going to need someone here to look after things. You're so bossy and in that white coat, everyone thinks you are our boss; an Inspector, or something. We can't think of any reason to tell them differently!" She grinned. "OK Governor?"

Alex looked down at his coat. He was wearing a cream colour gabardine raincoat. Immediately he took it off. "It's not white, its cream!" he said.

"Just don't go breaking anything else," she continued. "We'd hate to have to nick you!"

Alex nodded and they moved away to count the money. Back in the restaurant he stood beside Carol at the counter.

"Hey," he said. "Can you get some helpers and make up some sandwiches with this bread? We've got cheese, jam and stuff; you'll see. And see if we can make some hot drinks made; tea and coffee? It's going to be a long night."

Carol nodded. "We can do sandwiches, but have you found any milk? How we going to do tea and coffee without milk?" she asked. Alex thought back to the padlocked fridges and freezers in the back room. By now, they had searched most places and had found very little else. Alex stepped beyond the counter and clapped his hands.

"Could I have your attention everyone?" he shouted. Slowly the commotion died down, with several people shushing others. "Thank you everyone. Now we are likely to be here for some time. The snowploughs will be clearing the roads, but they are going to have difficulties getting through because of numerous broken down and abandoned vehicles. We are much safer in here, but it could be a long night. Now, we have some volunteers making sandwiches and chocolate will be on sale while stocks last. We are also making tea and coffee, but we don't have any milk. By any chance does anyone have any milk with them in their vehicles?"

There were numerous murmurings and people looked blankly at each other, until Alex realised a rather short, but muscular man was standing in front of him with his hand up. Alex felt like a schoolteacher with a pupil, waiting to speak. He pointed at the man and nodded.

"I got milk," the man began. "A whole bloody tanker full!" Laughter filled the room.

"Can you get it out?" Alex asked, feeling rather foolish.

"Yeah, there are drain holes," the driver explained. "I can bring it back in a bucket." There was more laughter. Alex turned to Paul the fireman and asked him to escort the man to his lorry.

"It's up the hill," the driver apologised. "I couldn't get it down in the snow."

In the event, two men went with the milkman and struggled up the hill in the heavy snow. Alex had ordered that they must stick together and not wander off. He watched as they went out into the night, wrapped up against the blizzard, armed with two torches.

"I'll take mine black," Alex turned to face the policewoman. "We're going to have to go out and search for bodies. We could use a hot coffee before we go. Gary takes sugar."

Two mugs were filled with hot coffee, one laden with sugar. They warmed their hands and stood talking to Alex. No one should leave, they explained. If it became necessary, take away their keys. No one should be allowed out until the rescue teams arrived. They would return every hour, or so, for a refill and to check everyone was OK.

"You're in charge, Governor." The policewoman smiled back at him as they disappeared into the snowy blackness. Carol looked at him quizzically. "Don't ask," he said. "I'll explain later."

At one o'clock in the morning someone turned on a radio. Everyone fell silent as they listened to the BBC radio pips. There were wars in the world, economic worries, and an MP had been caught with his mistress, but the news was as follows-

"This is the news from the BBC at one o'clock. It is estimated that more than one hundred people are trapped inside a restaurant, at Chicklade, on the A303, in Wiltshire, following severe snowstorms in the area. Police say snow ploughs are being hampered by the number of abandoned cars on the roads."

For a moment or two there was a stunned silence in the room; people looked blankly at each other. Soon this gave way to a few cheers. The general hum of chatter grew, before slowly fading into whispers.

People died that night; either frozen in their cars or overcome by exhaust fumes seeping into the car. Two very cold police officers returned several times, exhausted and tired, but they never gave up. Those officers rescued several stranded people that night. Alex was eventually sent a letter from the Chief Constable of Wiltshire, thanking him for his assistance. The snow ploughs finally got through at about 4.00am.

The old man sat thinking about his adventure. He was proud of his involvement and had always planned to return to the Little Chef to explain that it was he who had broken in to the restaurant in such perilous circumstances. He never did.

Maria sat in silence for several minutes before realising that the old man had again fallen asleep in his chair. He would often pause and closing his eyes, but this time the breathing had grown longer and deeper.

"Oh Captain," she whispered. "What are we going to do with you?" She placed a hand gently on his head and stroked his forehead. Then she pulled the blanket further over his legs and then slipped from the room. Tomorrow there would be another story.

Chapter 7: Charity in Blackpool

Alex Young had woken up to a strange grey light. Usually he enjoyed bright morning sunshine streaming in through the curtains, but not today. Occasionally he would hear footsteps in the corridor outside, but generally there was silence. He listened for the song birds outside, but he heard none. He forced himself up and staggered first to the toilet. His bladder felt full as usual. There was normally a need for a hasty visit to his little private bathroom. He felt relief, and then finally pleasure. A little shake, a brisk wash of the hands, and Alex was ready to inspect the greyness outside.

The room temperature was generally constant, but the dull light made him feel cold and he wrapped his dressing gown tightly about his body. He stood at the glass doors, moved the curtains and peered to the horizon. The clouds were dark and heavy, obscuring the hills that were normally his vista. The far vineyards, encroaching on elevated terraces below the line of straggly pine forest, were gone. It was going to rain!

Had it not rained yesterday? He tried to remember.

The long summer months in Spain were generally hot and very dry. Occasional rain was generally welcomed. Only the British are so pre-occupied with the daily weather to utter such comments as 'bloody rain again', 'what day is summer this year?' and 'I'm telling you, it's global warming'.

The grey clouds cast a foreboding shadow over the valley and Alex felt it too. He was tired, he was always tired nowadays, but today he felt a bit depressed and, perhaps a little frightened, although he did not know why. What was it that concerned him? He knew he had nothing to do today. He hadn't had anything to do for a long time now; no chores, no job and no appointments. Perhaps it was that making him feel empty, or even lonely.

Loneliness was Alex's greatest fear! His heart suddenly felt heavy, no, his whole body was sapped of strength. He could feel the pulse inside his arteries and veins racing with a fear and distress he did not understand. An almost child-like panic was slowly overwhelming him and tears began to fill his eyes. He was firmly rooted to the spot, confused and most of all, alone. He stood there for an eternity, time frozen, just as he was. His body began shaking as the tears fell down his cheeks.

"Good Morning, Captain!" Maria entered the room holding a tray with coffee and biscuits. With no response, she quickly placed the tray on the table and rushed to his side.

"Captain?" She put her arm around him and as he turned, he leaned towards her, burying his head into her shoulder.

"I'm frightened," he sobbed.

The old man was now dressed and sitting in his chair. His thoughts were everywhere and nowhere. Maria sat silently, watching him with more than a little concern. He was gradually settling down now, somewhat calmer than before. She was an experienced nurse, but it was hard to watch this. All she could do was…

"Maria?" There was a loud bang on the door that startled Alex. The door then flew open and a short, rather plump woman pushed her way into the room. "Le traje más café; está fresco." The woman had brought fresh coffee. Her eyes flashed towards Alex for just for a moment, then turned again towards Maria.

Alex had never seen this woman before and hoped he never would again! Her skin was leathery and wrinkled, worn by exposure to the Spanish sun. Her hair was dark and curly, but very thin. Alex watched her strangely. She was averting her eyes, keeping her head turned away from him. She gave the tray to Maria, who had stood up and turned to take it. The old lady then picked up the old tray on which stood the original coffee from earlier, now cold and untouched. She paused for just a second as Maria grabbed the biscuits from the old tray, placing them on the table too. The old lady flashed a second glance at Alex who, in turn, growled at her.

"Muchas gracias, Carmen. Esta bien." Maria, still standing, smiled and began re-arranging the tray before pouring the coffee. Alex was trying to look behind her to see the little fat woman comically scurrying towards the door. She was almost running, he thought. The door closed with a thud.

"What a strange woman!" Alex grunted. He leaned back in his chair. "Extraordinary!"

"Be kind!" Maria reprimanded, although she did retain her usual gentle smile. "Carmen is not a nurse Captain, but a helper from the local village. It is nice of her to make the coffee for us. Come, have your coffee and perhaps we can talk some more."

"She was still very strange!" Alex grumbled.

"Carmen is a kind person," Maria said gently. "She works here and also at the special school in the next village. She is a 'giver'."

"Special school?" Alex asked. "What sort of school?"

"This school is for handicapped children," Maria explained. "The children have such things as 'parálisis cerebral', how you say - cerebral palsy and must be looked after. Volunteers like Carmen are needed to help the staff and the families."

"Perhaps I could help?" Alex suggested.

"You? What would they want with a grumpy old man? You would scare the children!" Maria was smiling broadly at the thought.

"I was once a volunteer! I did many things." Alex sipped his coffee and thought back to those times. "I helped run a charity in my local community dealing with heritage matters. We preserved history and encouraged research, saving old buildings and running the local museum. It virtually took over my life. Later, I was even selected to be a magistrate in my community, but I had to stop when I moved to Spain."

"That must have been interesting," Maria commented.

"It was interesting, but also very demanding. But it all began with the children. Children with cerebral palsy..."

Alex had loved his life, flying around Europe and the UK, as a young First Officer. Yes, he had finally made it! He and Carol were married and now they owned their first house. She worked locally as a schoolteacher while he flew to cities such as Paris, Rome, Amsterdam and Berlin staying in first class hotels and eating in fine restaurants. He would fly with various Captains and the conversations could not have been more varied. Some talked about their experiences in the Royal Air Force, flying aircraft Alex had only ever seen in museums! Others spoke about their houses, their elaborate extensions and their huge gardens. Why was it that so many pilots were either building, or re-building their houses? Occasionally, usually after a few beers in the evening, some would complain about their home life, their wives or children, or their expensive divorces.

Then there was Captain Terry Keen. Terry was tall, good-looking and charismatic. He was also a big flirt who loved the ladies! Indeed, he was everything Alex wanted to be. Terry was a natural. He had a smile that could melt a stewardess's heart at six paces, a gentle charm and confidence that meant that everybody loved him. Well, everybody except his first wife! He had returned home one day to find his bags sitting on the doorstep outside. He swore to Alex that he was not guilty of the crime of which he was accused but someone, another pilot, had begun a whispering campaign against him. 'No smoke without fire' his wife had declared. He had been seen with a stewardess in a bar and they had left together.

"I'm getting divorced now," Terry explained. "So there's no reason to lie about it! I took her to her hotel room, pecked her on the cheek and said goodnight. Nothing happened. I wished it had, now!"

Several months later, Terry met that stewardess again. She had just finished her flights for the day and was walking to her car. He had to almost run to catch up with her.

"Good flight?" he asked with that charming smile.

"Hello Captain, how are you? It wasn't too bad really. Three days off now!" Tina was tall and elegant, with flowing locks of red hair. Today the hair was tied up, a requirement while in uniform, but she still looked beautiful.

"Well, I've got a bone to pick with you!" Terry grinned broadly. "Do you remember that night in Jersey? Few months ago?"

"Of course," she smiled. It had been a lovely evening and she had enjoyed his company. "It was with John McCann, Gail Tennant and Cathy Cord."

"How do you remember things like that?" Terry complained. "I can never remember all the names!"

"I flew with them for five days, I think. It was a good trip." Tina remembered most of her trips and the people she flew with. "So what have I done?"

"Well you haven't done anything really, but I was accused of having an affair with you and my wife has kicked me out!" Tina had now stopped walking and was staring straight back at Terry. He was still smiling.

"Well, you look pretty happy about it! You are joking, right?" she questioned.

"No, really. She really has kicked me out. Apparently I was having an affair with you!" Terry tried to look serious for a minute, but it was impossible.

"Oh, my God! Well, do you want me to talk to her? We had a drink and a meal - that's all. With Gail, Cathy and John." Tina still couldn't understand why Terry was looking so happy about it. It must be a joke.

"No, too late for that! It's all going through now, the divorce and everything, and she wouldn't believe you anyway. But you do owe me a coffee!"

Terry and Tina had their coffee in a hotel about three miles from the airport. Terry explained what had happened, the shouting, the recriminations, and the arguing, the denials and the accusations. Tina listened in disbelief as Terry told his sad story, describing the bitterness that had led to the lawyer's office, and an impending court case. Even his children were not talking to him!

About two years later Terry and Tina were married. This, of course, confirmed the suspicions of Terry's wife and the lawyers rubbed their hands with glee as the legal bills rose exponentially. Terry and Tina always denied any wrongdoing and Alex believed them. Why would they lie?

One day Terry and Tina were flying together, a rare but very enjoyable event. Alex was the First Officer, or co-pilot. He had flown with Terry before, but he had never met Tina and instantly fell in love with her! She was very beautiful and a perfect match for Terry, simply oozing personality.

"Ooooh, I like 'em young. Hello!" Tina joked when she was introduced to Alex. She offered her hand and Alex simply melted at her gentle handshake. Terry was always smiling and always confident, but forgot himself for a second and hesitated. The last thing he wanted was competition from some young fly-boy. He need not have worried. Alex made a hash of his moment with Tina, trying to flirt, but stumbling on his words. Terry smiled happily. However, Tina thought it endearing.

Sometime afterwards Terry began talking to Alex about his charitable work. A group of airline employees organised events such as a golfing tournament and the money raised allowed the charity to take underprivileged and handicapped children on a special flying trip. The pilots, cabin crew and other staff would offer their time for free, working on a day off. Shell or BP would offer the aircraft fuel for free. Would Alex be interested in giving up his valuable time for these children?

"Of course!" Alex was elated at being asked and couldn't wait to tell Carol of his good luck! It would be on a school day anyway so she shrugged her shoulders and told him it was up to him. He didn't mention that he had already accepted the role.

The first charity flight Alex flew was to Manchester. He and Terry checked the weather and planned the flight, while ground staff checked in the children and their helpers; one adult to every child. Alex watched as the first bus arrived at the aircraft steps, excited child jumping up and down at the very sight of an aircraft. Other children were brought to the aircraft in a 'High-Lift', a lorry that could raise its cargo of wheel-chaired children straight onto the aircraft. There was no schedule, no timetable, just care and efficiency to get the children and carers on board.

Alex listened on the radio and heard Air Traffic Control tell all the other aircraft that, due to airway congestion, delays of forty minutes could be expected. He touched Terry on the arm to gain his attention and told him. Terry nodded. Soon everyone was on board, the dispatcher took the final signed paperwork and the doors were closed. Extra cabin crew were working on the aircraft today and they walked the up and down the cabin, trying to secure all the seatbelts and bags. The noise was deafening!

"Forty-minutes of this and they'll be climbing the walls," Alex suggested. Terry simply smiled as he always did and called for start clearance.

"Charity Flyer request start for Manchester."

"Charity Flyer, cleared immediate start. There are no delays for you today! Good luck and have a great day. Change to Ground Frequency on one-two-nine decimal seven."

"Roger, Charity Flyer changing to Ground, thanks!" Terry beamed "Everybody pulling together. Bloody fantastic! Alex, start the engines please!"

The aircraft pushed back and taxied to the runway. There were all shapes and sizes at the holding point, lots of different airlines, all waiting to take-off.

"American 427 cleared take-off, wind two-seven-zero ten knots. Air India 302 hold position, we have a priority flight ready for take-off. Charity Flyer, confirm ready."

"Affirm, Charity Flyer fully ready," Alex said on the radio.

"Roger, Charity Flyer, You are cleared line-up and takeoff, wind two-eight-zero eight knots." Alex couldn't believe it as they passed all the other aircraft on the taxiway. The aircraft lined up and took off, climbing and turning gently right, following the published departure procedure. "Charity Flyer, change to departures. See you later!" The air traffic controller sounded like an old friend, wishing them well.

The flight to Manchester was short, about thirty-five minutes, and soon after takeoff Terry handed control to Alex.

"You have control," he said. "Your aircraft, your radio. Off the air."

Terry spoke to his passengers, giving them brief details about the flight. He was much less formal than normal, directly addressing the children.

"...and if you see a man in a funny hat, that's me." Alex heard him say. "OK, done. Are you alright if I go back and say hello Alex?" Alex nodded. "Ring the chimes if you need me."

Terry jumped up from his seat and put on his Captain's jacket and his hat. He opened the door and then was gone. It was a simple flight to Manchester and Alex continued climbing the aircraft to its cruising level, navigated the aircraft and did a fuel check. Several times he replied to instructions from Air Traffic Control. Behind him the excited children were talking to the Captain, a real Captain! One day that will be me, he thought, one day.

"Charity Flyer, change to Manchester now, one-three-two decimal four. Have a good one."

"Charity Flyer roger, change to Manchester, one-three-two decimal four," Alex changed the frequency box on his console. "Manchester good morning, Charity Flyer maintaining flight level two-four-zero."

"Charity Flyer good morning, fly heading three-three-zero, descend when ready flight level one-two-zero."

"Charity Flyer roger, fly heading three-three-zero and descend when ready flight level one-two-zero." Alex selected the radar heading on the autopilot and began the descent. He pulled out the checklist and made sure he had completed all the necessary checks. The air pressure within the cabin changed as soon as the aircraft began its' descent and Terry, the Captain, took that as his signal to return to the flight deck. Together they repeated the checklist, just to make sure, and made their approach towards Manchester.

"Charity Flyer, you are cleared to land runway two-four. After landing, clear the runway at Charlie and await your special escort." Terry acknowledged the call.

Terry flared, closed the thrust levers and the wheels gently kissed the tarmac. As they turned off the runway, Alex completed the after landing checks and read through the checklist. It was Terry who first noticed the blue flashing lights. Soon the aircraft was surrounded by six fire engines. Terry spoke to their excited passengers on the cabin address system.

"Hello everyone, well stage one of our journey is complete. Those of you near the windows can probably see there are lots of red fire engines surrounding the aircraft. This is our special escort and they are going to take us to our parking stand. It's very exciting, isn't it!" Terry switched off the cabin address and turned to Alex. "Anything?"

Alex shook his head. Tina burst into the flight deck and looked out of the window.

"Nice landing, darling," she said. "Oooh, firemen! I just love firemen!"

"Charity Flyer this is Fire One on one-two-one decimal six, how do you read?" The radio burst into life.

"Fire One, this is Charity Flyer. Good morning sir, what's the plan? We have lots of very excited children here, wanting to get off." Terry was being polite.

"Roger Charity Flyer. You are cleared to taxi to remote stand forty-six. My team will then assist with disembarkation to two coaches that are already waiting beside the stand. Over."

"Roger, Charity Flyer is cleared to taxi to remote stand forty-six." Terry pointed to Alex's side of the aircraft. "All clear right?" he asked.

Alex put his thumb up in acknowledgement and they began taxiing towards the stand. Sure enough, two coaches and two police cars were waiting for them.

"It must have been very exciting!" Maria exclaimed.

"It was Maria," the old man smiled. "The firemen carried the children down the steps of the aircraft and took them over for a quick look at the fire engines. They then carried them to the coaches, where their carers were anxiously waiting. Eventually, once everyone was settled, the coaches pulled away. We had a police escort from the Manchester Police, one car at the front, another at the back. Blue lights flashing, the lot! When we crossed the next county boundary, the Lancashire Police took over. They had police motorbike riders escorting us. It was so exciting!"

"It sounds wonderful," Maria said. "The children must have loved it!"

"It was," Alex smiled. "As we approached roundabouts, the police outriders would accelerate ahead of us and then stop the traffic on the roundabout so that we didn't have to stop. The coaches went straight through."

"Where were you going?" Maria asked.

"We went to Blackpool. It's a seaside resort with a famous tower, a bit like the Eiffel Tower. Below the tower is the Blackpool Ballroom and the complex, which included a children's playground. All the children had a fantastic time. Actually, so did I!" Alex closed his eyes and visualised the children's faces. They were so happy.

The following year Captain Terry Keen, First Officer Alex Young and Stewardess Tina Keen were amongst the crew of 'Charity Too'. This time the aircraft would be flying to the island of Jersey, visiting Gerald Durrell's zoo. In the lead up to this great event, Alex went to his manager and asked permission to wear clown's make-up and a wig for the day of the flight. He was flatly refused.

"He told me that, in the event of an emergency, the crew had to be instantly recognisable to the passengers!" Alex explained. "He said the authorities wouldn't allow it. Well, of course the children were definitely going to recognise a pilot wearing an orange wig and a red nose, weren't they?"

Maria chuckled at this prospect.

"Anyway," Alex continued, "I went to the Civil Aviation Authority and asked their permission directly. After that, my manager ran out of excuses. I wore my uniform with an orange wig, white face make-up, huge red lips painted across my face; it was great fun!"

The aircraft had taken off from Heathrow with a new set of needy, deserving children and flown down the long French coastline to the Channel Islands. At Jersey Airport the aircraft was met once again by the local firemen who assisted with the young passengers. Excited children pushed their noses to the windows as the coaches passed through the narrow lanes to the Zoo. Alex, still in clown's makeup sat with a well-known actor, star of the TV series 'Bergerac' about a Jersey policeman. He, too, had given up his time for these children, many of whom suffered from cerebral palsy.

"I thought actors were crazy," he had said, looking at Alex in an orange wig, in his airline uniform, in full clown's make-up!

At the zoo, Alex had noticed one mother who was having considerable problems with her children. She had two sons - Kevin was four years old and his brother Thomas was six. Thomas was desperate to follow the other children into the auditorium to watch a show, pulling at his mother's arm, while young Kevin flatly refused to go anywhere.

"I'll stay with him," Alex suggested. "Maybe I can get him to come in."

"Kevin's CP is quite severe. He might well throw a tantrum. He doesn't respond to people at all." The mother looked tired and exhausted.

"He'll be fine," Alex smiled. The mother hesitated but gave in to her other son, Thomas, who was dragging her into the auditorium behind them.

Alex bent down and looked at the little boy and made a face. Kevin looked away stubbornly. He wasn't going anywhere! Alex sat down on a low brick wall, bringing him almost level with Kevin's face. Kevin's head and eyes remained averted and so Alex moved slightly, almost turning his back on the boy. He kept perfectly still, carefully watching the child from his peripheral vision. It was a stalemate.

Alex was the first to give in. He examined his sleeve of his uniform and picked up an invisible insect in his fingers. He examined it for a few moments and then popped it in his mouth. Exaggerating his movements, he began searching the rest of his body for any more invisible insects. He found another tiny creature and examined it, holding it up to the sky. With Kevin watching he popped it into his mouth and began chewing. Suddenly he puffed up his painted cheeks and hiccupped. He removed the invisible insect from his mouth, smacked his hand, and then placed it back in his mouth. Then he swallowed.

Kevin stepped forward, staring at this very strange clown. Alex opened his mouth wide and Kevin peered inside. Alex stuck out his tongue and shrugged; nothing there. Kevin reached down and picked a non-existent insect from Alex's uniform. His tiny fingers reached forward and pushed the phantom insect into Alex's mouth. Alex chewed, swallowed and rubbed his tummy. Kevin stared at this strange man, but his expression never changed.

Alex reached out and offered his hand. Kevin shook it. Alex kept hold of the hand and stood up. Kevin held tight as Alex led him into the auditorium. Neither ever spoke. Dancers were spinning around the stage, while colourful lights flashed to the music, but little Kevin was too small to see. Alex lifted him upward and held him tight, supported against his waist. Somewhere in the darkness of the audience, Kevin's mother had looked across and seen a miracle. Her son was cradled in the arms of a clown and watching the show. She looked down at Thomas, sat beside her, and squeezed his hand gently. She smiled. It was a wonderful day.

Later in the day, with everybody back on board, the aircraft flew back to London. The ground staff involved with the charity had prepared a wonderful party. Each child was to be given a present, something to remember the day. Alex had slipped away to the toilets, removed his jacket and shirt, and scrubbed away at the makeup on his face. He was pleased to be rid of the orange wig, which had become hot and rather sticky. It had begun to feel as if all those little non-existent insects had hidden somewhere in the wig and he scratched his head rigorously. Finally, washed and refreshed, he returned to the party.

He was standing watching happy parents dancing with their children when he felt the pull on his trousers. He looked down to see young Kevin staring up at him. Alex lifted him up and felt the little arm around his neck. Kevin stared at him for a few moments and then began rubbing Alex's face with his little fingers. This strange man, who had had chalk white skin, now had pink skin. Kevin could not understand why and continued to gently stroke the face. Even stranger, Kevin thought, the clown's face was now very wet with tears rolling down the cheeks.

"It was very strange." The old man said, once again wiping tears from his eyes. "I felt such a massive sense of guilt. Everyone kept thanking me, time and again, for my help - everything I had done. Yet, for everything I gave, I got back so much more. It didn't seem fair. I was getting more out of it than they were."

"Oh Captain, you are a strange man." Maria stood up and leaned across the table. She placed a hand on the trembling man's shoulder and, with her other hand, wiped away the tears with a tissue. She bent forward and kissed his forehead. "Get some rest, Captain, you deserve it."

Chapter 8: Paris and Copenhagen

Generally (but not always) other pilots and cabin crew were easy to get on with. They were worldly, well travelled and generally not shy. It was acceptable to talk about a recent trip one might have flown, or a holiday one might have taken, without worrying about name-dropping. To those not working in the industry, talk about a weekend in New York or a night out in Paris simply sounded like boasting!

From the outside the job appeared romantic and glamorous and sometimes it actually was. However, those wonderful, lucky, but infrequent times were interspersed with tired flights, rough flights, boring flights and routine flights. Actually routine was good! Nobody wanted an exciting flight! Doing six days with early pick-ups was not much fun, either. It was particularly tiring. Sometimes there would be a series of long twelve hour, hard working days after which you would want to just fall into a chair (or your bed) and just sleep!

The same was true of the night-stops. Many night-stops were routine, tired crewmembers going to their rooms to rest and sleep. Some crew were known to study Open University down route, while others would be studying for their next air safety exam or simulator test. Sometimes a crewmember might simply be saving their money, ringing home to a loved one or just perhaps preferred to watch the television.

If you were lucky, likeable and fun, there was occasionally the chance that the crew would gel. If you were not, the crew might gel anyway, but you probably wouldn't know about it and they would go out without you. The last thing stewards and stewardess's want to hear about was airpanes, the pilots' union or your extra-large house extension. It was called leaving the hanger doors open!

Alex was lucky. As a First Officer, he felt he had met his fair share of nice Captains, fun-loving cabin crew and generally very nice people. It wasn't rocket science. If you were nice to people, they were nice to you. If you listened to their stories, they would listen to yours. Provided you didn't drag them to expensive restaurants, or expect them to subsidise your champagne bill, while they drank diet coke, then you would be fine. It was all about getting on and crews were experts at judging what sort of person you were.

Imagine flying to Geneva. On the ground they would spend forty minutes completing the departure checks before flying back to London. There they would have to wait, perhaps for an hour or two, sitting down with a cup of tea and relaxing before the next flight. Next, another briefing and another flight, this time a short hop to Paris. Transport out to the aircraft and meet the cabin crew. A hectic time checking the aircraft, completing security, planning the flight, and finalising the paperwork. Meanwhile the cabin crew would have their separate security checks to complete. Then they would check the cleanliness of the plane, count the catering and make ready for their passengers. Often they would even find the time to offer the pilots a cup of tea or coffee!

Paris

The night-stop was in a nice hotel, somewhere in the city. Passing well-known landmarks on the way, the tired would simply close their eyes, while others would perhaps chat about their day. If everyone was getting on, a plan might be suggested to meet in reception in thirty minutes. Too long in the room and there was always the risk of falling asleep or getting involved with a TV program. No, a quick shower and out was nearly always the best plan.

It is surprising how different people look when they are out of the uniforms we see every day and changed into normal clothes! Alex had stood in reception waiting for his crew. As he loitered in the lobby, he admired the two beautiful girls at reception flirting with the concierge. He watched as the concierge folded the map he had been drawing on and handed it to them with a smile. They thanked him, turned and saw Alex staring at them. He turned and looked away; he had been caught in the act! When he turned back the two girls were standing right in front of him.

"Hi Alex. Is the skipper not down yet?" It was the girl with the long blonde hair.

"No, not yet, late on parade," Alex said weakly. These were his crew! He simply had not recognised them with their hair down, their make- up and their smart clothes. They both looked fabulous. Alex found himself trying to remember their names.

"We've got the location of the restaurant," The blonde girl continued, seemingly not noticing his discomfort. "Dennis has friends here and has gone off to see them."

"Bon soir Amanda, bon soir Janette." Clive waltzed in with a charm that made Alex feel totally inadequate. "Is this us then?" he asked, winking at Alex. "Shall we go?"

The group of four stepped out into the Paris night air. They were in Paris! The street outside was bustling with people, while cars and scooters beeped at each other in a melody of impatient motorists. The combination of bright street lights, car headlights and illuminated windows made it feel like day but somewhere above, the stars and planets were twinkling to an unseeing metropolis. The girls appeared to be chatting incessantly to each other, but Alex had no idea how they could possibly hear anything amongst the din of the city. He and Clive just followed a few steps behind in silence. After two blocks they turned into a side street where the noise reduced to a gentle hum and darker shadows confirmed it was, indeed, nighttime.

Alex looked across at Clive who had his eyes firmly locked on the two bottoms, wiggling a short distance in front of him.

"Nice to have someone else doing the navigation," Clive said without moving his head or his eyes.

Alex agreed but he, too, had taken to focusing on the long legs and bottoms ahead of them. Amanda was wearing a flowing, light green, silk dress, which shone brightly each time they passed a lamppost. Janette was slimmer and taller and her dress, or was in a skirt and top, was tightly moulded to her lovely body. Both were wearing high-heeled shoes that looked as if they had been purchased from a very expensive fashion house. Alex did not see them refer to the map once, but soon they stopped outside a cafe-style restaurant.

The girls paused to look at the menu outside, but the lighting was too dim to read the small italic writing. Clive stepped ahead and opened the door.

"Ladies, after you." Clive took each of their hands and guided them in with a broad smile. He then followed them in, leaving Alex to grab the closing door. It was normal, he thought. First Officers are nearly always invisible.

The maitre d' guided them to a table near the window. The restaurant was only half full, but it was early and this was Paris. Menus were handed first to the ladies and then to the 'gentlemen'. Clive, as the senior gentleman was also handed a wine list. He said something to the maitre d' and suddenly a bottle of red wine was being opened at the table. Alex would have preferred a beer and was about to say so, when a waiter arrived to take the order. He frantically looked at the menu, all in French of course, as he heard the others selecting their first and second courses. He pointed to his selections and mumbled sufficiently that no one would hear his poor French. He added a 's'il vous plait' at the end and the waiter wrestled the menu from his hand.

To his astonishment both the girls then foraged into their handbags and took out cigarettes. He had been flying long enough to know that many cabin crew and even some of the normally health-conscious pilots smoked, but it was always a disappointment to him. He could not imagine kissing someone who smelt like an ashtray. However, as he stared across the table at the beautiful Amanda and Janette he was already considering making an exception. Alex had read somewhere that men thought about sex every six seconds and he had wondered what all the other men were thinking of for the other five seconds!

"You're very quiet young man," Amanda was looking across at him quizzically. "Get some of that wine down yer."

Alex reached down, picked up his glass, and said 'cheers'. The table conversation stopped with a suddenness, which startled him and he found three faces staring right at him.

"We did that about a minute ago," Amanda was wearing a teasing smile. "Keep up, will yer?" She drew on her cigarette and blew a cloud of smoke sideways over her shoulder. Alex was captivated and took a large mouthful of wine. His glass had barely touched the linen tablecloth before the waiter was again topping it up.

Clive talked about his yacht moored down on the Hamble. He had, he explained, picked up his French language skills sailing in and out of the harbours along the English Channel, or la Manche as the 'Froggies' called it. At that very moment Alex found a dish of frog's legs, fried and soaked in heavy garlic, placed in front of him. He sat and waited, wondering how bad could they be? He picked up his wine glass and took another swig. Pick-up wasn't until lunchtime, so a few glasses of wine would not go amiss. 'I'm going to need them', he thought.

The conversations were wide and varied. There was talk of yachts, then a discussion about cars and, of course, everybody else had a nice motor! Amanda had a Triumph Spitfire, new and shiny, which suited her glamorous look. Janette had two young children, she said, and her five-door BMW was perfect with the space. So while Clive talked about his Jaguar in much detail, Alex wondered how Janette could have two young children and still look like that. He thought about saying it, but thought better of it.

"What car you got Alex?" Amanda asked. He finished his mouthful of wine and wiped his mouth.

"I have an old Ford Cortina," he said. "It's OK, but all I can afford really."

"Cortina's alright," Amanda said kindly. "Are you married?"

"Er, yes," Alex replied with a nod.

"Well, either you are or you aren't," she continued. "Why don't you wear a wedding ring then? Think you'll get more shagging without one?"

Alex was rather taken by surprise at this sudden change of subject. "Well, I don't want to catch it on anything. I do a lot of DIY at home."

"What, wanking?" Amanda asked quizzically. The table erupted in laughter.

"Thinks he'll get more shagging without one," Janette assured the rest of the table.

"Personally I'd rather shag the married one's," Clive added. "It means they won't turn up on your doorstep!"

"You'd shag married men?" Alex asked directly at Clive. The girls laughed so loudly every table in the restaurant turned to see what was happening. Clive gave Alex a black look, but it slowly melted into a smile.

"You cheeky bugger!" was all Clive could say.

"You're alright lad!" Amanda raised her glass and pointed it to Alex. Janette did the same and after a moment's hesitation so did Clive. "Yeah, Ok. Here's to you Alex!"

The chat drifted from theme to theme, TV soaps such as Coronation Street and Crossroads were mentioned, everyone's last holiday, and where people lived. The banter continued and a second bottle of wine was ordered.

"Could I please have some still water, too?" Alex asked. The waiter responded with 'of course you can' in perfect English.

"Alex, if a stork delivers white babies, and a blackbird delivers black babies, what delivers no babies?" Amanda stared direct at him as she asked the question.

Alex considered the possibilities. He looked at Janette, who possibly already knew the answer, while Clive was looking skyward repeating the joke to himself.

"No, I'm sorry, I don't know," Alex shook his head.

"A swallow!" Amanda beamed at her victory and the laughter that followed.

Clive leaned in to the table and whispered to the two girls. "How do you stop a girl swallowing?" There was a brief shake of the heads. "Marry her!" There was an acknowledging smile and a 'ha, ha' from Amanda.

Clive got up from the table and asked "Ou sont les toilettes?" Alex watched where he went, just in case he needed to go (he had been drinking rather a lot of water).

"So does your wife swallow?" Alex nearly choked when Amanda asked him the question.

"What?" he looked over in astonishment. Amanda blew smoke rings from another cigarette.

"Well, does she?" Amanda had a big grin on her face, knowing she had embarrassed him. Janette was equally attentive.

"I'm not going to tell you that! People don't talk about that sort of thing!" Alex tried to appear cool, but it was not working.

"No, his 'Mrs' doesn't," Janette said, poking Amanda and grinning.

"Men may not talk about it darling, but women certainly do! Don't we Janette?" Amanda and Janette nodded to each other with a triumphant grin.

"Ooooh! Dirty Clive's coming back. I'll guess we'll never know!" Amanda nudged Janette and then waved at the waiter. "L'addition s'il vous plaît?"

The bill was divided equally, although Clive insisted in leaving the tip.

A nightcap on the house was turned down and after a lot of handshaking the crew stepped out into the street. After the impressive navigation by the girls in finding the restaurant, it was more than a little disappointing when, at the bottom of the steps, they turned the wrong way! Clive called after them and waved in the direction of the hotel. The girls turned, walked past him smiling, this time in the right direction and saluted their Captain.

Clive and Alex walked dutifully behind the girls, still focusing on their tight bottoms wiggling on ahead. The girls were whispering to each other and laughing loudly inbetween.

Finally Clive whispered to Alex - "I think you are definitely in there mate! The lovely Amanda!"

"What?" Alex looked at Clive in order to judge whether he was making a joke at his expense. "What makes you say that?"

"Oh, come on! The way she spoke to you, her eyes were all over you like a rash! Green light all the way, my dear boy, believe me!" Clive patted him on the shoulder and they then resumed their studies in silence.

At the hotel reception everyone collected their keys. At the lift Clive kissed each of the girls on each cheek and bade them both goodbye. He suggested breakfast, but the girls mumbled something about morning shopping. He then turned to Alex, shook his hand and wished him a good evening. It was a firm handshake. Both girls in turn then kissed Alex on both cheeks.

"Thanks for a really nice evening Alex," Amanda put a hand on his shoulder then touched his cheek gently with her finger. "You're a really nice man, once you loosen up. Hope I fly with you again."

Then it was Janette's turn. "Goodnight Alex. See you in the tomorrow. Ditto!"

At that moment the lift arrived and all four of them stepped in. The lift stopped at the fourth floor and both girls stepped out. "Goodnight!" they called.

Alex stepped out on Five and walked to his room. "Night!" he called as the lift doors closed. He entered his room and switched the lights on. He sat on his bed and looked at the hotel telephone. Beside it was the piece of paper he had been given at check-in with their wake-up time and the crew room numbers. He read the list and went to the bathroom and cleaned his teeth. Back in the bedroom he read the list once again, noting Amanda's room number. He rehearsed the conversation in his head several times but, every time, the call was followed by a rejection. Finally undressed, Alex slipped into the fresh sheets and closed his eyes.

Copenhagen

The night stop in Copenhagen held lots of promise, following a long three-sector day. The taxi had driven them straight from the aircraft to the city centre hotel where Geoffery Fielding, the captain, had given instructions that everybody was to report to the hotel bar in twenty minutes. Alex had carried his overnight bag to his room and was in the shower within five minutes. He was still trying to get used to the luxurious rooms that the airline put them in. The crews spent a significant part of their time in hotel rooms and it was important that the rooms were clean, quiet and had blackout curtains.

From his poor beginnings, Alex could not imagine a life where he would stay in such hotels where businessmen and posh holidaymakers routinely spent their days and nights. These hotels sported impressive reception areas, nice restaurants and bars, wide hallways and great rooms. Standard were large wide beds, matching heavy curtains at the windows, pictures on the walls and huge thick towels. Not all the hotels were this good of course, but Alex loved the experience. He showered quickly under the power shower using the complimentary fragrances to wash his hair and body. He dried himself quickly, got dressed and cleaned his teeth. He brushed his hair and checked in the mirror. He was generally disappointed with what he saw, he was no Adonis, but it would have to do.

The entire transformation from uniformed pilot in a twelve-hour old shirt, to a casual, clean civilian had taken just twenty-five minutes. He was really amazed, therefore, to see that everyone else was already at the bar. Geoff was standing at the bar, cigarette in hand, ordering a drink for his cabin crew.

"Glad you could join us," he smiled. "We thought you had fallen asleep in front of the TV!"

Everyone laughed and Alex knew it was futile to look at his watch, apologise or make some lame excuse. He just smiled at the joke and waited. "Beer?" Geoff had said with a wave of the finger and Alex nodded. His was the last drink to be served.

Alex could not help, but look at the cabin crew, his cabin crew. On the aircraft, dressed in regulation uniform, they had looked smart, but unassuming. Now they looked like models. Well, two of them definitely did. He tried not to stare, but probably did so anyway. He wondered how they could have got ready so quickly and look so great. Practice, he guessed. Geoff turned towards him, sporting two pints of beer. He had already handed the three girls their drinks.

"Good job everybody, another good day!" The captain raised his glass and toasted everyone. "Girls, you were in good hands today. Alex did a fine job! He's up from London on a temporary posting. If any of you are interested, he's a bit of a stud, and he will be flying out of Manchester all this month!"

Alex blushed at the lie, everyone laughed at the joke, and the evening settled into banter and general chit-chat. It was clear everyone else knew each other and much of the conversation related to mutual colleagues and friends Alex had never heard of. The Manchester base was expanding someone had said, although this was contradicted by someone else who had been told by a manager that they were losing several routes. Alex stepped up dutifully when it was time for the next round of drinks and he tried to hide his horror when he saw how much he was signing for.

'Had anyone seen Wendy since she'd been back at work,' someone had asked? 'She has miraculously increased her bust size by several inches and it wasn't through eating too much!'

'Let's hope they don't inflate at 30,000 feet!' someone else had said.

It was a short evening with a fairly early start the next day and after a couple of drinks it was time for bed. Geoff confirmed the pick-up time and everyone knew the hotel operator would ring them all an hour before that. Some were going round the corner to a tiny corner supermarket, which did soft drinks, sweets and light snacks. Apparently the mini-bar was a rip off!

Alex wandered to the lifts and pressed the button. An empty lift slowly opened its doors and he stepped in. He selected floor twelve, his plastic key card held in his left hand.

"Hi, room for a little one?" It was Valerie, who had barely spoken to him the whole evening. She stepped in and smiled. He stood slightly behind her so that he could look at her trim figure and her long flowing hair. The hair had been tied up during the day and the make-up had been a little more subtle. She turned and stared up at him. "Don't mind Geoff," she said, looking at him reassuringly. "He loves to have a laugh at someone else's expense, but he's a pussy cat really."

"Oh I don't mind really," Alex said unconvincingly. "It's just a bit strange when you all know each other so well. It's not really like that in London, being a bigger base."

"Ah well, it makes us all the more friendly," Valerie beamed. "It's just that everyone knows your business!"

The doors opened at the twelfth floor and Alex held the lift door and allowed Valerie to exit first.

"Thank you, kind sir," she said.

Alex reached his room first and stopped.

"Well, goodnight then," he said.

"Yeah, goodnight," she replied. She half waved a hand, but didn't look back.

Alex watched her for a second and then placed his key in the lock. He swiped the magnetic strip, but nothing happened. He tried a second time and then a third. He had never used one of these new keys before and cursed to himself.

"Isn't it working?" Valerie was standing three doors down in front of her door. "Have you got the right room?"

Alex looked at the room number. "Yep, room 1222. So much for technology!"

"Well come in and use the phone, luv," Valerie suggested. "They can send you up another key, save you going all that way downstairs again." She was smiling kindly at him.

He thanked her and walked down to where she standing. Valerie swiped her key and there was a loud magnetic click. She opened the door and Alex followed her into the room. Her cabin bag lay open on a chair and her uniform and clothes were hung neatly in the wardrobe.

"How did you get ready so quickly?" he asked, "…and get all your clothes hung up, and still beat me down to the bar?"

"It's years of practice, chuck. You'll get used to it. The phone is over there." She pointed to the bed.

Alex walked over and picked up the phone. A little note said dial '0' for the operator and the front desk. After a few seconds the phone started ringing. It rang for several minutes without reply. He replaced the receiver, picked it up and tried again.

"No answer?" Valerie asked. She took the receiver from his hand and replaced the handset on the phone. "Well, you'll just have to stay here then, won't you." She placed a hand on his chest and put her lips close to his. Instinctively, and without thinking, he bent down and kissed her. His hands moved to her back and he pulled her still closer. She lowered herself towards the bed and he followed. She had begun clawing at his shirt and pulled it from his body. They wrestled gently, kissing and touching, until finally their naked bodies pressed against each other. The pain of her nails sinking into his back lasted all but a second, but that was the moment he entered her.

The next morning Alex got dressed quickly and rushed down to reception. His clothes were heavily creased and he had not yet showered. He needed to get back into his own room. He was relieved to see that, at this early hour, there was no one else at reception. The night porter raised his head and smiled.

"Good morning sir, how may I help you?"

"My key isn't working. I am in room 1222." Alex flashed his airline I/D and the porter studied the photograph carefully. A new plastic key was placed in the machine and programmed accordingly.

"Your key, sir." The porter handed it to him with a knowing smile. "There was no malfunction, sir, this was not your key. Somehow your key was changed or swopped for another. Perhaps a little joke by your crew, sir?"

Alex dashed to the lifts and pressed the up buttons repeatedly. He tried to understand what the night porter had just said to him, but for now he only had thirty five minutes left in order to get ready. He almost ran down thc corridor and prayed that the key would work. The door latch clicked as he swiped the key and ran around the room like a headless chicken.

Thirty minutes later Alex exited the lift and stepped into a crowded lobby. A receptionist was ready to take his money, a bill for just one round of drinks, and he handed over his key. The rest of the crew were standing there waiting looking very smart in their uniforms. They smiled at him casually, almost disinterested, and began filing out to the little bus. There was no joke, no humiliation and Alex just felt relief. Valerie barely acknowledged him; perhaps a half-smile, perhaps not. He was not sure.

Geoff Fielding said nothing of interest on the flight home, a single sector back to Manchester. He was looking forward to a few days down in Nice, where he had a yacht. 'Gets me away from the Mrs," he joked.

With a firm handshake, the captain said goodbye to Alex and added that he would enjoy flying with him again. Alex looked on as the three stewardesses kissed Geoff goodbye. They all turned and waved Alex goodbye. In a second all three had turned away and began walking towards the car park, deep in conversation. While Alex waited for his bus to the hotel, it began to rain.

Chapter 9: Siddy and Charcoal

The rain was falling harder in Manchester and Alex sat in his room wondering what had happened the night before. Had someone switched his key? Had it been Valerie, or Geoff, the captain? Perhaps the whole crew had been in on it? Or perhaps the porter had been mistaken and there was no conspiracy at all? Finally he had to give up thinking about it.

Family history had a lot to answer for. These were the days before daytime television and there was no radio in the room. He had not thought to pack a reading book and the rain showed no signs of abating. What on earth was he going to do for the rest of the day? He opened a side drawer and pulled out a Gideon's bible. He opened up the pages, but quickly put in back. It reminded him too much of his childhood.

A second drawer revealed the Manchester telephone directory and he idly flicked through it. It was not going to be a good read. He opened it towards the back. There were not that many entries under X, Y and Z, although there were rather a lot listed under Young. Idly he turned back to the B's, paused and then went back a page. He ran his finger down the list. B – B – B – Burgum! He was surprised to see three Burgums listed in the phone directory. Burgum had been his grandfather's original name.

Alex had never understood why the family name had changed. Some whispered that there was a Jewish connection and that was the reason for change. But, Alex reasoned if the name was so rare, who would even know if it were Jewish? It didn't sound Jewish. Later in life, he investigated this and many other 'legends', only to find they had no basis in fact.

Alex's father had been christened Whittington because of the family connection with Dick Whittington, who became Lord Mayor of London. Yet Alex could find no proof of this at all; it was another fabrication. He wondered how these family myths and legends ever got started.

So why was the family name changed? Why, he wondered, had his grandfather sought to make himself anonymous? Was it criminal activity? Was it to hide from villains to whom he owed money? If any of these stories were really true, why would the family continue to risk exposing the subterfuge by speaking about it and mentioning the original name? For Alex it was a puzzle, mystifying and unresolved.

Alex rang his father that same day. He told him the surname Burgum was listed three times in the Manchester telephone directory and began questioning the Young and Burgum relationship again. His father was not evasive; he simply had no idea and had, apparently, never asked the question. There was too much other stuff going on, such as making a living and bringing up a family.

Alex had no choice but to accept that explanation and so he tried a different tack. He had been brought up on Burgum stories and not those of the family Young. It was always boasted that Burgum was an exclusive group, with just a few unique characters in the world. So who were these people in the Manchester directory then? Did he know them? His father could not offer any explanation, save that he had been told by his own parents that all the Burgums were their kin. It seemed to be a dead end.

Alex could not let it rest. Eventually the rain relented, slowing to gentle showers, and he made his way to Manchester Library. There he found a collection of telephone directories covering the whole of England and Wales. Mostly he drew a blank, but he continued to go through every directory, noting down names and addresses. Over two days he had found eighty listings of the name! This was a time when computers were mostly the preserve of larger businesses. Alex spent the next several weeks handwriting letters to every Burgum listed in his notebook. Each letter explained who he was and asking who were they? 'Were we related?'

So began a journey. Some wrote back saying they knew very little. Others identified brothers and sisters also in the phone directory and slowly, but surely, the seeds of family history research were sown.

Alex learned about certificates of birth, marriages and deaths, and the registers listing them all in London. He learned about census returns, parish registers and wills. With the advent of affordable desktop computers and laptops, his life was about to get somewhat easier. He began tracing back his own family, and others, back through the generations and recorded it in a database. The Internet was still in its' infancy and there were very few records online and not much else to go on. However, he did discover his own family of Burgums had lived for generations in the Forest of Dean, but he had no idea where that was!

Alex decided he needed to visit the Forest of Dean, in Gloucestershire. He stood at the small village of Flaxley where, he had recently discovered, his relatives had lived and worked. It was less of a village and more a number of farmsteads and cottages strewn along a few meandering country lanes. Standing in the so-called Vale of Castiard, he stared down the valley and was overcome by its' beauty, Alex felt a presence that was difficult to describe. Emotion overtook him and he felt a bond, a belonging, which remained with him most of his life. He could not know how, in the future, this would change the direction of his life forever.

Siddy

Alex had been sitting at his new computer. He was going through the copious notes he had made on his last visit to the Forest. He had trawled through the parish registers in the Gloucestershire Records Office. He had plucked randomly at parishes near to where his family had lived; Flaxley, Abenhall, Ruardean and Littledean. He was alarmed to find that the earlier records were partly, sometime wholly in Latin and the writing had been become much more difficult to read off the microfilm.

The local census returns had not been much better. Alex had spent ages reading and re-reading some enumerator's writing, trying to decipher the scrawl and misspellings. Having copied his findings into small notebooks, he was dismayed to discover his own writings, too, were proving difficult to interpret!

The ringing telephone had been a welcome distraction. It was his father. Alex's grandfather had been taken ill and his mother and father had travelled halfway across England to help the ailing parent.

"Alex, it's about your grandfather," Bill had explained. "He's quite weak. He has bronchial pneumonia and he has lost a lot of weight."

Alex said how sorry he was and asked for his best wishes to be passed on. He did not mention that he thought ninety-five was already a really good age! His father would probably not want to hear such things now, if indeed at all.

"Your grandfather has been asking about his brother," Bill continued. "He asked about Siddy. Well, I figure you bein' the family historian an' all."

Sidney had been born in the East End of London, in 1906, the seventh of ten children. While working at the Tate and Lyle sugar factory in 1926, he suffered a tragic accident. A large sack of sugar had fallen from a great height, striking him on the head, inflicting great physical and mental damage.

His parents, Fred and Mary, had wanted to keep him at home, but "Siddy" had become prone to violent mood swings and the task of looking after him became too great. With great regret he was committed to a mental home at Goodmayes Hospital, in Essex. To start with the visits were fairly regular but, over the years, the aging parents found it more and more difficult to visit him. The young man's brothers and sisters occasionally visited him, but gradually the visits become less and less frequent. Years turn into decades and memories fade.

Alex felt it was an impossible task. Siddy had been locked away over seventy years before. If he were still alive, he would be 93 years old. Alex rang the hospital, but they refused to discuss anything over the telephone. When that failed, Alex tried writing to the Local Health Authority, but the replies mentioned 'confidentiality', 'data-protection' and 'not known'.

"Dad?" The telephone had rung for ages and Alex was about to hang up. "Dad, are you there?"

"Hello son, I was in the toilet. Your muvvers not 'ere I'm afraid. She's working up the hospital."

"No, Dad, it's you I want to speak to. How is granddad?" Alex waited for the long story!

"Yeah, the Old Man's OK. He's gaining strength and gettin' a bit brighter. Fought he was goin' t' die, I reckon. Still moanin' all the time, though. We dropped everyfing, rushed up to help 'im and all he does is complain that we left him to go back 'ome!" Bill took a breath. "Bleedin' ungrateful really, but we can't stay up there forever!"

"Dad, it's about Siddy." Alex took a breath and waited for his father to interrupt, but there was silence at the other end. "Dad, Siddy is still alive!"

Alex waited for a reaction, but none came. "Dad, did you hear me? Siddy is still alive!"

There was another pause. "Well, that's really … really quite somethin' …" Alex thought he detected emotion in his father's voice, but he knew better than to say anything about it.

"I have had a letter from one of the nurses," Alex enthused. He was excited and he wanted others to share in this miracle. "She says they are all amazed. Dad, they can't believe Siddy has surviving relatives! Are you pleased?"

Bill had other things on his mind. His father Arthur had only just recovered from a serious illness. Only when he thought he was going to die, did he begin to ask questions about Siddy and his past. How would he react now?

Bill contacted a cousin who lived in the area. Sam listened quietly, as surprised as anybody about the news. Siddy was his uncle and, although he had heard the stories, the truth seemed so much more incredible. How long had he been in there? When did he last have a visitor? Would he still remember anything about the family?

Sam agreed to visit the hospital first to "get the lay of the land, so to speak." The nurses had asked Siddy about his family and he did recall his brother Arthur. The nurses were as excited as the family and arrangements were made for a family reunion.

Bill broke the news to his father at about the same time as Sam told his mother, Muriel, the day before the reunion was planned to take place.

"Thank Alex for me," Arthur kept repeating. "Thank Alex for me.

The family met in the hospital reception and nervously whispered greetings to each other while they waited for the nurse. Sarah Batchelor stepped into the room and welcomed them with a broad smile before taking them through towards Siddy's ward. The corridors were wide, bright and clean, with light flooding in through large sash windows.

"All the staff are so excited," Sarah confessed cheerfully. "Siddy is a very good patient," she continued, "albeit, he has good days and bad days but we all have those, don't we?"

She led them into a very large room resembling a ballroom. It wasn't quite the Kursaal, Billy thought, but some of the inmates were sitting on chairs around the edge of the room.

"Looks like they're waiting for someone to ask them to dance," Billy whispered to his father. Arthur looked nervously around, bewildered by the strange surroundings. He was clutching a large bag of sweets in one hand, while gripping Billy's arm with the other. They slowly walked across the room towards the large bay window. Billy could feel eyes from across the room watching them with curiosity.

A circle of armchairs occupied the recess and there sat Siddy. Billy recognised him immediately from the family resemblance. Siddy looked up and smiled at the sudden attention. There were kisses, the shaking of frail hands, and several rather clumsy hugs as Siddy had remained seated. Sarah Batchelor encouraged everybody to sit down.

A pale old man sat there before them, his face freckled and wrinkled by the passing of over nine decades. Siddy just sat quietly staring at the influx of strangers. Arthur had been placed in the seat beside his brother. Watching his father and uncle sitting there side by side was too much for Billy and he pulled a hanky from his pocket to dab his eyes.

"Hello Siddy," Arthur said softly. "I'm your bruvver Arthur. We used to play football down in Plaistow, we did. Then down the park, in Canning Town. Do you remember?"

Siddy nodded and smiled. Billy saw that the two brothers were now holding hands, both shaking ever so slightly. Siddy had become distracted by the bag of sweets he had been given and was sucking and chewing for all he was worth. He was wearing a blue shirt, which looked new, and a smart tie knotted at the collar. His trousers had an almost military crease down the legs and he was wearing shoes. Billy looked around the room. All the other patients were wearing slippers; the staff had spent some time preparing Siddy for his visitors!

"Siddy has been on several outings recently," Sarah said. "We have barbecues and family parties. Here's a picture of Siddy down at Southend on Sea, taken just a few weeks ago."

"Blimey, that's near where my Dad lives now," Billy said, "ain't it Dad." The picture was handed around and now Sam was showing it to his mother. Muriel just sat there sobbing, staring at her long lost brother.

Billy leaned over and spoke to Sarah, the nurse. "Those three there have nearly two hundred and seventy six years between them," he said proudly. "This is quite a reunion."

"It's a remarkable day," Sarah admitted. "We don't think Siddy has had a visitor for thirty or forty years!"

Three months later Billy heard from the hospital again. He and the family had been invited to the Mary Ward Christmas party! In the event Billy was unable to go, but he passed the invitation on to his brother George.

"Hello Dad, it's George. We're goin' out tomorrow. Fancy a little day out?"

He may have been an old man but, when George and his son arrived the next day, Arthur was sitting there waiting. He was clean and smartly dressed, his shoes highly polished.

"Where we goin' then?" Arthur asked.

"Well, it's nearly Christmas," George had joked. "We're goin' to see Father Christmas!"

"Arhh, you're daft!" Arthur grumbled. He sat quietly in the car, listening to George and his son Gary talking about Gary's football training, Southend United's loss at Hereford and the busy Christmas traffic. He stared out of the side window, watching the houses and factories flash past.

"That's Dagenham!" Arthur grunted. "That's near Siddy's hospital!" He was pointing at the huge Ford Motor Plant, which stretched for miles along the road in front of them.

"They reckon that's nearly five hundred acres just there Dad. Look at all those Fiestas. It's bleedin' massive!" George pointed to his left where row upon row of new cars waited patiently for distribution. "Anyway, that's where we're going."

"What to Fords? What we goin' there for?" Arthur asked, now bored with his day out.

"No, to Siddy's hospital, yer daft plonker. We're goin' t' see Siddy!" George beamed broadly.

"Used to live up this way," Arthur muttered as he recognised various landmarks passing by the window. "Siddy's 'ospital is up 'ere somewhere," he said to no one in particular.

There was disabled parking close to the front entrance of the hospital and George helped Arthur walk the short distance to the door. Gary stared up at the imposing building, nervous of what he might find inside. This was a mental hospital after all.

George pushed at the half open door and the three of them stepped inside. The lobby area was surprisingly small, with a glass door and partition separating them from a much larger hallway inside. A uniformed nurse with short blonde hair greeted them warmly and showed them to Mary Ward. Most of the doors along the corridor were open and Gary peered inside, looking for 'nutters'. To his relief everyone seemed rather normal, but he continued to examine every room just in case.

Loud music echoed from somewhere ahead of them and they passed through a set of double doors and into the large ward. George, Arthur and Gary stood in disbelief at the sight in front of them. Two ladies, dressed in top hats and tails, were tap dancing before them, both swinging a walking cane.

"Blimey, it's Fred Astaire and Ginger Rogers," Gary gasped.

"Wow, no, two Ginger Rogers more like!" George tugged at his father's arm, but Arthur was rooted to the spot, staring at the two women tapping their way through the dance routine. A man in his sixties was singing along to the music.

"I'm leaning on a lamppost at the corner of the street,
In case a certain little lady comes by.
Oh me, oh my, I hope the little lady comes by.
I don't know if she'll get away, She doesn't always get away,
But anyway I know that she'll try.
Oh me, oh my, I hope the little lady comes by...."

"In't that lovely Dad," George whispered to Arthur. "Just like the old days. Just look at those tap dancers!"

Arthur let go of George's hand and wandered a short distance across the room. He stood in front of an old man who was wearing a blue party hat and swaying from side to side in time to the music. Both men were unsteady on their feet. The man's eyes moved away from the dancers and looked directly at Arthur.

"Hello Sid," Arthur said. "How've you been?"

Siddy grinned broadly and half embraced his brother as best he could.

"Hello Siddy, I'm Arthur's son George and this young man is my son, Gary." George held out his hand, but Siddy was reluctant to let go of his long lost brother. Finally he did so and shook George's hand. His handshake was weak and his hand trembling. He then turned to Gary, looked down at the youngster's face and shook his hand too. He did not let go. He simply looked down and beamed.

"So, he's your great nephew," George continued. "Shall we sit down?"

The group found some armchairs and the nurses helped the two old men down into their comfy seats. George watched as the two brothers just stared at each other with tears in their eyes. Unnoticed, the two lady dancers had finished their routine, changed costumes and had just begun dancing to another song.

"Maybe it's because I'm a Londoner,
That I love London so,
Maybe it's because I'm a Londoner,
That I think of her wherever I go.
I get a funny feeling inside of me,
When walking up and down,
Maybe it's because I'm a Londoner,
That I love London Town."

Arthur listened to the songs, all of them reminding him of the good old days; his time with Siddy when they were young men and the evenings spent out together.

Gary reached across and took a packet of sweets from George's lap next to him.

"We bought these for you Uncle," Gary said. (Great Uncle seemed such a mouthful to say!). He placed the chocolates in Siddy's hand. Siddy smiled and picked up the bag, but his hands were too weak to open them. Gary slipped from his chair and opened the packet and took out a sweet. He took off the wrapper and placed it back in Siddy's hand. The wrinkled old hand lifted it to his mouth and Siddy began chewing. The soft chocolate melted in his mouth and he smiled with delight. Gary began unwrapping a second chocolate.

"Hold on Gary," George chastised. "He's not finished the first one yet!"

"My goodness, we didn't realise Siddy had so much family!" It was Sarah Batchelor, the nurse who had earlier greeted Arthur on his previous visit. "There are sandwiches and cakes," she said, "and some rather splendid trifle, nibbles and soft drinks on the table. Please help yourselves."

Gary needed no second bidding. He jumped up, walked across to the table and began piling sandwiches onto a plate.

"Oy, leave off!" George demanded. "Leave some for everyone else!"

"I was getting some for everybody," Gary protested.

"What, on one plate? Give over. Make up a little plate for Siddy and another for your Grandad. Go on then!" George paused to look at the two old men sitting together and felt a lump in his throat. "Bloody marvellous Gary, ain't it."

Gary nodded. He rushed over and placed the plates in each of the men's laps. He needed to get back for the trifle!

Alex was sitting, as he was most days, in his old armchair. The coarse fabric was badly worn on the armrests, but an extra booster cushion meant that it was particularly comfortable for his old body. His mind had been elsewhere as he tried to remember Siddy's astonishing story.

It was like something out of a Charles Dickens novel. How was it remotely possible that Siddy had been forgotten? After he had been institutionalised, his family had visited him regularly, but his brothers and sisters gradually moved away, got married and had their own families. It was left to their ageing mother and father to continue the visits until they were overcome by age and death. The visits simply stopped.

It was in June 1999 that Alex's father received a visit from the police. Siddy had passed away. Siddy had sat on the side of his bed, coughed once and then just lay back on his bed and died; his heart had failed. Siddy had been "locked away" for seventy-three years.

During his visit to Siddy, Billy had taken a short loo break, principally to get a cigarette. He had left his father with Sam, Muriel and, of course, Siddy. Sarah Batchelor had taken him into the gardens at the rear and waited with him.

"Can I bum one of those," she asked. "We're not meant to smoke here really."

Billy handed her a cigarette, lit it with his cigarette lighter and then lit his own. He took a long, deep drag.

"Has Siddy ever been a problem?" Billy asked. "He seems so calm!"

"Yeah, well he's on his medicine. As long as he's on that, he's a pussy cat." Sarah held the smoke in her lungs for a second or two before exhaling. "We all loved him," she smiled. "He was always calm, just as long as he took his medicine - although he did escape once!"

Billy stared back in horror, but Sarah continued to smile.

"He simply walked out of the hospital!" she explained. "The police searched and searched, scouring the streets in the local area. Naturally, they were looking for a strange man wandering the streets or looking suspicious, but to no avail. They couldn't find him."

Billy wondered how old Sarah actually was. He guessed she must be in her forties, but figured he could be wrong plus or minus ten years. She was difficult to judge.

"Siddy was eventually found in Canning Town, several miles away," she continued.

"That's where the family had lived," Billy nodded. "That was Siddy's home."

"Yes, that's right. So why had the police not spotted him?" she asked, smiling. "It turns out Siddy had picked up a broom and swept the streets all the way back to where he had lived forty or fifty years before! Of course, the police had passed the inconspicuous road sweeper several times, but had never thought to challenge him! After all, he was just a road sweeper!"

"Crafty old Siddy," Billy chuckled.

"Yes, crafty old Siddy," Sarah agreed. "Come on, we better go back in."

Fifty or sixty people attended Siddy's funeral at the hospital chapel. George and Gary attended with Arthur. Sam was also there with his mother Muriel. George had said it was a fantastic service and one of the nicest he had ever attended. Apparently Siddy had been a regular churchgoer and most of the congregation were from the church or his hospital ward.

Siddy had been 'locked away' for seventy-three years, although he had been taken out on the occasional visit. Just a few weeks before, he had been taken back down to Southend-on-Sea where a nurse had taken him for his favourite 'tipple', a glass of sherry. Siddy had insisted on buying the nurse one too! Siddy had also been allowed to buy a new baseball cap that day.

In the chapel Arthur had asked George whether he could go up to the coffin and touch it. 'Go on then,' George had told his father, 'He's your brother. You go up there.' Arthur walked slowly to the front of the chapel with his sister Muriel. On top of the coffin lay the baseball cap. Muriel picked up the cap, folded it up and gave it to Arthur. 'Go on,' she had said. 'You take it. He would have wanted you to have it.'

Alex continued staring out of the window. He had a tear in his eye. His favourite part of the story, he always kept to last. He looked around the room. He was alone and Maria had gone.

"The amazing thing, Maria," he said anyway, speaking into the empty room, "is that the nurses said that, since the family visits, Siddy had become more content; gentler and more mellow. He had found his family again. Siddy died, but he did not die alone. He had been reunited with his family and he will live on in their memories".

Charcoal

Family history had changed Alex's life and Siddy's story was just one of dozens of remarkable stories he had uncovered. Sometimes a story just landed in his lap, while others were put together one jigsaw piece at a time, perhaps taking years to put together. He discovered family he did not know he had. He had discovered his roots and moved to his beloved Forest of Dean, where his ancestors had walked, worked, married and died. Sometimes he even managed to see life through their eyes. His ancestors had drawn him here to his beloved Forest of Dean and now, as he sat here, he felt he could feel them and see them in the flames.

Perhaps they were here at this very moment, sitting beside him on the wooden hillside. They made the charcoal here. They worked at the furnaces and foundries as forgeman and ironworkers. They felt the heat on their faces, just as Alex was feeling it now.

Stones surrounded the small wood fire in a forest clearing, perched on hillside. Alex crouched down and stared at the crackling red embers as they warmed his face. The sun was falling further below the horizon now and in the twilight dark shadows began to chill the air. Alex craned his head up to the right, observing the white smoke billowing up through the trees thirty metres way over to his right. There were no red embers there, he thought, supping at his coffee. Not yet. Returning his gaze to the campfire, he considered the long night ahead. So this was it; this was to be his day, or rather night, to share the life of some of his ancestors as a charcoal burner.

Charcoal burning had played a significant part in the history of this area of England and charcoal had been essential to the ironworkers; its' forgemen and smiths. Alex's ancestors had mostly been 'Forge men' and he had been drawn to this area while researching his family roots; this was where **his** family had worked. Only months before, he had stood in the Vale of Castiard, looking up the valley at the slopes whose sides were still covered in thick woodland. This valley would once have been filled with the blue smoke of the charcoal stacks. He had felt very strange knowing that his family had, for many generations, lived and worked in this very valley. Now he was home!

The preparation of the charcoal stack had taken place several days before, using wood approximately three feet (one meter) in length. These pieces would be stacked upright, in a circular fashion, slanting towards a central flue. Roughly graded, more wood was placed on top of the stack until a dome-shape was made. The entire dome, or 'pit' was then encased in turf and earth, sealing it from the outside air. Finally the set was ignited with hot ashes via its central flue and the top itself was capped. Starved of oxygen, the wood would gently smoulder without burning, in a process called distillation. The process was controlled with a series of vent holes that were created, or blocked up, as was necessary.

Alex inspected the smoking stack with Emily, his companion for the night. She was slim, but very strong, and he had witnessed her potency and agility before. He had been invited to go potholing with a group of friends and found himself climbing through caves, small tunnels and vast caverns just a few miles from where they were now. Keeping up with Emily had been a considerable challenge!

Now she was wearing a boiler suit, tied at the waist, with her brown hair tied in a small ponytail behind her. They both watched the white smoke issuing from the vent holes and permeating through the top of the dome. All was well. Blue smoke would demand action with the sealing of an offending vent hole – they wanted charcoal, not ashes! They continued to study the rounded surface of the stack for future problems. They searched for cracks, or a thinning out of the outer earth casing. They both knew that the contents would slowly contract over time and the risk of a collapse would steadily increase. After a little tampering here and there, they returned to their own campfire and set about cooking supper.

Charcoal-burners led a lonely existence, remaining with their stack day and night until the process was complete, perhaps some five days later. Some of the burners were nomadic, raising their families in the Forest, while others travelled considerable distances offering their services to landowners and farmers. Accommodation tended to be a temporary conical hut, built by binding poles together and covering them with sacking, turf and twigs.

Alex looked across at his accommodation, which was similarly constructed, although the sacking was replaced with some tarpaulin sheeting, covered in twigs and fern. It reminded Alex of a primitive wigwam. This was to be their temporary home during the night. Doubt had been cast on how waterproof it might be, but the forecast was fair with a light, westerly wind. In the evening light, he and Emily sat by the campfire and watched the flames brown their food scraps.

Well, actually they were cooking steak and mushrooms, but Alex still felt he was back at one with nature! The food did smell good. They ate and drank and put the world to rights. They listened to the crackling fire and the active songbirds. Sometimes they heard a human voice, a child shouting from further up the valley or perhaps a barking dog. As darkness began to creep up on them, most of the sounds subsided. The rest of the world was gradually going to sleep, leaving them quite alone. They looked at each other for a while and smiled at the silence.

Emily listened politely as Alex began talking about nightfall. As a pilot, he had discovered that night rises, it does not fall! As the sun sets, he explained, shadows then darkness envelops the valleys. From the top of a hill, or from an aircraft, it was easy to see how night first captures the surface close to the ground. On high, it could still be light, at least for a while. Finally the darkness would rise to capture the whole sky. Ah, but then there was moonlight!

Emily cut Alex short and politely suggested they should make a final inspection of the charcoal stack. Maybe his analysis of nightfall was a little too deep or perhaps it just wasn't very interesting. Either way, they rose to their feet and walked over to the smoking stack. Both of them slowly circled it several times in complete silence. Then they walked back down the slope, where Emily placed a couple of small logs on the campfire. It provided light and security and would still be glowing when they next awoke. Finally they retired to their hut and their sleeping bags. The alarm was set for ninety minutes time.

Charcoal-burning is an ancient craft, dating back thousands of years to the bronze and iron age. The ancient Egyptians, the Greeks and the Romans all produced charcoal, the only fuel capable of raising temperatures sufficiently to smelt most metals.

The alarm clock rang out in the darkness waking Alex from a deep sleep. Was there a mistake? The time had gone so quickly! Emily was up first and scrambled up the hill towards the stack. The white smoke was now barely visible in the blackness of night. However, red embers, glowing gently just under the surface, indicated that holes were beginning to appear in areas around the dome. Tufts of grass and earth would be enough to affect the necessary repairs in complete silence. An inspection by torchlight revealed no further problems and soon they were back in their sleeping bags, awaiting the next ninety-minute call.

Emily was like a machine. She had jumped up, inspected and repaired the charcoal stack and then returned instantly to sleep. Alex lay back in his sleeping bag thinking about this evening. Occasionally the fire cracked outside. This was so different from his normal world. He spent his normal life delivering businessmen and holidaymakers to their destinations around Europe in large aluminium tubes. He tried to imagine a real charcoal burner, perhaps someone from his own family, looking up in the sixteen or seventeen hundreds and seeing his aircraft drawing a line across the sky. What would they have made of it?

Alex thought about the huge bulldozers and giant chainsaws of today's world, ripping and tearing at nature for profit - the massive destruction of the rainforest. He thought back to those simpler times when its inhabitants were skilfully managing the forest. Rather than fell or 'kill' trees, they used coppiced wood, which regenerating itself, providing self-sustaining growth. New shoots would rise from the stump, or stool, after the main stem had been felled providing more fuel for the future. But was it really that simple? The romantic image of sweet wood smoke drifting above the trees and through the vales was a valid one, but there were times in history when the demands for charcoal threatened to destroy the very forest itself. Some landowners sought quick profit, felling huge areas and, with high demand, woods and forests became thick with blue smoke. Intervention by King, Government and local lawmakers was inevitable.

The campfire still gave off a glow and Alex tied up his boots before walking up the slope once more. This time the news was not so good. An entire side had collapsed, revealing a strip of glowing wood. Glowing in the darkness, it reminded Alex of a volcano leaking lava, threatening to explode. There was no major fire, well not yet! They set to repairing the damage, laying ready-cut turfs over the scar. An earth covering sealed the edges. More turfs, earth and soil would still needed and Alex went off in search of a suitable grassy bank. Emily continued to effect repairs. It was almost dawn and it was slowly becoming easier to see. The air felt warm and Alex, digging into the hillside, was aching and soaking wet with sweat.

They worked for an hour and Alex realised he was having the time of his life. Finally, all the repairs were made and the dawn chorus had begun. He watched Emily make coffee and they sat by the campfire to discuss their drama. Maybe they could still get another ninety minutes sleep before breakfast. Once again, they set the clock and retired to their sleeping bags.

A thousand years ago this particular forest had, at least in part, been preserved and saved for royal recreation and the hunting of game. The early 1600's saw increased demand for charcoal with the introduction of blast furnaces into the area. Decades later it was Samuel Pepys, as Secretary to the Navy, who was demanding that these forest trees be preserved for naval ship-timber. These provoked preservation Acts to ensure the forest would endure. The production of charcoal slowed, then ceased at the beginning of the nineteenth century with the introduction of coke, although charcoal did continue to be produced in smaller quantities until the 1940's.

The alarm sounded for the last time. The birds outside were now deafening in their competition for attention. Bright light was streaming into the hut and Alex crawled out holding his boots in one hand. The air was still chilly and he reached back in for his jumper. Looking out at him was Emily, grinning broadly.

"What?" he asked.

"Your face!" she grinned. "You look like an army commando, all blacked up for a mission!"

Alex wiped his face, spreading more soot across his cheeks. Their repairs had held well and only minor work was required around the stack. Their mission was nearly over and someone else would soon take over.

Breakfast! A few chips of wood soon had their own campfire invigorated and warming the coffee. They sat and watched as the sausages turned brown. Eggs and buttered toast added to their morning feast. They were dirty, hungry and smelled of wood smoke, but beneath it all Alex felt elation. The experience, he reflected, was unusual, if not unique, and others might shake their heads sadly at his madness. He breathed in the bright morning air and began eating his sausages. He crouched down and stared at the crackling red embers as they warmed his face. He had felt a bond with Emily, with nature and with the Forest of Dean. His ancestors whispered to him, although he could not quite catch what they were saying.

The old man could still feel the glowing embers on his face. The Spanish sun was now hovering over the far hills and soon night would fall. He still called it night***fall***. He chuckled. He wondered if, out there somewhere, two people were settling down for the evening preparing for their task as charcoal-burners. Was there an Emily and an Alex preparing supper beside a camp fire, while a charcoal stack billowed smoke into the night air? He so wished he could be there, too.

Alex closed his eyes and imagined the forest. Tomorrow he would tell Maria that story. It was a little gem in his life, a moment that he would treasure forever. But there were so many gems, so many stories.

Chapter 10: Rumford and Concord

The old man was most difficult when it came to his washing and showering. A man should have his privacy and, while it was true he had a little difficulty these days, he certainly didn't need some nurse stripping away his dignity. There were a number of different nurses, male and female, who visited him each morning, preparing him for the day. Mostly they were workmen-like, if it were possible for nurses can be workman-like. But they rarely introduced themselves and were sometimes a little rude. None of them were pretty and they hardly ever smiled. Why were they always in so much of a hurry? It was the same battle every morning, with the same arguments and the same compromises.

Perhaps if he had spent a little more time learning Spanish? He spoke enough to get by, but he had never become fluent. It had always been a guilty disappointment to him. He could not roll an 'R' and some spoke so fast, it was like the speed of a machine gun! He had tried so hard, but it never really came naturally to him and time had always been the enemy. Blink and it was gone. Finally he would be clean and dressed and sitting in his chair ready for the day.

Another day.

"Good morning Captain," Maria smiled cheerily and she lit up the room. Maria was not just a nurse. She was his light, his fresh air, his friend and companion and she made great coffee. He had become very fond of this young woman with jet black hair. He had thought her plain at first, but now he saw a beauty with her dark features and, of course, those wonderful eyes.

The ritual was always the same. Other nurses had already been to ruffle him, harass him and ply him with pills. Maria, on the other hand, would talk to him and enquire of his health. She would talk about the weather as she checked that the room was clean and tidy. She would pour the coffee while standing over the table, pass a cup to him and then settle down. She had a habit of sitting down and then ironing out any wrinkles in her pristine blue and white uniform with her hands. Yes, she was beautiful.

"So Captain, what stories do you have for me today?" Maria smiled directly into his eyes and waited.

"Oh, I don't know. Those damn nurses! How can I remember anything?" Alex had made his point, but he did not labour it. After all, it was not Maria's fault. Maria, of course, said nothing. She just sat there, waiting.

"OK, now why don't you tell me more about your interest in family history," Maria said quietly. "You told me it changed your life, your journey to the Forest of Dean in search of your roots, and how it led to your involvement in museums and charcoal burning. Do you have more stories about your family history research? You studied it for years, no?"

"Yes, Maria, that is quite right; quite right." Alex's head rocked forward and back. "My search did take me to the Forest of Dean and eventually we moved there. I started my research that day in Manchester, of course, and began searching all over England for Burgums!" Alex paused again.

He tried to remember what story he had told Maria yesterday. Now his whole body was slowly rocking backwards and forwards as he gathered his thoughts. He had been aware for some time now that he would tell someone a story, only to realise he had already told them. Some would politely listen again, while others would cut him short with – 'I think you've already told me that one!'

"Well I spent years searching for those long lost relatives, Maria, but soon I realised I would have to extend my search to other countries beyond England and Wales. I never dreamed my search would extend around the world to America, Brazil, Australia and New Zealand. People used to ask me how many people I had found, or how far back had I got, but its not like collecting stamps you know! I used to uncover the stories behind the names. Where they worked, what they did and what happened to them. All families have stories, of course, it is just a case of uncovering them."

Alex looked up and saw that Maria was just staring at him in silence. He thought nothing of it and continued.

"Let me tell you a story about one visit to I America. I had travelled to New England where an ancestor of mine had settled. He had emigrated to America in 1851, with his ship docking in Boston, Massachusetts." Alex was now in his stride and related the story, only pausing to sip his coffee.

John was an artist and, soon after he arrived in Boston, he saw the highly decorated omnibus coaches hauled by two or four horses through the streets of the city. He found a police officer patrolling the streets and asked him about the coaches. They were manufactured in Boston, just a few miles from the bustling city centre. John asked for directions and eventually found the factory where these vehicles were built and painted. He entered the front gates and his life was about to change forever.

Soon John was working in that very same factory, adding his own elaborate designs to the production line. He drew his designs on thick tissue paper and offered them to his manager. When something was approved, as they usually were, John would place his design over the coach body and stick pins through the design. These would make small holes in the bodywork transferring his image to the wagon itself. He would then paint directly onto the bodywork using the pinholes as a guide.

This continued for some time until another company in a neighbouring state got to hear about the talented artist. John was headhunted and found himself moving to New Hampshire. Here, in the city of Concord, John began working on Concord stagecoaches. Eventually these stagecoaches would become famous and operate all across North America, into Mexico and South America. They were even exported to such places a South Africa and Australia!

Also living in Concord, at that time was Sarah Thompson, Countess Rumford, living in the old mansion she had inherited from her father, the late Benjamin Thompson, Count Rumford. Rumford had earned many titles and many roles including statesman, scientist, soldier and spy, and eventually became head of the Bavarian Army. The 'English Garden' in Munich, is so called in honour of the Count. President Roosevelt himself described Rumford as one of the three greatest minds America had ever produced! (Benjamin Franklin and Thomas Jefferson were the other two 'greats minds').

Benjamin Thompson had deserted Sarah, along with her mother, when he fled Concord, and then Boston in 1776, during the American War of Independence. Sympathetic to the State Governor and the Crown, he was forced to flee to England. The British initially rewarded him with a civil service job, taking a particular interest in science. He experimented with cannon, as he sought to improve the fire power of the British Navy. It became clear, however, that he was not entirely trusted. Had he not been a spy after all?

Benjamin Thompson left on a tour of Europe, finally settling in Munich. He offered his services to the Elector of Bavaria, and transformed the militia into an army through science, research and a profound self-belief in himself and his skills. He rose to become one of the most powerful men in Bavaria and a Count of the Holy Roman Empire.

The Count had left a wife and baby daughter in America and it was another twenty years before he was to see his daughter again! They were eventually reunited in Europe with Sarah travelling from the USA to London, Munich and Paris. She, too, was bestowed with the honour of Countess, as Count Rumford continued to transform his adopted country. While in Europe, Sarah had also adopted the first daughter of two of her servants. The daughter's name was Emma Gannell. When Sarah Thompson, the Countess Rumford, eventually returned to Concord, New Hampshire, she took Emma her young companion with her.

The Countess settled back into the old mansion and invited a promising young Concord artist to the Rolfe-Rumford house to view the Rumford collection of paintings. There he met Emma Gannell. They were both twenty-four years old and both took an immediate liking to each other. The Countess, however, was not impressed with John, convinced he was after their money, and so they kept their courtship a secret. Emma was told she would never receive a cent if she married John, but marry they did.

The Countess refused to attend the wedding claiming ill health. A year later Sarah Thompson, Countess Rumford died.

"You know Maria, they were married for fifty-five years!" Alex declared triumphantly. "I guess the Countess was wrong about John!"

"Fifty-five years is a long time," Maria acknowledged.

"Well they built a house in South State Street, Concord" Alex said, "and I actually went to New Hampshire to research the family. I spent my days searching through old papers looking for anything that might help. Then, after the library had closed, I would go and search the cemetery. In one I found the grave of Sarah, Countess Rumford. In another I found John and Emma, together with several members of their family."

"Was it sad?" Maria asked.

"No, it was beautiful," Alex replied. "It was exciting to find them. You have to remember I was spending my days and much of my evenings with this family. As I found more and more bits of the jigsaw I began to feel that I actually knew them."

"But they were dead, no?" Maria looked a little horrified.

"Oh yes, of course, but I was thinking about them a lot and learning more about them all the time. Let me give you an example - I found some of Emma's diaries. The entries were not very exciting. They were mostly routine weather reports or who had come to visit on a particular day, but then I discovered something very interesting. The first entry was innocent enough, saying that Mark was unwell." Alex took a deep breath.

"Mark was her grandson," he explained. "Two days later, the next entry said that Mark was very weak. Occcasionally she would record that the doctor had called. Emma and John would both visit, sometimes to read Mark a story. One entry said – 'Mark upstairs. He sat in his chair, then in his mother's arms, then propped up in bed playing with his buffalo toys.' The entries went on for about six weeks. Towards the end one entry read – 'Mark never spoke after midnight, his devoted mother at his side. At 9am God came for him'.

"So sad," Maria's voice was genuinely emotional.

"Yes. He was seven years old. While I was copying the diaries at the library a woman came over and asked if I was OK. Of course I said yes. 'I just wondered,' she had said, 'because you are crying'..." Alex grew another deep breath. "I had become so, so close to this family."

"My poor Captain," Maria whispered sympathetically.

"No, no, it was interesting," Alex said. "I had discovered this great story! That evening I went again and just stood outside the old wooden house in South State Street. I stood there, thinking about John and Emma, about Mark, and about the Countess. It felt very strange."

"She's in, you know."

Alex looked around to see a small boy standing close by.

"She's in," the boy repeated. "Why don't you knock on the door?"

Alex looked up at the house. He had thought about knocking, but really didn't think he could. Now he felt intimidated and he wished the little boy would go away. The little boy just stood there and Alex finally found himself walking up the short path to the house. The panelled wood was painted white, but there were trimmings in faded yellow. Two steps led up to the veranda and to an outside door covered in netting. Alex looked for a doorbell and now regretted walking up the pathway. 'Bloody kids,' he thought. He turned and looked across the street. The young boy was just standing there, still watching him.

Alex raised his hand and knocked against the door. It was not latched and banged against the inside door making a huge racket. His heart leapt. He wanted to run away, but he could already hear footsteps from inside. He heard a lock click and the door opened about an inch. There was a chain on the inside preventing the door from opening any further.

"Yes?" a woman's voice enquired from inside. He could not see her and found himself talking directly at the door.

"Ma'am, you don't know me, but my name is Alex Young."

"Ah, yes, Mr Young, I've been expecting you," the woman said. Suddenly the door closed shut. Alex stared at the shut door in amazement and for a second time that day considered running away. Then he heard the woman removing the chain and opening the door fully. Alex peered through the netting, trying to see the woman he was talking to.

"No, Ma'am, I think there's been a misunderstanding," Alex shuffled on the porch.

"Misunderstanding? I think not, Mr Young. Are you not here to ask about John and Emma?" She was still standing in the shadows, but Alex imagined an older woman. Probably mad.

"I'm sorry Ma'am, I don't understand," Alex's day seemed to be deteriorating rapidly. "Yes, I'm here to ask about John and Emma, but how...?"

"Why Emma told me, of course!" The woman pushed open the outside screen door. "Well, come in then," she said.

Alex automatically stepped in through the door, still confused by the conversation that had just taken place. The woman had already turned away, walking from the dark hallway into another room. He paused for a moment and wondered whether he should close the door behind him. He pushed it shut and hurriedly followed the woman into the sitting room.

"I'm sorry, Ma'am, who did you say told you I was coming?" Alex wondered whether someone from the History Library had called her.

"Emma Gannell," she said in a matter of fact way. "My name is Stella, by the way. You don't need to call me Ma'am. It sounds so old!"

"Ma'am; Stella. I believe Emma Gannell died in the 1920's!" Stella finally had turned to look at him, a pained expression of impatience across her face. She was a slim woman, perhaps in her mid-forties or fifties. She didn't look particularly mad.

"Emma Gannell haunts this house Mr Young," she said without emotion as if this were an every day conversation. "It's all right, she is a benign ghost."

Oh dear, she is mad, Alex thought and really did want to turn and run away.

"In fact, because I knew you were coming, I put something out to show you. Would you like some lemonade?"

Alex nodded and he watched as Stella turned and stepped back into the corridor, then through to the kitchen. He was left stranded, standing there in the middle of the room. He was cursing himself for knocking on the door. He had been bullied into it and now hugely regretted it. He looked around at the walls. Actually, he thought, he could easily have been transported back to the 1920's! In front of him the room was full of antique furniture, with old-fashioned faded carpets and heavy patterned curtains. There was no evidence of a television, radio or even a telephone. Perhaps they were in another room. The style definitely suited the room, but Alex felt he had stepped straight into a museum.

"Oh, do sit down," Stella rushed back into the room with a tray. On it stood a grand jug containing a strange opaque yellowish-grey liquid. His heart sank. Lemonade! Not the fizzy drink made to compete with Coke Cola, but the freshly made drink made with real lemons. Stella poured the liquid into two glasses and handed one to her visitor. She sat down and smiled. Alex, now sitting deep into the well-worn settee, felt duty-bound to take a mouthful of his drink, wondering how he could hide the grimace on his face. To his surprise the lemonade was sweet.

"It is really delicious," he said. "Really nice indeed." He was almost apologising for doubting Stella in the first place.

"Good," she said. "It's my own secret recipe, handed down from mother to daughter and probably from my grandmother before that. The only difference is I use a blender."

"How long have you lived in Concord?" Alex asked.

"All my life," Stella said. "Except for the time I spent at the university in Boston. Work keeps me here. I'm a computer analyst."

'*So much for my assessment of this poor lady*', Alex thought. Stella owns a blender and a computer. On the other hand, she has been speaking to someone who has been dead for about seventy years.

"So have you actually seen Emma?" he asked nervously. He wasn't nervous about the ghost, quite simply he didn't believe in them, but he was nervous about the embarrassment that might follow such a question.

"Good God, no," Stella laughed, "but I do feel her presence. Sometimes things move, or there's a strange noise. Even in a creaky house like this, there are some strange noises one would not normally expect."

"So what did you mean when you said you were expecting me?" Alex paused, trying not to be too sceptical.

"I sense when Emma is around and then I feel things. I sensed that I would be getting a visitor today, asking about the family who built this house and here you are. Now I am a little confused, are you a Burgum or a Young?" Stella smiled at him enquiringly.

"Actually, I'm confused too. I'm a Young, but I am related to all the Burgums. I'm not sure why I'm not also a Burgum." Alex sipped on his lemonade.

"The Burgums were on your mother's side perhaps," Stella suggested helpfully.

"I wish it was that simple," Alex admitted. "My grandfather changed the name and I haven't been able to find out why."

"Very mysterious, she said."

Alex tried to think what to say next. He could hear a faint ticking clock in another room and, aware of the silence, he tried to take another sip of lemonade without making a sound. He failed.

"Noisy lemonade," he explained pathetically.

"I've just remembered, that thing I have looked out to show you." She smiled excitedly as she scurried out of the room.

'Not mad,' Alex thought. 'Just a little bit crazy.' He was feeling a bit more relaxed now and took another gulp of his lemonade. It was a hot day and the drink was genuinely very good. The room felt a lot more comfortable now and he began to see that Stella was probably not another Miss Havisham. The last thing he needed was to find himself a character in a Dickens novel! She had clearly furnished the room to suit the original character of the place. Stella walked in and saw him looking around.

"Mostly garage sales," she explained. "They're much cheaper than antique shops. It's surprising what people want to get rid of you know. They say, one person's junk and all that. The house is nearly one hundred and fifty years old. I researched the house when I found out I was sharing it with someone. Over time, I began to realise it was Emma. I assume you know about the Countess, the Abbott-Downing Company and all that?"

"Yes," Alex nodded. "After the Historical Society today I went to the cemetery. I found several of the graves."

"Here, this is what I put aside to show you." Stella handed over a round block of wood. It was about twelve inches across and about one inch thick. There was a small hole at its' centre and he imagined it had been a lid. There were words inscribed upon it.

Alex examined the words and thought they had probably been burned into the wooden surface when it was first made. He read the words out loud. "Device for keeping Meat and Pickles under Brine, a Novel and Useful Invention Very Effective and Perfectly Simple in its Construction. Concord, N. H."

"This is truly amazing," Alex exclaimed. "I've read about this. John received an award for this from the American Institute of New York. It was about 1867, I think. See these holes? This is the lid of his invention. There would have been a handle and a screw device through the centre here. Before refrigerators, preserving food was always a problem. I imagine screwing this down tight would produce a vacuum, keeping it fairly fresh.

It's wonderful!" He looked up at Stella who was clearly delighted at Alex's enthusiasm. She sat there beaming all over her face.

"Would you ever consider selling this to me?" Alex asked, slightly embarrassed for asking.

"No, no, no," Stella's expression rapidly became more serious and he wished he had never asked her.

"No, it's far to close to my heart and to this house. I would never sell it!" Stella was shaking her head. Alex felt the discomfort of another long pause. "But I will give it you!"

Alex sat across from Maria, beaming all over his face.

"She actually gave it to you?" Maria asked.

"Yes she did. I still have it at home." Alex hesitated for a minute; where was home? Remembering the story he continued. "The lady showed me the house and then told me John had a painting hanging in the State Capitol Building, there in Concord. I visited it the very next day. Finally we said goodbye and she showed me to the door. I was still gripping John's invention in my hand, in case Stella changed her mind. I stepped off the porch then turned to thank her. Then she asked me the question."

"What? What did she ask you?" Maria moved forward in her seat.

"She asked me what had made me call at the house. Well, I told her about the little boy playing across the street who had cajoled me into knocking. She just stood there smiling broadly at me, her hands clasped in front of her." Alex looked up at Maria.

"What's so funny?" I had asked her.

"There are no children living in this road," she said to me. "Goodbye Mr Young."

"My God," Maria gasped. "It was Mark, wasn't it?"

"Perhaps, Maria" Alex smiled. "Perhaps it was."

Chapter 11: The Storm and the Travel

Alex rolled over in his bed and settled onto his back. Staring into the darkness he could just see the shadows of his ceiling. He was awake.

It was the noise of the rain that had awoken him. Hard, heavy rain was dropping thousands of feet from huge towering clouds, so heavy with moisture. In his mind he could see the giant cumulonimbus powerfully building. He knew, of course, about the incredible power that generated within this beast. Great currents of air swirled upwards within it holding tons of moisture. Tiny droplets grew, colliding with neighbouring droplets, soaring higher and higher within the thermal mass. Static electricity within the cloud slowly built within it, pulling and attracting, still soaring upwards within its centre.

At around thirty thousand feet the cloud reached the invisible barrier that is the tropopause. Above was the stratosphere where clouds could not go and the cumulus mass simply spread sideways forming an anvil shape. Alex had seen hundreds of anvil-shaped clouds like this, most spectacularly over Indonesia on his journeys south to Australia. Sure "CB's" (as they were called) occurred all over the world, but the biggest and most violent tended to form close to the equator. Flying through the darkness one would often see the flashes from the cockpit but, sometimes, more cloud might hide the buggers. Instead weather radar would send beams of radio waves ahead of the aircraft detecting the millions of molecules of water that make up the cloud. The larger the suspended droplets, the bigger and more powerful the cloud, and dramatic cells of red and purple would be painted on the radar.

Plans would be made from the cockpit to fly around these monsters so as not to spoil the flight of hundreds of passengers. Whether sleeping or watching their movies from within that darkened aircraft cabin, those on board would be oblivious to the aircraft gently banking left or right to find a safer and more comfortable route around the storm clouds. It was all part of the job of the steely-eyed pilots.

Tonight, however, a cumulonimbus cloud had drifted eastward over this part of Spain. It could no longer hold all the moisture that it had drawn up and decided to release it. The droplets of water now fell downward with such ferocity that it had woken Alex up. Raindrops smashed into the roof, forming streams of water that then cascaded down over his balcony. From there it would roll to the edge and so fall further, crashing onto the pavements and gardens below. Occasionally the cloud would flash, before growling and rumbling outside Alex's window.

"So you thought you could avoid me?" growled the storm cloud. "You have no radar now!" it thundered. "Think you are safe?"

The rain seemed to fall still harder. So much anger, so much energy, so much rain. Alex wondered whether aircraft overflying this part of Spain were studying their radar and diverting miles off course in order to avoid the menacing threat. But thankfully it was no longer his problem. He was an ex-Captain now, retired and spent. He had done his job, completed his duty, and grown old. That was the sad bit. He had grown old. All he had now were the memories, those wonderful memories, but life is cruel and even those were being stolen from him as he slowly drifted back into slumber.

"Good Morning Captain!" Maria stood at the door. "Have you had breakfast? Or is it just the coffee this morning?"

Alex hesitated. Maria did not wait for an answer and left the room as quickly as she had appeared. Alex was thirsty and needed his coffee. He looked down and saw he was dressed, but he could not remember if he had had breakfast. Indeed, he could not remember getting dressed. He had slept very deeply, but woken up before the sunlight had entered the room. He looked outside the window – it was another blue sky. He wondered what the time was, but did not have a watch. What had happened to that watch? The watch his wife had bought him.

Alex knew that the sun would soon set behind the mountains directly outside his window, but it was impossible for him judge time beyond that point. Time seemed to stand still here. Or was it that time simply did not matter? He tried to remember the days ticking by, but could not remember them. Perhaps he could go home soon. He could go back to his old life; his old routine. There was so much to do.

"Here we are," Maria said, pushing the door open wide open. Behind her Alex thought he could see something, people perhaps, walking along the corridor. There seemed to be several people. Did he know them? Who were they, he couldn't quite see. Then the door gently closed on its spring and they were gone. Maria busied herself pouring the coffee and arranging the biscuits.

"Now Captain. I must tell you," she took a deep breathe. "I have been talking again to my friends all about you adventures. I was telling them what a great storyteller you are!"

"No problem, Maria," Alex smiled. "I love sharing my stories. Are your friends here?"

"Oh no Captain, they are not here. They are all at work. They have jobs. But sometimes we meet in the evenings and talk about our days. I sometimes talk about you!"

"That's nice Maria, that's very nice indeed." He smiled.

"Well, today I want to hear more about all your travels. You have been to so many places. So many adventures! Please tell me about them." She was as breezy as ever.

Alex hesitated. He struggled to remember all the places he had been too. His heart began to race and he felt a sense of panic. Then he saw Maria's smile. She looked so serene and engaging. She simply waited and slowly random thoughts began to fill his mind. He could see pictures in his mind, but it took a few moments before he knew where those images were. Some were Europe, of course, but he had been to America, Africa, the Middle East, Asia and Japan, the list was endless; so many places. He took a deep breath and he began speaking again.

"The Great Wall of China, Maria, I shall begin there. I have stood and looked in wonder at the Great Wall of China, as it stretched far out before me, disappearing over the tops of mountains. It was simply amazing, but if you have no-one to share it with..."

Alex paused and wondered how best to explain. Maria wanted to hear about the beautiful places, the sunsets and vistas, the sights and adventures. How could he explain the feeling of being in a crowded room and still feeling lonely? How ever can you describe the vacuity of standing outside a temple knowing there was no hand to hold or no knowing smile to share at the marvel that was before their eyes. He knew that a photograph or a vivid description could never bring to life these moments, for it was incomplete. Emptiness.

Alex smiled at Maria and decided he would simply tell her what she wanted to hear.

"I have looked into the depths of the famous Grand Canyon, in Arizona, so deep that you can barely comprehend it!" Alex waved downwards towards the carpet. "The colours, the hues of orange and red, the rocks are breath-taking! I have swum on the Great Barrier Reef in Australia, in blue seas that you would think were impossible. We saw corals and fish that were beyond beauty. So many colours! Sometimes the fish would be all around you, swimming beside you, just going along on their way." He watched Maria's eyes grow wide.

"I have climbed ancient pyramids in Egypt and in Mexico," he continued. "Strange how they always put them in such hot, dusty places! I could not begin to comprehend the agony and the back-breaking feat of the labourers, nor the amazing ambition and skills of the engineers. Temples, churches and castles litter our planet Maria and they are all so amazing; and they all have a story! I have ridden the rapids of angry rivers in such places as New Zealand and the USA. Incredible!" Alex reminded himself to breath between sentences as he enthused over his travels.

"I have watched and shared the sunset over the African plains, with huge herds of Springbok silhouetted against the horizon. Now that was very special."

"Who did you share that with?" Maria asked gently.

Alex closed his eyes. He could see the Springbok in his mind, the warm low sun behind them. There were hundreds of them. It was their first safari and their tracker George had given them a glass of Amarula to toast their good fortune. There was just the two of them, standing there in wonderment. George sat high on the back of his seat, his rifle still in his lap, peering into the failing light searching for other animals. He had pointed quietly to the family of warthogs watching us from the bushes several metres to our left. We nodded eagerly. A small bat-eared fox had stepped out, watched us for a while curiously and then slipped away.

Carol placed her hand on Alex's arm and squeezed it gently. They had already seen giraffe, lion, elephant, rhino and zebra but there was something very special about this moment. There they were experiencing Africa together, while George and the jeep were lost in the shadows behind them.

For the ride back to the lodge George had given Alex a large electric spot light. Eyes stared back occasionally from the bush and George would slow down, or stop, to identify the beast. 'Kudu' George would whisper. "Look there, Impala!"

"It all sounds so wonderful," Maria exclaimed. "Tell me more!"

"Ah, well I was very lucky. I watched those large herds with my first wife Carol. It was new for both of us and we were in wonder. We would talk over dinner, then sit on the porch under the bright stars, listening to the sounds of insects in the night. Sometimes, if you were very quiet you could just hear the rustling of larger beings, but the temptation of talking about the days events was just too tempting and the wildlife moved largely unnoticed by us and the other guests."

Alex paused for a moment, took another deep breath and looked away. When he turned again to face his Spanish nurse, his eyes were filled with tears. He spoke in a quieter, more deliberate voice, his voice quavering.

"None of these wonderful things mean anything if you have no-one to share them with." he repeated, sniffing a little as he tried to regain his composure.

"Oh, but it does sound so wonderful though." Maria's eyes were wide with excitement. "I have never seen any of those things. You are so fortunate. Perhaps I should be a pilot, no?" Maria laughed at the prospect, but there was also gentleness in her voice. "D tell me more," she implored. "Please, do go on."

Alex sat quietly for a moment, regaining his composure. He lifted a tissue, tucked tightly in his hand, and wiped his eyes.

"For me, it was not about the places. There were special places that I loved to visit such as Singapore, Hong Kong, New York, Buenos Aires and Cape Town, but it was mostly about the people. It was about those moments when you were with a special person, or a great crew who really knew how to enjoy themselves.

"It did not happen too often, but when it did, how glorious it could be. I remember a party on the beach in Barbados. I was trying to impress a girl, but I was too competitive. I was young and trying too hard. I carried her on my back during a race along the beach, but then climbed a tree trying to get a coconut. I had probably drunk too much, but the chase; ah yes, the chase was everything! Sometimes the job was hard and tiring, but sometimes there was fun to be had." Alex chuckled to himself and Maria supposed he was laughing at untold elements of the story.

"And you had family holidays, too?" Maria asked.

"Oh yes, many," Alex admitted. "The United States was probably my favourite place with the children. It was so easy."

"Once," he continued, "we took our boys to the Ozark Mountains, in Arkansas. We had started down a river in two canoes, paddling across rapids and through deep narrow gorges, where the tops were covered in pine trees too high to even see. Drifting along the river, there was often complete silence, save for the water lapping at the river's edge, or our paddles splashing as we guided ourselves downstream. We would stop on small, but sunny river beaches where the sunlight had somehow reached down into the deep, almost impenetrable canyons or, sometimes, we would just sit and fish as we drifted further downstream. In a full, long day we neither saw nor heard another human being. It was so beautiful!"

Maria smiled warmly at the picture, formed in her mind.

"We drifted downstream, finally beaching by our cabin. That night," he chuckled, "the boys caught a big fish and we had no idea what to do with it! Then our youngest son, perhaps nine years old at the time, offered to help. He took a knife and filleted it as if he were a fishmonger! I had no idea he was capable of such things! We sat by the river and ate the barbecued fish and we could have been the only people on the planet!"

"When the boys were young," he continued, "I found myself laid off for a month without pay. It could be like that in the airline business you know. One morning we called our two young sons to the bedroom. One attended primary school, but the other went to nursery class. I held a globe and we talked about countries on the other side of the world. Then we told them we were going to those countries ***today***!"

"They must have been so excited," Maria gasped.

"Oh they were, but then so were we! We took nearly two months to fly around the world. The whole world, Maria, imagine that! Later that evening we flew to Singapore. Such a wonderful place; safe and magical, hot and atmospheric. A few days later we flew to Northern Queensland, in Australia. We spent three weeks just north of the city of Cairns in paradise, staying with one of Carol's relatives. Each day we woke up to blue skies and blue seas. Coffee, bananas and exotic fruits grew naturally in the garden. We swam on the Great Barrier Reef. We drove into the outback until there were no more roads or towns; there was nothing else but wilderness. We saw crocodiles, kangaroos, water buffalo and fruit bats."

"Eventually we flew to New Zealand and took a helicopter ride over a glacier and a glorious boat trip with dolphins down a fjord at Milford Sound, on the South Island. On the North Island we drove to an active volcano, but it was obscured by low cloud and rain. We booked into a mountain lodge overnight and were awoken by the sun steaming through the curtains. We pulled back the curtains to reveal Mount Ruapehu spitting lava, steam and smoke into the bluest sky I have ever seen. And we were so close!"

Alex took more coffee. He had been on a high, excited and telling his story with gusto, but now something was happening. His hands shook a little and he could feel something draining from his body. He took in a huge breath and the sigh resounded as if the wind had blown through the tightly closed windows and crossed the room. It was enough to cause Maria to hold her own breath and sit there in silence. The old man, with his eyes closed, did not move at all. Only a few seconds passed, but to Maria it seemed an eternity.

"A melancholy spirit came to rest just where I lay." the words were whispered, barely audible.

"Captain? Alex?" Maria leaned forward. "Are you alright?" There was concern in her voice.

"It was a poem I wrote a long, long time ago," he whispered staring at the woman sitting in front of him. "We had some great times, didn't we Carol? So many wonderful times." He looked up and stared into the eyes before him. "How could it have gone so badly wrong my darling?"

Tears were now rolling down his pale, wrinkled cheeks and he shook as the spirit seemed to drain from his body. Maria stood up quickly and took the coffee cup from his hands. She placed a hand on his shoulder and he reached up and touched it.

“I am so sorry Carol,” he said to her, patting her hand gently. “I am so sorry. I’m a little tired now, dear.”

Maria quietly returned to the table and placed the coffee cups on the tray. She turned to see Alex slumped asleep in his chair. She reached for his wrist and felt the pulse ticking away inside his weary body. The tear marks were still visible on his cheeks. She wiped a little tear away from her own face, straightened her uniform and walked back to pick up the tray; then, ever so quietly, she tip-toed from the room.

CHAPTER 12: NEAR DEATH

During those early days Alex was still feeling his way as a pilot, but loving every minute of it. Then the telephone rang. It was 4.45pm on a Friday afternoon. It was a man's voice that he did not recognise.

"Mr Young? Mr Alex Young?"

"Yes?" he said tentatively. It sounded rather serious!

"Mr Young, its the Chief Pilot's office here. How would you like a 747 course starting on Monday?"

A 747 course! Long haul!

"Well, I haven't bid for the 747." Alex began to explain.

"Mr Young, the 747 course. It's as a steward. Cabin crew. You have been redeployed."

Alex stood holding the telephone, trying to take in what was being said to him. "Do I have to take it?" he asked. Alex wanted to be a pilot. Nothing else!

"Well, if you don't Mr Young, you will be redeployed into an office!" The voice on the other end of the line was dispassionate; there was no emotion. This person could not have experienced the disappointment of being laid off for three years without pay. This person could not have experienced the steep mountain he had climbed to have achieved such heights from such a low beginning. His achievement had been incredible and unbelievable, not least to him! And now they were going to take it all away from him.

"Well, I've worked in an office. I certainly don't want to do that!" Alex was reeling.

"Well, report to the Training School Monday morning please. Registration is at 8.30am for a 9.00am start. Thank you Mr Young."

Alex tried to understand what had happened. He could not tell Carol. She was still at school, working late on some project or other. Alex went to the fridge and took out a beer.

The cabin crew training course turned out to be a massive laugh. The majority of the trainers were sympathetic, understanding and clever at getting the best out of a situation. The course went well, but Alex remained concerned how other 'real' cabin crew would react to working with redeployed pilots and engineers. He need not have worried. The stewards and stewardess's were warm and friendly and once they recognised that the 'Junior Jets' were hard workers, all was forgiven.

Alex had enjoyed flying around Europe, visiting cities from Glasgow to Rome, from Lisbon to Zargreb. Now he would be flying to the USA and the Caribbean; south to Johannesburg and Cape Town. Then there was the Middle East, Hong Kong and Singapore, Japan and even Australia!

The work was sometimes hard and tiring. He was used to dealing with people, but trying to recover an angry passenger with a grievance was sometimes very difficult. They might possibly be tired or even nervous of flying and they were, of course, the customer!

The lifestyle was completely different from short haul. There was more time away from home, more exotic destinations and sometimes more time off down route. Alex simply loved it. He loved the people, the travelling and the occasional parties. On one occasion a late 'Roman Toga' party in Nairobi had finished at about four in the morning. (What else do you do with two or three days in Nairobi?) Alex and the rest of the crew had worn nothing except their togas. When the party ended, Alex re-tied his toga before venturing back to his room, but however hard he tried, it no longer looked like a toga. It looked exactly like a bed sheet.

Alex walked quietly to the lift and pressed the up button. At that early hour the hotel was very quiet and still, save for the gentle humming of the lift. Finally the lift doors opened and, to his horror, he found six faces staring back at him. They were American tourists who had just arrived from Atlanta. He pulled the bed sheet still tighter and stepped into the lift. He reached over, selected the button for his floor and stared straight head at the lift doors. It was the slowest lift in the world! Behind him the Americans smiled to each other, then whispered and tittered.

"Wow, look what you can get on room service in this hotel!" joked one of the women.

Alex could not help but turn and look behind him. A blue-rinsed, middle-aged woman was grinning from ear to ear.

"Honey, can I have one?" someone asked.

"Looks like it was a good night buddy," said another.

"Hope she was worth it," another man said just as the lift was arriving at Alex's floor. Alex turned and answered the man.

"She ***was*** worth it sir, and she paid $200 for the privilege. Have a good night." Alex stepped from the lift to gasps and hoots of laughter. He could not help but smile as he walked along the corridor. He rummaged through his toga, just hoping he had not dropped his key!

Alex worked as a steward for just over a year. When the time came to return to his short haul fleet he asked whether he could do another year or two as a steward! The company politely declined. Soon he was flying around Europe again and, while he continued to enjoy the job, the call of long haul flying was too difficult to resist. Alex put his name on the annual bid list for the 747-400 and waited.

The years ticked by and Alex transitioned from the spring of his life into summer. The processes of career, home-making, marriage and socialising seemed enough. Life was comfortable and good. A house move gave Alex the opportunity to knock five walls down, building others and he excelled in his DIY skills. He could lay bricks, do plumbing and re-wire a house. Together with his job, the DIY projects and the parties and dinners, everything seemed warm and comfortable.

These were certainly the 'summer days'. He flew aircraft around Europe and continued to love his job. He enjoyed the night-stops, a meal and a couple of beers with people he had often not met before. Carol and Alex had been married nearly ten years when he finally asked the question. What on earth were they going to do about children?

They were both having a great time, they were lucky to have a large and active circle of friends and then there was the sport, cinema, theatre, holidays and dinners could keep them going for many years to come. To do nothing, he said, was effectively a decision not to have children. That seemed perfectly reasonable to both of them, but would they still feel the same way in another ten years. They were both getting older, perhaps more set in their ways. So, he said, let's think about 'yes' and think about 'no'.

Both Carol and Alex concluded that children would probably be a good idea sometime in the future but, having been on the pill for over a decade, it could take some time. Carol fell pregnant almost immediately! They had two sons, three years apart, who proved to be satisfying, straightforward and it did not change their lives as much as they had feared it might. The social life continued, with the young Youngs placed in baby baskets under a table when visiting friends for dinner. There was hardly ever a peep out of them.

The dream continued and eventually his bid to fly the mighty 747 Jumbo Jet came to pass. He was back to travelling to the four corners of the world. Initially his seniority allowed him to only fly the relatively shorter routes and he frequently found himself in New York, Boston, Washington, Philadelphia and Chicago. This meant he might only be away for three or four days at a time and, in terms of 'away from home' at least, it was not much different from his career flying around Europe. There was the jet lag of course but, while there was no cure as such, Alex learned how to cope with it. To Carol, nothing much had changed, except she rather envied his new travel experiences. It was not as if it was like a real job!

Gradually Alex's seniority in the company slowly improved as the older pilots hung up their wings and they spent their newly found freedom sipping gin and tonic or Mojitos on their retirement yachts. With a seniority based bidding system in place, he found his lot gradually improved and he could bid for the more lucrative and exotic destinations. He got to go to Buenos Aires and Rio de Janeiro, where beautiful steaks and red wine were the order of the day. Cape Town and Johannesburg were sociable, again with fine eating. Hong Kong and Bangkok were lots of fun with plenty to do, but Singapore was probably his favourite place. The crew hotel was wonderful, with great facilities, a beautiful swimming pool and tennis courts on the roof! The shopping was great and the food was terrific.

He also flew to Canada and the USA, the Middle East, India and Africa, Japan and Australia.

Alex loved the job, the flying and the destinations. At home and away, he continued his family history research and both he and Carol fell in love with the Forest of Dean in Gloucestershire during their visits there, seeking more information about his ancestors.

They finally found a beautiful house in the heart of the forest, quiet and isolated, with outstanding views of the River Severn and surrounding countryside. After the move, life in the Forest was idyllic and Alex immersed himself in a local charity preserving heritage and also worked as an instructor at the local Air Training Corps teaching young cadets about flying and aviation. He played sport, walked in the forest and the nearby Welsh mountains with friends and explored the labyrinth of cave systems that lay beneath the ground where they lived. Life was perfect! Well nearly…

Obviously things go wrong from time to time, but Alex and Carol could not imagine how their lives were about to be tested. The thing about disasters is they strike suddenly and unexpectedly; a storm, an accident or the death of a friend or loved one. Perhaps there are people who manage to get through life with the minimum of pain and disruption. There are others who seem to struggle at every turn.

Alex felt that he had been dealt a very good hand. True he had worked extremely hard to get where he had, but the resulting good fortune, his career, his family and his friends all pointed to him being very lucky. Occasionally there would be a little turbulence along the way, but on the whole he had been blessed with a good life.

The physical problem began quite surreptitiously. Alex was fit and played squash in a local league. He felt he did pretty well and he certainly enjoyed the competitive element of the game. He had found jogging on a running machine or along a road really quite boring, but chasing after this silly little ball on a squash court gave him so much pleasure. He was competitive, but he didn't mind losing to a better player provided he gave them a good game.

Trying to keep fit and remain consistent was difficult, given the nature of the job. Even after a long flight, with jet-lag and general tiredness, a good physical workout was a perfect way to unwind. However, frustration began to kick in as Alex went through a period of losing all his matches. No matter how hard he tried to hit the damn thing, he found getting the right length on the ball increasing difficult. He knew it was timing but, no matter how hard he ran, no matter how hard he tried, his playing game began to deteriorate. Was it a lack of fitness? Was middle age creeping up on him? As he tried harder, the pain started. Tennis elbow, pain in his neck and back; all signs that he was trying to hard. Or so he thought.

Perhaps the vacation would help him? Alex and Carol had planned a holiday to the United States to Washington DC, to Virginia, the Shenandoah Valley and Virginia Beach. As they planned the trip, the pain grew steadily worse and the painkillers increased. But how could they disappoint the boys?

The visit to Washington D.C. included a stay with a distant cousin who was a lobbyist in the political machine that was the capital of the United States. They were lucky enough to get a tour of the Senate, a grand and inspiring building steeped in a relatively short, but rich history.

They were also taken the short distance to Baltimore, to watch the Orioles play baseball against Detroit. The vast stadium stood close to the shoreline, where even the skyscrapers tried to catch a peek at the game. Alex was astonished at the family atmosphere. Money was passed along a long row of spectators with an order for beers and hotdogs. Shortly after, the food and drink was passed back down the line, together with the change!

Carol and Alex also took their two sons to stand outside the White House. They had stood at the foot of the towering Washington Monument, a huge white marble needle reaching up into the air. They saw the dignity of the Lincoln Memorial, where Alex read a section of the Gettysburg Address to his children, who were perhaps too young to appreciate "and that government of the people, by the people, for the people shall not perish from the earth."

The Smithsonian was interesting, the National Air and Space Museum was fun, and Arlington Cemetery with its rows of white crosses was sober, but beautiful. Alex took a few minutes to explain the significance of the eternal flame that flickered behind the plain flagstones of President Kennedy's grave. He told them briefly how JFK had been shot in Dallas.

"Was that the same as President Lincoln?" the eldest son James had asked. "They shot him, didn't they?"

"Why do they shoot the Presidents?" asked the younger son.

"Err, well it's complicated, Andy. Do you boys fancy an ice cream?" Alex's body was hurting more than ever and he needed to sit down.

Later that day, the family found themselves standing outside the J. Edgar Hoover Building, home of the FBI. Forever the tour guide, Alex had explained about the role of the FBI; finger prints, computer checks for local police forces and, of course, the G-Men. The boys wanted to go inside, but the long queue for the tour was substantial.

The FBI Building sits on one entire block, sandwiched by Pennsylvania Avenue and E Street, between 9th and 10th Street. The main entrance stood at one corner of a large crossroads, regulated by traffic lights and pedestrian crossings. There the family stood trying to decide what to do next.

"Look at that man," young Andy pointed across the road to the opposite corner of the street.

A man was searching through the street corner rubbish bin, seemingly sorting the contents as he went. He pulled out a newspaper and carefully refolded it, trying to iron out the creases. He placed it under his arm and continued to sift through the contents of the bin.

"What's he doing?" There was an element of disgust in James' voice.

"Searching for food," Carol whispered, barely audible above the local traffic.

"Yuck, that's gross!" Andy placed his fingers in his mouth and pretended to be sick.

"Andy, stop it! Shut up!" Alex's stare was enough for Andy to stop what he was doing, but the young boy then let out a gasp as the man took something from the bin and placed it in his mouth.

Alex and Carol just looked at each other, but said nothing. The four of them remained rooted to the spot as the man crossed the road to the next bin. Once again he sifted through the contents and, finding nothing, pressed the button to cross to the next corner; their corner! Alex suddenly looked down and realised they were standing close to another bin. He immediately ushered the boys back towards the FBI Building, then turned to watch old man.

The tramp walked slowly towards the bin and began his search. He was wearing a threadbare great coat, reaching well below his knees. He had old, worn out sneakers on his feet with no socks; indeed his legs were bare, as if he didn't even have trousers on. He appeared to have an old shirt tied around his neck, rather like a scarf, although the weather was warm.

Alex found himself walking forwards the man half-bent over the waste bin. His hand had already reached into his pocket and taken out a $10 note.

"Excuse me?" Alex said hesitantly; he was uncertain quite what reaction he would get. "Excuse me, sir!"

The man stood up slowly, turned his head, and looked Alex up and down.

"Excuse me. I was wondering whether you would accept this." Alex held out the $10 note. "I think it should be enough to get you something to eat and a drink."

The man looked down at the note, then looked up and smiled. He was not old after all, but very weathered. He was, perhaps, in his forties or fifties, his skin dried and burned by the sun. His smiling teeth were yellowy and chipped and he brushed long, dank hair from his face.

"Good afternoon," he said. "You are not a local man, are you?" he said. His voice was smooth and cultured.

"No, I am from England," Alex half –turned and pointed at Carol, who was holding her two children by the hand, close to the building. "We are on vacation."

"Ah, and how are you enjoying our fine city?" the man looked right into Alex's eyes and smiled.

"Oh, it's wonderful. Very interesting," Alex still had his hand extended with the $10 dollar bill, which the man appeared to ignore.

"I am so glad!" The man said. "It's a wonderful city and we are very proud of it. The White House, Arlington; have you been to Georgetown yet?"

"We've not been to Georgetown yet, but it is on our list," Alex felt for the first time that the conversation was almost normal!

"Georgetown is very pretty, it has lots of nice streets, old buildings, bars and restaurants. And, if you have the time, I would recommend you go to Monticello. It's about a hundred miles from here, but truly very beautiful; magical. Well worth the trip." The man looked across at Carol and the boys. "What a lovely family. I do hope you have a wonderful trip!"

The man turned to go.

"Sir," Alex extended his hand again, with the money.

"Treat your boys to an ice cream," the old man said warmly. "You have made my day, my boy. It was very nice to meet you."

The man turned and walked away slowly. Alex stood there and watched him go. Suddenly he felt a gentle arm around his waist and knew that Carol was standing beside him. He turned to look at her, with tears that welled in his eyes and then ran down his cheeks. He held up the $10 note still in his hand, but did not speak. He tried, but could not. Carol nodded and took her husband's hand, as they walked eastward towards Union Station. The two boys looked at each other but said nothing. They both had questions, but knew this was not the time.

A week later, following visits to the stunning Blue Ridge Mountains and the Shenandoah Valley, they had made their way to Monticello. It was the home of Thomas Jefferson, the author of the Declaration of Independence and third President of the United States. It was just as magical as the old tramp had described. Alex remained haunted by the memory of the poor man who, despite hard times, had retained dignity and pride.

The family passed Richmond on their way to Williamsburg and Jamestown, finally arriving at Virginia Beach. The boys grew excited. They had been very good and very patient, walking around old buildings and museums, but a few days by the sea with wonderful beaches and lots of sunshine; that was more like it!

Alex tried to keep things as normal as possible, but the pain in his back, neck and arm had increased significantly and the pills were proving less and less effective. Carol looked on with great concern, but had remained calm for the sake of the boys. They, in turn, were on their best behaviour, fully aware that things were more serious and getting worse by the day.

A day later, the family were all sitting in a Virginia hospital emergency unit waiting to be seen. The efficiency was breathtaking. Alex had been seen very quickly once the insurance details had been provided by Carol. He was examined, scanned, and immediately filled with morphine.

"You must take him home, Mrs Young. Your husband needs urgent medical treatment at home. The doctors will need to establish the cause of the pain and the paralysis." The doctor shook Carol's hand and bade her farewell. He explained that Alex would have to be taken to the car in a wheelchair and someone would be along very shortly. The boys would later relate a story about how their mother drove back to Washington with her husband almost unconscious in the passenger seat.

As she drove along the freeway northward, she did not notice that the three lanes were merging into two. With one huge truck to her left, and another to her right, the boys screamed at her in unison as her lane simply disappeared! She braked heavily as the gap between the two trucks narrowed to nothing.

Carol stared forward, urging herself to concentrate and be strong. She banged the steering wheel with her hand. 'I have to do this,' she thought. 'I have to do this!'

"It turned out to be a major back problem of the upper neck, Maria." Alex explained. "Apparently, if it had been left untreated, I would have become paralysed. Eventually I lost the use of my right arm, unable to even pick up a small piece of paper. The pain was so bad I was on the maximum amount of morphine that you could take as pills. On top of that, my doctor was calling at the house every day to give me a pethidine injection. They give that to women in childbirth for pain relief."

"Captain," Maria laughed and slapped her thigh. "Perhaps you forget I am a nurse!"

"Ah, of course," acknowledged Alex. "I'm sorry Maria. The pain was terrible. My skin had even turned grey. When I was finally taken to the hospital for my operation Carol was told I might become a paraplegic as a result of the operation, but I was already becoming paralysed. There was no choice."

"Carol left me at the hospital in Bristol where I was to have the operation and she drove to her mother's house where our eldest son was staying. He was about thirteen at the time. It was a long drive and Carol could not help, but worry about the possible outcome. She had watched me become more and more ill and knew the greying skin was a very bad sign. With so many drugs inside me, I did not realise how bad things were until a friend visited me. It was only when I saw the complete look of horror on his face did I realise how bad I must have looked! For my family, I must have been a terrible sight!"

"What was causing this pain?" Maria asked.

"A piece of bone on one of my vertebra in my neck was growing onto the next vertebra. It was cutting into some of the nerves in my body. Luckily the bone had only cut half way through the nerves and they were able to grow back." Again Alex paused as Maria interrupted again.

"This is very serious," Maria said. "Once they are cut through, they can never grow back."

"Correct Maria," Alex nodded. "Well, the surgeons went in through my neck, just here." Alex was pointing to his throat. The scar had long since healed even before the old man's skin had become so wrinkled and old.

Carol had driven to Salisbury, in Wiltshire, with the weight of the world on her shoulders. The two-hour journey seemed to pass in minutes. She could not remember anything of the drive, the entire thing a blur, but now she was entering the small city. She always felt that once she had passed Wilton House, she was virtually there. The traffic was heavier than normal and it was a relief when she eventually turned into the small road towards her mother's house.

Annoyingly the narrow road was almost blocked and she had to squeeze the car passed several utility vans all owned by the local electricity company. It was a ridiculous place to park. Finally she pulled up outside the three-storey town house, weary and tired. She was exhausted. She parked outside, gathered her handbag and the keys, got out and locked the car. She would take her overnight bag in later.

Her mother Mary opened the door as she approached and stepped into the street to greet her. There was an immediate embrace and Carol stood there for a moment while Mary held her tightly.

"Hello dear," her mother had said gently, but firmly. "Now look, he's all right!"

Carol suddenly felt a cold shiver. There was something in her mother's tone, but she was confused. Surely the operation hadn't taken place yet? It was scheduled for tomorrow. Had there been a problem with Alex?

Mary released her grip and stepped aside. Only then could Carol see into the narrow house and up the stairs. Her son James was standing at the top of the landing, leaning heavily on crutches, with huge bandages wrapped around both his legs. Carol simply burst into tears. She felt Mary's arms around her again and she was shaking. This was all too much.

"Oh my God!" Maria exclaimed. She crossed herself and looked towards heaven, quietly apologising for the outburst! "What on earth had happened?"

Mary had sat in the kitchen and watched as James devoured the huge breakfast. Her grandson was growing rapidly, but she was always astonished at the sheer volume of food this boy could consume. Every now and then, much to her relief, James paused, probably just to take a breath! The talk was of Mary's brand new car. It was less than two weeks old and it was her pride and joy. It drove beautifully and the leather interior smelt wonderful.

"It's the radio, you see dear," Mary explained. "Every time I switch it on, it blares out very loud pop music! I turn it down, of course, but next time I start the car it's very, very loud again. I've tried changing channels, but the radio simply doesn't remember them!"

"That's no problem Gran," James smiled back. "I can fix that for you. Just needs re-programming. It'll be a digital one. I'll do it after breakfast." He placed another large piece of toast into his mouth.

Mary was reassured and had full confidence in her thirteen year old grandson. He was bright and considerate and seemed to understand all these new gadgets and things. She sat and sipped at her coffee, keen that James should allow his breakfast to go down for a few minutes before embarking on any chores.

"Just let it go down, dear," she would say. "A few minutes won't hurt."

James dutifully sat with his grandmother, pleased that he would be able to assist her with this simple task. What was it with old people and electrical goods? TV's, video recorders, computers and mobile phones – even Mum and Dad didn't use all the facilities these things had to offer. Still, it was good to be useful!

Finally James concluded he had done his duty and sat still for five minutes, so he asked where the car keys were. Mary went to her handbag and stirred the contents until she felt the keys. She handed them to James, but then followed him down the hall and out of the front door. It was a new car, after all!

The car stood on an area of tarmac just along from the house. Mary didn't like having cars directly outside, perhaps because the hall door and side-panel had frosted glass and it cast a shadow into the hallway. Maybe there was another reason; James had no idea. He used the remote to unlock the doors and walked around to the passenger side. He opened the door and sat in the passenger seat. The car did smell nice and said so. He knew that would please her. He studied the car radio, which included a CD drive, and thought the buttons were ridiculously small. Naturally he didn't say anything about that!

The car wasn't the biggest, so James got out again and then lay across the passenger seat with his legs hanging out over the tarmac. His eyes were now just inches from the radio display and he went from button to button, working out what each was for. He could read the instructions, of course, but he felt it was much more impressive to simply punch a few buttons and complete the task. He began with the 'on' switch. Nothing happened.

"Oh Gran, can you put the key in the ignition?" he called. "There's no power to the radio!" James continued to study the tiny buttons, some had initials on them, but some meant nothing to him. He guessed there would be an automatic tuning mode and he would program Gran's favourite channels into the machine. AM/FM. Why did cars still have AM he wondered? Those rubbish channels, which always crackled and faded near buildings.

Mary had sat in the seat and closed the driver's door. She checked her rear view mirror.

"You just need to turn the key, Gran," James said trying not to sound impatient. He waited, ready to hear the radio come alive.

Everything else happened in a matter of a few seconds, but slow motion isn't really like that, is it? First James heard the engine spring into life. 'She' had turned the key too far! Then there was the sickening realisation that the car was moving. It lurched backwards. She had left the car in reverse gear and the hand brake was off! She quickly slammed her foot on the brake pedal ….. and missed!

Instead Mary's foot pressed the accelerator pedal flat to the floor and, in horror, she froze! The car accelerated backwards at speed. James held on tight to the seat he was lying on. He could feel his legs dragging along the floor outside the open passenger door. There was an almighty noise, but the car continued at speed. That was the sound of the passenger door being ripped clean off its hinges by a concrete bollard. Somehow it missed James' flaying legs.

James could not see anything, but he was aware the car was turning. The rear end had now turned through ninety degrees and the acceleration continued. He considered letting go, but he was uncertain whether he would end up somehow under the wheels. He gripped tighter. He could feel pain and stinging as the car drove backwards across two small, narrow gardens, bushes and debris slapping at the rear and underside of the car. The car was not in the least inhibited by the brick wall and punched straight through it.

The tall brick wall, now demolished, surrounded an electrical sub-station and that was the immovable object that had finally brought the car to a halt. The engine had stalled and the car was now silent. Mary just sat there in complete shock. James had taken the full force of the brick wall on his legs, which by now had been stripped of his jeans, his trainers and some of his skin. But he was alive; somehow they had both survived.

Only later were they told that when the emergency services and technicians had come to remove the car, they had found 11,000 volts running through it!

"The operation was a complete success," Alex continued to relate his own story. "I woke up about ten hours after the operation. I could not move, but that was not very surprising. I was lying on my back in a darkened room. I could see the television hanging on the wall in the corner. There was a painting on the wall and, of course, the door. I could see all of these things, but then something strange began to happen." Maria sat listening in silence. She nodded her head for him to continue.

"It was dark, but a strange black mist began to appear in front and above me. First of all I thought it was something in my eyes so I began to blink. Gradually the mist thickened so that I could no longer see the television, the picture or the door. Then I began to have trouble breathing. It was as if someone was putting a pillow over my face."

"Perhaps it was your first wife?" Maria joked!

Alex smiled. "No, she still liked me in those days! Anyway, I had started choking. I was struggling to breathe. My throat and lungs began to burn. Then, through the blackness I began to see a white light."

There was an audible gasp from Maria.

"Slowly I found myself moving towards the white light and soon I was entering a tunnel. I was floating. I then began seeing childhood memories, things I hadn't recalled since they happened all those years before. It was then I realised I was dying."

"Were you frightened? Maria asked.

"No," Alex replied. "I felt very calm and ready to die. I thought of my family and felt sorry for them, of course, the grief and the ordeal they would now go through. I thought of my life and my friends; it wasn't so bad. I had had a good life. Finally, I could see the end of the tunnel. I drifted towards the end of that tunnel and tried to see beyond it; just around the corner perhaps. Quite suddenly I began to hear bells, rather like a group of alarm clocks all ringing at the same time; lots and lots of alarm clocks! The sound was my heart monitor – my heart and breathing had stopped!"

"Captain. May I ask you, did you see God?" Maria was leaning even further forward, almost out of her chair.

"No, Maria," Alex's voice was quieter now. "I didn't see God. I don't believe in God; or ghosts, or spirits. Was it my optical nerve? Was it the sudden excess of carbon dioxide starving the brain? There are many theories. Two nurses had run into the room. One placed an oxygen mask over my mouth and nose, while another pushed at my heart. Nothing happened and several minutes passed until a doctor ran in to the room and stabbed me with an adrenaline pen. Of course, I didn't remember any of this. I was simply told the story later." Maria finally sat back in her chair.

"I was unconscious for another ten hours. When I work up a nurse was holding my hand. She spoke in a very slow and deliberate voice, which I thought very strange. She asked how I was. I replied in the same slow, deliberate voice that I was fine. I remember her saying 'thank goodness, thank goodness' and later telling me I would need counselling. She even asked if I wanted to see a priest."

"Many do see God," Maria almost whispered. "For many it is a life-changing experience."

"Oh, it was a life-changing experience Maria. I was told that there would be side effects. One, she said, would be that I would have to tell everyone about my experience. Well this was true and, of course, I am telling you. Another side effect was that I found I would cry much more easily. At movies, maybe a book or a piece of music, even a TV commercial; if it was sad I would ball my eyes out and cry. My tears even used to embarrass my children. However I began to appreciate things more. The glass, for me, is always half full. Not half empty. Things I took for granted suddenly seemed very special. A night out with friends, for example, a sunset or perhaps a moment; some special moment that meant something special. These things seemed much more meaningful than before." Alex looked across at his nurse and smiled. "The most profound change, I think, was in my attitude towards life. I was no longer frightened of dying. Sure, I am frightened of pain, but not of dying."

"It is a wonderful story Captain. I have heard of such stories, but it is good to hear your experience. I am just sorry you did not find God." Maria looked a little sad.

"I did not need to find God, Maria. I am surrounded by goodness and truth. I have the gifts of love and friendship. I have been blessed with a wonderful life. I have travelled the world. I have had a great career. I have met some amazing people and seen many incredible things. I have loved and lost; I have loved and won. Life and love, Maria, these are the real miracles. I think I am the luckiest person in the world. I even have the prettiest nurse!"

"Captain, you go too far!" Maria feigned a blush as she rose from her chair and brushed herself down. "You must rest now and I have things to do."

"But I'm not finished," Alex protested.

"For now, you are finished," Maria insisted. "A small siesta and then you can tell me more."

Maria cleared the table, placing cups and glasses on the plastic tray. She checked the room, which was tidy as always. She walked to the balcony windows and pulled the curtain partly closed to shield the sun. Returning to the table, she picked up the tray. Only then did she look down at her patient. He had closed his eyes and was breathing deeply.

'I bet you have some wonderful stories to tell,' she thought. 'God bless my Captain.'

Not for the first time, Maria found herself tip-toeing from the room. She would now go to the office and write up her notes. 'He sleeps more often now,' she would write. "I think he is growing weaker."

Chapter 13: Command and No Power

The old man had thought of his life as the four seasons; his entire life wrapped up in just one year. He had been born leading up to winter and his school days were exactly like a long, dreary winter to him. His childhood had been happy enough, but school had been a dark season educationally and, in relation to girls, the sun had hardly made it over the horizon. Later in life, he would smile when he heard people say that one's school days were the best days of your life. If it had not been for Mr Duncan and John Taylor, the two teachers amazing who had rescued him from oblivion, his whole life might have been winter!

The seeds sown by those schoolteachers were probably the beginning of the spring. They showed him that education, after all, could have a purpose and Alex pursued it with vigour and drive. That determination had led to his recruitment into a flying school and slowly he changed, as he grew into a more confident a person. He had already met Carol and then married her. Gradually he overcame his shyness and low self-esteem, slowly growing in confidence. At first he felt like an impostor, surrounded by clever, talented people and it took him time to realise he was one of them and he actually belonged.

The hard work had led to a glorious time with his new and successful career and, of course, his wife. The spring was long and fruitful. Those halcyon days included the incredible first ten years B.C. following their marriage (Before Children), where their social life was mad, busy and exciting! Theatre, movies, dinners, fun with wonderful friends, their lives were rich and full. They would not yet count themselves as wealthy, but they were certainly becoming a lot more 'comfortable'.

There were one or two hiccups on the way. That was probably to be expected, but Alex was doing what he had dreamed of since childhood. Flying around Europe was fun, but he had experienced the taste of longhaul and waited for his moment. Finally it came and Alex transferred to the vast 747 Jumbo. He had stood underneath the huge aircraft, parked outside a hanger, and looked up in awe. The aircraft was absolutely massive and he would be flying them around the world! He experienced new routes, new adventures and a new way of life. He would be away for longer, but he would also have more days off between trips. More time at home meant new opportunities and he immersed himself in his local community. The more he did, the greater the demands that were made of him, but he was appreciated and that made him give even more of his time.

Almost dying had been rather more than a hiccup, but Alex regarded it as being given a second chance. He began to appreciate things more; his family, friends, the beauty of nature and of life. He had been able to return to his career and even got back to playing squash again! He continued his life and career with a fresh impetus, basking in the comfort and rewards that were his happy existence. And it was just about to get even better.

Alex opened the big fat envelope, which contained the joining instructions for his Command Course. He was being given the chance to be an Airline Captain! His hand shook slightly with excitement. It was far from automatic, some did not make the grade, but he knew that with enough study and hard work, he would be good enough. It would begin with intense ground school training, numerous simulator details practising every potential emergency and flight procedure, and then a long series of operational flights where he was tested on his knowledge, professionalism and skills to the highest level.

At the end of his final check, consisting of two sectors to and from Tokyo's Narita Airport over several days, Alex finally taxied in at Heathrow. It had been a daunting, nerve-racking event, but it was over. The brakes were placed on, the engines were shut down and the checklists were quietly completed. As the passenger doors were opened and passengers began to disembark, there was an eerie silence on the flight deck.

Alex thought back over his decision-making during the past few hours. Had he made the correct decisions? There had been a tricky crosswind at the destination, unexpected delays in the holding pattern and difficult decisions had had to be made. Had he made a mistake? Had he blown it, faltering at the last hurdle? Why was there whispering and unusual activity behind him? His heart sank!

Finally there was movement and the Check Captain behind him reached over and placed a box on his lap. Alex picked it up and examined it. The picture showed that the box contained a bottle of Japanese wine. On the side was a label, which read 'Congratulations Captain Young'. Alex looked around at his colleagues sitting in the cockpit with him. They were all grinning from ear to ear.

"Well done, mate," said the pilot in the right-hand seat.

The relief washed his fears away. It was over! He was now an airline captain! There was paperwork to do, of course, and the other crewmembers offered to complete the final checks on the flight deck. Alex climbed out of his seat, picked up his jacket and stepped out and into the passenger cabin. The cabin crew were all standing there, either side of the aisle, and they applauded enthusiastically. Alex was overwhelmed and fought hard to keep his composure. There was a brisk shaking of hands, and one or two cheek-to-cheek kisses from the girls. Alex was a 747-400 jumbo jet captain!

Life could not be better. He was the luckiest man in the world! He had a wonderful wife, two fantastic sons and he lived in paradise. He had now fulfilled his lifetime ambition. How proud his parents would be! He would wear his four stripes with pride. His next stop was to be uniform stores!

Moving from the right-hand seat, where the First Officer or co-pilot sat, to the left hand seat of the Captain was a rather like his near-death experience. It was like being born again. As a Captain, he loved the responsibility and found he could create the mood for the flight. Being friendly, but firm, he found he could motivate his crews. There had always been a bit of 'them and us' between the cabin crew and the flight crew and he had hated it. On both sides there were some who didn't appreciate the others' perspective and occasionally expressed it.

"Bloody cabin crew," one First Officer had said to him. "They never come out!"

"I wonder why," Alex had retorted. He worked hard at smoothing things over, understanding both sides and it helped that he had been on both sides of the fence, having worked as a steward. He enjoyed dealing with the passengers too. So when things went wrong, such as an unexpected delay, he would put on his hat and jacket and go and speak to the passengers face to face, sometimes on the aircraft or when necessary in the terminal. The passengers normally loved it and the cabin crew appreciated it. He found being nice to people made them want to reciprocate – once again, it wasn't rocket science!

Alex also worked hard on his passenger address. He knew lots of people didn't listen to a droning voice so he tried very hard to make it more interesting. He injected humour and sometimes a bit of flattery. It was enough that the cabin crew would often mention it to him afterwards. The occasional sourpuss didn't get it but, on the whole, he achieved his objective. After landing, he would welcome his passengers to their destination, give them any important information necessary and end with his signature expression - "... and whatever you are doing for the rest of the day, do it well!"

The career was full-grown and he was now a successful 747 Captain travelling the world. Life was inevitably busy. He and Carol continued to enjoy an active social life. Carol was the consummate organiser and a great hostess and his days off would frequently be pre-booked with evening dinners, theatre trips and other fun-filled events. The volunteering also continued apace, gradually taking up more and more of his time. He was frequently reminded of the saying – 'Want something done? Ask a busy man!'

However, life in the fast lane was not without adventure.

Alex stood at the top of the Empire State Building looking north across the Manhattan skyline. This view was perhaps the most spectacular as is showed the enormous size of Central Park, a huge oasis set in a jungle of skyscrapers. The largest lake, named after Jackie Kennedy Onassis, showed up well but Alex was uncertain whether he could pick out the American Museum of Natural History from all the other buildings bordering its left side. Carol stood beside him, while the boys climbed the railings trying to look vertically down 86 floors to the ground. The family slowly walked around clockwise so, looking north-east, their vista included the beautiful Chrysler Building.

"That is my favourite building in New York," Alex announced to his sons. "That is the Chrysler Building. The design is art deco and it was the tallest building in the world for very nearly a year until the Empire State Building was constructed."

The boys looked at each other and then looked skywards. They were used to their father acting like an over-enthusiastic tour guide trying to find employment. Beyond the Chrysler Building stretched the East River and by the bridge was Roosevelt Island, which for reasons quite unexplained, fascinated Alex. They then moved to the south view where Wall Street and the other high finance buildings crowded the south end of the Island. Alex knew this was close to the Staten Island Ferry, as well as Fort Clinton, which was effectively the gateway to the Statue of Liberty and Ellis Island. Alex was desperate to share all his knowledge with his family, but he had already realised that they were only interested in the views, not in the history.

Alex could have spent a lot more time up here, but Carol had gently suggested the boys were becoming hungry and they had been promised lunch in Times Square. As the family stepped out onto 5th Avenue, Alex rubbed his hands together.

"OK guys, you now have a choice." Everyone looked at him patiently and waited for the momentous pronouncement. "We have two alternatives," he explained. "We can either get the subway train to Times Square, or we can cruise past the shops and walk there. It's not too far."

Everyone agreed that walking was the best option, so they headed north, following their 'personalised' tour guide. The shops on 5th Avenue were a little posh (aka boring!) and the day was very hot. They had barely walked five blocks or when suddenly office workers began filing out of offices, crowding the sidewalks. The family were growing tired and the traffic on the roads also appeared to be grinding to a halt.

"Strange, everyone seems to be finishing early today," Carol commented.

"There are no lights," James pointed out.

Alex looked through the shop windows and, sure enough, building after building seemed to be without electricity.

"And there's no traffic lights!" Andrew pointed at the street corner. The cars had all stopped because the traffic lights had all gone blank. Within seconds the crescendo from the traffic, cars, taxis, vans and trucks was simply enormous.

"There's no power at all," Alex exclaimed as they continued walking north towards Times Square. "This whole block is out," he said.

Steadily they walked through the ever-increasing crowds, who were blocking the sidewalks of New York. Traffic had come to a complete halt. Drivers were now standing outside their cars, waving their hands, some of them grabbing a quick cigarette. They need not have hurried! Eventually the family reached the corner with 42nd Street. Alex hesitated.

"OK, Times Square is that way," Alex pointed left, "but we are going this way." Carol knew not to argue when Alex was stressed and the boys watched the growing chaos on the streets with interest. They were walking east on West 43rd Street and, ahead, of them, a huge fire-truck was parked by the sidewalk. The road was filled with stationary cars going nowhere and hundreds of people were milling around the streets wondering what was going on.

Alex later discovered the mass exodus from the buildings had been because, on this hot August day when the electricity failed, the office air conditioning stopped working and the temperature in the buildings soared to unbelievable temperatures. The family reached the fire engine, which had two firemen perched on the top of the truck. Alex realised it was parked directly outside its own firehouse, a small stone building barely wide enough for the single engine. The building had a balcony above its narrow entrance, proudly boasting an elaborate stone motif with 'Engine Company' emblazoned upon it. This was the home of Engine Company No. 65. The four storey building was older, but far more beautiful than any of the surrounding buildings. Most of the windows were in rectangular sash frames, but on the third of the four floors, three arches proudly stood high with four stone circles above them. Inside each circle was a single letter spelling FDNY.

Although it was the middle of the day, the building was in darkness, the towering buildings surrounding it casting huge shadows everywhere. At that moment there was a loud electrical crackle and the radio came to life. The firefighters had connected a radio to the fire engine and the news commentator's voice bellowed loudly down the street. The radio faded for a moment as one fireman re-adjusted the volume, then the woman commentator's voice became more audible. The hubbub of noise fell to almost silence as people paused to listened to the news station.

"We are now going to our affiliate in Detroit where reporter Tony Siccarro is waiting to speak to us." The woman sounded very dramatic. "Hello Tony, tell us what is happening in Detroit."

"Good afternoon Susan. Well, I am standing in the Business District of Detroit and I understand the entire city is completely without power. Apparently back-up generators have failed to come online and the city streets are gridlocked. Generally there appears to be widespread confusion and anger in the streets. The failures began State-wide just after four pm and..."

"Tony, I am sorry to interrupt you, but we are getting reports that Toronto and wide areas of Ontario are without power. Are you aware of how extensive this problem is?" There appeared to be even more tension in Susan Tanner's voice.

"Yes Susan, we have also received those reports and Canadian Prime Minister Jean Chrétien has called for calm and announced a press conference for eight o'clock this evening. Susan, we are just hearing that Parliament Hill, in Ottawa, has been evacuated! Back to you Susan."

"Thank you, Tony. Well, initial reports indicate that the power has failed across New York City, Long Island and north all the way up towards Buffalo. Remain tuned to this station for further updates, this is Susan Tanner, WYNC." There was a dying cough on the radio and then silence.

There were a series of gasps from the crowd who had now surrounded the fire truck.

"Anyone got a cell phone signal?" a man shouted.

"I been tryin' for over an hour," someone else yelled.

"Payphones are working, at least they were!"

There was a surge as some people began pushing forward in search of a payphone further down the road.

"This can't happen," yelled a businessman who had already stripped off his jacket and tie, but continued to sweat profusely. "This is Nine Eleven all over again!"

There appeared to be general agreement that this was, most likely, a concerted and well-planned terrorist attack. People in the crowd experienced a myriad of emotions. Some cried, others shook, while others simply asking questions. How? Why? What's going on?

"Can't you get that radio fixed?" someone called.

"Nothing wrong with the radio sir," the fire fighter stood up, tall and authoritative, high on the back of the fire truck. "The radio keeps going on and off the air. I guess they are struggling with their power supply too. I can tell you we have received reports that all New York airports are closed, the subways are being evacuated and that all Manhattan has been closed to all inbound traffic."

"Hey, I just heard from my sister in Cleveland," an invisible voice shouted. "Ohio is also affected. It's the whole Eastern Seaboard and Mid-West!"

There were gasps and people began debating in small groups. Around them hundreds of workers were discussing the situation with fellow strangers on the street. Each had an opinion, advice and words of concern. Alex looked at Carol whose face carried all the concerns that he was feeling inside.

"Come on," he said, "let's get out of here."

The family pushed through the crowded sidewalks, the road still full of cars. Most were empty, the inhabitants beaten by the ninety-two degree temperatures that baked the city, its building and vehicles. They crossed Fifth Avenue easily. The wide thoroughfare had no traffic lights, but it also had no moving traffic; just stationary cars, vans and lorries. Later on the public would begin taking the law into their own hands and directing traffic themselves through the thousands of crossroads that made up the city, but for now, much of it was still gridlocked. Madison Avenue seemed to have fewer cars, but thousands of people were walking to somewhere.

Finally Alex and Carol were able to walk alongside each other, with their teenage sons striding behind them. Alex discussed the problem with his wife. They were staying with distant relatives in Brooklyn Heights, but how were they to get back there? The subway trains no longer worked. Thank goodness they had not chosen that mode of transport to get to Times Square! Stuck underground in a train, in the dark with no fans or air conditioning would have been awful! Buses and taxis were no longer viable; the roads were gridlocked. Alex estimated the distance would be about six or seven miles, so the walk could take them perhaps three hours or more on the congested streets.

Part of their journey would be in the dark. New York at night, with no lights; would it be safe? Would the criminals take advantage of the situation, mugging and looting their way through the night? What perils might lay before them? No, Alex reasoned, the safest thing to do would be to make their way to the airline hotel where some of the company's pilots and cabin crew stayed. At least, in the sanctuary of the lobby, they would be safe.

Ahead of them, and seemingly growing larger, stood the vast cathedralesque arched windows of Grand Central Station. Behind, Alex could just see the top section of the Chrysler Building. They turned right and left to go around the huge station complex. Alex told the boys that beneath the building lay forty-four railway platforms and so many train tracks, they had to be placed on two different levels underground. They walked under Park Avenue Bridge and then left onto Lexington. Alex's mind was racing, but he could not think of any other option. He grew more confident as they approached the hotel, but that changed to nervousness as they entered the foyer.

Inside, to his astonishment, some of his colleagues were standing in the foyer, checking out. They were at the desk, paying bills and checking accounts. Alex was relieved to see that he knew the First Officer and immediately approached him.

"Hello, Tom, how are you?" he said, reaching out a hand.

"Hello, Skipper. Didn't know you were in town. Really good, thanks. We're just off home now. What are you up to?" Tom held out his hand and accepted the handshake. "We've got a bit of a problem here, actually. The bloody power's off in this area and they can't do the credit card transactions. I think it's going to make us late."

Alex stared at Tom with incredulity. The crew, they didn't know.

"Actually Tom, I'm not here on a trip. I am on holiday with my family." Alex pointed back to his wife and two teenage boys standing by the door. "This outage isn't just for a few blocks Tom, it's the whole of the Eastern Seaboard. JFK is closed. Everywhere is closed, even the bridges and tunnels! Manhattan is cut off. You aren't going anywhere. If I were you, I would get your room back straight away before they sell it to someone else off the street."

"Are you sure?" Tom stared at him for a moment, but Alex's face remained grim. "OK, give me a minute Skipper, I need to tell our Captain."

Alex watched as Tom made his way back across the room and began speaking to his Captain. The heads turned towards Alex and another exchange took place. Tom made his way back to Alex with his Captain following.

"Captain Young, I'm Gerry Masters. I don't think we've met." Gerry had a firm handshake and was eyeing him up and down. "Tom tells me JFK is closed."

"Hi Gerry, Manhattan is closed! Have you tried ringing the airport? I don't think you will be getting any transport, the roads are 'chocker'. I have suggested to Tom that you secure the rooms just in case. If New Yorkers can't get home, they are going to be looking for hotel rooms." Alex spoke with authority and he knew Gerry that was taking him seriously.

Gerry went back to the hotel desk and began speaking with the hotel manager. The manager shrugged his shoulders, but then nodded intently. Gerry appeared to be giving him instructions, which in turn were passed on to his staff. The paperwork and plastic keys were all collected up and put to one side. The manager tried a phone, but then hung up. He then tried his cell phone, but that was dead too. The mobile phone companies had simply collapsed as every person in New York tried to ring out.

Alex knew that Gerry had to check the facts. The Captain's job carried a huge responsibility, which did not end when they got off of the aircraft. His duty was to get the aircraft away if that were at all possible but, if not, he had a duty of care to his crew. Word soon got around to the rest of the crew and they were busily discussing the problem. Their concerns varied from 'I need to get back' to 'will we get to keep our rooms?' or 'what could have happened for this failure to have occurred?'

Alex watched as the word went around from group to group. Some of the crew looked across at Alex, the messenger who had brought the unwelcome news. Could it be true? How could he know? The manager finally returned from the back office. It was true, he confirmed. Kennedy, La Guardia and Newark Airports were all closed. He had been unable to contact the airport, but he had got through on the landline to his sister hotel. Nothing was moving.

Apparently the governor of New York State, George Pataki, had declared a state of emergency while the New York City Mayor Michael Bloomberg had advised residents that they should open their windows, drink plenty of liquids in the heat, and not to forget their pets.

Captain Gerry Masters asked that the crew be given back their rooms immediately. The manager was nodding at the instructions, and Tom went off to tell the news to the CSD, the senior cabin crewmember. Alex looked back at his family, his expression begging for more patience. He had done his duty by the company, securing accommodation for this crew, but he still had no idea how they were going to get back to Brooklyn Heights.

One by one, the crewmembers queued up, re-signed a piece of paper and were issued a key. One or two of the cabin crew had recognised Alex and went over to speak to him. They asked him how he had come by the news and he explained about the fire fighters and their radio. He told them of his own dilemma - he was here with his own family with no way of getting back to Brooklyn. People drifted away, rescuing their suitcases from the hotel porters.

"Captain Young? How you doing? Colin Weslloski. We have done a couple of trips together. The last one was a Madras, about six months ago. A really good trip!"

"Hello Colin, good to see you again." Alex shook his hand and wondered how on earth this steward could not only remember him, but actually remember when and where the trip took place. He knew, of course, there was normally one Captain and perhaps fifteen cabin crew, so maybe that made it a little easier, but nevertheless... Alex remembered faces, but struggled to remember their names. He looked at the handsome young man now standing in front of him and certainly the face was familiar.

"Captain, I understand you don't have anywhere to stay?" Colin looked over at Alex's family, still frozen to the spot nearby.

"Yep, it's a problem! The hotel is apparently full, but we can't walk three hours in the dark." Alex smiled. "We'll sort it out."

"Well, I'm on married rosters with my girlfriend Pat," Colin explained. "We always take both rooms, in case we have an argument or one of us can't sleep. But the room is yours if you want it. I think we get smaller rooms than you. You can't really swing a cat in it, but you are welcome to it." He held out the key.

Alex stared down at the hand. Between the fingers of this young man was the solution to all his problems. He felt a confusing cocktail of emotions, but sought to control himself.

"Wow, Colin, I don't know what to say." He was visibly moved, but he now felt massive relief at the same time. "That's very generous Colin. Thank you!"

"No problem, sir." Colin simply turned and walked over to one of the stewardess. Together they looked around and smiled, the stewardess giving a slight nod of the head.

Alex squeezed the room key tightly in his fingers and turned towards his family. Three pairs of eyes were looking up at him in expectation. "We have a room!" he announced. "A steward has offered to double up with his girlfriend."

Carol let out a yelp of delight, while both boys grinned from ear to ear. All had understood the enormity and seriousness of their situation and Alex had come through for them. Alex found this sort of responsibility far more difficult than that of his job.

"James, here's some money." Alex thrust the US dollars into his hand. "There is a store just around the corner to the left. Take your brother and see if you can get some things. Er, some bottles of water, perhaps some toothbrushes in case the hotel hasn't got any. We won't need soap. Just get anything you think is necessary."

The two boys disappeared out of the hotel lobby and onto the street. It was beginning to get dark.

"Was that wise?" Carol asked. Her face carried concern for her children and relief for the room, all in one expression!

"Oh, they'll be alright. They've been really good, haven't they?" Alex put a hand on Carol's shoulder. "Darling, we've got a room! Yippee! Listen, can you go up and see what we need? Extra pillows, towels, that sort of thing. And could you see if the room phone is working. We should try and get a call to Margaret to let her know we are OK. I need to make sure there isn't a problem using this room. I'll sweet talk the manager!"

The manager explained that the room had been paid for by the company so provided the occupant was an employee of that company, he didn't really mind who occupied it. Alex realised the manager actually had a pile of much more important things to deal with and was not particularly bothered. For that, Alex was grateful. Carol had no success with the telephone; an operator had explained that all the outside lines appeared to be engaged. The boys returned with two carrier bags full of goodies. James had bought two torches and batteries, candles and matches, sweets and some soft drinks. The shop had not had toothbrushes, but the hotel was able to provide those.

The candles were placed on a windowsill in the bathroom and the family took it in turns to have a shower. It wasn't fun getting dressed in the clothes they had worn all day, but they were safe and well. Finally the candles were extinguished, the torches placed in pockets and the four of them walked down the seven flights of stairs. Small emergency lights lit the way, presumably run on batteries. They continued down to the basement level and stepped into the bar and restaurant area. To Alex's surprise the place was busy, bustling with people laughing and chatting about this remarkable day. Several gas lights burned by the bar and two barmen were busy serving customers in semi-darkness.

Just around the corner in the bar Alex found the crew. A little cheer rang out from several members of the crew as they recognised the family.

"Ah, you made it then Skipper." It was Colin, the steward who had so generously given up his room. Beside him sat his lovely girlfriend Pat. Alex concluded he, too, would give up his room to spend it with the stunning Patricia! About half of those present were ready for another round of drinks and Alex made his way to the bar.

In his absence the two boys searched for chairs, while Carol recounted the days adventure. How lucky were they, not to get stuck at the top of the Empire State Building! How fortunate that they had chosen to walk to Times Square rather than take the subway! What luck to find the Firehouse and hear the news on the radio! It had been inspirational that Alex thought about the crew hotel and lucky that the crew had actually been in the lobby at that very moment.

Alex returned with a tray of drinks. The group around table had just concluded that the Young family had experienced quite an adventure, but a lucky series of events had brought them here tonight. James had tried to argue for a beer, but this was the United States Alex had pointed out firmly, where James was two years shy of the legal drinking age of 21. It was an argument he had to repeat daily, but today he said it with humour and good grace.

The crew speculated about the possible causes of the blackout and its consequences. Was it sabotage, terrorism or just a bloody cock-up? The general consensus was that it must have had to be a series of terrorist attacks because of the area involved. Someone had heard that most of Canada, half of the United States and several other countries had been hit. Alex wondered how, without access to radio, televisions and telephones, these 'facts' could possibly be known, but he did not want to spoil the party.

Alex drank his beer very quickly. The temperature down in the bar area was already hot and sticky and, in the basement, there were no windows. The semi-darkness made the bar even cosier than normal. Alex watched as Carol, James and Andrew interacted with the crew exchanging stories, news and more speculation. The stories turned to what next. One stewardess, Alice, was distraught because she could not contact her babysitter to tell her she would be a day late. Alex wanted to tell her that he thought she would be extremely fortunate if they flew out tomorrow, given the scale of the problem, but thought better of it. At that moment Colin placed another beer in front of him. He picked it up and took a sip.

American beer was usually very cold and indeed his first beer had been cool and thirst-quenching. This beer was not warm, but…

"Guys," Alex said. "First of all, cheers! Secondly I think we are going to have to drink faster! The chillers are obviously off and the beer is going to get warm!"

"Bloody warm in here already!" someone said. Alex had been introduced to everyone, but now he could only remember a handful of names – Colin, the gorgeous Pat, the young mum Alice and the two pilots Tom and Gerry. Tom and Gerry! Alex wondered whether anyone had picked up on the fact their flight crew had the names of a cartoon cat and mouse! Best to say nothing, he thought.

The assembled group managed to get through another hour and several rounds of drinks before the heat became too unbearable and the beer simply too warm for consumption. Some crew members decided to call it a night, while some others decided to step outside and experience New York in darkness.

"Wow!" Andrew called loudly "Look at the sky!"

Everyone stopped in the road and stared upwards to the heavens. The sky was inky black and millions of stars twinkled overhead. Alex wondered if New York had ever even seen the stars before, since this city was normally emblazoned like a massive Christmas tree.

"Can we walk around the block?" James had asked. Alex had said yes, just before Carol was about to say no, so the two boys walked quickly away. The group, now down to about six people, stepped across the road for a better view. Alex sat down on the steps of the synagogue and leaned backwards. The tensions of the day had now entirely drained from his body. Margaret would guess that they had been stuck in the city. Alice's babysitter would hear about it on the news. The electricity would be back on soon and all would be well with the world.

Alex could not have known that the Northeast blackout, as it later became known, had affected large areas of the Northeast and Midwestern United States as well as the State of Ontario, in Canada. Thursday, August 14, 2003 would go down as the second most widespread blackout in history, affecting about forty-five million people in eight U.S. states, fourteen million of them in the New York area alone. The cascading failures of power plants across the North East, caused by high demand and overheated power lines, had resulted in a domino effect across a wide area. Inevitably a very angry public, and vociferous politicians, demanded to know 'how could this happen?' and 'how can we stop it happening again?'

"Dad, look what we've got!" Alex looked up to see his two teenage children holding two large carrier bags. "Beers!"

The boys had returned to the store around the corner, which had taken full advantage of the emergency. The prices of torches and batteries had increased five-fold. Even the price of the beers had doubled, but Alex did not care. They were even cold, having been tipped into a chest freezer amongst the spoiling, once frozen, peas and carrots. The boys handed them out to the group, who expressed thanks and admiration to the enterprising teenagers. Alex did not ask how they managed to buy them while under age, but assumed the storekeeper had given up asking for I/D in a darkened shop.

Alex gave the boys a nod and then raised his can to them as they gratefully opened their beers. Buying alcohol under age, drinking under age, drinking in public; Alex chuckled as he watched his boys enjoying the party. Carol was in deep conversation with one of the stewards, while sipping her beer from a can. He could not remember ever seeing Carol drinking beer from a can before, but this was a day of firsts. A day he would remember for a very long time!

Chapter 14: Going Wrong

Alex stepped off the ledge and felt himself falling. The air rushed passed him, loud in his ears. He remembered his childhood when he stuck his head out of the car window; the rush of the air had been similar. The roar in his ears grew ever deafening and the air was pounding the skin on his face. His clothing fluttered as it was buffeted by the wind. He was in free-fall, unyet he felt strangely calm as he continued his descent. Somewhere beneath him, far below, was the ground.

"Good morning Captain," said the voice. Alex looked all about him, but saw no one.

"I'm here," the voice said. Alex raised his head again and there, before him, was the face of an old man. "You look surprised," the old man smiled.

"Nothing surprises me anymore," Alex shouted with a sad, rather resigned tone to his voice. The old man seemed to be falling at the same speed as he was. Alex looked down beneath him, but he could see nothing.

"Perhaps you can't see it because of the mist," the old man said, stating the obvious. He looked down again. "Do you wonder how far it is to the bottom?"

"I'll know soon enough," Alex replied. He was thankful for the mist. All his life he had been afraid of heights, something that had amused others for as long as he could remember. 'But you're a pilot!' they would say. He would then sigh and begin again to explain the difference. 'In an aircraft, the floor of the aircraft is the ground,' he would expound, banging his foot as he did so. Several pilots he knew were also afraid of heights, which was why he reasoned, they were so safe! Very few people understood and now here he was – falling. But where was he falling from? He tried not to think about what he was falling towards!

This actually did seem extremely strange to him now, but he remained amazingly calm. There was no churning knot deep in his stomach, no sudden reflux burning a hole in his chest, nor a jelly-like weakness in his legs. There was no fear; just curiosity. He began to think back to how it all started.

"It started a long time ago," said the old man.

Alex looked startled. "What's that you say? How do you know what I am thinking?" he asked. "Can you read my mind?"

The old man chuckled. "I know what you are thinking," mused the old man, "but do you?"

Alex began to feel uneasy. What was happening and why? He was confused. The wind continued to rush against his face as he fell earthwards, but anxiety was beginning to seep into his body. It was not dying he was afraid of; it was the not knowing. It was not about where he was going; it was about where he had been. He remembered stepping off; off from somewhere. But where had that been?

"It doesn't really matter where you've been now, does it?" The old man stared straight at him, demanding an answer. "It's why you are here that matters and where you are going. Fancy a pilot being scared of heights!" The old man chuckled again at the thought, before looking down and pointing at the ground. "It may be misty, but the ground is still down there somewhere. Fancy another drink? Another bottle of wine perhaps?"

Alex just stared at the old man and wondered whether this was real or just in his mind. And, if it was in his mind, would it still hurt?

"Death and taxes, my friend." The old man sighed. "Have you ever noticed how people hardly ever speak of death? It's taboo, you know, yet it is the one certainty from the moment we are born. Some go prematurely; accidents, wars, those rather nasty illnesses. But, if you are lucky, you grow old. If you can count growing old as lucky, that is! Do you ever wonder how long you have left?" The old man pointed downwards. "Dare you speak about it now?"

Alex began to feel cold; so very, very cold.

"You watch the news and you read the newspapers!" the old man continued. "Someone famous dies every day and people speak with fondness about that person's achievements. Mostly, of course, it is old people but then you notice something different! He had a heart attack and he was only about fifty years old! That was your age at the time, do you remember? Then it gets worse. You become sixty! More announcements, more sad news; absent friends, remember? The age gaps narrows, but you pretend to ignore it. By the age of seventy, you become resigned to it as friends slowly begin disappearing around you. Will you be the last one left?"

For a moment Alex forgot about his free-fall. He suddenly became overwhelmed with emptiness; loneliness. It was not his own death he feared, but that of others. He felt alone, so very alone. Tears welled up inside him, with grief ripping at his insides; an unbearable sadness. That is why it is unspoken, he thought, it is too difficult to face. We build high walls around the cemeteries because we know that the flowers will also fade and then die. Left to decay and then they blow away on the wind. Dust to dust…

"So far, so good," teased the old man.

"What? What did you say?" Alex knew the ground must be down there somewhere and getting closer all the time. It was almost certainly racing up to meet him and he would eventually hit the ground. It was simply a matter of when. Strangely, there was still no fear. There was sadness tinged, perhaps, with disappointment and melancholy but no fear. He looked up as though a thought had just struck him, but no, there was no parachute. No, sadly that was not the answer.

"So far, so good," the old man repeated. "It doesn't hurt at the moment, does it?"

"Actually, it does," Alex replied. "It hurts very much." The old man looked at him curiously, as if examining his face for the first time.

"Ah, it hurts already!" the old man said. "Is that why you jumped?"

Suddenly the old man began falling faster than Alex, passing him on the downward plunge. He watched as the image, now below him, grew smaller fading into the mist below before finally disappearing completely. Just before the face disappeared, Alex had seen the Old Man's head tilted back, still staring back up at him. Those eyes, staring up and back towards him had looked unbearably sad.

"Tell me, did I jump?" Alex called down to the old man, every sinew tightening in his body. But now he was alone. Now he was afraid! "Why did I jump?" he screamed down into the mists below, but the old man had completely disappeared. There was only silence, save for the buffeting wind rattling in his clothes and face.

Suddenly there was a jolt, it was the sensation of a parachute opening, and Alex opened his eyes. He was shaking and sweating heavily. His heart was pounding very hard. He was lying in bed, hot and damp; but was it his bed? He moved his body slightly but his limbs felt very stiff and his fists were clenched incredibly tight. It was dark and he was still shaking as he tried to make out the room. It was inky black. There was no light and no sound, except for the blood coursing through his ears.

'Where am I?' he wondered.

"You're here,' whispered the voice of the old man.

Alex had woken up with a start. It was still dark and he felt confused and uncertain. His heart was racing and he was still shaking. He felt a tension, a real tightness in his body and he kicked off the covers. The room was unbearably hot. Had he been dreaming? What had startled him? He lay there for several minutes but he could not recall anything. He closed his eyes again and, breathing deeply, he drifted back into unsettled sleep.

It was early. Alex was only dozing, but now woken by two male nurses. They had helped him sit up and swung his legs out of the bed. They gave him a few seconds to get his breath, and then helped him to his feet. Carlos held his arm and guided him to the bathroom. It was then that Alex heard Bertrone pulling off the bedcovers and swearing behind him. There was a quick exchange in Spanish.

"That's a bloody lie!" Alex shouted, spinning around to look at Bertrone. Carlos held on to the old man's arm as best he could, but very nearly dropped him. For a moment Alex tried to wrestle free, but the strength was rapidly draining from his body. He was no match for the younger, stronger man.

"La cama está empapada. Él se orinó!" Bertrone repeated.

"That's a lie," yelled Alex indignantly. He began swinging his arms, but Carlos kept a firm hold.

"Es sudor, Bertrone. El anciano tiene fiebre." Carlos tried to pull Alex around towards the bathroom. "Callate y cambiar la cama!"

"Yes, it is sweat," Alex insisted, shouting angrily. "Do as he says Bertrone, keep quiet and strip the bed! Gracias Carlos, Gracias."

It took nearly an hour for Alex to go to the toilet, shave his face and then take an assisted shower. Carlos supervised, giving some privacy when necessary, but keeping a watchful eye on the old man.

'The old gentleman had some strength and might have stuck out had I not got a good hold of him,' Carlos thought to himself. This would need reporting, even if Bertrone had acted like an ass. Carlos had a family to feed and he would not hesitate to drop Bertrone in it, if it meant keeping his own job.

Carlos helped dress the old man, who could not reach down to his feet. How could such a man put on trousers, or his socks, or slippers he wondered?

"You are ready for the day, Capitán," Carlos stood up and made a point of admiring his patient. "Te ves muy bien," he said with an exaggerated wave. Before stepping out of the door he looked back and saw Alex staring silently through the window as usual.

How much time had passed, Alex could not tell. He had lost his watch and he found it very difficult to assess time. Five minutes, a day, a week, they all seemed the same to him. Sometimes he would tear his eyes away from the window and look at his home. Or was it his prison? He had no idea where he was or why he was here. He was a respected airline Captain, with someone to look after him.

Perhaps it was a hotel? He considered this carefully. He had spent much of his life in hotels all around the world. Some were breathtakingly beautiful, luxurious and decadent, while others were not much more than motel rooms, functional, but not much else. The location was important; there needed to be shops and something to do.

"Good morning, Captain." Maria breezed into the room as bright as usual. "Have we been a naughty boy today?" She smiled at him warmly.

"I'm sorry, Maria, I don't understand." He looked puzzled, his mind still full of hotels around the world.

"Is it possible you got a little angry today with Bertrone and Carlos?" Maria asked. The smile remained fixed and friendly.

Alex thought for a moment and tried to remember. There had been something. What was it? Had there been a bit of a flap? He thought of Carlos and felt warmth and kindness. Then he thought of Bertrone and suddenly his mood changed; he felt anger and hostility towards him. Then he remembered; the bed.

"It was nothing really, Maria." Alex smiled at his nurse who remained standing. "I had a fever and sweated heavily during the night. Bertrone said I had pissed in it and swore at me. I understand some Spanish Maria. He cannot talk to me like that!"

"Bertrone, he swore at you? What about Carlos?" she asked.

"Carlos is very kind, Maria. I like Carlos," he looked up and stared into that sweet young face. Maria gave nothing away except the compassion and warmth that came naturally to her.

"I will go and get the coffee Captain Young and, perhaps, some toast. Today we have the orange jam that you like. I will be back shortly." Maria saw no hostility in this old man, but a serious report had been made and it would have to stay on the file. She knew that the ramblings of an old man would not be taken seriously, but she also knew Carlos and she would establish exactly what happened. Then she would return for a story.

Life seemed sunny but, in those glorious and happy years of summer, Alex failed to see the grey skies that were forming on the horizon. Returning from a long flight, having spent a week or more away somewhere else in the world, created all sorts of problems. There was the tiredness, of course, often having been up flying through all of the night, followed by the long drive home. Then there was the jet-lag. Sometimes, arriving home mid-morning, Alex would fall into bed and grab a few hours sleep. To sleep for longer would be disastrous and would result in a night, sleepless, staring at the ceiling. So forcing himself up, still tired and exhausted, Alex sometimes found himself presented with a list of repairs, chores, bills to pay or letters to write.

However, it was in the evenings that the problems manifested themselves. Alex had mowed the large lawn and then spent an hour chopping wood. The bills and letters would have to wait – sometimes he felt so tired he could barely remember his own name, let alone fill in a cheque! Finally he slumped onto the settee and switched the TV on. He flicked through the channels, looking for something he and Carol could watch. Something light and simple. Carol had told him dinner would be in thirty minutes, so he settled for the BBC News.

Sure enough, thirty minutes later, a tray arrived offering fish in a white sauce, with peas and wild rice. The meals were always nicely presented. Alex took the tray gratefully and thanked his wife.

"What would you like to watch?" he asked.

"Oh, watch what you want," Carol said. "I'm out to aerobics tonight. I'll be home about ten thirty." She bent down, kissed the top of his head, and then walked from the room.

Alex was too tired to say or do anything else, other than lift the fork and begin eating his meal. He continued to flick through the channels. He rejected the sitcom on ITV; he just didn't find it funny. BBC 1 had a nature programme about insects, ants and beetles, while BBC 2 had an investigation called "A Life on the Dole". It featured a family about the single mother had never worked, but had lived on a lifetime of social security handouts. Now her seventeen year old and unmarried daughter, the eldest of five, had given birth to a baby girl and was demanding a council house of her own. Alex watched as the family watched DVD movies on their wide-screen TV, demanding the Government do more. He could stand it no more and changed channels again.

Finally he selected a film about two hapless police officers in Los Angeles. He had seen it before, but there was nothing else that could keep his attention. He moved the now empty tray onto the floor and slowly slipped lower and lower into the armchair. He felt his head drop and pushed himself higher into the seat. He stared ahead and saw that the final credits were passing up on the television screen in front of him. He had been asleep for about two hours and was now feeling worse than ever. After an extensive search he finally found the remote control on the carpet. He switched off the TV and picked up his dinner tray. As he wandered slowly towards the kitchen, he tried to remember how many days off he had this time around. He climbed the stairs to the bathroom, cleaned his teeth and fell into bed. A pile of untidy clothes lay beside him as he drifted swiftly off to sleep.

The next morning he awoke to find the bed empty beside him. Downstairs there was a crash and rattle as if someone had put all the plates and cups into the tumble drier, instead of the dishwasher. He slowly sat upright, found his slippers, and pulled on his dressing gown. He staggered out of the bedroom and went straight into the bathroom for a pee. Feeling only a little better, he slowly descending the stairs to the kitchen.

"Hi." Carol looked up from the dishwasher, where she was noisily rearranging the entire contents so that two extra cups might be accommodated. "Had to sleep in the guest room last night, you were snoring so loudly!"

Alex raised a hand in apology and staggered towards the kitchen table. His head was pounding through sheer tiredness. He needed a cup of tea.

"Tea?" Carol asked. After thirty years of marriage it was no longer necessary to ask. She placed a pile of letters in front of him and then turned to switch on the kettle.

Alex attempted to focus on the first letter, but his eyes were not yet working. Or maybe they were and it was his tired brain that was malfunctioning. Either way he still could not read the envelope even though it was his own name and address he was staring at.

"I do this job for the glamour," he muttered.

"I thought you did it for the money," she said sarcastically.

"Well someone has to pay all the bills." He retorted while shuffling the envelopes into a new order, but that didn't seem to help.

"There's a list of all the phone calls under that pile," she said. Carol was very well organised and each phone call included a date and time. "Oh, and the boys shower still isn't working properly. You promised you would fix it."

Alex nodded his head in acknowledgement, as a cup of tea was place on the table in front of him. He cupped his hands around the mug, but it took a few seconds before the heat began to scold his fingers. He did have some feeling in his body after all.

Following a long hot bath Alex set about fixing the boys shower. He switched off the electrics and stripped down the box. He was amazed the thing had water flowing through it at all; it was totally caked with lime scale. A failed attempt to clean it convinced him it would need replacing. More money and a trip to the shops; great!

By late afternoon Alex sat at his desk reading the list of chores he had been given. The new shower had been purchased and was now fully installed. All he had needed to do was attach the existing pipes and electrical wiring that had be connected to the old shower heater.

Wrong! He had even bought the same make but, incredibly, the manufacturers had decided to update the whole bloody thing by re-arranging its contents. Now the water supply needed to come in bottom left instead of bottom right. Now that could be corrected by moving the shower casing further right on the wall, but then the 6mm electrical cable would not reach. Bugger! Piss! Why was nothing ever easy?

Still, it was done. And he had cut the front lawn and he had cleared out the greenhouse for Carol's seedlings. Why couldn't she weed it herself? Creating the perfect environment for growing plants also made it the perfect place to grow weeds; hundreds of them!

Still Alex enjoyed physical work. You didn't have to think about it, just do it. Tomorrow his brain would have recovered enough for him to do the other chores, check the accounts and pay the bills. He was tired, but he could not sleep now. It was much too early. It was now late afternoon and he threw the list onto the desk and moved to the lounge and sat in front of the TV. Carol walked in with another tray.

"You're not going out again tonight, are you?" he asked. The tray was thrust into his hands.

"No! But I've got several hours of Eastenders to watch. I'll sit in the other room." Carol turned to go.

"Why didn't you watch it while I was away?" The volume of both their voices was steadily increasing and Alex knew he should shut up now.

"Because I was busy doing other things. Who you think does all the work around here? Who does your washing and cooks your food? Who drives the boys around ten times a day?" Carol stormed from the room.

Alex stabbed at his food. He continued the argument in his head and still lost every one of them!

The old man looked up. Maria was sitting there, quietly listening to his story. How could she understand? She is so young. How could he tell her how or why people drift apart when, the truth was, he did not fully understand it himself?

This person who had been his best friend, lover and wife now took him completely for granted. He had taken her away on trips, of course, and she had loved going out with the crew and having fun. They would have a nice meal, see some of the sights and perhaps go dancing. They would have lots of fun.

After a trip like that Carol would be tired and jet-lagged. But she had sat in a comfortable seat on the aircraft, drank a glass of champagne and watched a movie. Alex, of course, was working and flying the plane. She would probably have slept on the aircraft and still be exhausted. It would take her a week to recover from the jet lag! He, meanwhile, would sometimes only have a few days off at home before going back to work again.

"Remember how you feel now," Alex would say to her. "That's how I feel all of the time."

"Yeah, but you are used to it," she would say, dismissively.

"No! You never get used to it; you just learn how best to put up with it," he would reply a few decibels louder. It was so frustrating, why could she not understand?

"Well, you're probably tired because you were out partying half the night," she would say.

Then, there was a second, more insidious, problem. Over time Carol had begun creating her own life and she would find time to meet up with her friends or sometimes their friends. She would have her own routines, before settling down to a good book or an evening of television. Carol enjoyed the life she had created, but eventually she began to resent the disruption Alex caused by coming home at the end of a trip. Over the years 'her' world had become more attractive than 'their' world."

Cracks had begun to appear. Little arguments slowly became big arguments. They were disagreeing, more and more, on so many issues.

How dare he come home and suggest how she bring up the children! How dare he come home on the night when her best TV programme was on! How dare he come home at all!

Eventually the cracks grew too wide. Attempts to paste over those cracks proved futile; they had become fissures. They had tried marriage counselling, but the damage was already done.

"It's not working" Alex had said.

"No," she had conceded.

"Perhaps we should separate," Alex had suggested. There, he had said it.

"I think that is a good idea," she had replied without even hesitating or any further consideration. No argument at all!

Alex had been rather surprised at how 'matter a fact' Carol had sounded. After seemingly disagreeing on so many things, they had suddenly found something they could finally agree on.

"We managed to have an amicable separation and divorce," Alex told Maria. "We even stayed friends, and why not? After all, it had been a good marriage for many, many years. There had been so many happy times. It was just time, Maria. It was just time."

Maria smiled and stood up, but said nothing. He watched in disbelief as she walked towards the door. Had he offended her? Had he been too personal about his life? She opened the door and stepped from the room without even looking back.

'Extraordinary,' he thought. 'Most extraordinary!'

Chapter 15: Masami

"Good morning Captain!"

"Good morning Maria," the old man raised his head and smiled.

A male nurse had been in first and Alex had been given a wonderful bath and then a shave. There were several male nurses and Alex could never get to grips with their names. Carlos, Juan, Bertrone, none of them were particularly good with their English. He thought it was a complete disgrace! Still he was clean and dressed and ready for his coffee.

Maria rearranged the coffee cups and biscuits on the tray as usual. It was a ritual that she engaged in every morning and Alex watched her with interest. It reminded Alex of the Japanese Tea Ceremony. And that reminded him of Masami.

It was during the summer of his life that Alex Young met Masami. It was a strange time because he had always feared loneliness and now he had the perfect opportunity to meet people during his travels around the world. His aircraft would have a crew of fifteen or more, some he might have flown with before, but usually they were strangers. Some would remain strangers. At some destinations there would be several different crews staying there, somewhere else in the duty cycle. Some might be on their first rest day, some could be on their second. Some might be flying northbound, back to Europe, while others might be heading south, perhaps to Australia.

There were few opportunities to meet people actually on the aircraft. Alex would make a point of walking around the aircraft cabin before the passengers boarded, in order to say a personal 'hello' to all the crew members, but there were checks to be done and he could not linger. At a quiet time during the flight, he might go and stretch his legs in the cabin, but he could never be away from the flight deck for very long. Obviously he would choose a suitable time when the meal service had been completed and the passengers had either settled down to sleep or were watching a movie, but the crew would still need to attend to the passengers' needs. On very long flights the crew were allocated a rest break, taking it in turns to snatch a short sleep, hopefully making them fresher in the morning!

It was on one such flight to Narita, Japan, that Captain Alex Young left his First Officer to monitor the aircraft, record the flight, check the fuel, navigate the way and make the radio calls. There was just enough to do to make sure the pilot would not get bored! Alex put on his jacket, sporting his flying wings and the braided four stripes on his arms to indicate who he was. There was a name badge, too, for those who did not recognise the trimmings of power. The uniform was his camouflage, his shield, his protection.

The cabins were all dark, with just a low light. The occasional passenger would look up from his or her video screen and it was not unknown for some smart ass to ask who was flying the aircraft! He would smile and nod and most passengers were content with that. At the top of the stairs, a steward called Lawrence looked up from his crossword.

"Hello, Captain, would you like a cup of tea?" Lawrence put his crossword down.

"No thanks," Alex shook his head. "I'm just going to stretch my legs."

"Where are we then?" Lawrence asked.

"Siberia," Alex replied, "not far from the Arctic Circle. We've got Novosibirsk way to the south of us, Yakutsk off to our left in a few hours and then Khabarovsk about breakfast time."

"Blimey, a Captain who knows where he is!" Lawrence joked. Lawrence was old school; confident, efficient and respectful. "Usually they tell me to look at the moving map!"

"I only know because I checked just before I came out from the flight deck," Alex smiled. "We navigate by waypoints and airways, not always by cities and the lakes." Lawrence already knew this, of course, having heard it all before.

"Well, I'm popping downstairs," Alex said and tiptoed quietly down the steps. A stewardess was emptying a carton of orange juice into plastic cups as he stepped past the galley. She looked up and nodded towards him. Alex nodded back and pushed his way through the curtain down towards the back of the aircraft. It was much darker here; almost everybody was asleep. Someone was using a laptop in one corner, and a blue-white light reflected on the luggage racks above. Alex peered down ahead of him in the dark. Sometimes, the odd passenger had the habit of stretching their legs into the aisle. It was very unedifying to see the Captain sprawled on the floor and therefore being tripped up was best avoided.

Alex stepped through the next curtain and into the next galley. Standing, making a green tea for a Japanese woman passenger, was Masami. The airline employed National cabin crew on certain routes where language and culture demanded it. On the flight tonight, three of the cabin crew were Japanese based in Tokyo. Masami handed the tea to the old lady, smiled kindly at her and then helped her through the curtain. She then turned back to Alex and gave a slight bow of the head.

"Good morning Captain, would you like a cup of tea?" Masami tilted her head slightly and smiled.

"That would be very nice. Do you think I could have a normal tea? With milk?"

"Normal tea?" Masami giggled. "Ah, English tea. Hi!" The point was made. What was normal to the Japanese was very different from what was normal for the British.

Alex leaned over and snatched a glance at the name badge on her uniform. He had walked around the cabins when they first boarded the aircraft and shaken the hand of every single crewmember as usual. He had introduced himself to each person as Alex but each, in turn, offered their hand, said their name and then the words 'Hello Captain.' Occasionally someone might say 'Skipper' but rarely did anyone respond with his Christian name.

"Would you like to sit down Captain?" Masami offered a fold down double seat.

"That would be very nice," Alex smiled at her and sat down. Masami handed him the English white tea and then sat down herself with a Jasmine tea. "Masami is a lovely name," he said. "What does it mean?"

"It means elegant beauty," Masami blushed and immediately changed the subject. "Do you have any plans for Narita Captain?" she asked politely.

"Sleeping, eating and drinking, Masami," he said, blowing on his hot tea. "Then maybe a little more sleeping!" Masami giggled in polite acknowledgement of his joke. She knew Japan was a very tiring and punishing trip and each crew member battled with the fatigue in their own way. "And what will you be doing on your days off Masami?"

"I will also sleep!" she smiled. "Then I will visit my friends. And I have college."

"You have college? What are you studying?" he asked. He sipped his tea and checked at his watch.

"I am learning how to make tea!" Masami raised her own cup and took a sip. This time she had a huge grin on her face.

"You're learning how to make tea?" Alex teased. "I must tell them you have already passed the test, Masami!" He raised his cup and took another sip. "Ummm, yummy."

"No, I am learning the Japanese Tea Ceremony. It is a very important part of our Japanese culture. I learn about the history, the tradition and the special techniques; it is very symbolic to us." Masami remained polite but assertive.

"I mean no disrespect Masami," Alex was half-apologising. "It sounds very interesting. I confess I know very little about such things."

Masami sat quietly and looked at Alex. He needed to get back to the flight deck and extricate himself from this minor diplomatic incident.

"Would you like to see the Japanese Tea Ceremony?" Masami asked.

Alex wasn't sure what to say. If he said no, she might consider it rude. If he made a joke about it he might insult Masami and even perhaps the entire Japanese nation. He needed to get back to the flight deck.

"That would be very nice," Alex smiled and made to stand up. Masami stood up first.

"You will sleep most of today; perhaps tomorrow? I could pick you up at your hotel. Five o'clock in the afternoon?" Masami stared directly at him, looking a little serious.

Alex's heart sank. "That would be very nice," he smiled. "Five o'clock on Thursday. I will see you then Masami." She reached out and shook his hand.

"Bugger!" he muttered to himself as he made his way back to the flight deck. He had dug himself a hole and had fallen straight into it. He was not at all interested in Japanese tea-making, ceremony or no ceremony. He'd seen a few Japanese movies, of course, 'Shogun', 'Madame Butterfly' (was that Japanese?), and the 'Seven Samurai' but the culture was a difficult one for him. He didn't even get Karaoke.

"Sorry I was so long," he apologised as he took off his jacket and climbed back into his seat. He checked the fuel, their location and the next reporting point. He would talk to Masami tomorrow after their arrival in Narita. She probably had better things to do with her time anyway!

Alex pressed the ground floor button in the lift and the doors closed. He watched as the numbers counted down. The door opened and he walked around the corner to reception. Masami saw him coming and stood up, smiling broadly. She was clearly pleased to see him.

"You're here!" she beamed.

"Of course, I'm here." Alex shook the outstretched hand and smiled back at her. He had simply not been able to bring himself to cancel the appointment. Recriminations bounced around his head all day between fitful sleep and he finally got up and showered with the customary grit in his eyes. He had been out with a few of the crew the previous evening, eaten some Tamagoyaki or Japanese omelette, with rice, and washed it down with a couple of Ashari beers. He was back in his room by midnight, feeling fatigued, but knowing sleep would be impossible. He had slept for most of the day and he knew he was now facing a long night. There was only so much CNN Business Asia News one could take. Finally sleep had arrived at dawn.

Now here he was still in the middle of a handshake, in the lobby, desperate for a beer and not tea!

"Shall we go?" Masami led the way. Alex was over six foot tall, so most people seemed short to him. Masami was slim and probably a little taller than average by Japanese standards, and nicely fitted the tight designer jeans she was wearing. She wore a white blouse and he tried hard not to stare at her bra straps as he followed her to the door. They stepped outside and walked across the car park to a black Japanese sports car. Alex wondered if he would actually fit inside it. It looked brand new and smelt of leather on the inside. There was much more leg room than he imagined, although his hair was brushing against the roof. He pushed himself down a little lower in the seat.

"Nice car!" Alex said approvingly. Masami nodded proudly, smiled broadly and thanked him in Japanese, but repeated an English 'thank you' afterwards. She was nervous.

"So where are we going?" Alex asked quietly, trying to keep the conversation going.

"You will see," she replied. She started the car and pulled out of the car park and onto the road. The car had a gentle growl, rather like a leopard.

"Very nice car," he confirmed.

Alex was familiar with the first fifteen minutes of the journey. They were heading into town, following the route taken every two hours by the hotel bus. The traffic was heavy, so many people driving home from work or into town for the evening. Masami asked what Alex had done today.

"I had a bit of sleep and watched the news. I tried reading, but it was difficult to concentrate." In fact, Alex hadn't even opened his book and immediately regretted saying it. Little lies lead to big lies.

The conversation was largely made up of small talk. They spoke about the traffic and the weather. Masami had had a quiet day catching up on things. Then the car swung north and away from the city. Soon they were in a small suburb with little traditional houses, surrounded by postage stamp paddy fields. The farmers would plant these little fields that were surrounded by small dykes and drainage ditches, in order to control the level of water. How on earth you could make a living in this vast industrial economy, one of the largest in the world, with little plots of rice paddies was completely beyond Alex. Gradually the silences between the conversations grew longer, but Alex no longer felt the need to fill them. Perhaps he was too tired.

They turned into a dimly lit narrow road, with no pavement, but houses lined the street on both sides. Some of the houses had decorative lights while others stood dark and empty. Masami gently brought the car to a halt outside one darkened house and switched off the engine.

"Here we are," she smiled.

Alex looked around at the dark street. There were no cafes and no restaurants here as far as he could see. "Where are we?" he asked.

"This is where I live," Masami smiled.

Alex climbed out of the car. The area was completely silent, save for the grasshopper-like cicadas clicking away so loudly in the undergrowth. Dark hills flanked the farmland that backed onto the road. It was like a little oasis in the desert, with nobody home. Masami locked the car and walked towards the gate. There was a short path to the front door and Alex followed. She unlocked the door and entered. There was no hallway and they stepped straight into the traditional sitting room. Masami bent down and took off her shoes. Alex took his off too.

"It's beautiful," Alex said, still admiring the reddish-brown mahogany furniture, completely free from dust. It was like going into a cultural museum, but where all the items were brand new.

"Please, sit here." Masami pointed to a corner where scatter cushions lay on the floor and against the wall. Alex sat down and pulled himself backwards onto the cushions; they were surprising comfortable. Masami disappeared into another room. She returned with a glass on beer, with condensation dripping down the outside of the glass.

"Here's something to be getting on with," she said. "I'm sure you are very thirsty."

"Thank you, Masami," he beamed. He took a sip of the ice-cold beer and leaned back on the cushions. Masami gave another little nod and then scurried from the room. In the centre of the room was a table, but it was low to the floor. Rectangular cushions acted as little chairs around the sides. He sipped his beer very slowly and waited for the kettle to boil. No, that was cruel!

Masami was obviously taking this very seriously and he should not laugh at her or her traditions. He had expected to be taken to a tea house or some sort of café. He never dreamed Masami would take him to her house. Either she was rich, or extremely well paid, as everything looked so perfect. He wondered if there was another room with a television, computer and a telephone. Maybe she would return and press a button and walls would swivel James Bond style to reveal a more modern Japanese lifestyle.

Alex's beer was getting dangerously low despite his very best attempts to drink it slowly. An empty glass might be offensive, so he put it to one side lest he drink the remainder. Strong willpower and alcohol did not sit well together. A door then slid open and Masami walked back into the room. Alex was stunned. She was standing there in a beautiful Kimono, her hair set on top of her head, a large wooden pin holding it securely. She had elaborate little slippers on with tiny decorations adorning them. She had put on a different kind of make-up and just looked completely stunning. Alex stood up.

"Wow," he said. "You look..., you look magnificent!"

Masami smiled, or was it a blush? "You will sit here, please?" She took him by the hand and led him to the little table. "You can sit or kneel."

Alex's heart sank. He had been into restaurants before where they had similar tables to this and he had always found it incredibly uncomfortable. He could not get his long legs under the table and sitting cross-legged was not very easy for him. He was tall and lanky and, quite simply, built differently! He chose to kneel on the cushion placing his hands on his knees.

Masami shuffled back out to the kitchen and Japanese music began filling the room from unseen speakers. Within moments, Masami had returned with a tray, highly decorated, with what must have been the teapot and some cups. The teapot was small, while the cups looked more like dishes. Masami knelt down majestically and poured the water. It was steaming hot and, to Alex's great surprise, completely clear.

Masami reached across the table and asked for Alex's right hand. She then took a cloth, dipped in the water, and began washing his fingers and his hand. She then took his left hand and repeated the process. Her actions were gentle and felt extremely erotic. She poured more water and Alex hoped he would not have to drink it! She rose effortlessly from the floor, taking the tray with her. A large piece of material was tied tightly around her waist and he wondered how she could possibly breathe. She left the room for a moment and, shortly after, returned with a new tray.

Again she sat down as if supported by strings. It was a far more elegant teapot and the cups were wide with gold rims. He watched as she wiped just one side of bowl with tea, before turning the bowl through one hundred and eighty degrees. She then wiped the other side. She was reciting something in Japanese and he just sat and watched her lips move. They were rich with lipstick and he felt the urge to kiss them. He felt sure the opportunity would come, but this was probably not the moment. Finally she raised the dish, almost in prayer, and then lowered it again and poured in the liquid. She picked it up with two hands and reached out to Alex. He placed his hands together, palms up, balancing the sides with his fingers. He looked at her and she gestured for him to raise the bowl to his lips.

Alex raised the bowl slowly and solemnly, looking at her face the whole time. He doubted that this was ever intended to be a sexual experience but, as his lips met the rim of the bowl, and he took the tea, he imagined his lips against hers. He didn't have religion, but he felt religion and all the cynicism melted away. The tea tasted good, the droplets warming in his mouth and almost melting before slipping down his throat. He felt a warmth in his body and wondered what was physiological and what was psychological. Either way he was completely absorbed. He placed the bowl on the tray and waited. He wasn't sure what he should do next, but he was seriously considering the option of taking Masami in his arms, kissing her, and carrying her into the bedroom.

At that moment the entrance door opened. Masami looked up, smiled and said something in Japanese. She rose effortlessly to her feet and bowed in the direction of the door. Alex instinctively rose too and turned to see an elderly couple standing there smiling. He bowed at them.

"Alex, may I introduce my parents." Masami raised her arms to present them and then introduced Alex to them in Japanese. He was unsure whether to shake their hands and so bowed again. There appeared to be confusion as they closed the door and walked across to another room, removing their coats as they went. There were lots of exchanges, backwards and forwards, between Masami and the new arrivals. Alex wondered whether there was a problem explaining who on earth this western stranger was taking tea in their house.

"My parents wish to confirm you are staying for dinner. They would consider it a great honour to have you as their guest." Masami explained.

"Their guest? Is this their house?" Alex was completely taken aback by this turn of events. "I thought it was your house, Masami."

"It is the family home. It is my house and it is their house. Will you stay?" Masami looked up at him and put her hands on his chest. He was conscious of the physical contact and stared back down at her.

"Of course," Alex said. It was impossible to say no to her and, anyway, what possible excuse could he now invent.

Actually, dinner went off surprising well. Despite the language difficulties, the group laughed and joked and patiently waited as Masami translated in one direction or another. Sake was offered with the meal and there were numerous toasts and refills. Masami's father seemed determined to finish the bottle. Then Brandy was produced, an expensive one venerated for its age, but consumed with the same gusto as the sake. Alex's legs had long since gone to sleep underneath him as everyone rose from the low table.

"I should go. I can get a taxi back," suggested Alex. He was not used to drinking spirits, although wobbly dead legs proved to be a more honourable excuse.

"Taxi very difficult," Masami whispered back to him. "My parents have said they would like you to stay here as their guest. It is expected."

Alex acquiesced easily. Both parents came to him and shook his hand, each bowing their head like a slow nod.

"Arigatou gozaimasu" He said clumsily, but they seemed pleased with his Japanese thank you. He watched as they shuffled off to their bed, giggling to one another. Masami led Alex to a door, which slid effortlessly sideways to reveal a small bedroom. The bed appeared to be a mattress on the ground, but there was little else in the room. The walls had a translucent quality, with Japanese flowers and exotic birds painted on stretched paper. The door slid closed and Masami was gone.

'What a strange evening,' Alex thought. 'And with the parents coming back like that!' He was now unsure whether the parents had interrupted something, or whether the sexual tension that had built up was only in his imagination. He quietly undressed, climbing naked into the silk sheets. The pillow was a little low, but otherwise the bed was surprising comfortable. Japanese hotel beds tended to be on the hard side, but this felt like heaven. He lay there, staring at the ceiling, listening to the low whispering of the parents, who he guessed were next door. He was drifting nicely when he remembered the light. The light switch was behind his head, conveniently low to the floor. He lay in the darkness and planned his day tomorrow. 'More sleep,' he thought.

It was then that he heard the sound of the door at the end of the bed sliding open again. He peered down towards his feet and saw Masami standing in the doorway. She was silhouetted by a back-light, a faint orange glow from the sitting room. She was naked. He held his breath and looked at her in wonder. The kimono was gone and her hair released over her shoulders. She stepped into the room and closed the door behind her. There was darkness. Masami slipped in between the sheets and placed a hand upon his chest, caressing him. Alex turned and pulled the body towards him. Her skin felt cool and smooth against his. Their lips met in a passionate embrace and his hands began exploring her back, slowing moving down across her buttocks. He pulled her tight towards him. She gasped loudly.

"Masami," Alex whispered. He released his grip on her body.

"Yes?" Masami whispered back. "Is there something wrong?"

"I think your parents are next door. I think the walls are very thin."

Alex had his lips close to her ear, speaking as quietly as he could.

"Well, yes, of course. That is their bedroom. The walls are made of paper." Masami seemed very matter of fact about the whole thing.

"Masami, I can't do this with your parents lying just a few yards away, with just a paper wall between us. I'm very sorry." Alex caressed her affectionately and gave her a little kiss. In his imagination he imagined the parents holding their breath, wondering why there were no longer signs of passionate grunting.

"Please, do not be sorry Alex. It is not necessary." Masami whispered gently. She just lay there, very still in his arms. There was not a sound in the house, although Alex was sure he could hear his own heart pounding. He could just about hear Masami's breathing and he knew she was still awake. He wanted to explain, but such a conversation would be impossible. The parent's might not speak English, but they might understand the tone of such a conversation. What an evening! Had he offended Masami, and her parents, all in one go? His conscience battled with his dilemma until sleep finally overcame him.

The next morning Alex woke up uncertain about where he was. He felt the silk blankets and realised a woman was lying in his arms. He turned to see Masami lit by the sun that was streaming through cracks in the window blinds. She was awake and staring at him with those wide, beautiful eyes.

"Good morning," she said smiling quietly. "Did you sleep?"

"I did," he admitted. "What time is it?"

"It's early. You have plenty of time," Masami ran her hands across his chest provocatively. He wanted her so much. "My parents asked me to say they are very sorry, but they had to go out very early this morning. We are alone."

"Well, that was very nice of them" Alex grinned. "Are they likely to be back soon?"

"My parents are very understanding," Masami smiled. "They will not be back." She reached up, touched his lips with her fingers and then kissed him. As they embraced, she pulled at his body. The two bodies intertwined and were soon moving as one.

Alex never ever saw Masami again. Masami had cooked them breakfast and made coffee. She had driven him back to his hotel and they had chatted non-stop. They spoke about the job, the airline and the lifestyle. They had talked much about the tea ceremony, with Alex enthusing on the entire ritual. They spoke about dinner and her lovely parents, so relaxed, polite and strangely acquiescent. They both agreed they had had a wonderful evening and a magical morning. Masami blushed as Alex told her how beautiful she was. He did not mention the amazing sensuality that had so captivated him. Outside the hotel e-mail addresses were exchanged. She did not get out of the car, so he reached across from the passenger seat and kissed her. It all seemed so natural.

Yet all his emails went unanswered. Alex flew back to Japan several times during the next few months always hoping Masami would be part of the crew. He considered searching for her house, but knew it would be like looking for a needle in a haystack. Finally he abandoned the total discretion associated with such events and asked another Japanese crewmember if she knew how Masami was. There had been a cull, she said. The airline had decided to save money by reducing the National base in Japan and a number of crew had been made redundant. Masami had left the airline.

"I often think of her," Alex said.

"Ah, you've woken up!" Maria said. "You've been sleeping. Who is she, who do you think of?"

"Masami," the old man frowned. He blinked his eyes.

"Ah, well you were too tired to tell me a story today," Maria smiled sympathetically. "Another day you can tell me all about Masami."

The old man closed his eyes again and stared into the dark blackness behind his eyelids. A small light remained at their centre and it was there that Alex stared at the twinkling silhouette of Masami, her naked body lit from behind by the light from the sitting room.

"I've come back," she said gently, stepping into the room and climbing under the silk sheets. "I will never leave you again."

"I thought I'd lost you," Alex whispered.

"No, you silly man! I am still here, where I shall always be - in your thoughts."

Chapter 16: Meeting Laura

"Good morning Captain," Maria's smiling voice sounded so musical. "I hope I have not kept you waiting."

Alex was leaning against the chair back, practising standing on his feet. Too much of his time was spent either in bed or sitting in that bloody chair. He needed to go for more walks, he thought. Those hills in the distance looked very inviting. He had suggested to Maria that they should make a day of it, perhaps even taken a picnic. Maria had apologised and said she wasn't really up to walking. She had stood at the window and said she thought the hills looked far too challenging for her. Another time perhaps, when she was fitter?

Alex shifted his gaze from the window and turned to smile at his nurse. She was small but pleasantly elegant and, as usual, her eyes were smiling brightly. He inhaled quietly at this breath of fresh air.

"You haven't kept me waiting?" Alex smiled. "Maria, I have spent half my life waiting for women! If I was to add up every the minute I had spent waiting for my wife and was given them back, I would be half my age!"

"I am so sorry Captain. I had a meeting; so many things to do." Maria apologised again, making it impossible to be cross. In all honesty Alex found it hard to follow time. He rarely looked at his watch these days (where was his watch?) and only the hospital routine gave him any indication of the time. Even the sunrises and sunsets were often a blur to him. Sometimes the days seemed so very long and the nights fleeting while, at other times, it was the nights that felt endless.

"Your wife, she kept you waiting. No?" Maria asked.

"My wife, she kept me waiting – Yes, yes! Always! How long did I spend, standing at the door, waiting to leave? We would have somewhere to be, but there was always something else to put away, something to wash up, or something to find. Ten minutes here and half an hour there; if I was to add up all that time..." Alex looked up with his tired, old eyes and smiled. "Sometime we would decide it was time for bed; and perhaps we had been watching television. We would switch it off and I would go to the bathroom, wash and clean my teeth. Lying in bed I would hear the washing up being done. Then my wife would go into the bathroom and wash her face. It could take Laura 30 minutes, or more, to get ready for bed. Thirty minutes! Once I got up because she was taking so long and found she was washing the kitchen floor. It was about one o'clock in the morning!"

Maria smiled at the thought of such a thing.

"If I went to bed straight away, I would be asleep by the time she climbed between the sheets. I tried staying up, but I would then fall asleep in the chair, waking up later in the dark, in the middle of the night!" Alex was smiling as he complained. "I even tried doing the washing up myself, but then she would find something else to do. Leave it until morning, I would say, leave it until the morning!"

"I remember we had somewhere to be. We had got ready and I had reminded Laura we had to leave in fifteen minutes; then in ten minutes; then in five minutes. I told my wife I would turn the car around and sat there with the engine running. I sat there for ages and ages, but she did not come out. When I went back into the house, she was puffing up cushions and putting away magazines. We were always late!"

Alex tried to look cross, but could only smile again. He slapped his thigh. "It was exasperating Maria, but I did wait. Why? Because it was worth it! She was worth it! Of course it would annoy me on end, but I was blessed with a good life, a wonderful wife, and if I had to wait… Well, of course I would be cross. Sometimes I would be impatient. Often we would be late. It might not always have seemed so at the time, but perhaps the wait was worth it."

"Your wife must have been really special," Maria suggested.

"Special? Ah Maria, my wife could be irritating, frustrating, difficult and be wonderful, all at the same time. It drove me mad! My time with her made me so happy. Whether we were out with friends, or sitting alone together at home, the time was special. Often there were unspoken moments, just a smile or a look across a room." Alex paused and swallowed hard, tears welling up in his eyes.

How he missed her. He opened his mouth to speak, but no words would come. He stared across the room, but his vision had become blurred. He did not see that Maria had turned away to look out of the window. This was a private thing and she wanted to give him a moment to recover himself. He took a deep breath, but still the words would not come.

"The grapes will be good this year," she said. She often used this if she felt it necessary to begin or divert a conversation. Alex blinked, the tears fell down his cheeks and he squinted towards the window.

"It has been a fine year," he heard himself say. "Just enough rain, but not too much. It has been a fine season." He was talking again. He continued to stare out of the window and then whispered quietly; "I miss her." The tears welled up even more and he may even have sobbed.

Maria stood up slowly. "I think it is time for our coffee. What do you think, my Captain?" She did not wait for an answer, but moved towards the door. Only then did she turn, pausing to say "The cook has made a special cake today. Perhaps, if I am quick, there will be some left. I will only be a moment."

Alex watched her go, and then wiped his eyes. He continued to look out of the window, thinking about his wife, and the grapes, and then his wife again. Memories filled his mind; so many happy memories.

Alex had been a new young co-pilot sitting at the controls, on the flight deck of an aircraft, on the ground at Glasgow Airport, in Scotland. The checks were now complete and he was thinking about the three sectors they would be flying today. He had flown with this Captain before and he knew he would enjoy the day. Behind him the aircraft cabin was empty, waiting for the passengers to board.

"Quick toilet break?" Alex asked, rising from his seat as the Captain nodded his approval. Inconveniently the toilets were at the back on this ancient propeller aircraft, a Vickers Viscount 800, so it was best to go now before the passengers were on board. He walked down the aisle, looking at all the seats, all seventy of them. Each was dressed with a head cover supporting the company logo and his hands passed over them as he made his way rearwards. The toilet cubicles at the back were necessarily small and his height forced him to bend his knees to pee. The washbasin was so small he could only wash one hand at a time! He dried his hands and threw his paper towel into empty waste bin, knowing that bin would be full by the time they landed in Stornaway.

Alex slid the toilet door open and walked back through the cabin. As he approached the galley the cabin crew were boarding. They were all strangers to him and, anyway, they appeared to be in a deep discussion with each other. They simply acknowledged him with a nod as they stepped on board. Leading the way was a tall, rather large, buxom lady with curly black hair. Her uniform hat appeared tiny compared to her head. Indeed, the entire uniform seemed to have shrunk a couple of sizes as it clung desperately to her body.

"Good morning," he smiled. The chief stewardess seemed surprised by the interruption to her conversation and paused for a second. Alex's outstretched hand was treated with disdain and he lowered it after noticing that she had a handful of paperwork in one hand and an overnight bag in the other. Oops!

"Good morning, sonny." The accent was broad Glaswegian. Two other voices squeaked "morning" behind her, although Alex did not see their faces. He had to step back into the flight deck to make space as the three crew members filed on and into the galley and cabin area.

"That's the cabin crew," Alex announced to the Captain and he went to climb back into his seat. The flight deck was also very small with little spare room.

"Great, then perhaps we'll get a cup of tea then?" The Captain replied loudly. Alex thought he heard a grunt from the galley as the crew stowed their bags in empty trolleys before carrying out their safety equipment checks. Finally the terrifying stewardess appeared on the flight deck, her hat now safely hidden away.

"Good morning, Captain. I'm Jennifer." Jennifer offered her hand to the Captain who reached back, twisting his body to do so.

"Good morning, Jennifer." Captain James Briant was a charmer and broadly smiled as he greeted her. "This is Alex, a bit new." He gestured his hand towards his co-pilot.

"Aye, well we like a bit of new blood," Jennifer replied, promptly running her fingers through Alex's hair. Pity we aren't on a night stop!"

Alex forced a smile, trying to hide his discomfort. Actually he was petrified. This woman looked a little like his grandmother. He was about to explain that he wasn't that new, having been flying the Viscount for very nearly six months now, but he didn't get a chance.

"Tea or coffee?" Jennifer asked.

"Tea, white, one," James said in a practised manner.

"Tea with a half, please," Alex asked politely.

"Why a half?" Jennifer asked as if chastising him.

"Trying to give up," Alex smiled weakly, again wondering whether to take the explanation further. He rapidly decided against it as he could see he would be cut short.

"Right, one tea white, one sugar, for our lovely Captain. Tea, white no sugar for the boy." The boy squirmed in his seat as Jennifer swung around and left the flight deck. Every cup of tea Alex received that day contained no sugar, despite his gentle reminders. Every cup tasted awful, but he forced himself to drink them anyway. A day later, on another sector with another crew, he found that tea with a half a sugar was simply too sweet; he never had sugar again.

The flight to Stornaway was largely uneventful; uneventful to everyone except Alex. He marvelled at the scenery. The aircraft had turned to the west after takeoff and flown along the Clyde, climbing gently. The visibility was excellent and James had pointed out the Isle of Arran on the left before the aircraft turned northward, passing over lochs, islands and the sea on their journey towards the Isle of Lewis. Alex had seen it all before, but the clarity of the light was amazing. The modest little airport at Stornaway was right on the coast and they descended gently to cross low across the beach towards the runway. On a previous visit, with a longer turnaround, he had walked the short distance to this beach and seen the seals sunbathing. On that occasion they had taken lunch in a local hotel while the aircraft stood empty on the tarmac.

Today they would be on the ground for a short 45 minutes. Once the engines had been shut down, the silence was amazing. After the passengers had disembarked the cleaners dashed through the cabin, cleaning away the litter. The pilots left their tiny flight deck and moved into the cabin. By then the first few rows had been cleaned and they sat down in the passenger seats. Almost immediately Alex found a tray placed in front of him; lunch.

"Tea?" Alex looked up and saw the young stewardess standing before him. She was the most beautiful thing he had ever seen.

"Err, yes please, half a sugar," Alex stammered. He watched as the sublime beauty turned and disappeared into the galley. His heart sank when he realised that Jennifer was in the galley making the tea. No sugar, then. Sure enough the young stewardess returned with the tea.

"I hope it's not too strong," she said. Alex took a sip and told her it was perfect. He was lying.

That was the first time he had ever met Laura Cameron and that was probably the full extent of their conversation, other than hello and goodbye. He later asked someone her name, to be promptly told she was married. But then, so was he. Occasionally he would hear other crewmembers talking about her. She'd been to this party or that. She was, apparently, wild! All the boys loved her.

Some considerable time later, he had heard that Laura had been promoted to chief stewardess and, on another occasion, learned she had taken a management role. He saw her once or twice, but never to talk to. Anyway, what would he say? What could he say? For years after that he heard nothing.

Another twenty-five years passed before their paths were to cross again. The young shy co-pilot had now become a senior well-respected Captain flying Boeing 747 Jumbo jets around the world. The young, beautiful stewardess was still beautiful, leading a team of other cabin crew on board his 747 aircraft. Alex knew she would not remember the young co-pilot and chose not to remind her. He just hoped he would not say anything stupid. Just be professional, he thought. In all, he recalled, they flew together three or four times. He was careful to be respectful, never to flirt or say anything silly. Just don't be a jerk and don't try to impress her!

Several months passed and Alex found himself sitting in one of his favourite bars in Singapore with one or two members of his crew. Pilots and cabin crew tend to be creatures of habit and would, in the more popular destinations, often have a regular bar to meet up in. There were crew from several different flights in this particular bar on this particular night. The place was humming. Laura Cameron walked into that bar and saw Alex sitting with a few of his crew. She was with several of her own cabin crew. Laura surveyed the scene and then approached the bar.

"Good evening Alex." There was a bright, sprightliness to her voice. "How's life?"

For a few seconds Captain Alex Young had felt like the shy young co-pilot of twenty-five years before. However he collected himself quickly.

"Oh hello Laura," Alex smiled as he stood up and formally shook her hand. "Actually life is terrible! But you don't really want to know about that! Would you like a drink?" Laura turned around and looked over at her crew.

"Someone's buying me a drink already, thanks," she said. She turned back to face him. "What can be so terrible?"

"Well, for starters, my marriage is falling apart! I keep spoiling things by coming home at the end of trips!" Alex chuckled at his own little joke. He made light of the whole issue, but Laura persisted. At her request, he gave her the basic details, but soon he found himself talking about his failing marriage. The two of them just sat quietly at one end of the bar, undisturbed, and Laura spent much of the next two hours offering advice. 'No, nobody else was involved.' he had told her. 'Yes, we have spoken to a counsellor.'

The advice was mostly constructive but, in reality, a little too late. Finally Laura had to leave; dinner with her crew. Alex bent down and kissed her on the forehead, possibly taking her by surprise. He thanked her for the advice and all the kind words. The encounter was all very innocent, but Alex was grateful for having two hours with the beautiful Laura Cameron. 'Guess who I've just been speaking too!' he said to himself.

"I have fruit cake and hot coffee," Maria said, placing the tray on the table. "We are lucky it is so cool in here Captain. I had to go outside and it is very hot today. Much too hot!" Alex took a look outside the window. There was a bright blue sky and the sun was blazing down upon the vineyards and the distant hills beyond. The vines were used to being baked, sunshine a prime ingredient for good wine. He loved his wine. However one bottle was never enough, and two bottles was too much!

"So you were going to tell me how you first met your wife," Maria poured the coffee and pushed the cup towards the old man. He touched it with one hand, moved it slightly and then just stared into it.

"I had first seen her when she was very young. She was in her first year as a stewardess. I don't think I even spoke to her, but I heard things about her from time to time. She became a cabin crew manager for a time and was well liked. Then she went back to being a chief stewardess;

a Cabin Service Director. Then we had chatted in that bar in Singapore." Alex noticed that the cake had cherries and currents in it. He would have a piece in a minute.

"Months later I reported for work and found I was flying with Laura Cameron! I was excited in a schoolboy sort of way. Silly, I know, but I had a secret. Even though I was a mature grown man with a Captain's uniform, four stripes on my arm and my posh peaked cap, inside I was still a nervous, shy young man. We were flying to Japan, a long flight, which meant we would have two nights off when we got there. Could this be my opportunity to make friends with Laura Cameron? I confess, Maria, my thoughts were not honourable!" Alex looked up and chuckled.

"Captain, I'm sure I don't know what you mean!" Maria was pleased the old man was back to his old self.

"I don't remember much about the flight, but the crew were nice and we agreed to meet up that night. The pilots were staying in a different hotel (that happens sometimes) and after sleeping much of the day, one of my co-pilots and I made our way into town to join the cabin crew at their hotel. We arrived early and the bar was empty, so we ordered two beers and sat there chatting. We might even have had two rounds of beer because the cabin crew are always late!" Alex was again chuckling at his generalisation.

"Finally, over a period of about twenty minutes, a trickle of crew members came in to the bar and sat with us. I think, perhaps, six or seven of them, which is a good turn out for Japan." Alex reached forward and took a few sips of his coffee. His lips and throat were dry. He again glanced at the cake, but he was also enjoying his story.

"Laura was one of the last to join us. I stood up and greeted her. We had to rearrange the seating so that we could sit around the table. While that was happening I had stepped to the bar to buy a round of drinks. Laura Cameron drank gin and tonic," he announced, as if it was significant. "When I returned to the table, I found that my co-pilot had placed another chair next to his and Laura had sat there. I was at the other end of the table! This was not my plan at all!"

"Oh dear," exclaimed Laura. "What did you do?"

"What could I do? I talked to the other members of my crew and was forced to watch my co-pilot chatting up Laura Cameron. Eventually we went to dinner! It was a warm summer evening and we slowly walked to the restaurant. I am a gentleman, Maria, so naturally I allowed the girls to go through the door first. This was another big mistake! Once again my co-pilot had arranged it so that he sat next to Laura, while I sat at one end of the table. It was a disaster!" Alex took another sip of his coffee. It was not necessary to collect his thoughts; he had told this story many times before and he was well-practised at it!

"It was the same thing after dinner. There was a bar several miles away where the crew would go and sing. Do you what know Karaoke is?" Alex asked.

"Yes, of course," Maria said. "It is the same word in Spain. You sing into a microphone and it sounds terrible, no?"

"Yes Maria, its sounds terrible. Actually sometimes it sounds good. It sounds better when I do not sing!" Alex was pleased as Maria laughed out loud at this joke. "There was a special bus, the Truck Bus, to take us to this bar. By now, Laura was sitting on the co-pilot's lap!"

"Oh, no!" Maria gasped. "My poor Captain!"

"Anyway, there was also dancing and guess what happened? The co-pilot and Laura danced the night away! I think I maybe got one dance with her. At one point another stewardess whispered to me that I should bop him on the nose, but of course I couldn't. I just had to accept that the young, handsome co-pilot was preferred to the older, not quite so handsome Captain."

"But there is a happy ending, no?" Maria asked.

"We eventually returned to the cabin crew hotel. There was a football match on and it was being shown in the hotel. England were playing Portugal, or was it France? Anyway, I am sure you can guess! The co-pilot and my lovely stewardess sat together on a couch and, worst of all, they were holding hands! It was too much to bear! After a short while I went outside. There was a small supermarket nearby and I bought myself a can of Coke and a Mars Bar. I stood in the street and thought about my disastrous evening. In my mind, at least, the evening had showed so much promise. How wrong could I be? My fairy tale romance had never had a chance. Finally I decided to go back to my hotel. Before I did, I decided I should tell the crew I was going, in case they thought I had fallen into a ditch or something!"

"Does that happen very often? Falling into ditches?" Maria had raised one of her eyebrows in a questioning, theatrical way.

"It happens, but not too often," he grinned. "I walked back into the hotel and pressed the button for the lift. The TV room was on a lower floor. The lift doors opened and who should be standing there, but Laura Cameron!"

"Oh my God!" Maria exclaimed. "It was meant to be!"

"Where have you been?" Laura had asked.

"What do you care?" Alex retorted. He was tired and fed up.

"Of course I care!" Laura had insisted.

"You're more interested in the First Officer than you are in me," Alex had said.

"I'm not interested in the First Officer. He's like a limpet! He keeps grabbing my hand and pulling me onto his lap. It's you I'm interested in." Laura had looked up into his face apologetically, but Alex was still to be convinced.

"You've got a funny way of showing it!" he complained.

"Look, why don't we go to my room, well away from the First Officer and the rest of the crew. We can have a drink there." Laura had taken his arm. She tugged at it and smiled.

"Ok," he said. "A drink."

"Really, just a drink?" Maria asked. "You were a very naughty Captain! You were a married man!"

"No, no," Alex protested with a smile. "I was separated. My marriage was over. Anyway I found myself sitting on one corner of her bed. She sat on another corner and I was still a little cross with her. In my hand was my drink. Laura only had gin and tonic in her room and I hate gin and tonic! I hate the smell and the taste. I just don't like it. So, I was sitting there on the bed, sipping my drink, when it happened..."

"She kissed you?" Maria suggested.

"No, there was a loud knocking at the door," Alex smiled.

"Mother of Mary, the co-pilot!" Maria looked genuinely shocked.

"Yes, the co-pilot!" Alex grinned. He loved telling this story!

'Let me in!' the co-pilot had called.

Laura had told him to go away.

'Laura, let me in now!' he banged on the door again.

Once again Laura had again told him to go away.

'Laura, I'm not leaving until you let me in.'

"At that moment I got up and opened the door. Standing there, of course, was a very surprised first officer!" Alex grinned. "I stood there in the doorway and told him to piss off!"

"Oh my God! What did he do?" Maria was gripped.

"He had stood there for just for a second, his eyes popping from his head!" Alex was beaming over his face, triumphant at his storytelling. "Then he turned and ran away down the corridor yelling 'Argh! Argh! Argh! Argh!' I closed the door, faced Laura and we both burst out laughing. We laughed and laughed. The rest, as they say, is history!"

Maria drew a breath. She was smiling, no grinning, imagining the poor co-pilot running down the corridor making strange noises. Alex watched Maria laugh at the various images he had created in her mind.

"I think we deserve a piece of cake," Alex suggested.

They both took a few moments as the cake was cut, Maria placing the larger piece on a plate for the old man. She poured more coffee from the pot. It was only lukewarm, but that didn't seem to matter. Alex ate his cake, delighting as the cherries crushed in his mouth. The cake was delicious. Finally, he wiped his mouth with a serviette and continued his story.

When they arrived back in England after the trip, Alex and Laura had driven to a park. They sat, talking for hours and hours until it began to get dark. Alex drove home in deep thought, knowing his life had changed forever. He had given Laura his home telephone number and suggested she should ring him (if she wanted to!).

"Don't worry Alex, I wouldn't ever ring you at home," Laura had assured him. Alex was slightly surprised.

"Laura, if you have believed anything I have told you," Alex said gently, his hands on her shoulders, "you will ring!"

A week later Laura made the call. To her horror a woman, Carol, answered the telephone! 'Oh my God' she had thought, but quickly she regained her composure.

"Is Alex there please?" Laura had asked.

"Yes, is that Laura? Just a moment, I'll get him." Laura then heard Carol shouting through to another room. "Alex! It's Laura; it's your girlfriend!"

"She not my girlfriend!" he hissed and took the telephone.

Chapter 17: Surprises and Tears

It was another day and Maria was pouring the coffee. She had greeted her Captain in the normal way and he had greeted her back with a massive smile. She knew, at once, this would be a good day.

"So what shall we talk about today, Captain?"

Alex found the daily ritual fascinating. The tray was laid out carefully with the coffee pot, cups, spoons and biscuits on side plates arranged with military precision. It had not taken very long for him to become comfortable with Maria, and he had come to enjoy their chats. Their chats - more like his story telling - it was he who would relate those memories from his past, albeit with an occasional gentle prodding.

"For several months I remained in the family home," Alex began. "Carol and I had accepted some sort of truce. It was quite simple really. If Laura was away I would spend my time in the family home in the Forest of Dean. That allowed me to see my sons, carry on with my various voluntary duties in the community, and keep the grass down in our huge garden.

When Laura and I were in the UK at the same time I would go and stay with her at her house. However, on one occasion, Carol wanted to borrow my car while hers was being fixed in the garage. Initially I had said no as I was planning to visit Laura on my days off. So Carol suggest she would drive me up to Laura's house!"

"Oh no!" Maria exclaimed. "This is very strange, is it not?"

"Even I thought it was very strange Maria," Alex chuckled. "But you must understand Carol and I had already split up, even if we lived in the same house, and we had already accepted we were single people, with our own separate lives. I agreed to lend Carol my car and, sure enough, she drove me up to a pub car park, about half way between the two houses, to where Laura was waiting for me."

"Were you nervous? How did they feel, meeting each other?" Maria was sitting on the edge of her seat with her eyes wide open.

"Well, I was pretty nervous!" he said. "Laura's sports car was parked there, waiting. It was like a prisoner exchange. I stepped out of the car, took my bag from one car and placed it in the other. The two women both got out of the cars and stood there shaking hands and exchanging pleasantries. It was if they were the best of friends!"

"Remarkable!" Maria shook her head in disbelief.

Eventually Alex left his family home and moved in with Laura for good. The ending of his first marriage had been a slow and painful process and moving out was a relief for both sides. Moving in initially meant one suitcase, but unpacking his clothes and being allotted wardrobe space felt very strange indeed.

Living with a new person after so many years was exciting, but it felt very odd. The experience had a raw innocence to it. There was a sense of child-like ebullience as they giggled and laughed their way through each day, making house together.

Simple things like shopping had become a novelty and Alex remembered Laura buying him a pair of slippers to replace the ones he had forgotten to pack. Some would call it the honeymoon period, but this honeymoon lasted a very long time. In those early years, there were many special moments.

With a space in the wardrobe, Alex was gently reminded that this was where such items should be stored, not on the floor and not on a chair, and he was keen to please. One or two things in the house did not work and he earned extra 'brownie points' by fixing them. He tended to the garden and other such things, which he considered 'manly'. He disappointed in other ways, when Laura discovered his cooking skills were poor and that he was not as fastidious as she about everything being in **exactly** the right place.

Alex chuckled to himself. He recalled his somewhat juvenile attempts to please Laura at every opportunity. Well, mostly! He tried! Then there was the physical side of the relationship. These were a combination of the skills of mature experienced lovers and the energy and enthusiasm of young teenagers. The obvious chemistry had been confirmed very early on, but the hunger for sex was rather more than either of them had expected, but neither was complaining! However, it did rather limit the time they had for anything else! Still, they had the rest of their lives and, at this moment, nothing else could be as important.

Finally the first insurmountable barrier was reached. It was Laura who created the first real difficulty by saying – "By the way, I like flowers. Buy me lots of flowers."

The simple thing, of course, would have been to comply. However Alex was Alex and he found himself digging an ever deeper and deeper hole for himself. If he went out and bought flowers now, he explained, they would mean very little because it would not have been his idea. The gesture would be undermined with the knowledge that they had been requested; the idea would not have been his.

Laura reasserted that she liked and wanted flowers. Alex tried to explain that Laura should stop asking for them and, after a suitable, but short interval, he would buy them for her. They would then be his idea and an original thought; a far more caring present at that stage, surely? Laura did not understand and recognised the first childish flaw in her perfect man. Oh dear!

Weeks passed by and, their relationship was so great, this problem was forgotten. Well, maybe not forgotten, but…

Actually Alex had no real idea about Laura's feelings on this matter because both had diplomatically taken it off the agenda. The relationship was fresh and exciting to the extent that even a regular trip to the supermarket became a joint fun event, even though Alex had previously hated shopping!

Another difficulty, of course, was work. They both worked for an airline whose primary function appeared to be to ensure that they were on opposite sides of the world as frequently as possible! Occasionally there were real tears as rosters were compared with the realisation that they would not see each other for weeks at a time. It was little consolation that the reunions were that much more intense.

So it was that Laura returned home after a long flight from Chicago. She arrived tired and weary, to her beautiful house where her newly found lover had taken up residence. He met her on the driveway. After a big hug, and a huge lingering kiss, Alex removed the suitcase from her black, sexy sports car, while she staggered towards the front door of her welcoming house with a handbag, which could easily be claimed to exceed the normal weight limit for a suitcase.

Waiting in the kitchen was a gin and tonic, already charged with ice and a slice of lemon. The kitchen was filled with the aroma of dinner, not yet quite burnt, while upstairs Laura discovered a hot bath covered in bubble bath. A normal person would have stripped off and fallen straight into the inviting bath, but Laura carefully folded, smoothed and hung up her uniform. She unpack her case and placed everything in its correct location before finally allowing herself to slide into the deep, hot bath.

The image of romance was maintained by not going back downstairs to witness the blind panic as Alex ran about the kitchen trying to work out how everything could possibly be ready at the same time. He had already decided to abandon any pretence of control by hiding the massive amount of washing up under a big mountain of soapsuds. He also had no idea how he could possibly serve and eat a starter with his loved one, while the oven attempted to shrivel and burn his creation. His plan had finally been to have a longer interval between courses so they could "catch up on each others' news".

Laura may have been too much in love, or just too bloody tired to care, because to her the three-course dinner seemed perfect in every detail. They looked across from each other, hearts a'flutter, as they sipped the last of their red wine.

"Coffee in the garden?" Alex suggested.

"That would be lovely," Laura smiled. She sat and watched as Alex cleared away the plates while the kettle boiled. She noted that he had correctly selected the decaffeinated coffee and so the evening was not spoilt by a little terse correction. She had, of course, noticed that the washing up had not yet been completed, but this was too good an evening to spoil things. The coffee was placed on a tray and Laura opened the door to the front porch and stepped out. She had a little love seat, two seats separated by a little table, which looked out on the garden. She sat down.

It was a warm summer night and the air had not yet chilled. Anyway, she was full of love and watched as he fussed around her. She lifted her coffee and considered it a perfect evening. They both stared out on the dark garden, short shadows created by the hall light. Above they could just see the stars peeking through a mackerel sky. Alex reached down beside him and flicked the switch.

Suddenly the garden illuminated under the coloured lights of electric flowers. Red, blue, yellow and green flower petals shone across the lawn. Beneath the illuminations were scattered real cut flowers. Alex awaited a response, but there was none. Finally he turned his head towards Laura. Her eyes were full of tears and she could not speak. She mouthed the words "thank you" and smiled, causing the tears to run down her cheeks.

"Now you can have flowers," he said gently.

"Oh, my God," Maria gasped. "That is so romantic!"

Alex smiled. "The effect was far greater than I could have ever hoped for," he explained. "Our first Christmas was going to be a romantic, homely affair. There was always the possibility than we would have to work, but I was senior enough to bid for a nice trip if necessary. Laura decided to request a Christmas trip to Hong Kong. Most crew, of course, would want to be home with family and their loved-ones so it would work to our advantage to be away; at least we would be together."

Maria stared at Alex, smiling as ever. She appeared to really enjoy his stories. He continued.

Alex explained that Laura would receive her December roster sometime in early November. She had eagerly signed into the airline website with her staff number and password. The site was always frustratingly slow and one could imagine thousands of staff all trying to discover their work pattern over this crucial time. She tutted and groaned, but the response that followed had been a rather out-of-character growl of anger. Laura swore!

Alex had considered the possibilities. What could it be, he wondered; somewhere in darkest Africa, perhaps? Actually, that might be fun; maybe the non-drinking Middle East? Well, it could be worse. In fact, as he considered all the options; all that really mattered was that they were together. However, the news was far worse than he could have imagined. The company had given Laura standby for the whole of the month! Not even just part of it; the whole of the month!

Laura simply collapsed in tears and Alex, her strong reliable rock, sobbed with her. It would be impossible to organise a trip with her. She might be on standby, at home or at the airport, and she might be called out at a moment's notice. She could be away three days, or it might be nine days. She could be called away perhaps to the freezing snows of Canada or the heat of Singapore. Packing a suitcase was a nightmare!

They could not even co-ordinate any days off together, for she had none pre-planned. In this month, of all months, their first Christmas, they would likely be apart and not knowing the 'when' or the 'where' made it so much worse.

"I don't like this story," Maria complained. "You tell me a wonderful story about electric flowers, then you spoil it with a terrible story about this. It is horrible!"

Alex laughed. "Ah, well Maria, adversity can bring you closer together."

"Pardon me," Maria apologised. "I do not understand. What is this?"

"Adversity," Alex explained. "It is when sometimes something very bad happens. We felt the whole world was against us. We were upset naturally, but in the end we made it OK."

"How? How can you make this OK? Did they change Laura's roster?" Maria asked.

"No! They don't care about us! They paid us and we had to do what we were told! We could complain, of course, but they would just explain that someone had to do it. This time, that someone was to be Laura." Alex chuckled as Maria threw up her hands in disgust.

"Anyway, Laura finally got given a long trip lasting over a week and we knew she would have to have some days off after that. I had days off over the same period, so we decided we would have a special dinner at home."

It was the week just before Christmas. They sat in the kitchen having lunch, the mood frequently changing between laughter and sadness. They knew that, in a couple of day's time, they would both be facing the uncertainty of standby and being apart once again. They were both trying very hard to be upbeat, laughing and joking but, in the moments of silence, a sense of melancholy would fill the room. They washed up together while the kettle boiled for coffee. Cradling their mugs, they walked into the sitting room where a fire blazed in the fireplace. The lights of the Christmas tree sparkled invitingly and they both sat down on the settee.

"You go first," Laura invited. She had a childlike quality that made her both vulnerable and beautiful at the same time. Alex had stood up, walked up and down, passed the tree and stooped to pick up a present.

"Shall I open this one?" he asked.

"No! That's one of mine! Open one of your own presents," Laura protested.

"OK, how about this one?" He picked up a neatly wrapped gift and shook it. Laura was trying to remember what was in it. He sat down beside Laura and ripped open the paper.

"Don't rip it," Laura said. "Save it." Alex handed the now shredded wrapping paper to her. A box. He opened it up and found a leather wallet.

"Your old one is very tatty," Laura explained. "This one is bigger too; for all your money!"

"You mean it doesn't have any money in it? No, its what I've always wanted. A bigger wallet!" Alex kissed her on the lips; it was a slow, long kiss.

"OK, you choose a present," Alex said. "Any one at all."

Laura was sitting at the foot of the Christmas tree looking at the pile of presents, with their pretty paper and bows. Her hand floated over the top of them, first to the left and then to the right.

"Which one?" she asked jumping up and down like a little girl. "Which one shall I choose?" Her hand touched a present, but then she moved to another. "This one?"

Alex sat on the couch and watched as she lingered close to the Christmas tree. Her hands were behind her back and she lifted herself onto her toes as she stepped back and forth. They were only allowed to open just one present each; the rest would have to wait until after Christmas. At some stage they would find themselves with days off together and that would be ***their*** Christmas. In the meantime they would open only one present each.

Alex had always felt uncomfortable receiving and opening presents. Would it be something he wanted? Would he be able to hide the possible disappointment? What did he really need anyway? Frankly he preferred just to give presents. He was happy with his fashionable leather wallet. He knew many of the other presents would be something for him to wear. Laura had already begun systematically redressing Alex, gradually replacing his wardrobe with decidedly more modern or 'trendy' clothes.

"Ooooh, which one shall I chose?" she asked, still hovering close to the tree. The lights sparkled beautifully, even though it was mid-afternoon, the tree laden with reflective decorations. She bent down a couple of times, trying to decide which present she should select. "This one?" she asked, pointing to a large impressive box.

"Anyone you like, but it gets dark soon!" Alex chastised her. Thoughts of why they were here, having this 'mock' Christmas were temporarily forgotten as two middle-aged juveniles played at happy families; their first Christmas together.

"This one!" declared Laura, glancing over to seek some sign of approval for her choice. She hesitated, saw there was no protest, and began opening her prize.

"To my darling Laura," Laura read out loud. "I shall love you forever." First she carefully picked the bow from the top, and then she slid her long nails under the sticky tape, neatly opening the gift. The shape was a giveaway and she already knew it was probably a DVD. She took forever! Finally the coloured paper broke free and tumbled to the ground, while the little girl jumped up and down. She might easily have been nine years old again; she was so excited.

"Oh, I love Rod Stewart!" Laura squealed and she was still bouncing as she examined the DVD in her hand. "Rod Stewart's The Great American Song Book," she read out loud before dropping to her knees in front of the television. She began pushing buttons on the machine below and a little drawer politely opened. Then Laura tried to prise open the DVD box, not realising it was covered in a thin plastic film that enveloped it tightly. She scratched and tore at it, finally losing the patience she had shown up until now. Her fingers finally pulled the DVD case open and Alex flinched as fingers gripped the silver disc. 'Don't put your fingers all over the underside!' he wanted to say but, of course, he remained silent, not wishing to spoil the moment.

"Thank you!" she said, placing the disc onto the little drawer and pressing the 'close' button. Only then did Laura realise she was not using the remote control and there was now a selection page. She picked up the remote, all fingers and thumbs, and finally selected play. Suddenly Rod Stewart appeared on screen and began singing "You Go To My Head". Laura forgot herself for a minute, swaying gently from side to side in time with the music.

Alex looked whimsically at the little pile of Christmas paper on the floor and shook his head with an ironic smile. Laura was so tidy, always cleaning, always tidying up, but not today – instead she was lost in the romance of a song; a Rod Stewart song. The second track was called "They Can't Take That Away From Me" (one of Alex's favourites) and he marvelled at his good luck in meeting this remarkable girl. It took until halfway through the third track "The Way You Look Tonight" before Laura moved from her position barely twelve inches from the TV screen. She stood up, intending to join Alex on the settee, but she saw the little pile of crumpled paper. Alex knew she could not help herself and she picked it up.

A little piece of paper fluttered to the ground and Laura bent down to pick it up. It was a different colour to the wrapping and had writing on it. In her other hand she was already scrunching the Christmas paper into a small ball.

"What's this?" Laura asked.

Alex frowned. "I don't know. What is it?"

"Rod Stewart In Concert. The Great American Songbook. Earl's Court," she read. Laura simply stared down at the ticket and said nothing. She read it again and again.

"Alex, it's tonight, it says it's for tonight!" Laura looked for his confirmation as a broad grin came across his face.

"Now Laura, I need you to go and change," Alex explained firmly.

"You have less than an hour to get ready. We are going for a meal in Covent Garden and then the concert."

"But Alex..." Laura was swaying as she stared again at the ticket in her hand. "Alex, there must be over thirty presents under the tree. How could you possibly know I would pick that one?"

"Just lucky, I guess." Alex smiled. "Laura, you need to get ready now. But before you do, could you please unwrap the ball of rubbish in your hand. I think you might have killed the other ticket! Can you get ready in one hour?"

She assured him she could; no problem. An hour and twenty minutes later Alex was standing by the front door looking at his watch. They were going to be late for the dinner he had booked close to Covent Garden. He would have to rush down the motorway and hope the traffic was not too heavy.

"You are so romantic!" Maria's brilliant white teeth were beaming across at Alex. "But the presents? How did you know she would pick that one?"

"Psychology," he smiled. "A slightly larger bow perhaps, maybe a slightly different colour. Or the place where I placed it."

"Oh, you are so, so clever! Tell me about the dinner and the concert." Maria, too, could look child-like when she got excited. She leaned forward, sitting on the edge of her seat.

"The meal was terrific. Covent Garden is in a beautiful area of London, with lot of restaurants, cafes, markets and shops. In the end we had time to wander around for a while, hand-in-hand, just walking the streets waiting for the restaurant to open. We had more than enough time to get there. We then walked to the concert hall. Rod Stewart was brilliant! Before he sang his American love songs, he sang many of his old hits. Laura knew the words to most of his hit songs." Alex reflected for a moment, remembering the day. "Finally he sang those amazing songs from the movies of the 1930's, 1940's and 1950's. They were written by the likes of Cole Porter, George Gershwin, and Jerome Kern and once sung by Fred Astaire or Frank Sinatra."

"Sorry, Maria. I'm going on a bit about this. We had been so upset about spending our first Christmas apart and now here we were having the most wonderful romantic evening." Alex took a deep breath and wiped the tears from his eyes.

"Such an evening. Electric flowers and surprise concerts!" Maria slapped her thigh. "How could you ever top that?" she asked.

"I couldn't Maria," Alex smiled, "but Laura could!"

Missing the first Christmas together was hugely disappointing, but Alex and Laura were both used to the ups and downs of their job. It was highly rewarding in so many ways - travelling to great cities all around the world, then staying in wonderful hotels (sometimes!) and socialising with a good crew (occasionally). They both knew that there was no co-ordination at all between their rostering systems and there would be times when they were on the opposite sides of the world.

Of course there were also times when one was away and the other was at home, but that seemed more manageable. Potentially, however, there was another difficulty that was insidious but hard to talk about. Both had spoken about love, trust and commitment but the words 'doubt' and 'jealous' had remained unspoken. Why would you express misgivings when the relationship was so, so special and beyond anything either of them had experienced before?

Alex and Laura had both been flying a long time. They knew that travelling around the world staying in five-star hotels and going out with a ready-made crew far from home could sometimes lead to temptation. They had witnessed it many times and even experienced the intoxicating lure of an attractive person in an exotic location with hot balmy weather, alcohol and dancing.

After a week or more away, thousands of miles from home and reality, most would resist the enticement of a romantic moment; but not quite everyone. The job was generally tiring, often boring and frequently disappointing. However, Laura was a very attractive woman and, by her own admission, guys often 'came on' to her.

Their new life was exciting; they were gradually learning more and more about each other and they understood that the road was littered with those who had taken trust for granted. If it might be an issue they should, of course, talk about it, but they were very much in love, so why taint this magical relationship with mistrust?

Alex trusted Laura unreservedly, but trusting somebody ninety-nine per cent left at least a little doubt and they both knew the job and the temptations. It was not a big issue he told himself, so why spend time worrying about it. However, that trust was about to be severely tested.

Laura had been allocated a nine-day trip to Singapore and then down to Australia; nine days away from each other. Alex's heart sank when he heard the news. It was bad enough that they would be apart for nine days. But it was Singapore; hot, romantic and beautiful.

Laura had reassured him that it wouldn't be a problem. It would be a girlie trip, with shopping excursions, sessions in the beauty parlour and meetings with the girls for coffee. They would stay in touch by telephone and text. No problem at all.

Alex knew his disquiet was all of his own making. If he trusted Laura, what was earth the problem? Perhaps he should look to himself and examine the issues. He visualised himself standing in one of the bars, close to the crew hotel, with a pint of beer in his hand. 'Did you know the average guy thinks about sex every six seconds?' he could hear himself saying again. 'I wonder what the other guys are thinking about for the other five seconds?' This always got a laugh, but today it didn't seem very funny.

There were several weeks before the trip was to take place. There were other trips before it, of course, but these only lasted three or four days and were much less threatening. Their days off didn't usually coincide and there was no mechanism to rearrange trips. The pilots, unlike the cabin crew, were permitted to swap trips, but it was often very difficult to get a colleague to change both a trip and their days off. Instead days off alone became 'chore' days. Alex would busy himself chopping wood, fixing the washing machine or mowing the lawn while Laura was away. Laura would wash windows and scrub floors!

The days leading up to the nine-day trip were slightly tense. Alex had become quiet and Laura became irritable. It annoyed her that Alex could not put this behind him. So what was the problem? It was the nature of their jobs that they would spend time apart. Yes, it was nine days, but it would go quickly. She loved Singapore and Sydney; so why couldn't he just trust her? She loved him and it was relatively early days in their relationship, but why did he mistrust her so? She had assured him time and again, but his eyes always gave him away; he was unconvinced.

The day before she was due to leave Alex was packing to go to New York. It was a simple seven-hour flight and they both loved the Big Apple. He would go for a beer, maybe two, in a bar across from their Manhattan hotel. The next morning he would go for a hearty American breakfast consisting of bacon, sausage, scrambled egg and tomato. He prided himself on ordering in sufficient detail so that the waitress didn't have to ask any questions. 'What type of toast do you want?'

Laura was glad he was going first. She knew he would be thinking about his trip. It was a big responsibility being the Captain of a Boeing 747 and she did not want him distracted by silly, boyish jealousies. He packed his bag quickly, as always. Two white shirts, two sets of 'going out' clothes, wash bag, razor, shoes, socks, trousers, pants and a casual jacket for the evening. Even more important were passport, flying licence, identity card, hat and tie. As he was leaving she thrust some spare US dollars into his hand. 'I had these left over,' she said with a warm smile. 'Ring me.'

They kissed and held each other for a minute. 'Gotta go,' he said quietly. She stood at the door and watched him walk to the car in his smart Captain's uniform. He was so handsome, she thought.

Three days later Alex returned to the house. It felt empty. He had been up all day in New York and then flown through the night back to England. He was now very, very tired indeed. He took his flight bag and suitcase from the car and put them in the hallway. He would unpack later. He took his shoes off and then slowly climbed the stairs to the bedroom. Undressing, he carefully hung up his jacket and trousers. (Laura would be proud!) He removed the applets and name badge from his shirt, placing them carefully in the drawer beside the bed. The shirt, underpants and socks were dropped carefully into the washing basket. Even without Laura being here, he maintained the high standards of tidiness she expected. He climbed into the soft bed and pulled the luxurious duvet up to his neck. Within moments he was asleep.

Alex woke up to the sound of a tractor chugging up and down outside the house. They lived near a farm, but they were also close to a golf course, just across the road. Both had farm machinery and both regularly made a lot of noise. 'Its all part of being in the country,' Laura would say. Alex lay in the bed, staring at the vaulted ceiling. This was Laura's house and it still felt rather strange to him. He had been married over thirty years and now, here he was, in another woman's home; in her bed.

Starting again had been fun. The last few years had been stressful and full of arguments, but now here he was in another woman's house. 'I'm in another woman's house,' he thought to himself. 'I'm in another woman's house.' But it wasn't just any woman. It was Laura Cameron, sweet, beautiful, sexy Laura Cameron. He thought back to the first time he had seen her all those years ago, too afraid to even talk to her. She had looked stunning then, and she still looked bloody good now! His life had taken an unexpected turn, new and resurgent, and he was very, very happy.

Thoughts of mistrust were almost forgotten. Such thoughts were juvenile, immature and unnecessary. He jumped from the bed and searched for his slippers and dressing gown. Ah, the dressing gown, bought by Laura after he had forgotten to bring his own from the family home. It was thick and warm and he wrapped it tightly around him as he walked to the back window. The tractor was sitting just the other side of the hedge, still ticking over. It was doing bloody nothing and the driver was nowhere to be seen. He wanted to scream, but knew it was unreasonable to expect anything else. How can you explain to anyone what you are doing, in bed, sleeping (or trying to sleep) at midday?

Alex trudged down the stairs to the kitchen and put the kettle on. He was well accustomed to the feeling of grit in his eyes, but he knew that a coffee and a shower would make most of it go away. He stood in the immaculate kitchen waiting for the kettle to boil. He still had to search for various things, often opening several cupboards and drawers before finding what he needed. Of course Laura had the advantage of not having children who might leave half-eaten toast covered in sticky jam on the draining-board. Even the rubbish bin smelled new!

There was just him in the house, so he would make instant coffee. Huh, coffee! Laura had converted him very quickly from a tea drinker to a morning coffee person. He had adapted to please her, but already he could not imagine waking up to tea. 'Very interesting - but stupid!' he said out loud, using a German accent. Oh dear, now he was talking to himself! He took his coffee into the lounge, carefully took a coaster for his coffee, and sat down on the couch. His pointed the remote control at the TV and switched on the news. There was nothing much happening in the world, so Alex finished his coffee and went to shower.

The hot water was strong and beat down over his head. He began the mental calculation of the time change between the UK and Singapore. This one was relatively simple; the UK was plus one hour ahead while Singapore was GMT plus eight. Seven hours ahead and it was nearly one o'clock. What would Laura be doing at eight o'clock at night? Mostly likely she would be at Equinox, the New Asia bar near the top of the Raffles Stamford Hotel. The views from the seventy-first floor are stunning. The only question would be whether she was drinking gin and tonic or champagne.

Laura would be wearing a lovely summer dress to show off her amazing figure. Crew would often say how glamorous she looked and liken her to Marilyn Monroe. 'Yeah, but she's dead!' Laura would joke. 'Probably doesn't look so good now!' Actually with the short, blonde hair Alex thought she looked more like Jean Harlow. Younger crewmembers would look at him blankly when he suggested this. 'Jean who?' they would ask.

Laura and her crew would be talking about all manner of things, but eventually the subject of food would come up. The choices in Singapore were endless of course, but crew were creatures of habit and among the suggestions would be Sally's, Fatties, the Food Court, or the more upmarket Boat Key. The meal would be taken slowly, part of the entertainment, before a slow walk in the heat, back towards the hotel. At a crossroads nearby some of the crew would make their farewells and the party would split into two. Some would return to their rooms, while others would go to the bar. For a change of scenery they might venture to the Corner Bar and then perhaps to Ignition, which had a dance floor and a live band on the floor above.

Maybe not, thought Alex. Laura had said it would be a girlie trip. Perhaps she was wandering through the evening markets looking for bargains. It seemed to him that she had hundreds of pairs of shoes and lots and lots of clothes, but apparently not enough. She always looked great though, so he couldn't really complain. He got dry and then dressed but his thoughts were constantly of Laura. He went to his bedside drawer and opened it. He picked up his mobile phone and switched it on. There were two messages, both from Laura.

The first message read '***Had a good flight but very long. Nice crew. Quick shower, then meeting downstairs. Love you so much.***'

Alex selected the second message. '***Just had a call. Meeting up at Equinox. Back about one. Give me a ring then. XXXX.***'

Equinox; he was right! He looked at the digital clock radio on Laura's side of the bed. It was quarter past one here in the UK. One o'clock Singapore time was a respectable time to get in, given the time change, so he would ring her at six o'clock UK time. His thoughts turned to the garage that he had promised to clean out. There was barely enough room to park a car and Alex had agreed to tidy it up.

Several hours later Alex sat down with a well-earned can of beer. The garage was now tidy, but it had been a very dusty job and he had also become rather sweaty, so he had showered again. He now had his dressing gown and slippers on, feeling all nice and clean for the second time today. He opened the can and took a sip. He could taste the hops and savoured the moment.

The video machine indicated it was just approaching six o'clock. He had written the hotel telephone number on a post-it note and dialled the number into the phone. He listened to the crackles and clicks on the telephone and then, finally, it was ringing. Even at one o'clock in the morning the operator sounded very cheerful. 'I'll just put you through,' she said and the phone began ringing again. The telephone rang several times and then he heard Laura's voice.

Alex went to speak, but then realised it was an answerphone. She was clever! He'd been flying even longer than her, but still he had no idea how to personalise the recorded message in the hotel room. He waited for the beep.

"Hi darling, it's me. Ringing at one o'clock as requested. Hope you've had a nice evening. I'll call back in a while. Love you." Alex put the telephone down and flicked the television on. He was glad she was having a good night; he'd try again in half an hour.

"Hello, could you put me through to Laura Cameron's room please?" It was now three thirty in the morning and this was his sixth attempt at ringing her. He had rung every hour and half hour since his first attempt. The phone rang several times and he hung up before the answerphone clicked in. 'Wow, still out at three-thirty in the morning,' he thought. 'She must really be having a good time!"

An hour later there was still no answer. Four thirty in the morning - where could she be? Now he really was beginning to get worried. He had already sent a text to her mobile phone, but there was no answer from there either.

Singapore was one of the safest places in the world, so he didn't fear for her safety. He was more concerned about the length of time she had been out partying. He was a party animal, but even he had rarely been out until four-thirty in the morning. He began to feel sick. Of course, she might not still be out partying…

Surely not! He tried to put the bad thoughts from his mind. Was it possible? Surely she couldn't be in someone else's room?

Alex flicked through the channels, but there was nothing on the TV to hold his attention. It was only nine thirty in the UK, but this already felt like the longest evening he had ever experienced. He had made a pizza and eaten it between phone calls. He had done all the washing up and put everything away. He had made decaffeinated coffee during another break.

Later he had opened a bottle of red wine, but that was now empty. He was tempted to open another bottle, but he was already tired and jet-lagged and he feared he would fall asleep. He decided five o'clock

Singapore time would be his final attempt. His insides were now churning continuously and his mind was everywhere and nowhere. He was going crazy. He tried to judge whether he was being unreasonable, but had it not been Laura who had suggested that he ring her at one o'clock in the morning? He picked up the telephone and tried again.

Alex decided that five thirty Singapore time would be his last attempt. He felt tears welling up inside him when, again, there was no answer. He felt as if he wanted to shout something horrible onto the answerphone, but resisted the temptation. There's probably a rational explanation, he thought, but he couldn't think of one.

Six o'clock Singapore time would be his very last attempt!

Alex went up to the bathroom, cleaned his teeth and went to the loo. He already had his dressing gown on and so was ready for bed. He remembered he should have some milk by the bed and he went downstairs again to the kitchen. He opened the fridge and poured milk from the carton into a glass.

All reason had now left him. He was mentally and physically exhausted. He switched off the light downstairs, which was foolish and now found he was struggling on the stairs in the dark. 'Get a grip for God sake!' he muttered to himself has he felt his way up the stairs in pitch-blackness. He put his foot out for the last step, which was not there and almost dropped the milk. Approaching the bedroom door he finally found a light switch. As he climbed into bed he looked across at the clock radio staring back at him. It was eleven fifteen. He picked up the telephone and dialled the hotel number. He knew it off by heart now.

"Laura Cameron, please," he asked. There was no longer a pause from the operator; she didn't even need to look up the room number. She knew it off by heart, too! The telephone began ringing.

"Hello?" It was Laura!

"Laura?" Alex was almost shocked to have someone answer the phone. "Is that you?"

"Darling! How are you? Have you been ringing long?" Laura was slurring heavily.

"Laura, are you drunk?" Alex wasn't sure whether he should be relieved or angry.

"Not drunk darling! Just a little squiffy." There was the sound of several people laughing.

"Laura, who is that laughing? Who on earth is in your room at six fifteen in the morning?" There was confusion and indignation in Alex's voice,

"Is it really six fifteen?" she attempted to say. "Guys! Its six fifty, guys."

"Guys!" Alex was growing more and more impatient. "You've got several men in your room at that time of the morning and you are definitely drunk!"

"Only three guys darling," she slurred. "I've got three guys in my room."

"Laura, listen to me. Have you gone completely crazy? What are you doing with three guys in your hotel room at six fifteen in the morning?" Alex's heart was in his mouth.

"Oh, don't worry, it doesn't matter darling," Laura giggled. "They're Scottish!"

Laura's nine-day trip seemed to last forever. Alex had been to Delhi and back, a short three-day trip, in the interim. Alex and Laura had exchanged a number of texts in the meantime, but there had been no further phone calls. Alex was angry, but resolved to talk about the issue rationally and quietly on her return.

"They were friends," she explained. "They were old friends from Scotland." Apparently she had known them for years. At one stage she tried to explain that having three men in your room was much, much safer than one, but quickly abandoned that argument. She suggested that they had been looking after her because (maybe) she had, after all, been a little tipsy. That, too, sounded unconvincing. Of course she sympathised with Alex, but she could, and would not, not be responsible for his insecurities. It was his fault for not trusting her in the first place.

Alex, although frustrated, realized he was never going to win such an argument. He wanted to explain that this incident probably made him trust her less, not more! But it all fell on deaf ears.

The next day he operated to Cairo, in Egypt. He had a quick beer with some of his crew, but his mind was elsewhere and he retired to bed. He lay in bed waiting for sleep to come, but it didn't. He switched the TV on and flicked through the channels, but he couldn't find any English-speaking programmes. Finally he took his computer from his bag, plugged it in and sat in bed with it balancing on his lap. In the semi-darkness, he sat staring at flashing cursor.

Finally he began typing. The words did not come immediately and, every now and again, he would erase or edit, re-writing, cutting and pasting. He had lost all track of time, but finally his poem was complete. He read it through and, satisfied, considered a title. He called it – "It Hurts This Much"

Laura had busied herself spring-cleaning the house. This was their first crisis, but she wanted no part of it. She had nothing to apologise for. Wasn't she allowed to have a good time? She didn't get tipsy very often and if he had trusted her there would not be a problem!

Alex had returned home feeling a little happier, but he knew things might be a little difficult once he had entered the door. The issue was unresolved and they needed to talk. However, he also knew that Laura would not want to talk and, when they finally did, it might well lead to shouting. The house was always spotless, but even Alex could see the house sparkle. Laura had been busy indeed.

"Can I read you something?" he asked about an hour after he had got home. He was showered and changed and Laura was in the kitchen preparing dinner. His laptop was under his arm. He sat down at the table and opened his computer. The poem was already there on the page.

"If you must," she said tersely. She remained at the sink, scrubbing vegetables.

She did not turn around and, head down, continued to punish the poor vegetables as if it were their fault.

"It's called – It Hurts This Much," he said. She said nothing. Alex began to read...

"How could it happen? What could it mean?
A misunderstanding; creating a scene.
He looks at the phone, no message to see.
Out dancing and drinking at three fifty-three.

Sick in the stomach, he wipes sweat from his face,
He takes a deep breath; his heart beats a pace.
He picks up the phone; his nerves feeling raw,
Still out on the town at quarter past four.

Not a problem, he thinks, she loves only me.
Partying and drinking at four twenty-three.
He's been out of course and done just the same,
Now she's hurting him back and he's going insane.

But if he's done it to her, then she's felt it too;
The anguish and heartache at four forty-two.
It's silly to worry, there's nothing to fear.
Now out for nine hours, on wine and the beer.

He's seen her like this, when the words start to slur;
Out dancing and drinking, the night's just a blur.
She can look after herself, he knows she'll be fine,
Still out on the town at four fifty-nine.

They trust each other, but these times they're apart,
Put strain on their love; a strain on the heart.
Our differences settled, but he'd done nothing wrong,
At quarter past five, the night's been so long.

He does not want her to stop. She does her own thing,
Don't pull of her wings - Oh please God, just ring!
He swallows hard, wipes a tear from his eye.
He looks at the phone; he's started to cry.

"OK, I get it," he pleads up to heaven,
"Please now please stop the pain." It's five twenty-seven.
He swallows, then chokes; can't take any more,
He's sick in his stomach. It's five thirty-four.
He lies in his bed, unable to sleep.
He cannot compete with the hours she keeps.
She loves to party, she does it for kicks,
And he lies there in pain at five thirty-six.

"Can't do this," he murmurs. "The pain is too great.
This cannot go on." Its five thirty-eight.
He whispers a prayer. "Show me a sign,
Please stop the hurt." It's five thirty-nine.

Finally a message, she's had a long night.
She loves him, she says. Everything is alright.
He's glad, but he's sad, but can she not see?
He can't live with this pain, at five fifty-three.

Does she know that it hurts? A twist of the knife.
"I cannot do this for the rest of my life."
He can't take the anguish, the tears or the hurt any more,
He turns off his phone at five fifty-four.

Alex looked up from his laptop and then closed the lid. Laura remained at the sink with her back to him. He sat there quietly and waited. Finally she turned and looked at him. Her eyes were full of tears.

"OK, I get it," she whispered. "I'm sorry."

Alex got up from the kitchen table and put his arms around her.

"I love you so much, Laura. Maybe that's why it hurts." He held her tight. Laura never ever partied that heavily again.

CHAPTER 18: SINGAPORE

Loving someone this much, Alex reasoned, hurt from time to time, but surely that would pass. The 'up-side' was so incredibly wonderful that missing Laura when she was away was just something he would have to put up with. Perhaps the pain would gradually fade as they grew ever closer and more familiar with each other. He chastised himself for his immaturity, acting like a love-sick puppy.

This all meant that their new-found relationship had to be managed. The couple were still learning about each other, their likes and dislikes but, with the intensity of their love, almost anything could be forgiven. They learned that it was OK to have a good time down route, without the other being there. One could not be expected to sit in a hotel room pining for your loved one when so much time was spent away from home. It did make sense to meet up with fellow crewmembers for a meal or a few drinks. A walk around the shops, or the park, or the street was sometimes essential for ones' sanity!

However, it was still early days in the relationship and when the airline rostering system delivered nearly two weeks apart from each other, it proved to be a difficult experience. This time it was Alex's turn to fly a long trip down to Singapore and then Sydney, Australia. With rest days down route the trip would last nine days.

Meanwhile Laura had been given a Hong Kong trip, which would be five days away from home. As if that were not bad enough, by the time Alex returned home, Laura would have completed her rest days off at home and would be back out again, this time to New York.

Being dealt another blow like this was a challenge, but it was one they would rise to. You have to bear in mind this was a couple who wanted to spend every minute of every day together. How long they would continue to feel like that, neither of them knew but, for now, it was a problem.

Both Laura and Alex tried to put on a brave face, but the day of their conflicting trips got closer and closer. Both of them were very professional people, both doing very important jobs. Arriving at work, Alex concentrated on his preparation and briefing for his flight. Laura would equally be very busy.

The flight to Singapore would be long (about twelve and a half hours) and tiring, but when Alex arrived in his hotel room he rang Hong Kong. Laura's flight would be just a little shorter, but she had stayed in, waiting for his call.

Yes, it had been a very busy flight. Yes, there had been the occasional difficult passenger or problem to deal with, but none of that mattered now.

Would Alex go out? Probably; he would go and drown his sorrows with some noodles and a few beers.

Would Laura go out? Yes, the girls were planning to go to the Ladies Market. They had promised their pilots they would check the bar on their return, just in case the pilots were still stuck in there!

For Alex, the rest of the evening was pleasant enough. He met up with his fellow pilots and a few of the cabin crew and chatted about life, the job and where they should eat. Normally the consensus would be that there was no consensus. The pilots might suggest one restaurant, while the cabin crew were set on another. Cost and the distance away were often factors in these decisions. Cabin crew were paid less than pilots and, generally, did not want to walk two miles in high heeled shoes. Yes, they might meet back in the bar later; it would depend.

The next day Alex slept until late morning, switched on the television on and just lay in his bed. By lunchtime he began to get hungry and looked out of the window. It was a sunny day. Should he go for a walk in the hot, sticky heat and find somewhere to eat? Or should he go to the huge, air-conditioned shopping centre within the hotel complex and eat there? Should he go to the swimming pool and allow his tummy to rumble all afternoon? While he lay there thinking about all those things, he fell back to sleep again.

Alex was awoken by CNN television, telling the same old news every fifteen minutes. It was now four o'clock in the afternoon. He noticed the message light flashing on his telephone and his heart fluttered. Laura! He picked up the telephone and pressed the message light.

"You have one call waiting. One call, left by a guest, at 3.30pm today."

'Hi Alex, Terry here. A group of us are meeting for tennis at five o'clock; we've booked a court. See you then.'

"No more messages. To repeat the message, press three." Alex hit three and erased the message. "Message deleted".

Alex listened to the CNN news again, sure that it was the same exact news he had heard last week. Curiously his stomach was no longer rumbling, so he drank a full bottle of bottled water instead and had a shower. Yes, he was about to sweat more than a Turkish Bath attendant, but smelling on court would be much worse. So he showered, cleaned his teeth, put on his white shorts, white top, socks and air tennis shoes and found another bottle of water. Wallet, hotel key and airline I/D and he was ready. At five to five he took the lift to the eighth floor and walked past the swimming pool and bar on the way to the tennis courts. The swimming pool was a good place to see who else was in town.

Two hours later and Alex's sports gear was completely drenched through. It was hot and humid. He had run like a madman, attempting to compete with younger men who clearly practised every day! He was an ex-squash player, lacking the finesse of backspin and topspin. Also a squash court was smaller and the game only lasted 45 minutes. Nevertheless he was still reasonably fit (for his age). The guys thanked him, primarily because one against two would have made it an even more challenging game for them in temperatures of thirty-three degrees Celsius. They all congratulated each other on how well they had played, slightly grateful there had been no witnesses.

"See you in 'Jane's Bar' in an hour," the four sweaty bodies agreed. Alex lay on his bed for another twenty minutes with the air conditioning on full before having another shower. Thankfully this was a posh hotel with a good supply of towels. He lay naked on the bed, again with the air-con on full, before getting dressed. He was exhausted but it does you good, doesn't it? Finally dressed, Alex sat by his bed and rang Hong Kong.

"How was your day?" he asked. Laura began by saying how she and the girls had popped into the bar on returning to the hotel. Yes, the pilots had still been there. Someone had made a plan to go to a local dance bar and, of course, you can't let your colleagues down. Laura had tried to explain that she had just met this gorgeous Captain and was madly in love, but that did not stop the guys from flirting with her. A couple of guys even knew Alex, but that didn't stop them flirting either! Finally the girls got bored and had taken a taxi back to the hotel.

Today she had been tired. Apparently jetlag makes you tired, but dancing until 3.00am doesn't. She had awoken at mid-day and watched a movie on the TV; it was a girlie-flick. In the afternoon she had been for a pedicure with one of the girls and tonight they were meeting about eight. They both spoke about missing each other, but the lack of intimacy at one thousand six hundred miles distance made the telephone conversation difficult. There were pauses. How can you say 'yes, I'm going out, but do you have to go?'

"I love you Laura," Alex whispered.

"I love you too," she whispered back.

"Are we going to spend our lives, wishing the days away, until the next time we are together?" Alex asked. "Is it always going to be this torturous?"

"I don't know," Laura said quietly. "Let's not do this..."

Ten minutes later Alex walked into the bar. "Late on parade!" someone said. "Too tired to get in the shower?" Alex smiled and soon after, a beer was being thrust into his hand. "Maybe you should play golf, its slower," someone else suggested, but Alex knew they all practised that, too.

The two rest nights in Singapore passed very slowly and Alex found himself flying his Jumbo jet down to Sydney, Australia. It was early morning when he got to his hotel room in Sydney. He stood looking out on the Sydney Harbour Bridge behind the towering office blocks. He knew that just to the right, obscured by another apartment block was the Sydney Opera House. He was a long way from home and a long way from Laura. He felt very lonely. He was very tired, but stood there waiting for his suitcase to be delivered to the room. It was the wrong time to ring Hong Kong, even earlier in the morning there, but he could send a text. She would get it when she woke up.

Alex found it very difficult to sleep. He was still less than half way through his trip. Laura would be leaving Hong Kong tonight, flying back through the night and arriving back in London tomorrow morning. He tried to work out what time she would be back home at the house, but his brain hurt. Would it be before he departed Sydney, on his return trip to Singapore? Plus ten on GMT he thought… And my pick up time is…..? How far away would she be then? At least ten thousand miles he calculated. Still more jumbled thoughts filled his mind. Living with a stewardess was, perhaps, a bad idea. How many times would he have to go through this frustration and torment? Would he ever get used to it?

Alex listened as an ambulance or police car raced along the city street. Cars were sounding their horns and, in the far distance, someone was digging up the road. This bloody hotel needs double-glazing, he thought. Light was streaming through the windows. He rolled over and squinted at the radio clock beside the bed. It was two o'clock in the afternoon. He had slept after all, but his head felt very heavy and eyes felt full of grit once again. He was very familiar with these sensations of course, all part of the job, but the depression was new to him. The excitement of meeting a new woman, the wonderful romance, the new life, eventually moving in with her; all of this seemed a high price to pay for the pain he now felt. He was sad, fed up and empty inside. How come it hurts this much, he wondered?

Alex reached across to his telephone and switched it on. It seemed to take an eternity to turn on and find a signal. No messages. Did that mean Laura was still asleep in Hong Kong? That was highly possible; it would be Noon there.

Noon.

At Noon, in Causeway Bay, Hong Kong, just along from the Yacht Club, a cannon would be fired to mark 12 o'clock midday. It was a tradition from the colonial days, but the Chinese had carried on the custom. Would she just be waking up to the sound of the Noon Gun?

Alex checked the mobile phone once again. Yes, he did have a signal. If he put the phone down, was it more likely to ring? He considered whether to send another text, but that might seem a little desperate. Actually, he was desperate. He was hurting like hell and he didn't like it. He wanted it to stop. He put the phone on the bedside table and picked up the TV remote. He was well practised at turning a TV on without looking at the buttons. The television in Australia was awful, especially during the day. The choice included low budget soaps, Australian and American, a downmarket chat show showing you how to scramble eggs, a cartoon channel, local news and a DIY program.

Alex paused at the DIY channel.

'So Mark, that looks really great! Did you really do all that in fifteen minutes?'

'Well, yes Sheila, I did.'

"Well, yes Sheila, I did," Alex said out loud. "And you've been standing there watching me do it, so why are you asking such a bloody stupid question?"

'Well, that really is amazing Mark. How did you do it?'

"Sheila, are you thick or something?" Alex shouted at the television.

'Well Sheila, I used this new handy device from Gadget Inc. Those clever people have designed a hand-tool that virtually does it all by itself.'

"No, Mark, it doesn't," Alex complained to the TV. "You have to do it once you've put on those stupid safety glasses and the ear defenders. I bet you can buy those from Gadget Inc. too!"

'Wow Mark, those people at Gadget Inc. have really done it this time, haven't they?'

Alex wondered why the women on these shows always had that terrible whining accent that could rattle a wine glass.

'Yes Sheila, they certainly have. Only this time, if you ring in the next two hours, they will give you another one completely free!'

"Why would you need two of these Mark?" Alex shouted at the television. "Unless the first one breaks after the first day!"

'Now, I noticed you've created a little mess on the floor Mark. Does Gadget Inc. have a tool for that too?' After every inane question Sheila would show her bright white teeth to the camera.

"Yes!" Alex shouted. "It's called a bloody vacuum cleaner, you toss pot!"

This type of dumb, absurd programme would go on for thirty minutes, sometimes an hour, pretending to be a home improvement programme when clearly it was one long advertisement. Were people really that stupid? Evidently, yes.

On the bedside table, the mobile phone sang a short tune. It was a text! Alex hit the mute button He then realised this was a little odd given that it was only a text on his mobile. He picked it up and selected his 'Inbox'. Yes! It was a text from Laura. His heart beat loudly as he scrolled down.

'Late night. Walked home at sunrise. Off to bed. Talk later.'

Alex stared at the message, reading it over and over. He checked the clock on his phone, then at the bedside. It was 2.14pm. 12.14pm in Hong Kong. Off to bed? He pushed himself into a proper sitting position in the bed and re-focused on the message. Then he scrolled down still further. Sent today at 06.00am!

The excitement drained from his body. The text was six hours old. She had been out partying while he had been breaking his heart. Upset, empty, angry; these emotions flashed through his body and through his mind, none lasting for more than a few seconds but now he felt numb.

It the shower hot water poured over his body, but he felt nothing and everything. He washed away the soap and then just stood there, slowly turning in the falling water. Then he absent-mindedly picked up the soap and began all over again. He had tried to analyse his emotions but there was simply too much going on inside his head. He was tired and perhaps he was being unreasonable. On the other hand, was she not feeling the empty hollowness that he felt? He was missing her so much. Too much!

Out in the streets it was a warm muggy day, with a fair breeze blowing between the skyscrapers. But the wind was warm too, failing to cool him down. Swirls of dust spun at street corners, stinging his eyes. Where others saw beautiful Sydney on a summer's day, Alex saw full waste bins and doorsteps littered with cigarette butts.

At every street crossing the little man flashed red. DO NOT CROSS. Cars, taxis, buses and lorries all desperately raced through green traffic lights at speed, vying for position and pushing up even more dust. Another street, even more speeding traffic, all in a hurry for what? The city blocks seemed small, meaning frequent roads to cross, and they were always on red. DO NOT CROSS!

Finally he reached the sanctuary of Sydney's Royal Botanical Gardens. The sound of the traffic was lost on the wind and paths led him to isolated parts, surrounded by large, exotic trees and bushes. The roses were probably at their best, but they went unnoticed as Alex made his way along the curiously named Mrs Macquaries Road at one side of the park. A large sandstone rock, carved into a bench by convicts nearly two hundred years before, was also named after the wife of the then New South Wales Governor. He strode past it with barely a glance. Eventually he could see across Farm Cove to the wonderful Sydney Opera House, with Sydney Harbour Bridge framed behind it. To his right dozens of ferries, boats and ships hurried across the harbour, linking coves and points and bays that were part of this amazing city.

Alex began to breathe deeply now, wishing he could share this with the one he loved. Years later, he was able to do exactly that. By then the insecurities and the pain had given way to happiness and peace, contentment and eventually old age.

Back at the hotel, Alex sat on his bed and rang Hong Kong. It was mostly small talk. He spoke about his long, but uneventful flight down from Singapore. No, not many of his crew were planning to meet up, all complaining about the time-change and never sleeping well in Australia. Laura said she had had a nice evening, but neither of them mentioned the text or her late night. Alex just kept repeating that he was missing her and wished this whole month would be over.

Text me when you get home, he instructed, and he would ring her before he flew back to Singapore tomorrow afternoon. He told her to have a good flight and then there was a pause. A long pause. 'I love you' and 'I love you too' were then said very quietly and Alex found himself listening to the dialling tone.

"Text as soon as you get home." Alex re-read the text and pressed 'send'. It took an hour before the short reply came back.

"OK" was all it said.

Alex had a quiet evening. He met his First Officer Malcolm Peacock in the bar just down the street from the hotel. Once again, because crew were creatures of habit, Sydney too had a recognised meeting place for the crew to meet up. Or not, if they didn't meet up at all!

Soon Brian, a purser, joined them. Together the three of them put the world to rights. Brian described his co-workers as 'crap'. He was glad they hadn't come out. Malcolm and Alex glanced at each other, but made no comment. It was risky slagging off the crew. There was a strong possibility that anything mentioned tonight might be repeated by Brian on the flight home tomorrow. Safer then to say nothing! Alex also wondered if the crew were all out somewhere else having a great night, avoiding Brian ***and*** the pilots.

The usual subjects were all given a quick mention - How long had they had been flying? Why was longhaul was less tiring than short-haul?

Hadn't the Unions made a mess of things and why was it the management didn't care about its' staff?

Brian was married with young children, which was a surprise causing another silent glance between the pilots, who both had thought he was gay. As if to reinforce his manliness, Brian then began to talk about football and his wonderful soccer club, Chelsea. He talked about the players, the manager and the fact that he could no longer afford to be a season ticket holder at Stamford Bridge. He himself played in midfield for a club in South London, but he found it difficult to keep his place in the team because he was away all the time. Still they trained twice a week and replaced all the muscle tone with beer after each training session or match.

Alex was asked which team he supported. He began by way of an apology. His great-great-grandfather, he said, had been a forgeman working with iron for a company called Thames Ironworks. Thames Ironworks built big wooden ships and then clad them with iron plates so that cannon balls would bounce off. That company had formed its' own works football team and, as they worked with iron, they were nicknamed the Hammers. This, Alex explained, made his great-great-grandfather a founder member of West Ham Football Club.

Brian nodded knowledgeably and they both turned to Malcolm, who was just finishing his pint of Victoria Bitter.

"I fucking hate football," he said, thrusting his empty glass towards Brian and banging it on the table. Alex hastily picked it up and strode quickly towards the bar. He returned five minutes later with three more VB's, hoping the subject of the conversation might have changed, but it hadn't. Brian was explaining why rugby was a game for poofs, unaware that Malcolm's face was getting redder and redder.

"Are we eating tonight?" Alex asked.

If anything was going to change the subject, food was. To his relief both the boys were starving and his suggestion of a steak at Phillips Foote, a restaurant in the Rocks area near the harbour, went down well. Thirty years before, Alex had been urged to visit 'The Rocks', because it was the oldest part of the city of Sydney! He had been distinctly unimpressed, given that his own house was a hundred years older than any building there.

Now, older and wiser, he loved the charm and the history of this corner of Sydney. It was just a short walk away and the novelty of cooking your own juicy steak on the Barbie began to distract the boys, especially with the prospect of some good red wine. Football and other sports were, thankfully, not mentioned at all for the rest of that evening.

The next afternoon Alex was sitting on his bed, holding his mobile telephone in his hand. He had eaten a late breakfast and pickup was only a few hours away. It was a beautiful sunny day, with light winds and a very blue sky. He should be out walking, he thought, but he had returned to his room to await the all-important message from Laura. He had allowed for the large time change, of course, and calculated the time to disembark the passengers in London (a 747 takes forever!), her trip to the car park and her journey home. She must be home by now. Finally he could wait no longer.

"Are you home yet?" he typed clumsily into the phone. He imagined the question leaving his phone and travelling to a mast somewhere close by in the city. Down the mast and then to where, he wondered? Clearly there was not a wire going all the way from Sydney to London, under the sea, or was there? Perhaps it was beamed to a satellite, but what then? London was on the other side of the world. Was it like a relay team, passing the baton or in this case his message from one athlete to another?

'Pist, are you home yet? – Pass it on!'

'Just got a message from the satellite behind me; Alex wants to know if you are home yet – pass it on!'

Was his message being passed satellite to satellite around the world? Or was there really a telephone wire under the oceans and across the continents? 'I'm an airline captain,' he thought, 'and I don't even know the answer to this!' Suddenly the phone trilled at him to indicate a text had arrived.

'Just having a coffee with someone at the airport. Home soon.' It read.

Alex stared at his mobile phone in disbelief. He read, and then re-read the message. He had stayed in most of the day, a beautiful sunny day in Sydney, waiting to call her and she was having a bloody coffee with a friend. He just could not believe it. He did not know whether to be angry or upset and, instead, he just sat there in total bewilderment. He looked at his watch. There would be no time to go out now. In forty minutes his hotel telephone would ring to tell him there was one hour to pick-up. In that hour he would have to shower, change into his uniform and do his little 'checks'. Make sure his bag was fully packed. Nothing left hanging in the wardrobe. Computer away, mobile charger, and electric razor unplugged from the wall and all put away. Under the bed, in the bathroom and then (he could not help himself) ONE FINAL CHECK!

There would now be little or no time for a romantic chat back to home. He decided to shower now. Of course he had showered this morning, but he had been out since then and got more than a little sweaty. Hygiene was incredibly important because he would be sitting next to Malcolm for the next eight hours or more and the prospect of body odour appalled him. Bad breath would be equally unacceptable. The flight deck was an incredibly confined space. The stewardess's would come in and ask if you wanted a drink. Any horrible spells would be noticed at once.

These were the sort of thoughts that went through his head as he scrubbed and scrubbed at his body concentrating, of course, under his armpits and his private parts. It would mean he would be sitting in his room in his uniform for longer than he would have liked, but how else could he snatch a few extra minutes, creating the time to make his telephone call. 'Coffee with a friend indeed!' She knew he was waiting in his room!

'You must be home by now?' he questioned sometime later. He held his sent message in his hand. He sat there, incredulous, as he waited for a reply. A couple of times he stood up and checked his room. The suitcase was packed and by the door, as was his briefcase. He walked in to the bathroom. Wash bag and razor packed. He walked back into the bedroom and checked the electrical sockets, the side tables and under the pillows.

Finally he took one more look in the wardrobe. He had done these checks already, but another look around never really hurt. He sat back down on the bed and checked the phone again. There was nothing, no message at all. Finally he picked up the telephone and dialled the number. It rang five times before it was answered.

"Hi, we can't get to the phone right now but, if you leave a message, we'll get back to you." Laura's recorded voice was chirpy and bright. Alex was feeling far from chirpy and bright and, therefore, did not leave a message.

Twenty minutes later he was sitting on a bus taking the crew to the airport. Behind him several cheerful conversations were taking place, while one or two others sat with things over their ears, listening to iPods. Several times on the journey he checked his mobile phone, but there was still nothing.

"Hello Skipper, how was that for you then?" The CSD, or head steward, was on the kerbside in front of the airport terminal building waiting for his suitcase to be unloaded.

"Not too bad, John, thank you," Alex smiled back. "We're on the return journey now John, heading in the right direction at least."

"Yes, Skipper. Bloody long trips these; exhausting!." John stepped forward, took his bag and wheeled it towards the terminal.

On board Alex searched the flight deck, part of the security checks, while Malcolm walked around the outside of the aircraft in the sunshine. A scan of the flight deck panels, clicking various switches in sequence, ensured the aircraft would soon be ready for departure. There were hundreds of switches on the overhead panels, on the side panels and on the central console. However, to the trained eye, it only took a few minutes to scan them all and somehow the human brain could detect if a switch was in the wrong position. Small computers were programmed, by telling them where in the world they were and then typing in the route stage by stage, waypoint by waypoint, from Sydney to Singapore.

"All good on the outside," Malcolm reported, as he returned to the flight deck and hung up the bright yellow tabard that he had worn, making him conspicuous to the various vehicles that attend to an aircraft's arrival and departure. The fuel trucks, cargo lorries, the baggage vehicles and the 'honey wagon' that emptied the toilets; all were potential hazards.

"The route is loaded - just the winds to put in," Alex stated. As Malcolm fell into his seat Alex stood up and climbed out.

"Back in five," he said. Alex disappeared into the toilet sited conveniently on the flight deck for the pilots. Inside the narrow space, his head against the curving wall of the ceiling, he took his mobile from his pocket. A small flashing red light indicated that a message had been received.

Yes! A message!

'Home! Next door have invited me to a panto with their kids. If I go, I'll be back about 11. C U Laura.'

'Well it's too late now', he thought. He re-read the message several times before he noticed the time above the text. It had been sent over two hours ago, but he had only just received it! He switched off his phone, washed his hands and walked back onto the flight deck. The engineer was standing, waiting with the tech log in his hands open at the page that required a signature. Alex read the page and checked the fuel amount and oils before signing the page in the box at the bottom.

"Thanks Skip, speak to you on the headset. See yer next time." The engineer brushed by him in the narrow space and left the flight deck.

"Right, let's go to Singapore," Alex said as he dropped back into his seat. "You ready for some checks Malcolm?"

The flight proved to be quite busy. There was CAT (clear air turbulence) over Australia, especially in the area of Alice Springs. It was not dangerous, but definitely uncomfortable for the passengers and crew. The pilots talked with the air traffic controllers at Brisbane Centre, but they were told that the bumps were being reported by other aircraft were at all levels. The seat belt signs remained on for several hours so the tea and coffee service was cancelled. Cold drinks only! Beyond the Australian coast near Broome, the turbulence settled down for a while.

"What do you think, Boss?" Malcolm asked. "OK for the seatbelt signs?" Alex nodded and watched as his co-pilot switched them off. A chime echoed through the aircraft. Night had fallen by now and pilots were studying the weather radar. Ahead, in the far, far distance, flashes could be seen on the horizon. Eventually little green patches appeared on their radar screens. Beyond these appeared some orange and yellow ink blots, and occasionally the centres showed red.

"Left or right?" Malcolm asked. Alex adjusted the range on his screen.

"Right, I reckon. There might be a gap through there." He pointed and then pressed to transmit. "Bali, Bali, Speedbird One Six. Request up to three zero miles right of track due weather."

"Speedbird One Six roger. Three zero miles right of track is approved." The radio crackled and then fell silent. Malcolm selected the heading bug, pressed it once and turned it to the right. Three hundred tons of aircraft dipped its' right wing, moving away from the airway centreline. Alex tapped at his navigation computer and typed R-3-0. A dashed line appeared thirty miles right of their planned track and parallel to it. The flashes grew ever nearer as the Boeing 747-400 approached at a closing speed of about five hundred and thirty miles an hour. Alex reached across and switched the seatbelt signs back on again.

"Just in case you balls it up!" he grinned.

"Thanks," replied Malcolm, turning the Jumbo another five degrees right and squinting out of the window. Tall towering cumulus clouds flashed threateningly around them, whole clouds ignited like a light bulb, before dimming once again to black. They both knew it was a bad idea to get anywhere near one of these evil things. They were currently at thirty five thousand feet, but the anvil tops reached far above them. They managed to keep it reasonably smooth, with most of the passengers and crew oblivious to these monsters that could swallow them up, toss them around and spit them out with an unbelievable force.

It was another ninety minutes before they were back on track again. By now they were talking to Jakarta Air Traffic Control. The moon now reflected on the odd cloud, while Alex studied the rows of lights on the

Java Sea beneath them. He could see Indonesian fishing vessels trawling their nets through the night seven miles below them. Suddenly there was just an hour to go and the two pilots began the briefing for landing, talking about the approach and landing into Singapore. Both had flown approaches into Singapore many, many times before but, before every departure at every airport and before every approach onto every runway, the pilots would brief each other about what they were going to do, down to the finest detail.

Only once they were on the ground and in the car transport taking them to the hotel in Singapore, did Alex switch on his mobile phone. He knew it would take a few minutes to find a connection and he took the time to look out of the window. Singapore was a beautiful city and one of his most favourite places in the whole world. It was clean, very safe and it had some great bars, shops and restaurants. He favoured "Fat Sams", where the tables were all outside on the street. Spring rolls to start, then black pepper beef, sizzling prawns or salted prawns (sometimes both!), pak choy and loads of egg fried rice. Yummy!

In his hand, his telephone began vibrating and he watched a message came through with excitement.

'Welcome to Singapore Roaming. To receive your messages...'

Alex deleted the message and stared at the mobile. Then he made a pact with himself. If there were no more messages by the time they arrived at the hotel, he would not even try to ring home. He stared out of the window and watched as the familiar buildings passed the window. Between the food courts on the left he could see the harbour with cargo ships and tugs brightly lit up. The mobile phone remained silent.

Check-in at the hotel was quick and efficient. In his room he had switched on his TV and closed the curtains. CNN news was broadcasting Asia Business News again, the most boring thing on TV, but Alex had not wasted time surfing the channels. His bag had just arrived, he had tipped the porter, and now he was in the shower. He had promised Malcolm he would be in the bar thirty minutes after his bag arrived.

The Singapore flight from Australia landed quite late in the evening. There would be several crews in Singapore, as there were every night. Most of them would have met up with colleagues and been out to eat. Some would then call it a night and go to bed. Others would have wandered back to 'Jane's Bar' to see what was happening. He wondered who was in town.

Alex stepped out of the shower and picked up a small towel. It was his habit to wipe the surplus water from his body with a small towel first. Then the larger towel remained drier for longer to actually dry his tall long body. He walked into the huge bedroom he had been given, a privilege of his status, and he sat on the bed. He had time to just sit and cool down in the efficient air conditioning before getting dressed and stepping into the hot sticky night air. He had already shaved and cleaned his teeth.

Now he took his lightweight black slacks and a very cool black top from the suitcase. Normally he would unpack his case and hang everything up, but he was in a big rush to get to the bar tonight. He was thirsty! Finally he returned to the bathroom and took a tube of hair gel from his wash bag. He pushed his fingers through the fringe of his hair so that the front stood up just a little. At his age he could still look a little trendy!

He switched off the television, placed his credit cards in the safe and locked it. Wallet in pocket, tissues in left-hand pocket, plastic door key – checked! He looked at his watch. It was thirty-two minutes since the porter had delivered his suitcase. Alex did not even attempt to look at his mobile phone, which was charging on a desk across the room. Certainly there was no time for a recriminating telephone call home. Beer time!

The lifts often took a while. There were a lot of floors in this hotel and Alex reckoned they turned a couple of the lifts off during less busy times like now. Most people, businessmen and tourists, would be in their beds by now ready for an early start tomorrow. Lots of crew, on the other hand, approximated to UK time in an attempt to preserve sleep patterns and minimise jetlag. It was a good theory anyway!

The lift arrived and Alex stepped in. The interior was highly polished with mirrors around the walls. An advertisement talked about the hotel

Jazz Bar, but it was expensive and not the sort of place crew would frequent. He looked in the mirror and hoped he looked OK. He was a senior Captain in a large airline, but he was no longer wearing the protective uniform that gave him authority and assurance. It was hard to explain the little element of uncertainty he felt, a small lack of confidence in a social setting. He knew that once he was there and drinking his first beer, he would be fine but, for now, he just hoped he didn't look a prat!.

Stepping out of the lift, Alex entered the hotel lobby area. As expected there were only a few people there, just a few very weary travellers with heavy suitcases or backpackers seeking a bed for the night. Actually they must have had a booking in a hotel like this, he thought, you would not just turn up unannounced. The desks were fully manned with probably the best-trained staff in the world. Service was everything here! A porter was crossing the floor walking towards him.

"Good evening, Captain. Have a good evening." The porter beamed a smile at him. There must be hundreds of people passing through this hotel at any one time but, even out of uniform, the hotel staff always seemed to know who he was. Incredible! He also knew that when he walked into Jane's Bar just a block away from here, the staff would greet him by his first name.

'Hello Alex, jug of Tiger?' they would ask. If Jane was there, she would come over and kiss him on both cheeks as a long lost friend. The hotel lobby was cool and peaceful with just the sound of a water feature, stunningly effective in the outer hallway. The concierge nodded with a smile as he approached the double doors. Alex knew it would be hot and muggy as the electric glass doors slid open. He stepped outside.

A hotel doorman still guarded the taxi rank, but he would know, or guess, that Alex was walking to the corner to cross one block into the complex of bars and restaurants that housed Jane's Bar. Then he stopped just outside the hotel door.

What was it? What was wrong? What had just happened?

Alex turned and instinctively walked back into the hotel lobby.

Standing there in the hotel lobby was Laura! Of course, it was impossible. She was back home in England, having recently got back from Hong Kong. Yet here she was, standing in the middle of the lobby in all her splendour! The apparition looked beautiful, wearing a gorgeous white dress. Yet she was staring straight at him, smiling.

"Hello darling!" It was the voice of an angel; his angel.

Alex just stood there, frozen to the spot. This was impossible. She took two steps towards him.

"Beast! You weren't meant to see me!" she said. "I was going to follow you across to the bar. The staff have been fantastic, they were all in on it."

Alex looked around to see the concierge, the porters and the check-in staff all beaming goodwill towards him from across the lobby. Laura was really standing there immediately in front of him.

"You weren't meant to turn around!" she admonished him.

Alex reached out to touch her. She was real. He found himself rocking very slightly as he held her in his arms. Then he released her and stood staring at her, still not speaking. His eyes were filled with tears. He tried to talk, but nothing happened; there was no sound. He was, quite simply, overwhelmed.

"Come on," Laura said, taking him by the hand. Together they walked back out into the humid night air. "I'm sorry about the texts. When I landed at the airport I had a coffee while I waited for the Singapore Airlines desk to open. We had an embargo, so I couldn't fly out with the company. Then I dashed home to change my suitcase and get new clothes. The neighbours really did invite me to the pantomime! Then I went back and caught the Singapore flight. Right down the back, I'll have you know! Did you know they have a row 58! Luckily it wasn't busy and they let me move into a row of empty seats."

They paused for a moment at the traffic lights, which then obligingly turned green so that they could cross the road.

"And the facilities at Changi Airport are really fantastic!" Laura continued. "They have wonderful showers and changing rooms. The hotel staff were great, too! They looked after my bag and then told me when you would be checking in. You seemed to be ages! I was going to follow you across and walk into the bar to surprise you. Someone asked what I would do if I walked in and you had your arm around another girl! Well, you are so friendly and flirty anyway, but I hadn't honestly thought about it before then."

Alex smiled as Laura chatted away excitedly. She had hardly paused for a breath. His eyes were still misty with tears and he could not speak. He was still in a state of shock. Laura was more than able to make enough conversation for both of them and so it was. Several of his crew were in the bar when he walked in and they were curious to know who this glamorous girl was. Word soon got around that she had actually flown halfway around the world to be with her loved one AND immediately after a Hong Kong trip! They all understood the sacrifice and fatigue that had been involved.

'It's so romantic!'

'He's so lucky!'

'Hope he was worth it!'

'God, it must be love!'

Overwhelming bewilderment slowly gave way to ecstasy and pleasure, and pride, and happiness and ......love. So much love.

After a while several of the crew moved upstairs to another bar. Another venue. Late on in the evening a live band played there and Laura and Alex, the talk of the town tonight, joined them to drink and dance the night away. It proved necessary to repeat their story several times, but they did not mind a bit. Laura talked about electric flowers, the Rod Stewart surprise concert and flying halfway around the world to surprise her boyfriend. Girls eyed this Captain in a new light, while guys scoffed and suggested such things gave men a bad name!

"What can you do to ever beat that?" one girl asked him. "She flew round the world for you."

"Absolutely nothing!" Alex replied, the tears again welling up inside. "Absolutely nothing."

CHAPTER 19: NIGHTMARE EXPRESS

Alex had been searching back through his mind. He could no longer recall things at will. Sometimes half a thought would take him and he would go through the alphabet from A to Z (occasionally more than once) to recall someone or some place. That seemed to be enough to push open a memory and the details would come flooding back. Well, sometimes.

Penang had been a charming place to visit. It had reminded Alex of how Singapore might have looked fifty years ago. Singapore had, of course, prospered greatly and become rich and modern. It had demolished many of its historical buildings in the name of progress before it woke up to the fact that its history and colonial past was part of the reason the tourists went there in the first place. Towering monoliths of banks, corporations and hotels continued to be built, dominating the cityscape, but streets of colonial facsimiles now gave the impression, at least, that Singapore finally understood its historical heritage.

Some development had taken place in Penang, with luxury apartments and hotels climbing high above the city and beyond. However George Town's colonial heritage had, so far, been preserved more by chance than wisdom. It had been the lack of money that had slowed down the developers, thereby inadvertently creating a living museum, part of which was eventually granted World Heritage Status. Many of the buildings remained dilapidated, desperately in need of love and investment, but gradually the balance between progress and tradition would preserve the city for future generations.

Alex and Laura had wondered at Penang the beguiling island, a cosmopolitan mix of Malay, Chinese and Indian, peppered with Siamese and Filipino, British Expats and Japanese. A melting pot where Islamists lived alongside Buddhists, Chinese Taoists, Sikhs and Christians. Some successful Malays had become the new colonialists, playing golf, attending tennis clubs and having dinner parties with the expats, almost more British than the British themselves.

Stories would be told about the tsunami that hit in 2004. The tragedy of fishing villages totally wiped out. There was the miracle of the mosque on the seashore, untouched by the huge devastating waves. The wall of water had arrived very tall and super powerful, sweeping past it on either side, before draining away again to leave it dry, untouched and intact. Then there was the young baby, asleep on a mattress, cruelly plucked from her open bedroom window and out to sea. The baby's family were still mourning at the waters' edge, when the incoming tide returned the floating mattress with the baby on top of it, still alive and asleep.

Great meals with friends, old stories from the distant past and companionship had made it a trip to remember, but it was the return journey from Penang back to Bangkok that was burned into Alex's memory. They could have easily returned to Bangkok by air, but they had chosen adventure and the long, enduring journey by rail.

After the crossing from the island, it had been a short walk from the ferry pier to the Butterworth Railway Station. Actually the old station, with all its imperial splendour, had been demolished in the name of progress. Not everything could be saved! In its place stood a small corrugated building, built sturdily enough to wait patiently for the construction of the new station. Whether it was to be constructed sympathetically in the old colonial style for its' Orient Express visitors remained to be seen.

Alex and Laura purchased their tickets at the corrugated makeshift ticket counter, but the man behind the glass explained, with a smile, that he could only sell them a ticket as far as the Malaysia-Thailand border. After passing Padang Besar another ticket had to be purchased. This would take them as far as Hat Yai across in Thailand. From there, a restaurant car would be added to the train, together with a first class carriage, which would provide comfortable private sleeping accommodation for the overnight journey. Alex had booked that ticket back in Thailand.

Passengers assembled in the metal shed with such 'mod-cons' as wooden seats and a badly over-worked air-conditioning unit. Five minutes before departure Alex approached a uniformed member of the station staff and asked which platform would be used for the Bangkok departure.

"Yes Sir," grinned the station attendant, determined to please.

"We board soon?" Alex asked. He wiped away the sweat from his face and yearned to be on his way.

"Yes Sir. Definitely!" It was certainly customer service with a smile.

"Soon?" Alex persisted.

"Yes Sir." Today Pradesh was really earning his money. "Maybe depart at 3.00pm."

"What? Are you saying we are forty-five minutes late?" Alex could not help the disappointment in his voice.

"Yes Sir, definitely maybe!" The station attendant then moved away, proud to have been of service. How he loved his job!

In the event, it was another ninety-five minutes before the train finally began moving out of the station. The seats were a little hard, but the carriage was cool, with large windows providing a huge vista. Beyond the glass was the hot sweaty exterior, resplendently green and lush, providing a panorama of plants and trees producing goods such as rubber, coconuts, pineapples, purple mangosteens and palm oil. Occasionally a clearing appeared, a field of shallow water, divided into unequal plots, roughly half the size of a football pitch. It was impossible to tell whether the occasional person wading knee-deep in the murky water planting rice, was a woman or a man, a huge netted veil draped over a large, wide-brimmed hat.

Occasionally the rich tropical greenery would fall away to show or reveal an old factory building, rusting under corrugated tin, reflecting the lack of money in the struggling economy. This would contrast starkly with the iniquitous presence of a towering building, perhaps apartments or offices, rising proudly and boasting a new age that was leaving so many others behind. Near some of the towns new orange earth, cleared and flattened, demonstrated the new exciting construction and infrastructure paid for by the government; new roads or new, better railways for the developing Malaysia. It had of course always been developing but, sometimes at a trickle, sometimes at pace, and most often in the coastal plains, near the beaches where the rich wanted to live and the tourists wanted to visit.

Cities benefited from development, while elsewhere survival was sometimes a constant imperative. Parts of this amazing country had so much promise and so little money. With a minimum wage, not always enforced, of 300 ringgits or £60 per month, the future held little prospect for many in the countryside or those who had flooded to the factories in the new growing towns and cities. It was indeed a beautiful country, full of contrasts and contradictions, a real blend of ethnics and nationalities, with mosques, temples and churches, each steeped in history, prayer and philanthropy.

Alex turned from the window, a sort of Discovery Channel with sound but no narration, to look at Laura. Her blonde hair was perhaps even blonder, bleached by the Malaysian sun. He looked at her skin, brown and beautiful, draped in a Desigual dress of black and white, descending into rich reds, pinks and fuchsias below the waist. It was elegant, but fashionable; a suitable refection of Laura herself.

She sat staring down at her crossword, perhaps saving the suduko for later. As she pondered 'nine across' she stared out at the palm trees, the drainage ditches and smallholdings. Sometimes a little moped chugged alongside, straddling a single-track road, a blue and grey mist spilling from its exhaust. Then the train would pull away, changing the picture for something new, as if changing TV channels with a remote control. Next was an innocuous hill of igneous rock, sticking out of the flat wetlands, its steep sides packed tightly with impenetrable rain forest.

The sun was slowly sinking towards the horizon but, before it did so, high powdery clouds began to hide the blue ozone of the day. The small delicate clouds were slowly replaced by grey, bubbly clouds, sufficient to shield the weakening sun. The passing scenery seemed cool from the air-conditioned carriage, but Alex knew the countryside remained very hot and humid. He wondered whether this would soon convert into a rainstorm. Not that it mattered, he thought. Dusk would soon fall, night would come and later still the border with Thailand. Beyond the border was the promise of a restaurant car, a first class cabin and, ultimately, a bed and sleep.

About three hours into the journey, night had fully cloaked the rural landscape. Occasionally a single light shone above a small farmhouse, hidden amongst the trees between the wider expanse of farmland, wetlands and fields. These single lights seemed more like dim beacons, showing the farmer the way back across the fields to sanctuary and home. Totally in shadow, a building passed stealthily by the window; then another and, more frequently, another. The train began to slow. They were approaching Padang Besar and the border.

At Padang Besar passengers began getting off the train to go through immigration. Alex went to pick up their bags, but train staff ushered them off the train shouting 'leave bags' over and over again. He felt rather uneasy about leaving their possessions on the train as numerous personnel had boarded the train behind them. Caterers, cleaners, and relatives of the train staff, the carriages were a swarm of activity.

On the platform, Alex and Laura followed the huge crowd of passengers who ambled slowly into the station building. Inside the scene was equally chaotic. People were being ushered in numerous different directions as if the train's arrival had been a massive surprise.

Alex looked back nervously at the train through the station window, while Laura held his arm trying to reassure him. He looked down at her and she smiled a familiar smile, which meant 'chill, it will all be OK.' The line moved painfully slowly, with one single man apparently dealing with all the passports. First he studied the passport, checking the picture and the details. Then he thumbed through the pages, examining each stamp or mark in the small red book. Finally he began typing into his computer, seemingly writing an extended essay on each passenger in turn.

"Deep breaths," Laura whispered. "It won't go without us."

Alex had no such worries. He was more concerned about the contents of their bags finishing the journey with them and he chided himself for not at least bringing the IPad and the camera with them. They were hidden from view, but a professional thief would find them soon enough. Alex hated being outside his comfort zone, in a situation where he was not in control. This all seemed much worse because no one here appeared to be in control. Eventually their turn came. Laura smiled and said hello to the Thai uniformed official, who immediately melted and smiled back. 'Where have you come from?' 'Where are you going?' the man asked.

'No, stop,' Alex wanted to say. No-one else was asked these questions. 'Just stamp the bloody passports' he thought, but dared not say. The official again beamed and smiled at Laura as he handed her both passports. As they stepped away, they found themselves herded towards a second queue. This time it was Thai Immigration. More staff, more urgency, faster queues; it wasn't rocket science!

"We still need a ticket from here to Hat Yai," Laura reminded Alex. "Shall I go and buy it while you dash back and check the bags?" she asked.

Alex needed no second bidding and hurried back to the train. Dozens of officials continued to walk up and down the train, but the faces and the uniforms had mostly changed. The Malay staff had all got off and now the Thai staff had taken charge. Laura returned and tried to explain to Alex why she had not bought any railway tickets for the next part of the journey. The ticket man, she said, would come on board and explain to the staff why we did not need a ticket. Alex wanted to know his name, who had he spoken to and why was a ticket unnecessary? No answers were forthcoming. What if we get going and the train guard demands our tickets? What will we do then? Will we be arrested if they do not believe us?

Alex felt his blood pressure slowly rising to high levels again. This was totally disorganised. They were planning to travel further on the train without buying the tickets they were told they would need to buy. And why? Because a man (unknown, but presumably something to do with the railway or ticket office back in Padang Besar) had said he didn't think we needed a ticket for this journey. He had supposedly passed this information onto someone else on the train, also not known to us!

Why couldn't Laura understand this was crazy? Alex hated the uncertainty, while Laura just smiled and said it would be OK. In the event, it was OK. The bags were intact, no tickets were purchased and no-one seemed to mind. Somewhere from the platform a whistle blew, the engine beeped a loud acknowledgement and the train began to pull away. Alex remained tense; Laura smiled again and went back to her book. They were now in Thailand and on their way.

About thirty minutes later a ticket inspector entered into the carriage and began checking tickets. Alex closed his eyes, frustrated and doubtful. He passed the tickets to the official.

"You come!" The ticket inspector ushered Alex and Laura from their seats. "Bring," he said, pointing to the luggage and bags. There was no attempt to assist them. "Come now!" he persisted.

Alex lifted the suitcase and one bag, while Laura took the smaller holdall and her handbag. They struggled down the narrow aisle, while the ticket collector hurried them like a goat herder. Other passengers eyed them curiously as they stumbled along the carriage.

'It's because we haven't got a bloody ticket!' he wanted to say to them. 'We tried to explain, but no one would listen!' In reality, of course, he said nothing.

At the end of the carriage was a door and, through its' little window, Alex could see the next carriage twisting and turning like a snake ahead of them.

"Press," barked the official. "Press!"

Alex put the suitcase down and pressed the little green button near the roof. Instantly the door slid open to reveal the intense heat and a cacophony of train sounds, including grinding metal. Below, in a gap between the two carriages, the railway sleepers flashed by menacingly. The two carriages continued to wrestle with each other, swinging wildly this way and that. Alex and Laura struggled to keep their feet as they hauled their bags and stepped across the divide.

Instead of a first class carriage, or even a carriage at all, they found themselves in a sort of baggage car. The walls and floor were wooden and of poor quality. A passage led still further and around a corner until the wagon opened up to the full width of the train. Four men sat either on the floor, or on boxes, and they looked up at the visitors curiously. To step further into the wagon required them to pass a fully open door, perhaps two metres wide, protected by a small, flimsy cotton tape. Despite the darkness, Alex could see the countryside flashing passed them at considerable speed. He hesitated.

"This can't be right," he called back loudly to Laura above the noise of the train. "I'm not walking past there!" He pointed to the huge open door. He fought hard to keep his balance, his hands full of baggage, as the racing train continued to sway sharply from side to side.

"Let's go back," Laura implored. Alex watched as trees and bushes continued to dangerously speed passed the train, with just that cotton tape between them and certain death. Alex needed no second bidding. They both turned unsteadily, trying to keep their feet, and they finally staggered back through the sliding door to the safety of second class and relative peace. They moved back to an empty seat and sat down. Five minutes later the ticket inspector returned. He was not happy!

"No, you go, you go now!" The official aggressively waved his hands towards towards the door.

"How long to Hat Yai?" Alex asked. "How long?"

"Twenty minutes," the official said, who had become even more agitated.

"Then we go in twenty minutes!" Alex waved his hand back towards the exasperated ticket man. "No! Twenty minutes!"

The ticket man turned on his heels and walked away. Laura and Alex looked at each other with some relief.

"Well, that was interesting!" She said. They both held on to their bags and rocked left and right, bounced by the speeding train. "We've never had this much turbulence on an aircraft! That can't have been right Alex," she said and then smiled. "Gosh, your face looked fierce. I thought you were going to shout at him!"

Alex smiled back. He still hated being outside his comfort zone, but he did admire how Laura just took everything in her stride. She was his rock. He liked everything to be smooth, correct and right. Slowly he began to relax again, but that was not to last for long. A short fifteen minutes later, a well-dressed Thai woman in her thirties approached them.

"Excuse me," she said politely. "My husband works for the railway." She pointed behind her where a security guard, dressed in a tan brown uniform, stood looking very stern glaring at them. "They ask please that you bring your things. We must go to the next carriage to transfer to First Class at the next station."

"But there isn't another carriage," Alex explained. "Just a sort of wagon; a storage place."

"Yes but, at the next station, it will be disconnected. Please come with me." Her English was very good and she sounded kind and helpful.

Alex and Laura dutifully stood up and again staggered to the end of the carriage. The woman walked gracefully, but then she did have two hands to steady herself. She opened the door, and looked back and smiled reassuringly at them before stepping through to the baggage car. Alex and Laura followed her through with their bags, once again standing in the rough, wooden wagon. This was not an intended place for the public to stand!

"Stop here," she said, raising her voice against the loud train noise. "We must wait. We are approaching Hat Yai. It is necessary." She went on to explain why she was travelling with her husband. A medical issue, she had said, a throat problem; she ran her fingers down her slender neck. It was one of several visits she had had to make. She engaged them in small talk. 'Where had they been?' 'Where were they going?'

"There will be a restaurant car, won't there?" Alex asked. "It's my wife's birthday today and I promised her a nice dinner!"

The Thai girl looked at Laura from head to toe. "How old are you?" she asked disarmingly.

"I am fifty-five," Laura smiled confidently.

"No!" The Thai girl showed a polite look of astonishment. "Much less, surely! And how old are you, sir?" she asked Alex.

"I'm fifty-eight; very old. Why, how old are you?" he pointed back at the young woman rather indignantly.

"I am thirty-eight sir. I have a sixteen year old daughter," she said proudly.

"No! Thirty-eight, that can't be possible!" Alex looked back at her unmockingly and she acknowledged the compliment with a smile and a nod. Out of the corner of his eye he also saw Laura's wry smile. Alex was forever flirting.

At that moment the train began braking. It was approaching the station of Hat Yai. There were no handrails and the rough, wooden walls looked unclean. There was nothing to hold on to, but they braced themselves as best they could. The train braked sharply, coming to a halt in the station, before a loud speaker bellowed something inexplicable in Thai from the platform. Several men brushed by them, while others called instructions from the platform. Within minutes the wagon was separated from the carriages behind and pulled away. The second-class carriage, and the sliding door that had divided them, remained stationary at the platform, growing smaller through the door as the train pulled their wagon further along the tracks.

Their baggage car had no such door, indeed there appeared to be nothing between them and the railway lines below. It continued out of the station, while the rest of the carriages sat temporarily moved and abandoned by the platform.

Alex had put down his bags and stepped forward tentatively to watch the manoeuvring, before noticing a man standing on the lower step of an open side door. The man, in royal blue overalls, beckoned him forward, to stand at the edge. Alex pulled a camera from his pocket and took a picture of the train tracks below and the disappearing second-class carriage behind them.

Two hundred metres up the line the train stopped abruptly. Alex grabbed the open doorway to prevent himself falling out. The railway worker laughed heartily. After a few moments the train began reversing backwards, shunting sideways onto another line and another platform. A different carriage, presumably their first class carriage, grew ever closer. Finally with an almighty crash, the two sections of train became one. Men on the tracks feverishly began attaching the electrics and hydraulics between the two sides of the train, and calling instructions to each other with some urgency.

The first class carriage had the luxury of a sliding door and it slid sideways to reveal another ticket inspector. This man was taller, wider, stern-faced and heavily moustached. He beckoned, but did not speak.

"He wants you to follow him now," our newly acquired Thai girl explained. "Cabin 19 and 20."

Alex and Laura thanked the young woman and stepped across the gap on the, thankfully, stationary train. Suddenly someone stepped forward and took the suitcase. 'Ah,' Alex thought. 'First Class!' A smiling face waved them into number 19/20.

The beds were already made up, upstairs and down, just like bunk beds. There were clean pillows, sheets, one blanket each and a small sink with two tiny bars of soap. Second class had been pleasant enough, but the constant chat, the ringing of mobile phones and other extraneous noises would have made the long journey seem so much longer! Again the seats converted into bunk beds, but a thin curtain was all that protected you in Second Class from the constant patrolling of explorers and bored passengers. In the First Class private cabin, in an oasis of calm, they would be able to relax and finally sleep. They found a corner for the suitcase and then sat down on the lower bunk together.

"Happy birthday Laura," Alex took her hand and kissed her. She smiled back at him with those beautiful eyes on this biggest of adventures. Of course the Air Asia flight would have been the easier and simpler way to go, but this way they would experience Malaysia and Thailand, rural and urban, culturally and idiosyncratically.

"Sir, Madam, can I give you the menu?" A steward stood at the open door and pulled two paper menus from his pocket. There were four choices of dinner, 190 baht; four choices of breakfast, 200 baht.

"Do we order now or in the restaurant car?" Laura asked.

"Restaurant fully booked," the steward replied politely. "You must eat here."

Alex looked down at the lower bunk. A tiny table was perched under the window at one end, but that was all.

"No, no," Alex said firmly. "We are not sitting on a low bed, without a proper table. I can't even sit upright under there! Anyway it is my wife's birthday and I wish to take her for a special meal in the restaurant."

"Restaurant fully booked. Only six tables." The steward was adamant.

"Are these First Class passengers?" Alex asked.

"No, Second Class," the steward replied. "You are the only First Class passengers."

"Then we will wait," Laura interjected. "We will wait until a table is free. We wish to sit in the restaurant. I would like the chicken with cashew nuts and a beer."

"I would like the chicken with cashew nuts and two beers," Alex added. "In the restaurant."

The steward became flustered and stepped out of the cabin, disappearing down the corridor. Alex and Laura two looked at each other, uncertain whether they had won or lost the argument.

"Well, I will not forget this birthday in a hurry!" Laura said with a wry smile. Alex sat down beside her, put his arm around her shoulder and squeezed. They both looked out of the window to see a tiny hamlet flash by. "Well, it is different," she said.

Forty-five minutes later the steward returned.

"You must come," he said. "Dinner."

Laura grabbed her handbag and the two of them leapt up to see the steward rapidly disappearing down the corridor; they followed. It was a long walk through three second-class cabins to the restaurant car towards the rear. The rows of seats had all been converted to bunk beds, lining either side of the corridor. Some already had little blue curtains pulled shut, concealing the early sleepers. Others were playing cards, or listening to music through headphones, reading or simply chatting. It was a very long way to the restaurant car!

Alex and Laura stepped through another sliding door to reveal six or seven tables, each with two seats either side of it. The first table on the left was vacant and they were taken to it. Almost immediately two plates were laid before them, a fork and a spoon, and a series of bowls. Soup, sauces, rice, chicken with cashew nuts and a very modest garnish made up the bulk of the meal. It wasn't the Ritz, but it was good enough, adding to the whole quirky experience. Two large Singha beers were also placed on the table, with two tiny glasses.

Alex poured the drinks and looked around him. Very few of the other tables in the carriage were actually full and only one other person was actually eating. The other occupants were just sitting there drinking beers and smoking, trying to converse over the rather loud television that sat on the bar, at the far end. Most of the people who standing near the bar appeared to be staff and several were glued to the TV. An American couple opposite called for their bill while they were draining the last of their glasses. The table did not remain empty for long. Another couple, German perhaps, entered and sat down and ordered drinks. They had asked what was available and the steward reeled off the list – 'Beer, vodka, Smirnoff, juice or water'. Two beers and two glasses were swiftly delivered.

Alex raised his glass. "To a very strange birthday," he said. "This is totally unreal!"

As if to prove his point, one of the stewards plonked himself down opposite the bemused German couple and began drinking his own alcoholic drink. Laura paused to watch the spectacle with amazement, before returning her attention to the soup.

"Well it tastes good. Thank you darling, you only take me to the nicest places!" She took a mouthful of beer. "Ah, a very good year!"

Alex wanted to ask – 'You or the beer?' but thought better of it. Their adventure was bizarre and quirky, but they were together, in love and having fun. Alex raised his half-empty glass to his lips as the train continued rocking wildly, this way and that. He deliberately missed his mouth, raising the glass to one cheek and then the other, taking care not to tip it down himself. His clown-like actions caused Laura to laugh out loud and she mimed with her lips – 'I love you'.

They returned to their cabin with two more large Singha beers and they sat together again on the lower bunk. Laura took Alex's hand and thanked him.

"It's not over yet," he said, "pointing out of the window." Laura turned to see the fireworks lighting up the sky - starbursts of white, exploding rockets of red and flashing ambers.

"Oh, they're beautiful," she whispered. "Thank you darling."

And that was the incredible thing; in the middle of a rural Thailand, fireworks were lighting up the sky on Laura's birthday in the middle of nowhere. A similar random event had occurred on their honeymoon, on the back of a yacht at Antibes, near Nice in France. Serendipity, Alex would explain. Strange, random events had occurred to them frequently since they had met and both accepted the magic as part of their amazing courtship, relationship and marriage – not perfect, by any means, but sprinkled with fairy dust. When the cabin light was eventually switched out, Laura whispered 'good night' and another 'I love you' for good measure. 'I love you too' Alex had d before drifting off to sleep.

Alex woke with a start. The train had braked hard, sending the carriages crashing into each other. There was an enormous grinding of metal, wheel against rails. Alex felt his heart pounding for several seconds before realising they were still moving and still on the tracks. He tried breathing deeply, but the G-force he felt as they sped too fast around a bend left him breathless. The train protested, groaning and screaming for sanity and more moderate driving, but the pleas were ignored by the driver. The carriages rattled, swinging left and right without unity, struggling to break free.

Alex was thankful for the guardrail, which had prevented him falling out of the bed altogether, but he turned onto his left side, then his right side, trying to find some sort of comfort. He rolled onto his back, but still his body rolled one-way and then another. 'Now I know what it must be like in a tumble drier', he thought.

Alex loved rollercoasters, but this was madness. He reached for his bottle of water, but he found himself mimicking his earlier joke as he struggled to put the bottle to his mouth to quench his dry throat. And so it continued, hour after hour, shaking and tumbling, banging and scraping, until he finally resigned himself to not sleeping any more. Sleep is a luxury, he reasoned; please just get us safely to Bangkok!

The next morning Alex lay on the top bunk staring at the low ceiling. He was completely exhausted.

"Good morning," Laura said from the lower bunk. Alex turned and realised she could see him reflected in the mirror above the tiny sink.

"Morning," he grunted. "I hope you feel better that I do!"

"Wasn't it awful! I thought we were going to die!" Laura laughed. "I think my whole body has been shaken to pieces!" They had endured, survived and experienced a great adventure and she felt strangely elated.

"Are you going to get up first, or shall I?" Laura asked. Alex looked back down at Laura through the mirror and the tiny little basin beneath it.

"I'm sure if you pass me my toothbrush," he said, "I could spit from here!"

Laura roared with laughter and Alex could not help, but smile. He remembered the story he had sometimes told to friends earlier in their holiday – 'If I was approached by some being and offered two choices - they could make me happy every day for the rest of my life, or they could make my wife happy every day for the rest of my life, which would I choose. I would choose my wife of course, because if she is happy, I am happy!' That's how it was now. Laura was lying there giggling and Alex felt warm and happy inside.

Alex slipped on some shorts and flip-flops and left the cabin to go to the toilet. He bumped his way along the corridor towards the front. He saw several staff exiting other cabins, somewhat dishevelled, clearly having been taking advantage of the vacant first class cabins. It appeared they too had struggled to sleep despite the relative comfort of first class. There were two toilets at the end of the carriage. One was a western style sit down toilet, but the floor was completely soaked. A shower hose hung close to the toilet and Alex hoped the puddles were the result of someone showering, rather than spraying their dirty bottom. The alternative toilet was a hole in the floor with a place either side to put your feet. It was fine for a pee, he concluded, but squatting for anything else would be hazardous given the violent swaying of the carriage.

Alex returned and tried washing his hands, and then the rest of his body, from the tiny sink. Behind him, Laura was still sitting in her bed, staring at the crossword. She was bobbing up and down in time with the train, as if she were riding a horse at the gallop, her hands holding the newspaper to her raised knees. Half an hour later they were sitting together looking out of the window.

There were far more buildings along the track now and they knew that in another hour or two they would be back in Bangkok. They asked a member of the train staff, and there were many, whether someone could convert their beds back into a bench seat for the last few hours of their journey. Soon after that, breakfast was brought to the cabin. An egg, bacon, one slice of toast and some strange-looking beans proved to be tastier than it looked and the coffee was delicious. The steward even returned to offer them a second cup; now that really was first class treatment.

One station before Bangkok Central, the train pulled into a station in the suburbs. One or two passengers alighted, but Alex watched curiously at the other activity on the platform. Numerous stewards and other train personnel were rushing around, unloading boxes. These were stacked carefully across on the opposite platform. Each box was double wrapped in black polythene. An old man had been designated as a minder to guard the boxes.

"Watch this," Alex said to Laura, pointing to the comic, but intense activity that was going on. "That's the scam."

Laura looked out, puzzled. "What am I looking at?" she asked.

"Do you remember how the steward was pushing for us to have lots of beers here in our cabin?" he asked. "And then again, in the restaurant car? Have more beers, have more beers!"

"Well, yes," she said. "The beers turned out to actually more more expensive than the meal!"

"Well that's it!" Alex pointed triumphantly. "That's the scam. Those boxes contain beers. I saw someone wrapping some of them up this morning. So why unload them here? So they don't go all the way back to Bangkok for the company to see! The train will be cleaned in Bangkok and re-stocked. Then its' first stop will be back here. Here, where the crew will re-load their own beers, purchased at a fraction of the price, to be sold to the passengers on board. The owners probably have no idea why the sale of their own beers is so poor. I bet they make a fortune!"

"Oh, you are so cynical," Laura exclaimed. "There could be another reason why they are unloading them here."

"Like what?" Alex asked. "Look at all that the activity; that is the fastest we've seen any of the staff move the whole trip! Come on, that is because they are doing it for themselves."

"Well, maybe they are not paid very much," Laura suggested. "Anyway, the staff have probably made a few bob out of you then, haven't they?"

Alex chuckled. A whistle blew and, suddenly, the staff began running back onto the train. Just one solitary old man stood guarding the contraband. In an hour or two, the train would return and the warm beers would be re-loaded into the chillers.

Enterprise at its best!

Chapter 20: Birthday and the Cow

It was a fine sunny day. It was September, but it was still hot. Alex's chair had been placed in the shade away from the strong Spanish sun. The children were in the pool swimming, dropping something heavy to the bottom and then diving down to get it. Occasionally they would get out and dive from the side. Alex wished they wouldn't do that. They could easily hit their head and, anyway, each splash sent even more spray onto the pathway. It was a waste of water and the pool would need topping up again tomorrow.

The childrens' father Andrew was standing over the barbeque, cooking burgers and sausages, peppers and courgettes. He had a beer in his hand and seemed to be able to cook, talk and drink all at the same time.

It was a wonderful day and Alex was surrounded by his family and friends. On the decking below another group were sitting in a circle, animated in discussion. Alex felt a hand on his shoulder.

"It's for you," Laura stood in front of him, smiling kindly. She looked terrific in her light summer dress and sunglasses. "It's Carol." She handed him the telephone.

"Hello?" Alex spoke into the phone and waited.

"Hello Alex, happy birthday!"

"Hello Carol, thank you," he said.

"I'm sorry I can't be with you today, but I'm in Amritsar, in the Punjab." Carol's voice was surprisingly clear. "I visited the Golden Temple today, it was simply breath-taking! "You know how much I love India."

Alex smiled. Carol had always put him and Laura to shame. She was always traveling - a week in the Caribbean; a weekend in the city of Prague, or a tour of the Greek Islands. 'How could she ever afford it?' he wondered.

"What time is it there?" he asked.

"It's about six o'clock," she said. "We are just meeting, going downstairs to try the curry. It's a fabulous hotel. Ah, I have to go now. Sorry, have a nice party won't you. Bye."

Alex said goodbye and looked around him. Laura had dashed back upstairs to finish preparing the salad, so he placed the telephone on the table in front of him. Behind he heard the thud from the room behind him. It was the sound of a ball being pocketed at the pool table. There were so many people here; so many friends.

Alex closed his eyes and thought about Carol in India. He had married his college sweetheart and they had made house together. The struggles of their early years had now become distant memories, replaced by nostalgic recollections of amazing parties, wonderful friends and exciting holidays.

Together they had brought two magnificent sons into the world and the rest, as they say, is history. His two little boys were now both successful men, raising their own families. Andrew and James now had flourishing careers and he was so proud of them. One had flown from the other side of the world to be here today, while the other had taken the short hop from Milan.

A language teacher with his own school in Thailand and an airline captain, following in his father's footsteps – Alex was so, so proud. He chuckled again at Carol. Happy birthday from India! More than three decades they had spent together before they quite simply drifted apart.

Their friendship had endured and now, here she was, ringing him up from India! Whatever next!

Laura came down the outside stairs holding a tray - plates, serviettes, knives and folks, mayonnaise and ketchup. She placed it on the table and looked over at her husband. The smile and the look were sufficient. They could now communicate without words.

'Yes, I'm fine,' he smiled silently.

'I'll be back down soon my wonderful husband,' she smiled back without uttering a single word.

Alex had been given at least two second chances in his life. One was life itself; a near death experience, which had profoundly changed his outlook on life. The second was his chance meeting with Laura, twenty-five years after he had first flown with her on a Viscount in Scotland. It was meant to be. He remembered that even the airline company newspaper had got in on the fairy tale at the time with the headline –

AT LAST – SHY CAPTAIN FINALLY MARRIES HIS CSD

Now here they were. The decision to move from the UK had been a bold one, but it was a decision they had never regretted. They spent their time jointly between their two homes, a large apartment in Andorra, close to the ski slopes and the mountains, and their Spanish home by the Garraf, near Barcelona.

In these two locations, Alex and Laura had enjoyed a long and blissful retirement. They relished the visits from the family and there were always friends from the UK wanting to come and visit them. Locally they had made new friends, close friends and casual friends. Perhaps, and perhaps more importantly these days, they enjoyed their own company.

There were the usual daily chores, of course, cleaning, going shopping, more cleaning and cooking. Laura had her radio for the BBC and her TV programmes. Alex had his computer, his worked on his family history and his writing. Both of them enjoyed golf; it was something they could share together and with friends. There were occasional lunches taking the day, the whole day, to do just one thing. It was very Spanish. Summer months relaxing, reading, chilling and sunbathing, sometimes on their deck, sometimes at the beach.

The convertible sports car had been an extravagance, but it gave them a feeling that they had actually finally made it. It had also made the three-hour journey between their two lovely homes so much more comfortable. There was no more rattling and bumping, listening to a scratchy radio as they had previously endured. Their travels had extended to various parts of Spain. They visited the north; Pamplona, San Sebastian, Santander and Bilbao. They drove west to Madrid and, sometimes, even further west into Portugal.

They had ventured south too, although on longer journeys they chose to fly and hire a car. Very slowly, their Spanish finally had began to improve. Well, Laura's did anyway! They could get just get by. Catalan in Andorra proved a little trickier, although sometimes they found themselves speaking it, without even realising it!

'Oh, you speak Catalan,' someone might say. Alex would smile; he thought he was speaking Spanish!

Holidays came and went. Alex had always wanted to take Laura to the United States to visit Yellowstone National Park. They had travelled to North Dakota to visit relatives, and then continued the trip to Wyoming, Montana, Idaho and Washington State. When in Yellowstone they had seen so much wild life - bears, bison, moose and elk. The trip had been 'awesome' and Alex felt he had finally found himself again.

South Africa had been a favourite of both of them, but the trips changed over the years. They had begun as frenetic adventurers fitting in as much as possible but, over time, they became more sedate as befitted a more mature couple.

Cruises were sedate and seductive. Occasional trips around the Mediterranean had proved very relaxing, while the Iceberg cruise to Alaska had been adventurous and beautiful, but rather tiring.

Slowly they discovered that mostly, they enjoyed their time at home. Whether in Andorra, with the summer mountain walks and the winter skiing, or in the Spanish sun, their homes were where they felt most relaxed. Often they would conduct separate activities during the day, but they would come together each lunchtime and every evening. They had become comfortable with their own company and the company of each other. They could sit and read, then look up and smile. Nothing needed to be said, except with that look or that smile.

Living together twenty-four, seven had begun as a challenge but, over time, instead of fighting the imperfections, they grew to gently tolerate them. The complaints became fewer, the discussions became shorter and the knowing smiles became more frequent. 'Warts and all' Alex used to think. They were too old to change, and their relationship too important to tamper with. The odd crossword was quickly forgotten.

Alex and Laura spent much of their time talking together. Alex was a storyteller and Laura had heard most of his stories one hundred times before. But she listened patiently to his stories about family history and his latest online discovery; some remarkable fact he had uncovered about an ancestor from hundreds of years ago. They both read avidly (Laura perhaps more than Alex) and they talked about their experiences, their discoveries and the latest masterpiece they had discovered from the shelves.

Alex had maintained his links with the Forest of Dean, and continued to read local authors. Occasionally he would pick up a Winifred Foley or a Cyril Hart book to read again. It was the beauty of getting old that he could discover a book all over again. He had discovered that Laurie Lee, who had written one of his favourites books 'Cider with Rosie' based in the Cotswolds, had also written about his time in Spain before and during the Civil War. Then there was the Spanish author Carlos Ruiz Zafon, who had created the most amazing series of books based in Barcelona and elsewhere in Spain. Old age had become a little less active, a little less frenetic, but still it was a joy.

"Give me your glass mate, I'll get you a little top up." Alex looked up and saw Ross standing over him. He handed over his glass and watched

Ross disappear back towards the bar. Another ball dropped into a pocket on the pool table, then rolled noisily down a ramp towards the other potted balls.

"Hurry up," he heard Ross call loudly inside. "I'm playing the winner!"

It was Ross who had introduced them to Andorra and all the offerings it provided– tranquility, mountain scenery, the rivers and, in the winter, the snow. Alex and Laura had especially loved the skiing, but now their old bones were a little too fragile, their knees a little too weak.

Alex thought back to one particular day when the forecast had been particularly poor. It was grey and the clouds were laden with snow. It was early and the ski lift had been eerily quiet. He and Laura, together with Ross and others, had skied down the slopes in limited visibility but they knew the mountain well. Just before 10.30am they had alighted from the ski lift and stood at the top once again. They skied down the first part of the slope, where the run either continued straight on or turned left towards La Coma.

Alex pointed to the ground. The only tracks in the snow were those they had made earlier. It was a rare moment; they were alone on the mountain.

"Great," Ross had said, "means there won't be a queue. I fancy a carajillo!"

A carajillo was a coffee, normally an espresso spiked with brandy or whiskey. It was a warming drink, just perfect to help you thaw out. Ross had launched himself down the slope. In the poor visibility he had quickly disappeared but the mountain around them echoed with his call of 'yippee!'

Alex smiled at the thought of Ross disappearing down that slope.

"One ice cold beer. Happy birthday Alex." Ross raised his own glass to Alex and touched him gently on the shoulder. "To all those happy memories!"

Happy memories; Alex was still remembering that amazing call of 'yippee!' on the mountain, when another story came into his mind. It had brought many hoots of laughter when he told it but now everyone was busy talking and catching up on the family news. There was no one left to tell.

It was during the long warm summer months when he and Ross had decided to cross over one of the mountains to Os de Civis, in Spain. The winter snow had long since melted from the ski slopes of Pal and the chair lifts had been removed from the high cables above them and stored locally. The ski slopes in summer were hardly recognisable and now the grassy inclines were well behind them. Somewhere above and ahead of them was the invisible border that separated Andorra from its Spanish neighbour.

Grass and beautiful alpine flowers covered the mountainside like a carpet spreading up the slope ahead of them. Alex wiped the sweat from his eyes and continued, simply placing one foot in front of the other. It was a warm summer's day, with barely a cloud in the sky. Ross was striding on ahead, more acclimatised to the altitude than he.

Ahead of Ross was Jessica, a German Shepherd with lots of astonishing energy. She was bounding on ahead and then stopping, sniffing at the ground, free from her leash. Occasionally she would come back, checking to make sure her human companions were just about keeping up with her. Sometimes she would run back towards them, her huge tongue hanging from her jaw.

"Vine aqui!" Ross would cry out every so often, calling the dog back to him. "Vine aqui!"

Alex was puffing hard. In the distance he could hear cowbells in the welcome breeze and, as they reached the rise, he could finally see the herd.

"We're going this way, down over that ditch, and then over the next col," Ross had said, pointing downwards to the right. He had removed a bottle of water from his knapsack and took a swig. "Bloody hot!" he gasped.

Alex was relieved to see Ross was also finding it hard going. Ross was several years younger than Alex and was considerably fitter. Alex looked up at the next ridge still high above them. There always seemed to be one more ridge. It was a cruelty of nature, creating the illusion that the next ridge was the last. Then, as you reached the crest, another would reveal itself. 'You're not finished yet' it would whisper.

Jessica had already run down towards the ditch, but now she had noticed the herd of cows. She began barking.

"Jessica!" Ross called and began jogging gently towards the dog.

"Vine agui!" he yelled.

Alex followed, trying to maintain a brisk walking pace. Jessica had stopped and was deciding what to do next. She looked longingly at the cows and wanted to chase them. However, she could hear Ross calling for her. Should she risk it? She took a few steps towards the herd, barked and then stopped. Ross appeared to be getting angry and that was not good. Perhaps she should just stay put...

Ross was suddenly upon her and grabbed her collar. He gave her a short, sharp pull, admonishing her for not coming when called. He pulled the lead from his pocket and clipped it on. Ross was breathless and looked back to see Alex striding towards him.

"Alex run"! Ross called.

"I'm much too old for all that!" Alex called back, grinning but already out of breath.

"No, Alex. Run! Look behind you!"

Alex turned to see a cow with horns jogging towards him and he needed no second warning. Actually the cow was not chasing him, she was chasing Jessica, but he was in the way and he would do for a start! Ross had taken a few seconds to assess the situation and had realised that Jessica was the target.

Jessica had also come to the same conclusion and was again barking excitedly. This was jolly good fun! Ross turned and began running down the hill, pulling the reluctant dog behind him. He turned to check on Alex, who appeared to be straying further to the right.

"Alex, come this way!" Ross called.

Alex continued further right and turned his head to see their pursuer. Right enough, the angry cow was now losing interest in him, focusing instead on the noisy four-legged critter who had threatened her herd.

Ross was going to reach the ditch first and found it to be rather steep. He moved slightly to his right and carefully made his way down diagonally to the trench to the bottom. There was no point in breaking an ankle and, anyway, he needed to keep a grip of Jessica who was now enjoying the challenge. He had time to glance right and saw Alex approach the ditch further up.

Alex was now walking more slowly, satisfied he was no longer a target. He scrambled down into the ditch, sliding on the greasy grass. In a few strides he was at the bottom. Climbing the opposite bank was rather more challenging so he decided to ascend on all fours. Safe on the other side, he wiped his hands on his wet, sweaty tee-shirt and began walking towards Ross and the dog.

"Fuck!" Ross gasped, pulling Jessica closer to him. Both of them were panting heavily. "You OK?" he wheezed.

Alex nodded. They both stood there looking across the ditch. The mad cow was standing on the other side watching them. Jessica had stopped barking, but remained very excited. Ross pulled at her lead and began walking towards the ridge.

"We still have to climb that bloody thing!" Ross gasped, still trying to catch his breath, and pointed at the crest of the mountain still ahead of them.

Jessica was now pulling on her collar, wanting to be the first to the top. Ross held her tightly. Alex followed on at a slower pace. He needed to recover and knew the next ascent would be a killer. He would need to pace himself. He looked behind to check on the cow. It had turned its back on them and was walking along the top of the ditch in the other direction. He paused and took his bottle of water from his pouch on his belt. He was hot and tired; his lungs were sore and painful. His leg muscles were beginning to tighten. 'This is meant to be fun!' he thought grimly.

He stood and watched Ross striding on ahead, Jessica virtually pulling him up the steep slope. He took a second mouthful of water, clicked the lid shut and placed it back in the pouch. Then something made him look back again and, for a moment, his body froze.

The cow had walked along the top of the ditch and found a shallower incline. She had crossed the ditch, climbed onto their side and was now jogging gently towards them; towards him!

Alex turned on his heels and with more than some difficulty, began running again. Immediately his heart began complaining and he could feel it tightening against his chest. He called to Ross who stopped abruptly and turned. Jessica almost pulled him over. He stared back at Alex and then beyond him in disbelief. He hesitated. His instinct was to run too, but Alex was some way behind him, and staggering rather than running. By now Jessica had realised what was going on and had begun barking again. She was having a great time!

Alex stumbled towards him one step at a time, albeit rather slowly. The cow was now slowing to a trot. It seemed to be having second thoughts. Alex was now coughing and breathing very deeply. He was fighting for his breath.

"Just walk Alex," Ross called. "The cow's knackered too! Hey, Jessica, shut up!"

Alex tried to reached out for Ross's arm and bent himself double. He swung his head backwards to see the cow still walking slowly towards them. It then stopped and simply watched them. It looked longingly back up the hill towards the rest of the herd and back at them again. She concluded she had done her job and chased away the trespassers. She let out an angry 'moo' of rebuke and then turned away.

The two men just looked at each other and burst out laughing. Well, Ross laughed. Alex let out a rasping splutter, air and oxygen still hard to come by. It was a snort of relief; a release of tension.

"That's the last ridge," Ross gasped. "After that, it's mostly downhill. Somewhere over there is Spain and a lovely ice-cold beer."

Alex nodded and they began the rest of the climb in silence. They would certainly have something to tell the girls when they reached Os de Civis.

Alex was still chuckling to himself. He took a sip of his beer and watched young Penny pointing in his direction.

"Granddad is just telling himself a funny story," James was explaining to his little girl. "Shall we go and give him a birthday kiss?"

Chapter 21: The Final Checklist

"How is he today?" the woman asked. She was wearing an elegant summer dress and smart shoes. An expensive pearl necklace hung from her neck. Modest, but effective makeup made her look much younger than her years. Maria thought she was beautiful. She always looked so glamorous. If only she, too, could afford such clothes.

"Our Captain is doing very well today," Maria reassured her. She smiled warmly to re-affirm her statement. "He wakes early, as always. He sits by that window and just watches the fields and the hills. I think he enjoys the blue sky and the sunshine."

"Well he is in the right place for that!" the woman said. There was a silence as they both looked over at the old man sitting in his chair. "Does he ever speak?"

"No, Madam." There was a hush in Maria's voice. "It is, as it has always been since I have been here. I take him his coffee; he loves his coffee and the biscuits. Then I ask him to tell me stories, as we agreed. He smiles at me, making noises, and I do honestly believe he is communicating.

Sometimes he pauses and chuckles to himself; then he begins to grunt again. Small, little sounds."

"Do you think he is talking? Do you think he might actually remember anything?" The woman was now almost whispering.

"We cannot be sure, Señora. We know he does not remember how to speak, but he can get himself out of bed. He still manages the bathroom. He seems happy and, if I were to make a guess, I would say he was remembering his life. I speak to him about such things and, sometimes, I think he is reacting. He smiles and makes noises in the right places. I am his nurse Señora and, to care for him, I must believe. He is still Captain Alex Young, my patient, and of course, your husband."

"Dear Maria, You make me feel so guilty." Laura tried to control the emotion that was welling up inside her.

"There must be no guilt, Señora. You looked after him for as long as was possible. You must continue to be strong. Even if he is uncertain who you are, and we can't be sure of that, he does detect our emotions. He laughs when we laugh; perhaps he would cry if we cried. We do not find it strange to talk to a dog or a cat. We speak with them and believe they understand us. We sense them react to us, even though they cannot speak. This is normal, no? So it is, here. He can sense us, perhaps understand us." Maria placed a reassuring hand on Laura's arm.

"I have cats Maria and, of course, I understand." Laura was trying to regain her composure. She always found these visits difficult and distressing. She and Maria had had similar conversations many, many times before, but the visits never ever got any easier. "You are a saint Maria. I don't know how I would manage without you. I love my husband, which is why I find it so, so difficult."

"It is my honour, Señora. It is my, how you say, my privilege. Now I must leave you for a while. I will bring some coffee for you both a little later. What are you going to read for him today?"

"I am reading a book about a seagull, Maria." Laura held up the book. "It is about a bird learning to fly! It is very funny, written by a pilot."

"Go to your pilot, Señora," Maria said. "Go to your Captain."

The door clicked shut behind her and Laura walked over to the table.

"Hello darling," Laura kissed the old man on his forehead and sat down. "Have you been well? I have a new book to read to you today. It's about a seagull called Jonathan Livingston Seagull learning to fly."

Laura watched as Alex looked over at her with his old, tired eyes. She began reading to him, her eyes moving line by line down the page. Alex watched her for a minute and then turned back towards his window.

Alex lay in his bed. Eating and drinking had been difficult these last few days and the dryness in his throat was sore, each breath burning as he exhaled. The breathing was intense; he was almost snoring! His heart was pounding, unusually strong and loud. The nurse lifted the sheet that shielded his body. His feet were no longer pink; they were grey. Other parts of his skin had turned purple and, like the shadows cast after a setting sun, the extremities of his body were darkening.

The heart beat still harder and faster. It could no longer reach the extremities. The heart, the lungs and the brain; these had to be preserved and the body had no choice but to shut down the non-essentials such as the feet. It was a slow, but inevitable process. Slowly the hands had also begun to darken. They, too, had become a victim of the bodies' defensive systems, shutting down to preserve the vital organs. The breathing had become harsh. There was a coarseness and a rasping to the struggle that was fighting to control the situation.

This was an emergency.

"Get the QRH" a voice ordered.

"Which checklist?" a desperate voice asked.

"The emergency checklist!" someone ordered urgently.

"Which one?" another voice asked.

"It's a bloody emergency! The emergency checklist!" someone shouted. That someone thumbed through the checklist, but found nothing relevant to the current problem.

"We are doctors, we not pilots!" the young Spaniard said in English, which was curious because it was the language of the patient; only the patient. The nurses just stared down at the old man in the bed. "This is not an engine failure," he shouted "There is no checklist!"

Something was lost in the translation. The nurses looked at each other in bewilderment, with no clue to the words uttered by this young intern. He seemed emotionally absorbed by the processes that confronted the small group, but the nurses had seen this so many times before. This was incredibly sad, but there was no cure for what they now observed before them. Inevitability is exactly that; no more, no less.

"Good morning Captain," Maria was standing by the door. She looked radiant.

"Hola, Maria." Alex smiled.

"What would you like to do today?" Maria asked. "Perhaps a walk in the mountains?"

Alex looked out of the window. The hills in the distance looked more beautiful than he had ever seen them. The sky was blue, but fluffy white clouds capped the peaks. Below the tree line the vines were full of grapes and the fields were green. A walk in the fields would be wonderful.

In an instant his mind flashed back over the hundreds of walks he had done in the past. He could remember every one of them. The sweaty steep peaks of Lantau in Hong Kong, the beautiful rolling hills in France, the chocolate box mountains of Switzerland, the gargantuan towering Rocky Mountains and his beloved Andorra; remarkably he could remember every one, every step.

"Great," Alex said. "I'll get ready."

"You are ready."

Alex looked around his room and hesitated. He had not been outside these walls for some time and he felt nervous. He looked at the chair where he spent his days, where he waited for the days to tick by. The room felt secure and safe.

"Come now, Captain, it's time to go." Maria held out her hand.

"I'm frightened. Where are we going?" Alex was frozen to the spot.

"Alex, your tea is ready!" a voice called.

"Mother?" Alex looked to the window, trying to confirm where he was.

"Alex! Come in when your mother calls you!"

"Dad?" Alex looked around, trying to trace the origin of his father's voice.

"Don't do as I do, do as I say!" his father's voice boomed. "Come on, son, every time you talk, you miss a mouthful."

"I love you lots," his mother called. "Drive safely, fly safely."

"You are so handsome." It was Laura's voice. He spun around and looked around the room. He was standing in a hotel room with his hand in his pocket. He pulled out a dollar and gave it to the bell boy. Alex watched him leave and turned back towards Laura. She was in her uniform, her arms outstretched towards him.

"My wonderful husband," she said. "Shall I run a bath?"

Alex looked down at the four rings on his arm. He looked in the mirror and saw he was standing in his uniform, with his hat tucked under his arm. He was so proud of that uniform, but had he not handed it back when he retired? This did not make any sense at all. He looked around the room. He recognised it immediately; it was Cape Town.

Alex turned to smile at his wife. Laura was now standing across the room in a turquoise dress; that turquoise dress. The light silk material clung tightly to her body and the curves of her breasts and hips were simply perfect. Singapore! He watched as she walked into the bar in that dress and all the heads turned to look at her. He was so proud.

"Listen to the waves," she said. They were sitting on the beach and Laura was allowing the sand to run through her hands. The moon glistened on the sea and Alex looked up to see the bright stars over Barbados. But then they were gone.

"Laura, I'm frightened!" Alex stared up at the night sky, but only saw darkness. The stars had gone.

"There's nothing to be afraid of, my Captain. Everything will be fine." It was Maria's comforting voice.

Alex stared back at the blackness, afraid. "Laura!" he shouted.

"Maria, help me!" he cried. He began to sob. He could feel himself shaking and he felt very cold. He was gripped by melancholy and felt an overwhelming sense of loneliness. He shivered and gasped for a breath, but nothing came. He felt a mild burning in his throat, yet there was no pain. It was too late for pain. He blinked his eyes to clear away the tears.

Then, through the cloudy dark mist he saw a star; a single light. He stared as it came closer, growing brighter; dazzlingly brighter.

Suddenly it surrounded him and he felt himself floating. He was flying high above the ground, over the fields and forest, but there was no aircraft. There were no controls or instruments. He was flying like a bird, like Jonathan Livingston Seagull, soaring through the sky. It was at that moment that he finally understood…

"Do you understand?" the voice asked. "What is your legacy?"

"Yes," he replied with a little surprise. "I do understand it now. I am my own legacy."

"Yes," a voice said. "Now it's time. Don't be afraid."

"I know," Alex replied calmly. "I'm not afraid, I've been here before." His mind was full again. There were so many amazing memories - so many great recollections and now he could remember them all. What a wonderful life! So many wonderful people and so much love!

"Laura, I love you so much!" he heard himself calling. "I shall miss her," he said to no one in particular. "I shall miss them all."

"They'll miss you," the voice said. "That is your legacy."

Alex felt calm and happy. Memory after memory flooded through his mind. The whiteness was now so bright, he could not see anything beyond it, but the rich emotions still filled his heart.

Laughter, love and tenderness.

Contentment; yes, great contentment.

"I'm here darling," he heard a voice saying. "I'm here."

This was a wonderful dream; so wonderful he never ever wanted to wake up…